Gabriella

Book Six
The Sacred Women's Circle Series

Judith Ashley

Windtree Press
HILLSBORO, OREGON

Windtree Press
Hillsboro, OR
http://windtreepress.com

Publisher's Note: This is a work of fiction. Names, characters, places, and incidents are a product of the author's imagination. Locales and public names are sometimes used for atmospheric purposes. Any resemblance to actual people, living or dead, or to businesses, companies, events, institutions, or locales is completely coincidental.

Book Layout ©2013 BookDesignTemplates.com
Book Cover by Christy Caughie
Editing Services by Kelly Schaub

Ordering Information:
Quantity sales. Special discounts are available on quantity purchases by corporations, associations, and others. For details, contact the "Special Sales Department" at the address above.

Gabriella/Judith Ashley – 1st Edition
ISBN 9781940064611

This book is dedicated to:

Those who work with homeless and at-risk youth including those who are aging out of foster care with no family to call their own. I especially want to recognize three women whose dedication and commitment to at-risk youth is commendable: Rosemary Iavenditti, Lois Neuman and Diane Egger. The number of lives the three of you have positively impacted is many more than any statistic shows.

Acknowledgements:

My village for *Gabriella* includes my first reader, Lois, who continued to support me and this book even when Life hit her hard. My friend Michele, who initiated the first treatment program in Oregon for sexually abused children who were in foster care.

Without the skill of Hand and Microsurgery Dr. Mark J. Buehler, MD, my writing life would have taken a downward turn.

Last but in no ways least, to the #RCRWFTB group and the Goal Writing Challenge group. You help me keep my tush in the chair and my fingers on the keyboard.

To Jump or Not

Wednesday
September 21, 2005
Mabon – Fall Equinox

Tap, tap, tap, tap, tap—*tap, tap, tap, tap, tap*—Gabriella Moncrief turned from the rim of the canyon toward the sound. Scanning the nearby trees, she searched for its source. Unable to find it from where she stood, caution marked her movements as she moved back from the brink. A sigh escaped and tears welled when her feet left the unstable rocky point and found purchase on solid ground. The effigy she held in her hand dropped to the ground. *Was I really thinking of tossing myself off the cliff along with it?*

Arms folded over her waist, Gabby looked again for the woodpecker she knew was nearby. Her eyes inspected the trunks of trees in the direction from where the tap, tap, tapping came. Subtle light flowing through the needled branches created a shifting montage much like when she watched the flow of water over a high cliff.

Intrigued, she stepped closer until she was sheltered under the branches of an eighty foot Douglas fir. A fallen cone caught her eye and she bent to pick it up. The needles on the forest floor seemed to form a design, the nearby fern's fronds created a magical pattern. Sitting on the raised tree root, she studied the cone and the way it resembled a flower. It looked different than the other cones littering the forest floor around her. *It isn't a Doug fir cone. I wonder what tree it belongs to and how it got here?*

Tap, tap, tap, tap, tap—tap, tap, tap, tap, tap—the woodpecker's search for food was persistent. In truth, if the bird gave up it would die. Is that what would happen to her if she gave up the hardest part of her healing process?

Her head told her she'd come so far and had done enough… but her heart? Her heart told her she was still broken, damaged goods, and on top of that, a coward. When she considered the journeys of the women in her sacred women's circle, she and Sophia were the only ones not in a loving, committed relationship. And, Sophia had been happily married to Jonathan for years before his death.

It wasn't that she hadn't any friends. She had The Circle and both her head and heart told her they would always be there for her. But—

Tap, tap, tap, tap, tap—tap, tap, tap, tap, tap—Gabby saw the small bird ten feet up the next tree. A downy woodpecker—black and white with a spot of red on its head. Industrious, persistent, ever seeking the next meal. She'd been persistent in her own healing work until she'd found The Circle. The acceptance and the resulting friendships gave her a foundation and a haven—she'd stopped moving forward with her own inner work.

Why was it important?

Why did the woodpecker keep moving around the forest instead of staying with the same tree? What did the woodpecker know that she didn't? What was she missing?

A shaft of sunlight speared through the fir's branches illuminating the cone in her hand. Mesmerized by the repetition of the petals, Gabby slipped into a light trance.

Tap, tap, tap, tap, tap—she waited for the second series but only heard quiet. The woodpecker was gone. What was the message the small bird wanted her to hear? Standing, she brushed off the seat of her pants and started back to the cabin leaving behind the effigy.

Something's Changed

The forest floor muted her footsteps as she took the long way back. As she neared the hideaway, glimpses of the cabin peeked from between tree trunks. The contrasting barks of the Douglas fir and Western Red Cedar caught her attention as never before. Something was happening around her. What, she didn't know.

Pausing at the cabin door, she slowly turned, letting her gaze sweep the clearing and the woods beyond. It was early September and the summer had been hotter than usual so she saw the signs of fall on the maple and oak leaves. The asters and zinnias were blooming as was the Armistead salvia. Gabby soaked in the ambiance, the quiet, the sense of place and safety before going inside.

The cabin was on the rustic side, not to the point of hauling water from a well and using an outhouse but there was no cell reception or computer hook-up. The kitchen was a simple L-shape. The living area had a massive stone fire-place that was often used on cooler evenings. One bathroom and two bedrooms completed the structure.

When she'd found Hunter's missing daughter, Logan, it was the natural place to bring her. *Running away doesn't solve anything. Why is it so hard for me to take my own advice?*

Gabby toed off her sturdy walking shoes and crossed the room to the refrigerator. Pouring herself a glass of lemonade, she plopped down on the chair facing the picture window. Framed within its borders was the blooming garden in the foreground and the woods beyond. She pulled a hassock closer and rested her feet on the multi-colored throw covering it.

Setting the lemonade aside, she closed her eyes. *I came here to finish my work and yet I've been here two days and have accomplished little.* Peeking from under her lashes, she noted the clutter on the side table and sighed. *Well, I did accomplish completing the effigy of my abusers. But I never finished the rest of the process—throwing it over the cliff onto the rocks below.* A sad smile flitted across her face. *A fitting end for them but I didn't even get that done. Instead I almost tossed myself over the cliff.*

Breath strangled in her chest as the reality of what she'd almost done to herself loomed in her mind. *Who'd care if I had?*

When she'd decided to spend a week or so here at the cabin, she'd reminded herself she was loved by many. In reality, her list was short—six people. "That's not true!" she muttered the scold under her breath. "I am loved by Lily, Diana, Ashley, Sophia, Hunter and Elizabeth but I'm also loved by Jackson and Charlie, Matthew and Bill, Daniel and Rose, Anthony and James. I'm especially loved by Logan and

Grant. And, my bond with Elizabeth's Michael and Maeve is strong. So, that's a lot more than six!"

Even ticking the eighteen names off on her fingers left her feeling hollow inside. "Eleanor, I'd forgotten Eleanor. I'm at nineteen now. And Doc S. If I asked her, I know she'd say she loved me."

Being able to list twenty names of people who loved her eased the sense of loneliness Gabby battled almost every day. *If The Circle knew I felt this way most of the time, they'd be surprised—maybe even shocked. I've always had my mask in place. No one sees the real me. She's buried so deep I'm not sure I'd even recognize her.*

Through an open window, the song of a bird drifted into the quiet. Gabby rested her head against the back of the chair and closed her eyes. In the deep recesses of her mind, she saw a little auburn-haired girl clutching a teddy bear, hiding behind a couch, eyes wide with fright. The little girl dropped the stuffed animal and clamped her hands over her ears and squeezed her eyes tight.

It really didn't help. The screams as the man hit her mom over and over still filtered through her fingers. The policeman took her out of the house and her life was forever changed—but was it for the better? When she allowed herself to reflect on the years spent revolving in and out of foster care, in and out of her mom's home before she'd had enough and fled to the streets—not really.

Who would that little girl be if her dad hadn't left, if her mom hadn't thought she needed a man to survive, if she'd been allowed to stay with the first foster family or even the second?

Will I ever know?

Do I have the strength, the courage to try and find her?

Can I do this alone?

And who would I ask if I can't?

Lily was traveling with her husband, Jackson, and Ashley was recovered enough from her mastectomy to help with Lily's clients when she was out-of-town, but she also had a new husband and three kids to care for.

Diana was back to teaching her classes and while Matthew was a great dad, Madison Michelle wasn't even a year old. And Hunter? Right now, Hunt was back in Rhode Island trying to figure out her relationship with Grant.

Sophia? School started this week and she's got her dying friend who seems to get worse every day. She doesn't think he'll make it to Samhain. I can't ask her.

I've been closest to Elizabeth but she's in Ireland and Maeve is only three months old. I can't impose on her to sit with me, to listen to my babbling as I try to figure out my way forward.

The abyss of loneliness and the darkness that came with it was winning.

And this is why I stood on the edge of the cliff and wanted to throw myself and the effigy into the void.

Why didn't I?

Someone would have found me and I couldn't do that to someone. Seeing death is horrible when it isn't natural.

A choked laughed erupted. Of course it would be natural to be dead at the bottom of a canyon when you threw yourself off the top. But she knew people hiked the canyon and some were high school age. She'd seen a street friend murdered and had nightmares for years afterward. And to be honest, since going out on the streets and finding Logan, the nightmares from that life had been back.

I'm not a coward. Doc S reminds me that I'm a brave woman who has come a long way. Only a little bit left to do.

Yeah, but what's left is the hardest of it all.
You came here to do the work and now seem stuck.
What does the woodpecker do when it is stuck? Moves on.
To what?
To where?

The internal dialogue raged as Gabby debated her path.

No closer to an answer, when her stomach growled for the third time, she patted it and shifted to stand.

Food first and then I'll figure out what I'm going to do. I've taken two months off so I've time.

In the kitchen, she cut an apple and noticed the pentacle sign in the way the seeds were formed. She'd learned about the pentacle in the apple since becoming part of The Circle.

She chopped a tomato and saw how the different parts were connected. The veins in the lettuce caught her attention and delayed her chopping some up for her salad.

Looking out the kitchen window, the sun's light made designs on the ground as it streamed through the tree branches.

Beauty was all around her and while she was generally an observant person, this level of awareness was new. She saw in the natural world designs, patterns and configurations she'd never seen before.

When the Stellar blue jay, her own personal totem, swooped into the yard a few feet from where she stood, she barely contained her whoop of delight.

Maybe my way is being shown to me. I'm certainly seeing everything around me here in a different way.

Standing at the window, Gabby watched the sun dance across the land as the jay pecked at seeds under the sun flowers. She'd been at the cabin for three days and even though she'd not finished what she came for, it was time to go.

The Circle was meeting tomorrow and being there this time was critically important.

Why, she wasn't sure, but with the natural world around her seeming to agree, she was going to trust in the urge to pack up and return to Fremont. The option to return to the cabin was still there. *And this way, Doc S can have the place to herself this weekend. I'll call and let her know I won't be here tomorrow when I get within range of a cell tower.*

With her salad and a piece of bread in hand, Gabby went outside to sit at the picnic table. The air smelled cleaner. The lettuce was crispier, the tomatoes sweeter...all the ingredients tasted fresher. Munching a piece of the rustic peasant bread, she saw a shimmering glow envelop everything.

Life is good right now. And that truth sustained her into the night.

Hunter's News

Saturday
September 24, 2005

The last to arrive, Gabby parked across the street from Sophia's house. Grabbing her potluck contribution of a plate containing the rest of the loaf of rustic bread and a cube of Kerry Gold Irish Butter, she headed toward the house.

One knock and she opened the door, calling out a greeting as she stepped inside. Excited voices from the family room area pulled her forward. At the entrance to the kitchen/family room, she paused, entranced by the scene before her.

Hunter was radiant and the center of attention.

Gabby rushed to put her plate on the kitchen counter and join the others.

"What's going on?" A burst of excitement flashed as she focused on Hunter.

"Hunt, you've got to tell Gabby!" Ashley exclaimed.

"Tell me what?" Gabby's hand reached out to her circle sister. "What's happened?"

"This!" Hunter waved a hand in front of her face.

Confused, Gabby stepped back. "I don't understand?"

Lily stood beside her. "Look closely at her hand."

"Oh My!" Gabby shrieked. "You and Grant?"

Hunter nodded, her turquoise eyes bright with tears.

"When?"

Sophia tapped a metal spoon to a pan and the room became silent. "Now that everyone is here, we need to gather. The day is lovely so we can be outside in the living circle. What do you want to do, Hunt?"

"Outside, please." Hunter pirouetted before dancing the two-step across the room and opening the door to the backyard.

Once everyone was smudged with sage and settled on the grass, a piece of snowflake obsidian was picked up off the living altar and handed to Hunter.

"You go first," Sophia said, handing the fist-sized stone to Hunter.

Taking the stone, Hunter held it in one hand, her other gesturing widely as she talked.

"When I flew back to Rhode Island, I wasn't sure it was the right thing to do. I just knew I needed to see if it was possible for Grant and me to recapture what we'd had that summer. I learned Grant had been thinking about moving to Fremont to be closer to Logan, so he could be more involved in her life but hadn't decided because she was still considering attending Smith. When she made the final decision to come back here and go to the UofO—well, the way it happened, he didn't see a place for him.

"But he'd already decided to take a chance on us and had given his notice to the firm when I said I was coming out and to meet me at the shore.

"It just happened. Grant and I were walking along the beach and it felt so right. We decided we wanted to get married on the Equinox and so we just did it. We asked another couple who was waiting with us to be our witnesses and to take a ton of pictures." She brushed her chestnut hair back from her face in an elegant gesture. "We did go down to see Logan and tell her in person. We are going to have a reception, we think. We're still figuring things out. Grant isn't someone to sit around and do nothing so he's exploring different ideas and we're looking at whether we want to continue living above the studio."

Incredulous looks followed by big grins and nods were on each face. "He wants to buy a house and thinks Allyssa could move into the apartment. Or, since Max, another friend of mine from LA, has said he would love to come to Fremont and help with the studio, maybe he could live there.

"So many decisions! And we've only been married for four days!"

Happiness radiated from the new bride as she shared how frightened she was but how glad she was to take the leap. "Remember how I was just a few weeks ago at 14th Moon?"

Gabby did remember the somber almost ghost-like vision of her vibrant friend. She also remembered the Crone who'd spoken about the wisdom to know what of the past to try to reclaim and what to let go of. At least that is how she remembered it.

Was that what she was supposed to be doing?

Was that part of her healing process?

Letting go of the dark and remembering the light? There was light. Doc S was part of the light. Her mom working with child protective services to get her back was part of the light. *But she was never able to sustain it. I was never enough.*

A hand rested on her back, rubbing in gentle circles. Lily…

.

Weariness weighed her down and the urge to rest her head on Lily's shoulder was strong but she resisted. A glance and a soft smile toward her circle sister. Lily nodded, her blond hair swishing forward, hiding what Gabby knew were blue eyes.

The stone made its way around the circle.

Diana's violet blue eyes sparkled as she shared Madison Michelle's latest exploits. "I thought I'd have a bald spot, she held on so tight." Diana pointed to a lock of her dark brown hair near her right ear.

Ashley's soft Alabama drawl followed Diana's more business-like tone. "Everyone's settled in their new classes. Can't believe James is in high school. Anthony still wants to go live with his dad and Daniel thinks we need to seriously consider at least a visit. We already see the testing starting. Ms. Muir says it won't get better without counseling and Anthony totally refuses that." She shook her head, her forehead over grey eyes pinched with worry. "Don't seem to be any good answer so we're just living it day-by-day."

As Gabby took the stone from Ashley, she reached over and tucked stray strands of Ashley's fluffy blond hair behind her ear. "You'll find your way through this, Ash. No matter what, your kids always know you love them and that's more important than anything.

"I've been staying at my friend's cabin for the past few days working on a long term project I've let slide for several years. I know I said I might not make it this week but the urge to be here was strong. I'm very glad I paid attention." She leaned forward towards Hunter. "I'm so very glad you followed your heart. You glow with the light of love and it becomes you." Sitting back, she handed the stone to Lily.

"And Rose?" Lily directed the question to Ashley. "I can't believe you didn't mention her." She held the stone out and Ashley took it.

"My Rose is her normal powerhouse. She has decided to build me something and she and Daniel are out working in the shop every day. She comes in dusty and smiling. He comes in shaking his head. I've been informed that she's going to be a carpenter or maybe an architect or maybe—well, depending on where they are in the project it changes. Daniel won't say too much other than that she's amazing and that she is doing it all by herself. Actually insists on it."

Soft chuckles sounded around the circle.

"That certainly sounds like Rose," Lily said, the stone now back in her hand. "And I want you to know that whenever she can go with you to visit clients, she's more than welcome. Everyone who's met her loves her energy and kindness.

"And Jackson is grateful you are healthy enough to check on people this next week. We're flying down to Carmel and checking in on former clients just to see how things are going. He particularly wants to get feedback on the house totems and wants me there in case there are questions. It'll be great to see everyone again. Two of the families are having receptions at their homes for us. I can hardly believe that three years ago I didn't even know Jackson. Now I can't imagine what my life would be without him."

Sophia now had the stone. She tossed it from hand-to-hand appearing to gather her thoughts before she spoke. "My friend is nearing the end of his days. We continue to march to his own music and that won't change. I've made peace with the reality that all I can do is be his friend, be there whenever I can and listen when he needs to talk.

"As you know, the garden is in full harvest and I've bags of fresh vegetables and fruits for you each to take home. If anyone wants to stay after and make a bunch of apple pies, I'd welcome the company and the help." Her dark brown gaze traveled the circle seeing heads nod.

"Elizabeth is expecting all of us for Samhain so think about working that into your plans," Sophia added, pulling out a piece of paper from a skirt pocket. Flattening it out she read an email from their circle sister in Ireland. "The Lady sends her blessing upon you all. Maeve is growing and is already lurching forward into a more upright sitting position. No longer can she be left for a second without a hand on her. Of course there is no lack of hands!

"Michael is so taken with her and he is hinting that maybe we'd like to try for another soon. He has totally forgotten his vow during Maeve's birth that she would be raised an only child. I am smiling as I write this. I never believed he was serious but it is a little too soon for me. Maybe after Solstice?

"We miss you ever so much. Connecting energetically is better than nothing but not the same as a hug. Please try to come for Samhain. Michael and I are planning on being in Fremont for Winter Solstice. Maeve will be six months old and I won't be so anxious to travel with her by then. In love and light! E."

Gabby did stay and help with the pies knowing she'd take one home with her. Would that be back to the cabin or to the Murphy's house where she lived as caretaker? She chatted with Lily and Hunter who'd also stayed to prepare apples for the filling while Sophia made the pie crust.

Opportunities were not readily available to talk about her problems. She did know that all she had to do was say something and she'd have everyone's total attention.

But she didn't.

When she left, she had two pies in hand. One for the freezer at the Murphy's and one for herself—or that was the plan. There was something about Sophia's pie crust that made abstinence a challenge. Maybe? There was no 'maybe' about it. She'd not lie to herself and say the pie would be in the freezer in December. Her promise was that the pie would be in the freezer now. That promise she'd keep.

It was late and the better decision was to stay at Murphy House but after depositing the pie in the freezer, Gabby was back in the car and headed out-of-town. It was about an hour's drive to the turnoff to the cabin. She wasn't sleepy and the thought crossed her mind that maybe the drive would help her sort things out.

It was midnight when she pulled to a halt in front of the cabin. Lights were on which meant Doc S was there and still up. Pie in hand, she headed toward the front door. It opened as her feet hit the porch.

"I wondered if you would come back tonight," Doc S said, holding the door wide.

"Pie. Sophia's apple pie. I think we have some vanilla ice cream in the freezer." Gabby breezed in and headed straight for the kitchen.

"You've things in the car?"

"Nothing that can't wait until after pie. Do you know what a torturous drive it was smelling the deliciousness of this pie all the way here?"

"I'll get the plates while you get the ice cream," Doc S said.

A few minutes later they sat in front of the glowing embers of a fading fire relishing the decadent dessert.

As the last few bites were eaten, Doc S commented. "I went for a walk today and saw something of yours by the canyon. Just so you know, I left it there figuring there was a reason it was in that place instead of somewhere else."

"It fell from my hand when I tried to find the woodpecker."

"And did you find it?"

"I did find the woodpecker and…. . I don't exactly know how to explain it but something happened and now the world around me looks, smells and tastes different." Gabby sat up straight and looked right at Doc S. "Do you see all the patterns when you look at the world around you out here?"

"I'm not sure what you mean?"

Gabby reached over to the side table and picked up the cone she'd noticed when searching for the woodpecker. "This. Look at it from the top down and even from the side. It isn't a Douglas fir cone but I found it under one. And the way a tomato is put together. Even apples when cut through the middle show the pentagram."

Doc S took the cone. "It's spruce. Unusual place to find one because there are no spruce trees in that area." Doc S handed the cone back to Gabby. Her head tilted, she added. "But you knew that about apples."

"I did know that about apples and I know I've noticed or seen everything I saw but somehow yesterday it all seemed different. It seems so important right now to understand what this is all about."

"More important than finishing your journey?"

"I'm wondering if this is part of that process, part of my healing. Why was the spruce cone under a Douglas fir? Is it a message? Something for me to explore? Or am I using it to distract myself, to protect myself from what lies ahead?"

Seeing a New World

Hiking through the woods the next day, Gabby searched for spruce trees. Altogether she found seven on the property, none were even close to the canyon. It didn't seem plausible the wind could have carried it to where she found it because it was under the branches of a huge Douglas fir. Squirrels were a remote possibility. But there was no reason for a squirrel to haul something almost its own size that far.

Back at the cabin, she chopped vegetables for the stir-fry Doc S was fixing.

"We'll have pie for dessert, but we used the last of the ice cream." Doc S tossed carrots into the wok.

"Or I can make an ice cream run to the store?"

"Or we can do it together. Your choice. I know that pie is calling out for vanilla ice cream." Doc added onion. When it was translucent, she added the celery.

"I'll get the bean sprouts ready for you."

"And the noodles. This is going to be a great veggie stir fry." The noodles went in next with spinach, sugar peas and bean sprouts last. When a few stirs later everything was hot, Doc moved the wok off the heat.

"Here are bowls." Gabby placed two large bowls on the counter next to the stove. "I've set the table and put the soy and hoisin sauces out."

As they finished their meal, Doc S brought up the topic of ice cream. "I think we should both go to the store. I'd like to get a few things."

"That's fine with me, or you could give me a list."

"I could but then I wouldn't be the one picking out the other flavors of ice cream."

"So true. You'd have to live with whatever I brought back."

Curled up, covers tucked under her chin, Gabby's mind whirled with unanswered questions. *Tomorrow I'll go out with my camera.* She also knew if she went along the main path to the canyon she'd see the effigy she'd spent hours making as part of her healing process. Wrapping her arms around her knees, she pulled into a tighter ball. *I know this is the hardest part. I'm so tired of facing the pain, of dealing with the nightmares that come from digging it all up again.*

As exhaustion claimed her, so did the nightmares. In an effort to extinguish them, Gabby concentrated on the mental picture of the spruce cone, seeing it from the top down, seeing in it a pattern that soothed. If she stayed focused on that image, she relaxed and rested. If she drifted into sleep, the nightmares came.

When the light of morning bathed the room in a soft light, Gabby was awake. As the room brightened, she paid attention to how the familiar nooks and crannies, paintings on the wall, the vase of flowers on the dresser were transformed. She was seeing the world around her in a new way. A new way she hoped would help her in the final part of her healing.

The Noumenal World

Wednesday
September 28, 2005
Montgomery House

Giovanni Migliori lounged against the kitchen island, his eyes on the auburn-haired beauty across the great room. He was visiting his friend, Jackson Montgomery and his wife, Lily, who was hostess to an informal gathering of The Circle.

Jackson was busy stirring his marinara sauce. The ice cream maker with a new batch of vanilla was churning in the background. Even with the constant humming of the machine, Giovanni could still hear bits and pieces of the women's conversation. Perhaps he should turn away and focus his attention on what his friend was doing but he didn't. There was something about the way Gabriella sat, the way she held her head. Intuitively he knew something was wrong.

It wasn't just intuition. Over the past three years, he'd watched her from a distance and at other times up close. He knew her moods and body language well enough he knew she was distressed.

They must be taking turns talking because he could see no actual on-going conversation.

When Gabriella leaned forward, he found himself leaning towards her. Unable to hear her soft voice from where he stood, he strolled in her direction as if drawn by an invisible string. When he heard her, he stopped.

"I don't know how to explain it. It's as if I see the world differently. It started with the spruce cone I found under a Douglas fir tree and it's expanded from there. There are times I see patterns or certain configurations that are repeated. It's magical."

"It is sacred geometry." Giovanni stood behind Lily, directly across from Gabriella. His Italian accent added a musical cadence to his words.

"I don't know what that is?" Gabriella's brows puckered and confusion showed in her hazel eyes.

"I know I intrude. But if you wish, I will explain." Giovanni waited until he saw nods of agreement. "In times past, the belief was that numbers were more than just for counting. They had a special meanings that held the keys to understanding how everything worked."

"I remember reading about how the geometry of numbers is used in composing music. There's something about harmonics that have to do with numbers and fractions and things like that," Diana added.

"That is true." Giovanni took the few steps so he was next to the fireplace mantle. Leaning against it, he continued. "Sacred geometry was used in creating the Great Pyramids in

Egypt as well as the temples in Greece and Rome. Cubits, which are one of the measures in Sacred Geometry, is talked about in the Bible."

Perplexed, Gabriella said, "I don't really understand how my fascination with a spruce cone and the swirls in a sunflower fits in with pyramids and temples."

"Temples, stone circles, cathedrals, pyramids are all man-made using the principles of sacred geometry. Your cone and flower are made by God and that is where the sacred comes in." He paused before adding. "Why do you call yourselves a sacred women's circle?"

"I believe we do that because our spiritual practices are an integral part of our circle," Sophia replied. "What do the rest of you think?"

"And we honor the female as well as the male, calling upon the Goddess as well as the Gods or God," Ashley added. "Oh, we also use the phrase 'The Universe' and 'Great Spirit'. I've never thought about why we use different words at different times but we do."

"We suspend our minds and open ourselves to what comes to us," Lily said. "And we trust the words will come and they will be the right ones for that time and space."

"You are talking about concept of *noumenal*—where you feel something you cannot really explain or prove." Giovanni watched Gabriella absorb what was being said. "It is what Jackson and I do at some point in our work. We just know an idea is right for that particular time and space. We don't try to figure out why. We just do it." He looked over at Jackson who now stood across from him behind the couch. "It is true?"

"It is true," Jackson affirmed. "When you feel something and know its truth but are unable to prove it, you are touching the sacred."

"B-b-but…," Gabriella stammered, "I still don't understand how the spruce cone got where I found it."

Giovanni answered, "That is part of the mystery of life. Accept that it was where it needed to be for you to find it and become intrigued with it. After all, the unknown is part of the mystery of life and our lives are richer because of it."

"I think it's important to trust that the unknown, the mystery, is not harmful." Lily tapped a finger on the arm of the chair. "It is easy to become afraid of what we don't know or to fear what hasn't happened. It is our fear of "what if" that keeps us bound to the present, anchored to the past, unable to move forward."

"And when you look at the cone or the sunflower, what do you feel?" Giovanni's casual stance masked his unerring interest in Gabriella's answer.

"I've a mental picture of looking at the cone from the top down that I meditate on. I don't know why exactly, but I find it soothing, almost like repeating a mantra. It sounds sort of foolish but… ." her voice trailed off, her unfocused gaze far away.

"Then that is all that matters." He straightened and turned to Jackson. "The aroma of my bread is filling the air. The dinner, it is almost ready?"

"Dinner is almost ready. That is if you ladies are hungry. I can keep it warm if you need more time."

"Do we need more time?" Lily asked the group. Seeing everyone shake their head or murmur 'no' and begin to stand, she turned to her husband. "We're coming. Do you need help getting things out?"

"It's all done, Lily my love. Giovanni is getting the bread sliced, I've drained the pasta. Just need to get the salad from the refrigerator. Plates, etc. are already on the counter."

"Have I told you lately how much I love you?" Lily said crossing the room.

"It's my spaghetti that did it," Jackson replied. "Well, my spaghetti and other things." He waggled his eyebrows and leered.

Lily laughed. "Your spaghetti and homemade ice cream?"

Jackson slipped around the counter and pulled Lily into his arms. "If you've forgotten about the 'other things', I'll have to remind you." His lips captured hers in a searing kiss. "That will have to do until later."

A flush-faced Lily reached for the counter to steady herself. "I will pay you back for that, Jackson."

"And I'll be looking forward to it."

"Dinner is served," Giovanni said putting the baskets of bread on the counter next to the salad. "I made some garlic croutons," he pointed to a cloth lined bowl.

Gabriella hung back until everyone else had served themselves. She was thinking about what Giovanni said about the concept of noumenal and the sacred. She'd like to know more and knew he had the knowledge to help her. *But to be around him, to be close to him. As attractive as he is, I need to remember men aren't trustworthy.* Dishing up her plate, Gabriella found a seat as far away from Giovanni as possible.

Nightmares and Giovanni

Although it is said that hindsight is 20/20, Gabby couldn't figure out why she'd stayed when everyone else had left—stayed so long that the mega-storm struck. At Lily and Jackson's urging, she agreed to spend the night. Lights flickered as thunder and lightning struck close by. When they went out, she fretted because she should have gone home to Murphy House. After all she was supposed to be the caretaker. Even though she'd lived there almost three years, ever since Elizabeth moved to Ireland, since taking time off from work, she'd been staying at the cabin, coming in to town for The Circle gatherings, to check mail and get groceries.

Three weeks of her leave was gone and she'd come no closer to finishing her healing process. She had it mapped out. It was written down on a sheet of paper attached to the cabin refrigerator with a magnet. The first half of the list, the part about making the effigy and infusing it with her anger and angst had been done.

Where was the effigy? As far as she knew it was still on the ground by the canyon rim. *Or maybe not if a critter hauled it off.* A shiver surged up her spine at the thought of the people from her past the effigy represented being mauled by a bear or maybe a mountain lion. *They are out there. And coyotes? Wolves? I've heard their howls.*

As she crawled into the bed in the guest room on the lower floor, she was glad she wasn't alone in a big house right then. Initially staying at Murphy House was a treat because it was so much bigger than her old apartment. But when she couldn't sleep, when the nightmares came, being so separate from other people, being so alone was torture. And, with Sophia the only one of The Circle not married to the love-of-her-life, the idea of staying with anyone else, even though they all had room enough for her, was uncomfortable. *They need that time with their husbands. And Soph? She spends most of her free time with her sick friend. She doesn't need to come home and find moody me there.*

The vision of the spruce cone vivid in her mind's eye, Gabby wrapped herself around an extra pillow and pulled the covers to her chin. A flash of lightning illuminated the room through the closed blinds. Three seconds later, the bed shook with the clap of thunder. The brilliant lightning and rumbling thunder faded as the storm moved off. Gabby dozed, keeping the spruce cone vision strong, warding off the nightmares.

A scream woke her.

Thrashing she struggled to throw off the covers.

Trapped.

Air stalled in her lungs as panic struck.

She had to get lose, get away, get to safety.

A loud rap-rap-rap rang through the night.

"Who is it?" But the words sounded in her head. No air to say them aloud.

"Gabriella?"

Giovanni's voice.

"What is happening to you?"

She wanted to answer, to tell him she was okay and to go away but as she gasped for air, for enough to say even one word, he called out again.

"I am counting to ten. If I do not hear your voice, I am coming in. *Uno, due, tre, quattro, cinque, sei, sette, otto, nove, dieci.*"

Slowly the door opened until it was pushed back against the wall. Giovanni stood in the opening, his hair sleep-tousled, the shadow of a beard covering his cheeks and chin, his forehead wrinkled in a worried frown. "You screamed."

Giovanni didn't move for several seconds waiting for Gabriella to say something or maybe even throw something at him and order him out.

But she didn't.

He flipped the switch and the bedside table lamp came on.

It was then he noticed her gulping for air.

Her mouth was moving like a fish out of water. The harsh sound of labored breathing filled the room and he wondered why he hadn't hear it before he opened the door.

Crossing the room, he reached out but held back from actually touching her. Something was wrong and he didn't want to make it worse. Without a paper bag for her to breath into, he hoped bending over would help.

"*Il mio Gabriella*, we try this to help you." He rested his hand on the back of her head. The soft curls seems to embrace his fingers. "I help you to bend your head a little, like the runners do at the end of a race. Maybe it helps? Maybe not, but we try. Okay?"

Gabby nodded her head but confined as she was in the tangle of sheets, she made no further moves.

Sensing what was wrong, Giovanni carefully pulled and tugged until Gabriella's arms were free. She grasped his arm, the wild look in her eyes speared his heart.

Pushing the rest of the covers aside, he helped her shift so her legs were over the side of the bed.

"We do this together," he said sitting beside her and bending over. "Like this." He sat up and watched her looking for a slight nod. Her breathing was still labored but not as harsh as when he'd first come into the room a few minutes ago. "Ready?"

Giovanni bent forward, looking sideways to see if she did the same.

She did.

It didn't help.

"We try it this way." Giovanni held out his hand, inviting her to stand next to him.

Once she was on her feet, he bent at the waist putting his hands on his thighs.

Gabby followed his lead and felt her breathing ease a bit more. Was it the bending or the fact she wasn't alone or she wasn't in the dark?

Still shaky, she managed a "Thank" breath "You."

"Prego."

"I-I-I'm" breath "all right." Breath "You don't ne-e-ed" Breath. "to stay." Breath "I-I'm fine."

"You do not look fine." He waited for a sarcastic comeback and his worry meter rose when it didn't come.

"I-I mean I'll be all right."

Her words were shaky but she was getting her breath back. Now she only had to take a deep breath at the end of a short sentence instead of between every word or two.

"I wait until you breathe normal." Giovanni stood and crossed to the chair under the windows.

She wanted to scream at him to get out and she wanted to beg him to stay, maybe hold her and tell her it would be okay. Either option took more air than she had. Concentrating on her breathing helped. The terror that spiked when the idea to ask him to stay eased.

Her hand flew to her chest. *OMG! I woke him up.*

Giovanni held his hand up when her mouth opened.

"Do not apologize."

"Arrogant—who said I was," Gabby's chin was in the air, imperiousness cooled her tone.

Giovanni smiled. "Aahh, I see the Gabriella I know is back." He leaned back and crossed his ankles, folded his hands on his stomach. "So, you talk to me now."

"No, I don't talk to you now." Gabby bristled and turned away from him to straighten the bed. She had to remake it as the fitted bottom sheet was the only thing remotely in place.

Finished she debated whether to make a grand gesture and order him out, pointing dramatically to the door or just sit down on the bed, her back to the headboard and wait him out.

Too tired for the grand gesture, she climbed back on the bed and sat cross-legged in the middle. "I truly am sorry I woke you. And, I really am much better. Sometimes I have nightmares and maybe it was the thunder and lightning that triggered this one."

He said nothing. Just waited, his dark chocolate brown eyes calm and understanding.

"Do you ever have nightmares?" she asked.

He shook his head. And waited. Those eyes never left her and yet it didn't feel like he stared.

"I hadn't had them for a long time but—well, since spring and more recently they seem to come more frequently. This one was one of the worst because I couldn't breathe. Usually I wake up before—." Gabby half-smiled. "You can't honestly be interested in my ramblings."

"But you would be wrong. I don't hear you rambling. And, I am a good listener. If talking helps you, I will listen."

"But, Giovanni—." Gabby began to protest.

"You tell me these nightmares have come back since last spring but I do not believe you have talked to any of the others about it.—I see by the way you look, I am right.—So, I ask myself, 'Giovanni, why would Gabriella not talk to any of the others? Why would she keep this all to herself?'"

"And what is your answer?" Her heart pounded as she waited for this all too discerning man to guess her secrets.

"I have many answers in my head but they are not your answers. I am only interested in your answer not my speculation."

Her hand clamped over her mouth to stifle a yawn.

"Perhaps a conversation for another time, *mio cara*." He stood and ambled to the door. "You will feel better and maybe the nightmares will go away if you talk about what is the problem. If not me," he flashed a devastating smile her way, "then perhaps your friends. Or perhaps, you prefer the nightmares?"

He turned off the light and pulled the door closed when he left.

Gabriella crossed the room to the chair he'd just vacated. The seat was still warm and the scent of cloves and sandalwood, his scent, remained. Curled into the chair, Gabby closed her eyes. Some of what Giovanni had said was true. The nightmares were the same ones she used to have. Ever since she prowled the streets to find Logan, they'd returned. That was six months ago.

She was losing the battle to contain them.

They were more frequent and she didn't wake up until the start of the horror.

But would talking to anyone really help?

In her mind, the spruce cone glowed. "Relax," she whispered over and over as she focused on the repeating patterns.

Safety in Numbers

Trees were down but Montgomery House had electricity because Jackson had had a generator installed. Who knew how many hours or even days it would take to get the city of Fremont back up and running? The downside to living in older neighborhoods and where trees were abundant and valued was the possibility of limbs or whole trees coming down and taking out power lines.

Gabby hoped the cabin was okay. When Doc S had found the place, she'd done what she could to protect it. She'd had trees harvested back far enough that if one came down it would most likely not hit the place. The ground around the house was either well-watered or gravel. No bark dust or bushes close to the house. An alarm system that included a state-of-the-art smoke detector was another important safeguard. Days went by when no one was there so a fire either from within or without would be devastating.

Sitting in front of the roaring fire in the Montgomery's great room, Gabby pondered whether to go back to the cabin after she checked Murphy House and updated Elizabeth and Michael on how it had fared or just stay there. She thought it might be prudent to stay in Fremont for a few days, until most of the storm's damage could be cleared up.

The scent of cloves and sandalwood announced Giovanni was nearby. She turned to see him standing a few feet away.

"You sleep with no more nightmares?" His forehead wrinkled and worry showed in his dark brown eyes.

Gabriella's cheeks flushed. "Yes, for the most part, I did. And thank you for your help. I'm sure I would have managed but I know I recovered more quickly because of you."

His concern did not abate with her statement. In fact he moved closer, sitting in the chair at a right angle to her. "I am still a good listener," he said in a soft voice only she could hear.

The sounds and smells of breakfast being made, Jackson and Lily's banter drifted across the great room but in that moment in time, it felt as if she and Giovanni were alone. Disarmed, discombobulated and disoriented, Gabby floundered. What had happened to her defenses when it came to men?

Giovanni wasn't mean or harsh or abusive. Instinctively she knew he was more like Jackson and the other men her circle sisters had married but he was still a man and that meant, for her, she had to be on guard.

Men had so many faces they showed women depending on what they wanted. They could turn on you in a moment. The loving, caring guy instantly replaced by a demanding, abusive one who didn't really care about you, your feelings much less your body. Giovanni was a man and bottom line, he wasn't a safe person.

"Breakfast is ready, you two," Lily called out.

"Coming." Gabriella stood, grateful that Giovanni did also and that he'd stepped aside so she could pass. Or was she grateful? The scent of cloves and sandalwood filled her lungs as she hurried her steps and sought safety in numbers.

Assessing the Damage

By the next morning, the roads were clear and she could make her way to Murphy house. Her home yet not really her home. The idea of having her own place was in the back of her mind. She thought of asking Lily about renting her little house. *A little farther to work but easy enough for me to keep up. But I could also check out buying a house of my own. Right now my being a caretaker of Elizabeth and Michael's house works but when E and Michael and little Maeve come to visit? I know I'll feel in their way. And Maeve will have a brother or sister in a few years.*

She'd been putting money in savings and with the last bonus check she probably had enough for a down payment on a place but—. One of her dreams was to travel, to finish her book and get it published. The agent she'd had never did sell her first book before she retired earlier this year. Although she had an option to go with another agent, she hadn't and with the big project at work, finding Logan and all that had raised, it was probably a good thing. But last month when she had a restless or sleepless night, she got up and wrote.

A little voice told her she needed to finish her healing process before she could move forward with her book. She'd started on her plan, but now was stuck. Just thinking about returning to the cabin to finish her plan caused physical pain and contributed to the nightmares.

What was she going to do?

"Gabby?" Lily's voice broke into her thoughts.

Focusing, she saw Lily standing next to where she sat on the couch. "What are your plans for the day?"

"Oh, I didn't realize the time had passed. I'll be out of your way in no time." Gabby jumped up and started past Lily.

"Wait!" Lily held her hand out. "Wait a minute, Gabby. Jackson, Giovanni and I were talking about checking on Sophia's because she's at her friend's house. And I want to go by the little house just to make sure it's okay. We thought if you went along, we'd go by Murphy House. Maybe find a place to have lunch?"

The flight-response that galvanized her to her feet slowly ebbed. "Oh, okay, I can do that." The words were barely out of her mouth when panic struck. She clutched her elbows and took a deep breath to quell the urge to bolt. Hours in the car with Giovanni? What was wrong with her?

"When do you want to leave?" she asked, pleased her voice was fairly normal in tone and cadence.

"Jackson and Giovanni are restless so whenever you're ready, I think we're good to go."

"Just let me get my things." Gabby headed toward the stairs and the guest room. Back upstairs, she checked her phone as they were heading out the door. A text message from Doc S *When you get this, let me know how the cabin is. Too busy here to check myself.*

Relief warred with Gabby. Here was her out. "Doc S has asked me to check on the cabin."

"Not a problem," Jackson said. "We'll just add it to our list."

"That's a great idea, Jackson." Lily stood on her tiptoes and kissed his cheek.

Gabby noted that Giovanni said nothing. He just opened the car door for her. She was sitting behind Jackson and diagonally from Lily. After shutting her door, Giovanni strolled to the other side and slipped into the back seat next to her. Suddenly she was enveloped in his clove and sandalwood scent.

Murphy House was unscathed although there was a lot of smaller tree debris. Something the landscape maintenance people would clean up later in the week. The little house was also undamaged. Lily had a yard service and they would take care of the leaves and twigs that littered the yard and driveway. Sophia's was a different story. While there was no damage to the house, two of her fruit trees had lost limbs and the wind had decimated the tomatoes, beans, peas–well, anything that wasn't on the ground.

Lily called and described the scene to Sophia. "It will be whatever it will be," Sophia had said. "I don't think my friend will make it many more days."

"She's taken this next week off from school she is so sure this is the end," Lily reported when the call ended.

"We can have a work party and at least clean things up," Gabby suggested.

"Or, hire an expert who can maybe save some of it," Jackson said. He was already on the phone with Daniel and Matthew who said they'd follow up and find someone as well as come over and survey the damage themselves. Both had amazing Victorian gardens at their homes and contacts to call.

"Lunch or the cabin next?" Lily called out over her shoulder as she led the way through the house to the front door.

Lunch everyone agreed was the next order of business. They stopped at a deli not far from Sophia's and ordered sandwiches to go along with coffee for Jackson and Giovanni and hot tea for Lily and Gabriella.

Turning on to the road to the cabin, Gabriella was alarmed at the destruction. About a quarter of a mile in, the road was blocked by a downed tree.

"I'll hike in from here. You'll have your hands full turning the car around." Gabby was out of the car and heading toward the tree.

"We'll come with you," Jackson said striding to her side.

"It's about a quarter of a mile further and we've no idea what other problems we'll encounter and your car?"

"My car has reverse. When we're done, I'll just back out to the highway."

"Don't argue, Gabby, he's in his 'take charge and take care of the little lady mode'. It's better to go along until he figures out you know what you're doing." Lily patted Jackson's arm.

Gabby led the way. They came across three more downed trees. Her heart was beating overtime as they neared the clearing both because of the exertion required to get there and her apprehension over what she'd find.

Pushing past the last of the smaller limbs that covered the ground Gabby's breath whooshed out as the cabin came into view. The ground was littered with tree branches of various sizes—some six to eight inches in diameter some less than an inch. One larger tree was down, held up by two other trees.

She tilted her head to see whether if it fell the rest of the way it would hit the house.

Clove and sandalwood mixed with the scent of evergreen trees and overturned soil. Giovanni stood beside her. "It will miss."

"How do you know?"

"It is a matter of geometry—the angles and triangles."

"Is it part of the sacred geometry you talked about?"

"*Si e No.* The cabin, it will be spared but the garden will not."

Gabby made her way across the space to the cabin. Fishing the key from her pocket, she unlocked the door and let everyone inside. A flick of the switch and lights came on. "The generator still works." She checked that the refrigerator and freezer were working. And looking around the place, knew her decision had been made for her.

"Let me pack up the perishables and take them with us. I'm not sure how long it will take to clear the road and clean the mess up. And, if the power goes off, this will be a horrible mess."

She got a cooler out from a cupboard and put milk, ice cream, cheese and lettuce, tomatoes and avocadoes inside. She packed up the bread but left the condiments. As she closed the cooler and tried to lift it, she rethought her plan.

"I'm going to dump this," she said taking the milk and ice cream out of the cooler. "It'll be lighter without these."

Giovanni poked through cupboards until he came to where sacks were stored. "If you do not take the ice cream, we can put the rest in these sacks and more easily carry."

"I think we need to leave the milk, too."

With an economy of movement, Giovanni transferred the vegetables, cheese and bread into four small sacks while

Gabby heated some water in the microwave and used it to melt the ice cream and wash it and the milk down the drain. For good measure, she heated another quart of water and poured it down also.

"I think that will take care of it." Gabby put the pitcher on the counter and wiped her hands on the kitchen towel.

While she was dealing with the perishables, Jackson and Lily had been busy. Debris on the porch had been cleared away and they had righted the rose trellis next to the house.

"Thank you," Gabby said, giving Lily and then Jackson a hug. "It was so much easier with your help." Steeling her resolve, she turned to Giovanni who was starting toward the road, two sacks in hand. She hurried to catch up. Taking a sack from him, she shifted it to her other arm and rested her hand on his. "Thank you for all your help."

He stopped then, directed that smile that warmed her toes directly at her. "Do I get a hug?"

Gabby nodded.

Giovanni frowned.

"What's wrong?"

He took the sack from her and placed them both on the ground.

"Now, now it is time to hug."

His arms opened and Gabby stepped into his scent, his warmth. He was strong and gentle and held her as if she were fragile china. Her mind fogged as one hand stroked her back and the other cradled her against him.

"Ah, *mia cara*," he whispered into her hair. "*La mia Bella Gabriella*."

He eased his hold on her but she still staggered a bit before gaining her equilibrium. Now steady on her feet, her face flamed with embarrassment. Where are Lily and

Jackson? Her gaze darted around until she saw them, already moving up the road. Not that they hadn't seen that hug. She was certain they had but at least they were polite enough to pretend otherwise.

Without words, Gabby picked up her sack and started after them. She thought she heard a soft chuckle but she wouldn't give Giovanni the satisfaction of looking back.

He said nothing as he helped her across the trees or held the door open for her when they reached the car. Grateful for the silence, Gabby regained much of her composure. Composure that was rattled by his every touch.

The tea and coffee were long gone but they hadn't eaten the sandwiches thinking they'd have them at the cabin. They'd left them in the car and so decided to stop at the little store down the road. They went through the coffee kiosk in the parking lot and sat at the picnic benches outside to enjoy the warming day.

Although she'd stopped at the store here in the last couple of weeks, the memories that assaulted her were of when she and Logan had sat at this very same bench. A gentle pressure on her thigh reconnected her to the conversation.

How does he know?

Sandwiches and drinks finished, they piled back into the car and headed for Fremont. When they got within cell range, Gabby called Doc S and gave her the news. They decided that first the road needed to be cleared. Doc S was going to call the people who took down the trees she thinned out every couple of years. Once that was done, she and Gabby would spend a weekend cleaning up the rest.

"We could make it a work party," Gabby said. "Maybe Sophia could contribute her chocolate cake and her pecan sticky buns."

Jackson said he'd volunteer if he could have a whole cake and a pan of buns. Giovanni said he'd come back to help if he could have the same. Doc S heard them and said she'd contract with Sophia for as many cakes and pecan sticky buns and maybe the chocolate peanut butter cookies that would entice a weekend work party.

Gabby was smiling as Jackson drove into Fremont and to Montgomery House. She was still smiling when she hugged Lily, Jackson and Giovanni and said her good-byes.

Jackson and Lily's invitation that she come for spaghetti dinner tomorrow night was accepted. As she drove to Murphy House, she cursed herself for accepting the invitation. Giovanni would be there. Her body hummed with the memory of his arms wrapped her, his taut body pressed against hers, his clove and sandalwood scent surrounding her.

He Knows

A weary Gabby trudged to the front door, opened it and faced a concerned Lily on the other side.

"What's wrong?" Lily stepped into the house, closed the door with one hand as she wrapped the other around Gabby for a hug.

"Didn't sleep well." Gabby pulled away before she clung to Lily showing a weakness she kept carefully hidden.

"So you said. I'd have thought with all the hiking around we did yesterday, you'd have slept soundly." Lily took Gabby's hand and pulled her through the house to the kitchen. There she put on a kettle to boil and got out cups, milk and sugar. Lily said nothing else as she busied herself around the kitchen but Gabby was cognizant Lily was very aware of her.

"You know, some nights are just like that. For whatever reason, just couldn't sleep."

"I know you will want to say 'no' but I'm asking you to seriously consider the dinner invitation. You know you can come as you are in ratty sweats and no one will think anything of it. You don't have to stay late and you don't have to drive—probably shouldn't as tired as you look.

"I'll drive and bring you back whenever you say so. But the offer to spend the night and I'll bring you home in the morning is also being made. And, I'm sure there will be plenty so you can leave with a container of spaghetti and some bread."

Gabby smiled. Lily was in her 'take charge' mode. She might stay with her and have Jackson bring food over here if she didn't go with her. "When I called to cancel you said Jackson had peppermint ice cream with a new mint chocolate sauce."

"And, he'll send some of that home with you too. I promise."

"How can you make a promise for Jackson?"

With a saucy smile and a flirtatious tone, Lily said, "I have my ways of convincing him to do most anything I want."

Gabriella laughed. She had an idea of what methods Lily would employ and knew it wouldn't take much or even be a hardship. "He's that much of a pushover?"

"Not really a 'pushover'. He's asked me to travel with him on his next trip to California. I told him I'd have to see how things were going. What he doesn't know is that Ashley and I've worked something out and I'll be free to go with him in two weeks."

"Lily Hughes!" Gabby was laughing. "You have a manipulative streak in you I've never seen!"

"Of course you have. I plan ahead. You know that about me. You saw me try all sorts of tricks to get Dr. Mark to release me when I wanted to go home after that accident."

"But none of that worked."

"No, but it was good practice. I know Jackson's weaknesses—"

"And he knows yours—." Gabby interrupted.

Lily laughed. "It's a mutual strength we have that we only use on a win-win basis. He'll have strings attached to your bringing ice cream and the new sauce home."

"Of course, I'll have to guard it with my life and praise it to the heavens. He and Grant are getting a little competitive with their ice cream contest."

"And it's all to our benefit."

"Well, to our emotional benefit. I'm not sure it's to my physical benefit."

"You actually look like you've lost some weight," Lily said scrutinizing Gabby. "You look good but I wouldn't lose any more if I were you.

"So are you coming?"

"Okay, I'll come but—."

"No buts. Grab a nightgown and toothbrush. You don't have to stay but that gives you the option. Always better to plan ahead, to have options so you don't get caught and cornered."

Gabby did as Lily suggested—well, ordered was more like it. But disguised as a suggestion, she amended to herself.

Of course Giovanni was there. She wasn't sure why because he usually only stayed for a couple of days, maybe a week at the most but this time he seemed settled in. Jackson, Daniel, Matthew, Grant and Giovanni were often together.

He was friendly toward her, held the chair out for her at the table and made small talk to fill in the silences when she stared into space. But there was also a knowingness in his eyes as if he'd been there last night as she woke, the screams caught in her throat like a barbed hook in a fish.

Of course he didn't really know what had happened but that notion was dispelled when he leaned toward her and said in a lowered voice, "Ah *mia cara*, the nightmares come again. It is bad for you to be alone at such times. You stay here tonight and it will be better. If they come, Giovanni will chase them away."

What Are They Up To?

Was it because she was so tired when she went to bed or was it just a night off—whatever it was, Gabby was pleased she'd slept the whole night through—well, almost the whole night. Her new normal seemed to be six full hours of sleep. It was better than the nights of two or three hours but still way off what she needed to be at her best in her job.

When she turned on her phone, she had a text from Jordan, the leader of the Seattle team she'd been assigned to last spring. He was going to be in Fremont and hoped to see her.

Her brow scrunched in how to respond, she startled when Giovanni greeted her.

"*Buongiorno, mia Cara.*"

His voice always reminded her of melted chocolate, the kind you drizzled over coffee ice cream before adding the whipped cream. Decadent... .

Gabby swung around to face him, flushed with where her thoughts were headed. She was battling her past. She needed no entanglements now. With a sudden clarity, she quickly texted "Not a good time. On personal—." She stopped. Not wanting anyone to know why she took the leave, she deleted the last two words and added "Maybe next time."

She had an instant reply. "I'll look forward to it." Another followed. "When will you be back to work?"

"Not sure right now."

Tucking her phone in her sweat pants pocket, she followed her nose to the kitchen where Jackson was scrambling eggs and bacon was already on a plate along with Giovanni's left-over bread that had been made into French toast.

"How many people are you expecting for breakfast?" Gabby watched with amazement as Jackson finished the eggs off with a dash of cream and a large cube of cream cheese. She perched on one of the chairs set around the far side of the kitchen island and sighed at the mouthwatering food set before her.

Lily came in and after giving Jackson a serious good-morning kiss, sat next to her.

She and Lily dished up leaving an enormous amount of food on the platters. Before she finished swallowing her first bite, the doorbell rang and in strode Matthew, Daniel and Grant.

While the men grabbed plates and dove into the food, she noticed again how tight they'd become. Although Daniel and Jackson had been friends as had Giovanni and Jackson, the other men, Matthew, Grant and even Michael in Ireland had not known one another.

It occurred to her that what brought them together was the women they loved. She stopped in her mental tracks because that didn't apply to Giovanni. But he and Jackson go way back, she reminded herself. They were friends before Jackson ever knew Lily.

"They make an interesting group, don't they?" Lily observed as the men moved to sit at the dining room table.

Gabby nodded, pulling her gaze from them to find her cup of tea. Taking a sip, she took another bite of French toast. The bread had a chewy texture that she really enjoyed. After savoring another bite, she turned toward Lily. "What are they doing? They seem so business-like right now."

"They've come up with some project."

"Do you know what the project is?"

"Top secret. Nothing I do will loosen his lips. He just smiles or laughs and enjoys my efforts but—."

"Same with Diana, Ashley and Hunter?"

"Exactly the same. In this one thing, those men are united and will not give even a hint to any of us. Of course they know we are comparing notes to see if we can figure anything out but they've come up with standard answers to all questions having to do with the project so we are drawing blanks."

"Have you asked Elizabeth if Michael knows anything about it?"

"We have, he does and he won't tell either."

"How come I'm just learning about this?" Gabby turned on her stool toward Lily, her face scrunched in a frustrated frown.

"What would we have said to either you or Sophia? We don't know what they're doing.

"And, Sophia is wrapped up in these final weeks of her friend's life and you've been struggling with something." Lily laid her hand on Gabby's arm. "We weren't keeping anything from you or Soph. We just, I guess individually because we haven't talked about it, didn't say anything to either of you.

Believe me when I say, if I learn anything, you will certainly be included. And if you have any ideas, please share."

"It has to do with The Circle." Gabby pushed aside the thought to deny anything was wrong. They'd become so energetically attuned to each other, Lily would know it was a lie. "And it has to do with a building."

"Because?"

"Because that is what binds them together and that is where their strengths lie."

"Makes sense…," Lily paused and then a grin blossomed. "You've given me other ideas how to worm some more information out of Jackson."

"Or you could just let them do what they're doing. It might even be more challenging for them if you stop asking."

"Very clever idea. We should let the others know."

"They are enjoying whatever they are planning and I'm positive that whatever it is, The Circle will be delighted. I can't even wrap my mind around those men ever doing something to hurt anyone in The Circle."

"You're right. Let's see if the others can get together for lunch? It's time we start planning on Samhain in Ireland and we can add leaving the men to their project to the agenda."

Death Changes All

A call from Sophia usurped the idea of lunch and talk of Ireland. Her friend was in ICU and not expected to make it through the next 24 hours. Even though that prognosis had been made before, she believed it to be true this time.

He wanted to go.

He was comfortable in a coma from the morphine and she was by his side, holding his hand and assuring him she'd stay until he passed over.

They freed up their schedules and headed to Sophia's. Each of them remembering a time when, without asking, The Circle showed up in their lives. Help, support, to make sure they weren't alone in a difficult time—whatever was needed, they'd made sure it got done.

Diana dropped Madison Michelle off with Matthew at a construction site on her way. Daniel would see that the children were home from school and okay, which freed Ashley up. They took charge of the laundry—stripping linens from the bed, towels from the bathroom and kitchen to start the laundry.

Lily and Gabriella tackled the garden, pulling weeds, discarding rotting fruits and vegetables—filling a yard debris bin which they put out at the curb for pick-up.

Hunter showed up, Grant with her. Together they dusted and vacuumed.

Lily called Jackson and asked him to put together a container of his spaghetti. Giovanni offered to bake another loaf of bread to go with it.

When Sophia came home, her house would be clean, her bed changed, her garden tidied and food would be waiting.

After checking in at the hospital and learning there was no change, the women adjourned to Sophia's living room, her sacred space, while Grant finished sorting the recycling and rolled that bin and the garbage bin to the curb.

Smudging themselves, they created a circle and raised their arms in silent prayer. With the smudge stick still smoldering, Diana led them through the house, cleansing each room with the smoke and prayers.

"May you be held in the light of love as you complete this part of your journey."

"May you be held in the light of gratitude as you bear-witness to another's passing."

"May you know you are from the light and that love flows through you to the outer world."

"May you feel our presence as we send love to you at this special time."

"May you know the Goddess is with you this day and forever more."

Gabriella shivered as a blend of light and shadow passed through her. "He's gone." She looked at the others and knew they'd felt the same thing. Turning to Lily, Gabby asked, "What do you think is the best thing for us to do? I'm more than willing to stay until she comes home or even go to the hospital and bring her back."

"Let's see what she wants to do." Lily pulled out her cell phone and called the hospital asking for the ICUnit. After asking the clerk who answered if talking to Sophia was possible, they all waited.

"Hi Soph, we got your message. We're all here at your place." Lily said. "Yes, we felt him pass.

"How can we support you at this time?" Lily nodded and gestured to the others, who stood in a semi-circle around her.

"Here are some ideas. We can come and get you, bring you and your car home. We can come and just be with you while you take however much time you need to be there.

"Yes, our leaving you alone is an option and if that is what you truly need, we will honor it."

Diana took the phone from Lily. "Soph, it's Diana. While I totally understand why Lily is being so neutral about all this, I am coming to be with you. You can order me to leave, but I will be there and I will give you a hug before I go."

"Guess you're going to have to deal with a few more hugs," Ashley said, taking the phone from Diana, "because I'm coming with Diana. And just so you know, Hunter and Gabby are nodding their heads."

Handing the phone back to Lily, Ashley headed to the laundry. "Got a load of laundry to fold before I go."

"Soph, Lily again. Yes, you are not being totally listened to but remember the insurrection is being done with love. And, Jackson is sending over his special spaghetti along with Giovanni's freshly baked bread so there is nothing for you to do once you are home.

"Okay, I'll pass that along. Always know you are loved by many, Soph."

Hanging up Lily called out. "Soph will be ready to come home in an hour. She is willing to have someone drive her car as she admits she is really tired. She doesn't know if she wants company or not."

"Do you think Jackson can make enough food to feed us all if she does want us to be here? I've never seen her freezer so bare. She hasn't been cooking like she normally does." Hunter paced to the freezer and checked the contents again.

"Lily, why don't you check with Jackson and Giovanni and see if they can put enough food together for everyone. If she doesn't want company, we can put it in her freezer." Diana was already making a list. "We need to check the cupboard and make sure she has tea and if the dishwasher is clean unload it or run it if not."

"Ash and I'll go get Sophia," Gabby volunteered. "That will leave the three of you to take care of everything here and make a grocery store run if need."

"We've got a plan," Lily said. "I'll check in with Jackson and Giovanni now."

"Ash, I've volunteered you to come with me to bring Sophia home," Gabby said to Ashley who had come in from the laundry area.

"There were some towels not quite dry. I've put them back for another fifteen minutes or so." Ashley picked up her purse and headed toward the front door after Gabby.

Gabby volunteered to stay the night with Sophia but was sent home. In hindsight, while she wanted to be there for her circle sister, it was probably better in case the nightmares came again. It wasn't Sophia's job to take care of her.

It was interesting to watch as everyone said their 'good byes' and left except Lily. Lily didn't even ask about staying. When Jackson arrived with the food, he had a small basket with Lily's nightgown, toothbrush, etc. Of course, of all of them, Lily could relate better to what Sophia might be feeling because of her work. One of the things that made her a sought after guardian and geriatric case manager was her ability to build solid relationships with her clients.

In her bedroom at the Murphy House, Gabby readied herself for bed. She decided to leave her salt crystal and selenite lamps on. Their soft light might help keep the nightmares away and if they came, waking to their healing light would be better than the dark. Or so she hoped.

Again she held the vison of the spruce cone in her mind's eye as she drifted into the dark.

In Support of Sophia

The nightmares didn't come. Was it the lights or her exhaustion? She spent the next day with Sophia because Lily had a court hearing.

Ashley came over once while the children were in school and brought several different dark chocolate bars. After chopping them up and mixing the pieces in a bowl, she fixed herself a cup of tea and joined Gabby and Sophia on the patio.

It was a cool day and the outdoor heater wasn't set up yet. Instead of wrestling with it or even calling Daniel or Matthew, they covered up with blankets from the family room and let the beauty and peace of a fall garden surround them.

The chrysanthemums and asters that had survived the storm were blooming. Pumpkin orange peeked out from under large green leaves further back in the vegetable patch. Gabby was glad they'd made an effort to clean the garden up a bit—certainly not up to Sophia's standards, but the amount of damaged plants and spoiled and dead fruit, vegetables and flowers would make a dark day even worse.

"More tea?" Ashley stood with cup in hand. "I'm ready for another cup."

Gabby held her cup up for Ashley to take. A glance showed her that Sophia's cup was half-full and clutched in white-knuckled hands.

"Soph." Gabby touched her friend's arm. "Soph, Ash is going to freshen up your tea." With her free hand, Gabby reached for the cup. As she pulled it from Sophia's grasp, her friend startled.

"What?" As if waking up from a deep sleep, Sophia's movements were jerky. She clutched the cup to her chest and swiveled toward Gabby and Ashley. "What?"

"Ash is getting us fresh tea," Gabby explained. "And, she's brought us some great chocolate." She nodded to the bowl on the small table nearby.

"Oh, okay." Sophia handed her cup to Ashley. "Sorry. I don't know... ."

"No apology needed, Soph," Ashley said. "I'm going to get that tea now and be right back." She paused in the doorway. "Anything else I can get y'all?"

"Are we good, Soph?"

When Sophia nodded, Ashley called out. "Be right back."

Gabby stood and took a few steps so she stood behind Sophia's chair. Bending over she put her arms around her and hugged. "Hard time right now. Thought maybe a hug would help."

Sophia raised a hand and held Gabby's. "He's gone and yet he isn't. I still hear him talking to me."

"What's he saying?"

Her grip on Gabby's hand tightened. "Take care of myself. And 'thank you'. I made a difference in his life."

The wetness on her hand, the shuddering shoulders, the bowed head, Gabby shifted to the side and half-held Sophia. Ashley appeared on the other side, wrapped her arms around Soph and rocked.

"Her friend—," Gabby started.

"I heard." Ashley kissed Sophia's temple. "Let's go inside, Soph. I'm going to pick a bouquet of chrysanthemums and asters for the table so you'll still be able to see them."

"Let's shift the couch so it looks directly out on the garden. If that's okay with you, Soph."

Just then the doorbell rang, Gabby stood. "I'll see—."

"I'm back," Lily called out, "and I've brought men and food."

Gabby turned back to Sophia. "What about the couch? Would you like to sit there and see the garden?"

Sophia whispered "I'd like that". She took a deep breath and scrubbed her hands over her face in an effort to erase the tears.

Gabby half-smiled. *It isn't working. Lily already knows and she isn't even all the way out here.*

Her hand resting on Sophia's shoulder, Gabby turned to a concerned Lily, seeing Jackson and Giovanni just behind. "We're grateful you're here, guys. Need some muscle."

"What needs doing?" Jackson paused in the door way deciding not to follow Lily onto the patio.

"The outdoor heater is in the garage and it's cool enough now it needs to be set up here. And, we want to rearrange the family room furniture so Soph can more easily see into her garden when she's relaxing on the couch."

"We do furniture first." Giovanni turned back to the family room scrutinizing the arrangement. He said something to Jackson, who also looked around and nodded.

They moved the dining room table in front of the fireplace. Next they set the couch, chair and recliner in a u-shape around the low coffee table. The furniture was not really in a conversation configuration because regardless of where you sat you saw into some part of the garden.

"What do you think?" Lily held Sophia's hand as they came into the house.

A watery smile and slight nod was all Sophia managed in reply. But she did come in and sit in the swivel rocker recliner now positioned to see out the sliding glass doors.

Giovanni stood beside Sophia. "You have beautiful garden. But you have a problem. An idea for you to consider to fix the problem. Glass sliders." He strode to the door and gestured how they'd work.

"Jackson?"

"I'm listening. And I will agree it is an excellent suggestion. It would create a totally indoor-outdoor portal."

"You think about it, *si*?" Giovanni patted Sophia's shoulder as he passed. "We get the heater now?"

"*Si*, we get the heater now. We'll bring it around the side of the house." Jackson led the way toward the garage.

Moments later he was back. "To get to it, we need to move your car."

"I'll do it," Gabriella volunteered. She picked up the car keys from the hall table where they were always kept and went out to the garage. Before she moved the car she approached Jackson and Giovanni. "How much would it cost to put in that glass door thing you're talking about?"

Giovanni flashed a smile in her direction. "*Si*, Jackson and I ordered it just now. Matthew and Daniel will help us install."

"What if she doesn't—,"

"Breathe, Gabby," Jackson interrupted. "She'll be okay with it. I've heard her comment on how much she likes the one Matthew put in at their place."

"Do you think that means she'll like it at her place?"

"We won't install it without her approval."

"Who's paying for it?"

"Us guys and Giovanni. It's our way of making a partial payment for all she's done for us." Jackson smiled and added. "You do know what she's given each of us, don't you?"

"Actually, I do. But she's also given each of us pretty much the same thing."

Jackson's forehead wrinkled.

"She gives you each other," Giovanni said. "She give the guys their wives but she gives each of you the others."

Gabby's breath clogged her lungs, her feet tripped over each other as she spun around to push the button to open the garage door. "I'll move the car."

Change is Coming

It was his perceptiveness that rattled her almost as much as the masculine energy that emanated or was it oozed from each pore. Whatever it was it screamed *Danger, Danger, Danger.* She couldn't help but think of him because whenever his scent of cloves and sandalwood touched her senses, she was consumed by a heightened awareness of his every move.

The car moved to the driveway, Gabby headed back into the house. Lily was sitting on the couch, a calm presence in the somberness that had invaded Sophia's usually bright and lively home. She patted the place next to her.

A quizzical quirk of her brow and Lily leaned towards her. "Jackson and Giovanni have an idea. I'd like your input first."

Gabby nodded and tilted her head to better hear Lily's soft voice.

"They think it a good idea for her to take a few weeks off, bereavement leave if possible, to rest and relax. Giovanni has offered the use of his villa on the Italian coast. Since his schedule is uncertain, the idea is for someone else to be there as well."

It didn't take a psychic to know who that 'someone' was to be. Gabby knew everyone else had families to care for. And, the reality was, she still had four more weeks of leave which meant she actually could go without doing anything other than asking one of the others to check on Murphy House.

As if reading her mind, Lily continued, "Jackson or I will stop by Murphy House every day and take in the mail, etc."

"I can hear you, you know."

Gabby looked up to see Sophia had swiveled her chair around and was glaring at them. A second glance and Gabby knew it wasn't a real glare; the pain radiating from the depths was so stark, so dark it took her breath away.

"It's more than the death of your friend, isn't it?" Gabby moved the few feet and knelt next to Sophia's chair. "I know he became important to you and you devoted so much time to his well-being and care especially in the last few months but…"

"I tried to give him what I couldn't give to Jonathan." Tears streamed down Sophia's face.

Lily, now on the other side of the chair, put her arm around Sophia's shoulder. "And so you did. Never forget that Jonathan knows what you did here. Never forget that your loving care mattered to not only your friend but to those around him who saw your dedication."

"Do you really think I should leave here for a while?" Sophia clutched Gabriella's hand and turned to Lily.

"Yes, I do." Lily hugged Sophia. "It would be healing for you to not be here for a few weeks. To have no responsibilities except to just be.

"Your garden is past its prime and the rest of us can manage, especially if you give us a list of what needs to be done. Diana and Matthew live closest to you and they are willing to stop by and check on your house every day."

"This has been decided?"

"No, it is your decision. We just want you to know that we are ready to support you if the answer is 'yes'."

"Do you think Hunter and Grant would be willing to stay here if I go? Someone living here would—."

"They would be delighted," Lily interrupted. "You know they are trying to figure out whether to launch a major renovation of the spaces above the studio or just buy or build a place. This would give them a taste of what it would be like to have a house and yard."

Gabby had kept silent, letting the two talk. Sophia had kept ahold of her hand through it all. Her grip tightened and she turned toward her. "And would you come with me? Cheer me out of the doldrums if I get too far down?"

"You mean like race you to the end of the pool? Or challenge you to how much wine we can drink at dinner?"

Sophia smiled. A sad smile but Gabby was glad to see it. Over Sophia's head, she saw Lily give her a bright smile and quick nod.

"I'm sure we'll figure things out as we go, Soph. From what I remember Diana saying about her stay last year, it is a grand place and the staff are wonderful. There are little villages to explore or if we prefer, nothing at all to do.

"When was the last time you had nothing to do? No papers to grade? No garden to weed or water? No pecan sticky buns to bake?"

Giovanni and Jackson had come in from the patio as Gabriella was asking these questions.

"Ahh, *mia Sophia*," Giovanni picked Sophia's hand up and kissed the back. "We pack a suitcase of your pecan buns and maybe a chocolate cake?"

Sophia chuckled. "I believe your villa has a kitchen."

"A kitchen with a temperamental chef." Giovanni winked at Sophia. "This is why I come to visit my friend, Jackson. He always has a supply of your decadence in his freezer."

"And I thought it was for my marvelous spaghetti, better than any you can find in Italy." Jackson pouted, an exaggerated look of hurt on his face.

"No, I come to add my bread so your dismal spaghetti looks better."

"You will come with me if I agree to go?" Sophia stared at Gabby.

"I will go with you." Gabby looked over at Jackson and Giovanni, "And do you have a plan for when this trip is taking place?"

"Of course we do. In three days. Giovanni has already contacted the embassy and made arrangements for tourist visas. We've checked and there are tickets available on the same flight back he is taking." Jackson rocked back on his heels. "That gives the two of you time to pack and take care of whatever else you need to do."

"Don't look so pleased with yourself, Jackson," Lily cautioned.

"Seriously, Sophia, I think both you and Gabriella could use a vacation where the only thing you have to do is relax, enjoy the sun and let other people look after you. Giovanni's villa is the perfect place to do that. Talk to Diana. I'm sure she'll agree."

Gabby remembered Diana describing the villa as a peaceful place where she had time to reflect, time to sort things out and decide on her forward path. *Maybe this will help me sort out what I need to do to finish my healing and move forward with my life.*

Italy

The heat of Rome was in stark contrast to the cool fall air of Fremont. Gabby stayed close to Giovanni who had Sophia's arm as they made their way to baggage claim and then on through the airport to the outside. Almost instantly a limousine pulled up and as the trunk opened, a man jumped out of the driver's side and hurried around to the back of the car.

Gabby had no idea what the words being said meant but the action was clear. Efficiently luggage was loaded into the trunk by the driver while Giovanni ushered them in to the backseat.

An open bottle of champagne was waiting along with fresh fruit, bread and cheese. A small door opened and damp towels were inside. "Something to freshen up with," Giovanni said.

It was surreal in many ways but Gabby was determined to appear sophisticated enough so her mouth wouldn't hang open and she wouldn't disgrace herself.

"We spend a few days here in Roma," Giovanni said, gesturing to the city outside as the car made its way through the crowded streets. "After we rest, we have dinner at a little restaurant I know well."

And so it was. Sumptuous rooms overlooking a walled garden filled with flowers; dinner at an intimate restaurant that not only did Giovanni know well but where he was well known. The next day they walked through narrow streets and wide plazas and stopped at an outdoor café for a snack. No rushing about, they took their time. At the Trevi Fountain they made a wish and threw coins over their shoulders. Gabby's wish was the healing of her past to be done so she could move forward with her life.

That night dinner was at his home. The chef created a magical dish of fresh fish, vegetables, rice and a sponge cake soaked in amaretto and brandy that Gabby fell in love with. Of course there was wine—a different one for each course and each was delicious. Only by sheer force of will did she only have a half-glass with each course – six in all which meant three glasses of wine.

As a precaution, she took a couple of aspirin when she went to bed to, hopefully, ward off the headaches she always got when she drank wine.

The aspirin did work.

And the next day more sightseeing followed a breakfast of fresh pastry, still warm from the oven; fresh fruit and the fresh squeezed juice that Diana had raved about. Stops at the museums with lunch at a little bistro on a side street where no one spoke English, but with Giovanni there it didn't matter.

The third morning, Giovanni announced that he had business to attend to. They could stay and do more sightseeing with Antonia as tour guide, or they would be taken to his villa on the coast. He'd join them there for the weekend.

Although Gabriella remembered Antonia from Diana's description of her time in Italy, the ever darkening circles under Sophia's eyes were a testimony to sleepless nights. Gabby suggested they go to his villa. Maybe in his home overlooking the Mediterranean Sea, Sophia might be able to nap during the day.

When they pulled into the drive of Giovanni's villa, Gabriella's breath caught in her throat. She'd been referring to this magnificent place as 'his home'. It was stunning and overwhelming and inviting and peaceful all at the same time.

That evening she and Sophia sat at a small table on a veranda overlooking the sea. The scent of flowers in the air and quiet music added to the calm, peaceful and relaxing ambiance.

"This is an amazing place. It almost doesn't seem real." Gabby lifted her glass of champagne toward Sophia. "To healing."

"To healing" Sophia touched her glass to Gabriella's. "To healing and storytelling. I'm glad we insisted you bring your laptop. This is a perfect place to write."

"We'll see. Right now I'm full of wonderful food, relaxed with a tiny buzz from the champagne and yawning. I was so tempted to lie down on that bed but knew if I did I'd miss dinner. And speaking of 'glad'. I'm glad you brought your swimsuit. The pool looks heavenly."

They wandered through the garden and watched the sunset. When they were back in the house, the maid, Margretta, gave them a message from Giovanni. "Signore Migliori say *"Enjoy my home! I see you Saturday. If you want, you ask. My people are at your command."*

Margretta's dark brown hair was pulled into a soft twist on the back of her head. She was around five feet six in shoes and of medium build. The black pants and white blouse, a kind of uniform all the staff wore, was conservative, attractive but not sexy.

"Doesn't it both you to be referred to as "my people"? Gabriella asked the young woman.

Margretta's dark brown eyes sparkled, her lips turned up in a smile. "Signore Migliori is good employer. It is a pleasure to work here for him."

Gabby sat in the lounge chair on the balcony outside her bedroom. The stars in the inky blackness fought to claim the night from the moon. The beam of the lighthouse on a distant point swathed a path across the water. The rolling sea engaged in its timeless battle with the rocks, its sound soothed.

Tired. So tired from the long journey and the time change. As tension leached from her body, exhaustion claimed her. Her heightened state of stress had been upon her for a very long time.

Now stress free.

No, not stress free. But being here in the villa, the pressure to finish her healing process eased.

Eyes drooped shut, her head nodded as her body relaxed. Before falling asleep, she got up from the lounge chair and went inside. Leaving the door open, she hoped the soft sound of the surf would keep her demons at bay. Crawling into bed, she pulled the covers up to her chin. With the clear vision of the spruce cone held in her mind's eye, Gabby closed her eyes and prayed.

"Goddess hear your child. I ask you to be with me this night. To show me my path to peace. I feel it near at hand but I've no idea how to claim it for my own. Blessed Be."

Settling In and A Plan

Hearing the soft sound of surf that had lulled her to sleep was the first sense that registered. Although she was on her side and curled around a pillow, there was no tension in her body. A mild lethargy, aches and nausea were the next signs her body was relaxed. Sleeping so deeply she'd drooled on the pillow, Gabby welcomed the normally unsettling physical sensations. To her they meant she had let go of the toxins her muscles had clamped onto when she was stressed, anxious, frustrated and panicky.

Moments passed while she laid in bed relishing the peacefulness and calm. Finally she stretched, marveled at how neat the linens were after a night's sleep, and climbed out of bed.

Before her shower, she stood on the balcony, the dark blue sea before her, the sky a light blue. White caps danced on the peaks of the waves, seagulls swirled high and low, the scent of flowers from the garden drifted on the light breeze. The sun was already high in the sky when she finally noticed it.

"Oh my! What time is it?" Gabby dashed to the bathroom and took a quick shower before tossing on a skirt and top. Barefoot, she charged down the stairs stopping only when she reached the doorway to the veranda.

Sophia, a dreamy smile on her face, was sitting on a chaise lounge, a glass in one hand. Gabby paused before intruding.

"I know you're there," Sophia said without turning. With her free hand she motioned Gabby forward.

Plopping down on the chaise next to Sophia, Gabby sat to the side so she could see her friend's face.

Eyes still closed, Sophia said, "I've not been up that long. Guess we both needed an extraordinarily long sleep."

Margretta appeared next to her. "May I get you something?"

Gabby looked up, noting her smooth skin, trim figure and sparkling eyes where happiness glowed. *Of course he would be surrounded by beautiful women. I wonder if—.* She stopped herself from completing the thought. "I don't want to bother—,"

Margretta raised her hand, palm out. "Signore Migliori says to do as you request."

"This orange juice is divine." Sophia took another sip. "Ambrosia of the goddess."

"I think I need something more than juice," Gabby said when her stomach growled.

"I bring you tray with fruit, cheese and pastry."

"That sounds wonderful. And, the juice please?"

"*Si*, I put a pitcher of juice on the tray. Oh, and Adolpho, our cook, wants to know when you want to eat?

"I think she means when we want to have a real meal." Sophia opened her eyes and sat up. "I find I'm hungry but I'm not really hungry, so you can decide, at least today."

"What time is it now?" Gabby asked the maid.

"Does it make any difference what time it is?" Sophia answered.

"Maybe it doesn't, at least today." Gabby smiled and winked. Turning to Margretta she said, "We would like something in three or four hours if that is okay."

"*Va bene, si,* it will be *bene,* good." Margretta's face flushed. "My English not so good."

"Your English is much better than my Italian," Gabby assured her.

A slight curtsy, a dip of her head and Margretta turned back to the house.

"This is like a dream and if it turns out to really be one, I'm glad I'm sharing it with you." Sophia reached over and patted Gabby's knee. "I did think at one point to check on you but then decided not to because of how hard I slept. No nightmares, no dreams—a peaceful night's sleep."

"I didn't know you had nightmares, Soph."

"Not usually but with my friend getting sicker and sicker and my knowing he was dying, they came back."

"That's right, you did have them after Jonathan died." Gabby held Sophia's hand. "I'm glad I'm here with you, too."

Margretta returned with the promised tray of fruit, cheese and pastry along with slices of bread and the pitcher of juice from oranges growing on the property.

"No wonder it tastes so different. Mere minutes from being picked to being in our glasses makes a huge difference. Even better than squeezing oranges purchased at the grocery store."

Finished with the meal, they walked past the pool and down the path to cliff's edge. As they settled down on a bench along the balustrade, Gabby pointed out the distant lighthouse.

The sound of waves doing battle with the cliffs below drew their attention away from the lighthouse.

Sophia leaned over the railing to get a better look below. "Imagine how many centuries, how many eons the water has worked to take down the cliff."

"If you look over there," Gabby pointed to the right, "you can see where it has made more progress. There's a cave. Do you think it was used for smuggling?"

"If you look beyond it, there's sort of a path leading from the top of the cliff down. I wonder if at low tide there is beach and you can access the cave."

"A place for star-crossed but improbable lovers."

"You could write their story, Gabby. Do think about it.

"What do you think their background is?"

"He is the second son of the man who owns the villa and she is a maid?"

"Why isn't he the first son, the heir?"

"Oh, because as the second son he has more to lose. His father probably wouldn't disown or disinherit the first son but the second son is expected to also marry to improve the fortunes of the family."

"You've a great idea, Soph. I think you should write the story."

"I'll write my story if you also write," Sophia bargained. "So, if this isn't your story, what is?"

"The owner of the villa is a successful business man. So successful he has his choice of companions and never lacks for anyone to share his bed."

"Okay, but who is the one who captures his heart?"

"I don't know. Maybe a tourist. Maybe a servant. Maybe the daughter, make that a really young daughter of his best friend and business partner?"

Sophia put her hand out. "Let's shake on it. We'll set aside a couple of hours each day to write and see what we come up with by the time we head home."

Gabby was shaking Sophia's hand before her better judgement caught up with her. *I've tried writing stories but even my agent gave up on trying to sell them. Why am I doing this?* But when she saw the spark of excitement growing in Sophia, she knew why. *I'm here to help her find her way back from the edge, to help her find peace and to help her rest and recuperate.*

Elizabeth's Visit and The Plan

The fifth day they were in Italy, they had company. Elizabeth and little Maeve came to visit. Traveling with a four month old baby from Ireland to Italy wasn't the challenge traveling from Ireland to Oregon in the United States would be.

Having the distraction of the baby helped in many ways. Elizabeth was an amazing mother as Gabby knew she'd be. Her favorite time to hold the squirming, grinning, babbling bundle was after E had fed her and welcomed a few moments to put herself back together. Being a nursing mom meant no matter what, when Maeve was hungry, she stopped and fed her. To Gabby breast feeding seemed like a huge commitment but the look on E's face when Maeve, cradled in E's arms, her small hand on E's breast, was mesmerizing.

Would she ever have children? A glance at the misty look on Sophia's face brought home that neither would her circle sister. *Would I want children?* For the first time in her life, Gabby actually wondered if that was something she'd miss, really miss, because to do it the way she'd want to—it was a full time job.

I don't think I have the temperament to be a mom, especially to a new baby who can't tell me what's wrong.

Three days later Michael flew down to escort Elizabeth and Maeve home. He had access to a private jet and although his wife and daughter had flown first class, he wanted E to be able to feed Maeve without anyone else, well, other than him, around. His grin as he held his daughter, an arm around his wife, telegraphed that in his world all was as it should be.

Of course the invitation was for them to stop by in Ireland on their way home. Michael would change tickets out if that was agreeable to them.

While the discussion was still taking place, Giovanni arrived. His hair in disarray, a day's growth of beard shadowing his face, he took Gabby's breath away.

"You do not steal my guests." Giovanni stood with his feet apart and hands on his hips as he glared at Michael.

"We could share," Michael offered, a grin mitigating his no-nonsense stance.

"Excuse me," Gabby interjected. "I do hope neither of you are referring to either Sophia or me." She glared at the two men who were way too amused with this conversation.

Giovanni shifted, his gaze now locked with hers.

She cocked a brow and waited.

"I invite you to stay here." He paused but instead of going on, he turned and strode away.

She'd seen the tiredness and stress in his eyes. And underneath, it was as if she could see past the surface and into the darkness within. Underneath was a pain that she doubted he let anyone see. *But I saw it.*

"Michael, Giovanni is right. He did invite us to stay here and it seems to be important to him." Gabriella wasn't sure why she needed to speak up on Giovanni's behalf but the words just tumbled out.

"Gabby is right," Sophia added. "He did invite both of us to stay for three weeks. We've been here a week now and the change has been wonderful. I wasn't even aware how tired and drained I'd become.

"However, if you can get my ticket changed so I fly into Shannon on the twenty-second, I will tell him I want to travel to Ireland a little early so I can help get things ready for Samhain. Otherwise Gabby and I'll see you in two weeks for Samhain."

They didn't see Giovanni at dinner and Michael, Elizabeth and Maeve left at daylight.

Giovanni saw her sitting on the white balustrade overlooking the sea. Silhouetted against the bright blue of the water, the breeze ruffling her auburn curls, she took his breath away. His feet shuffled to find their balance.

He'd been too exhausted, too raw to spend the evening with everyone last night. Today was better. He wasn't good but he was better—good enough to spend time with Sophia and Gabriella and keep things lighthearted.

"I find you in my favorite place."

"This is your favorite place?" She turned toward him, her face uplifted so their gazes met.

"*Si*, when I want time to think, when I need inspiration, this is my favorite place." Her hazel eyes turned from green to grey to blue in an instant. *They reflect her emotions, I think.*

Remaining seated, Gabby gestured to the cave. "Does that cave have a history, a story?"

He laughed. "You want to know about Sophia's story?"

Her indignation flared.

He knew when she realized he joked because the bristly energy around her softened.

"There are so many spots around here that have a long history. In Fremont, any history more than a few hundred years old, if even that, is lost."

"It was used for smuggling at one time. During World War II, it was a place for the resistance fighters to get new supplies. The cave is very deep and there is an incline a few yards inside so it is safe from the tide."

"Have you ever been in it?"

"*Si*, a few times. But I much prefer the light to the dark."

Except for the background of the sea, a companionable silence surrounded them as they looked out toward the horizon. Multi-colored sails flitted across the waves as sailboats traveled to unknown ports.

"We come back to watch the sunset. Bring wine."

"And Sophia."

"*Si*, and Sophia."

He extended his hand, pleased that she took it. Tucking it in his elbow they started back up the path. "Adolpho has fresh fish he is fixing special for you."

"Fresh fish and fresh bread and fresh salad and fresh cheese. I don't think I've had anything that is even a day old since I arrived."

"You like?"

"I love."

"There you two are." Sophia stood on the veranda, a hand up to shade her eyes from the sun peeking through the lattice roof. "Dinner is actually ready whenever you are."

"I want to wash up and then I'll be right back." Gabby dashed off toward the stairs.

"Giovanni, if you have a minute," Sophia gestured to a chair at the table.

He sat, not surprised when she told him her change in plans. What did surprise him was when she asked him to help her persuade Gabriella to remain.

"She needs more time here. I see a side of her I've not seen for a very long time, if at all. And, she isn't due back to work until the first week in November."

Gabby saw the two of them, heads together, deep in conversation when she came out to the veranda. When they noticed her, they broke apart. Giovanni rose. "I return *un minuto.*"

"What was that all about?" Gabby asked as she sat down.

"A plot to keep you here for another week after I leave." Sophia reached out and held Gabby's hand. "Please consider it. I've no memory of you being so at ease, so relaxed."

Margretta and Silvio, another servant who also doubled as Giovanni's driver, brought in the meal as Giovanni returned to the table.

Her emotions rocketed, her head swirled with 'what ifs'.

Holly's Story Begins

She was thirteen when her mom brought home Uncle Henry. She was fourteen when she realized that his walking in while she was taking a shower was not an accident. She was fifteen when he raped her. She was fifteen when telling her mom got her a slap in the face. She was fifteen when she took to the streets.

Gabby looked at the words on the page from a surreal distance. She was dissociating because she watched her other self sitting at the table on the balcony outside her bedroom typing.

The dream last night was so vivid, so real when she woke she wasn't sure she'd even been asleep or if she'd been lost in memories. After her shower, she understood it was a dream. A dream that made her heart pound, her stomach churn and her other self separate for safety. Even though physically, viscerally she was back in her own childhood, there was something different about Holly. Holly didn't go into foster care. Holly didn't have to go home to another abusive boyfriend. Holly just took off for the streets, somehow knowing her mom would never choose her first, would never protect her.

Oh, honey. It's all right. He only wanted your first time to be with someone who loved you. So many boys out there are only after one thing—sex. Henry wanted something different for you.

Gabby dashed for the bathroom and clung to the toilet as the orange juice she'd had emptied from her belly. In that moment she wasn't sure she could write *Holly's Story*. Wiping the sweat from her forehead and rinsing her mouth with cool water, she brushed her teeth, gargled with mouthwash and returned to the balcony.

The sea dazzled gold and white under the intense sun. Brightly colored spots of sails flew back and forth across the water. Gabby leaned on the balcony railing, drinking in the view and the scented air. Her mind flew with the story, *Holly's Story*.

How could she write this story so people would understand the twisted, crazy-making logic of Holly's mother? And at times her own mother?

Like Holly's mother, her mother also slapped her face, also blamed her for being raped by several of her boyfriends. She'd started Holly's sexual abuse at thirteen but her abuse had started much earlier. The fondling at five she remembered.

Her stomach churned at the memories.

Maybe tea will help

Gabby turned from the view and went inside to find Adolfo and see what was available.

At the bottom of the stairs, she spied Giovanni relaxing on the veranda. He looked up as she started across the wide hall toward the kitchen. He said something in Italian and immediately Margretta appeared.

"How I help you?"

"I am going to the kitchen to see about tea."

"I get for you."

"Thank you, but no. I want to see what's available."

Margretta smiled and gestured toward the archway. "I go with you. When you decide, I bring to you. Signore say you write. You tell Margretta what you need and I bring to you."

"I don't need to be waited on." Gabby paused knowing her tone was harsh. "I mean, it is good for me to get up and move about when I'm writing."

"*Si*, but now you can walk in the garden. I can get tea for you."

Adolfo had no herbal teas but said he'd fix her a pot of orange mint for now and get something else she liked later. She perched on a stool and watched as the chef expertly chopped up mint and zested orange peel. Steeping the mixture in boiling water, he also juiced the orange and added it at the end just as he fixed the cup. She'd asked for a large cup and he'd obliged with a pottery mug with glazes that matched the blues of the sea.

A sip of the brew and she was transported. An elixir of peace. "This is fantastic!"

"You like!" Adolfo beamed.

"*Si*, I like very much."

He nodded, a cheerful smile tipped his mouth. "I fix more?"

"*Si*, this is perfect."

Topping off her mug, she turned and almost dumped her drink all over Giovanni. "Do you have to creep up on a body like that? This is hot. You could have been burned."

"You worry about me?"

The twinkle in his eyes fired Gabby's response. She glared and snapped, "No, I do not worry about you. I don't want to make more work for your staff. You know laundry, mopping floors, making me another."

She sailed past him lowering her chin when she neared the stairs. No point in stumbling or worse yet, falling because she was making a point. With effort she slowed her pace and walked up the steps at a sedate pace. Once back in her room, she sat in front of the laptop, sipping her drink.

A soft knock on the door. "Come in."

Margretta stuck her head inside. "You ring when you want more tea. I get for you. Adolfo makes so you can have anytime."

Turning toward the door, Gabby smiled. "*Grazie.*"

Once she was alone, she stared at the page. Deciding not to reread what she'd already written, she started a new chapter. *The Streets.*

As Gabby continued typing, Holly became a composite of many of the young girls she'd known. It was important to her to convey that homeless youth were there because other options weren't safe—or they didn't perceive them to be safe.

She'd returned home three times before she left for good. Every time she went into foster care, her mom kicked the guy out, swore she'd never let anyone hurt her again, went to the parenting classes, did everything asked of her. But within a month of her return, there would be someone new.

How her mom could only find pedophiles was a thought for another day—or maybe something to let go. Was it important for her to know this? Would it make a difference?

When, with Doc S's help, she came in off the streets, she vowed to never see her mom again. She'd kept that promise for fifteen years.

Starting another chapter, Gabby wrote about Holly being badly beaten when she wouldn't prostitute herself for her latest boyfriend. Of course this was when she met Doc S, her guardian angel, her mentor, her savior.

Where to go next with the story?

Another chapter later Gabby reached a point where, while she still had the story fresh in her mind, she needed to stop. This was a story she needed to tell and it was a story only she could tell but it was also an emotional, gut-wrenching story. A story that would be written, but in segments.

Today's segment was finished.

Tomorrow's segment would start with Holly making the decision to leave the streets and move her life in a different direction.

Tomorrow's segment would be the beginning of a new life.

Tomorrow's segment would show Holly leaving her past behind her.

Fact? or Fiction?

Leaving her past behind. Gabby reread the sentence two more times before her fingers hovered over the keys and the new chapter began.

"You got in." Doc S's words echoed in Holly's mind.

"I got in?" Her breath whooshed out on a shaky exhale.

"You did. You have a place to stay. A small studio apartment but there are locks on the door and staff on duty twenty-four hours a day."

"I-I-I really got in?" Holly could barely believe the news. She'd been staying in the back room of a restaurant that she worked at. Some nights she slept curled up in the graveyard of a nearby church. She knew the priest knew she was there because sometimes there was a brown paper bag with a muffin or a bagel at the gate.

That was the second turning point or maybe the third. If you counted when she decided to take to the streets to protect herself as the first one, and the decision to leave the streets the second one, then this was the third. A safe place, school, work—always working. Sometimes Holly worked two or three jobs, studying on her breaks, staying up late to finish a paper. Doc S got her a used typewriter and a ream of paper as a gift when she passed her GED and was admitted to Fremont Community College.

Gabby stood and stretched. She was getting things mixed up. *Holly's Story* was not her story. *Holly's Story* was a composite of the stories of several young girls she knew or had known.

Leaning on the balcony railing she noticed more boats on the water. They looked small and vulnerable in the vast sea. In the light of day, the safety the lighthouse could afford was lost. The sea stretched in front of her to the horizon. She'd never been on a sailboat and wondered how it would feel to be so exposed to the elements.

Would she relish the sea's spray spattering her cheeks?

Would the smell of the salty air be stronger when she was on the water?

Would the wind be worrisome to the point she'd be fearful and close her eyes and pray?

Would it be an adventure? Freeing? Fantastic? Fun?

Giovanni strolled down the garden path past the pool toward the balustrade. He stood, feet spread as if bracing himself for something. His hands were tucked into his pockets and that posture told her he was at ease. For several minutes he remained in one spot. If his eyes were open, he was looking out to sea. If they were closed—Gabby closed her eyes and let herself experience this time and place through her senses.

The soft breeze caressed her cheeks. The floral scent flowed around her. The warmth of the sun found her, even though she was shaded by the balcony roof. A layer of tension lifted and for a moment she lost her balance.

Sophia's words penetrated her drifting mind. "I've never seen you so relaxed." *That's because I've never been this relaxed.* When she left the streets, finished her education, got a more professional job, had her own place, could pay her bills without having to decide between rent, utilities and food—even when she reached that place in her life she'd never felt so relaxed, so safe.

Even within The Circle there was always the thought that if they really knew her, really knew what she'd done, what had happened to her she'd be cast out. Last spring when she witnessed how her circle sisters and their husbands, even Giovanni, had rallied around Logan, that fear had lessened but it was not totally gone. What had happened to Logan was horrific but what had happened to her had been worse.

Worse because she'd lived that life for four years.

Worse because she'd stayed even when she could have gone back into foster care.

Worse because she thought that was the life she deserved.

So much healing left to do. She opened her eyes. Giovanni had turned away from the sea and was watching her. He was far enough away she couldn't see his eyes but she felt them.

Always from the beginning she knew where he was in any room.

Always from the beginning there was something about him that called to her.

Always from the beginning she knew she had to stay away. She was a girl from the streets. He was a successful architect with clients all over Italy and also in the Balkans, France, Monaco and who knew where else. No, if he really knew who she was, he'd only want one thing—a fling. Since leaving the street, she'd abstained from sexual contact of any kind.

Gabby lifted her hand in acknowledgement. He did the same. She turned back to the laptop on the table. After saving today's work again, she turned the machine off and closed the top. Tomorrow was another day.

Sophia was leaving in the morning. Earlier she'd gone to see the gardens of some of Giovanni's friends. Hopefully she was back and they could sit by the pool or maybe just stay in the shade of the veranda and have something cool to drink. *I wonder if the orange and mint drink would taste as good cold.*

Sophia Leaves

At the last minute and because Sophia had asked her to come, Gabby found herself in the car with Giovanni when he took Sophia to Rome and the airport. The clincher was when Sophia confided she'd not slept well the last two nights.

"But you didn't say anything earlier." Gabby had sighed with frustration. "Adolfo would have fixed you something natural that would have helped, I'm sure."

"I'd thought for sure spending time yesterday in beautiful gardens would help. Even with all the walking I did and how tired I was—sleep would not come. I'm restless, at loose ends. Somehow my garden and teaching is no longer enough."

They'd emailed the others for updates. Of course everything was going smoothly. Elizabeth and Michael were excited she was coming in early. E would meet her this afternoon at Shannon airport. Maeve and Michael would be waiting when they reached The Manor.

In Rome, they went directly to the airport so Sophia could catch her flight to Limerick. After hugs and good-byes were said, Gabby settled back in the car with Giovanni still at the wheel.

"Are we driving back to the villa?" Gabby thought it possible because there was so much daylight.

"Would you like to see more of Rome?"

Gabby looked over as Giovanni started the car and backed out of the parking space. Something wasn't right but she had no idea what it might be.

"You've done the driving. I can help with that once out of Rome but I think whether we stay the night or go back should be your decision."

Giovanni was tired but not too tired to drive back to his villa. There was something about Gabriella that called to him. Always had and maybe always would. What would happen if they spent a day or two in Rome, saw more sights, had dinner at his favorite restaurants? Very aware she had not brought a suitcase or a change of clothes, he made a decision.

"*Si*, I am tired. We stay but you must agree to allow me to buy you clothes for tomorrow."

"That isn't necessary... ."

"That is the agreement. I am tired but I will drive us back to the villa unless you agree."

"I can drive once we are out of Rome."

"No, the roads are narrow, we Italian drivers can be reckless. It would be better if I did the driving." He drove out of the airport, letting the silence build. "Something simple…you choose."

Gabriella knew Giovanni was tired. It showed around his eyes and his voice had no energy. She thought she could drive once out of Rome. But, she remembered the first time Elizabeth had driven her car. She was on edge the entire time. If Giovanni could not relax if she was driving then there was no point in leaving tonight.

She always lived "light". All her clothes fit in one medium sized wheeled suitcase. All her sacred items nestled in her backpack with room in the side pockets for two water bottles. When she got ready to move on, she always wore her cargo pants, pockets filled with matches, Swiss Army knives, energy bars and her identification. Of course she had other things: books, furniture, bedding but she considered them ancillary to her life. *Why do I?* But she knew why. Being able to get away, taking what was most important to her at a moment's notice fueled her simple lifestyle.

But when I moved to Elizabeth and Michael's house it was different. She'd taken her bedding and books and realized then that since she had a car, there were more of her personal possessions she could keep. *When I finish my healing process, will this part of my life be different? Will I feel like I can settle down in one place? Will I always be restless?*

As Giovanni drove through the streets, she looked at the passing scenes. Here she'd never run into someone who knew her from her time on the streets. Because she volunteered at the Youth Shelter, every now and then she'd see someone from her past and turn away to avoid being noticed.

Leaving that part of her life behind her while still volunteering was difficult. She wasn't ready to stop or was she? *Can I finish my healing and still volunteer?*

"Do we go to the villa or stay in Roma?"

Gabriella visibly jumped at his voice.

"Ah, you find Roma beckons?"

Her hand on her chest over her racing heart, Gabby shifted to see Giovanni more clearly. "We will stay here tonight but tomorrow we go to a thrift shop for the clothes."

His brow raised in question, he glanced in her direction before refocusing on his driving. "What?"

"A second-hand clothing store. Used clothes. I don't need anything new."

Giovanni, his forehead furrowed, the space between his brows wrinkled, drove on.

A few minutes later, they parked at his Rome house. They'd been going in circles while she was lost in thought, figuring out what to do.

Inside, he spoke Italian to the housekeeper, a middle-aged woman who wore a black skirt and white blouse. She nodded and hurried away.

"You will have something to wear to sleep when you get to your room." He grinned and a light sparked briefly in his tired eyes. "I would offer one of my shirts but I think you would refuse."

She tried to glare but he'd already turned away. A wave over his shoulder accompanied. "I see you at breakfast."

The idea of sleeping in one of his shirts, no doubt made of the finest cotton, wrapped in his clove and sandalwood scent would ensure a sleepless night. The idea of sleeping naked on cool sheets with him just down the hall would ensure a sleepless night. The idea of being alone in the house with him—yes, that also ensured a sleepless night.

Upstairs she found a plain white cotton sleeveless shift that reached mid-thigh. Utilitarian.

Crawling into bed, she pulled the sheet up to her waist, turned on her side, hugged a pillow and closed her eyes. Her last thought before she came upstairs about being in the house alone with Giovanni popped into her mind.

Several of the staff lived in and although their rooms were in another wing she really wasn't alone with him. She'd met him in the early months of 2003 when Lily was at Montgomery House recovering from the hit and run accident. Over the intervening years she'd spent hours with him around. He came to Ireland when they were all there. He never missed a wedding—well, they'd all missed Hunter and Grant's.

She still knew where, in relationship to her, he was at those times they were in the same room. And, she knew he paid attention to what she was doing or saying. Most recently he'd talked to her about sacred geometry and the concept of noumenal. But he didn't flirt with her as he had at first, he didn't invade her personal space. Things had changed between them.

Tomorrow as they toured around Rome, she'd ask him to tell her more about sacred geometry. The image of the spruce cone bright in her mind, she slept.

A Day in Rome

Gabriella was transfixed by the sight before her. The cathedral was beautiful. A grandiose structure built to please God. Giovanni pointed out the smallest of details, explaining how the symmetry fit into the concept of sacred geometry. A wave of dizziness swept through her and in that moment she exhaled. Stunned that she had unknowingly held her breath, Gabby focused on her breathing until her head cleared and she was steady on her feet.

"But this is all man-made sacred geometry. When you first talked to me about it, I was explaining how I'd found a spruce cone under a Douglas fir tree."

"*Si.* That is so. But in ancient times, the people were curious about their environment. They discover the geometry of nature: circles, cubes, triangles. Then they find the correlation to mathematics. Even today, astrophysicists use the basic concepts of sacred geometry's mathematics to explore the universe."

As they strolled through side streets, Giovanni described how sacred geometry fit in the building of Rome as a city as well as the art and architecture for which the city was renowned.

They had lunch at a small outdoor café and dinner at a hide-a-way restaurant that served pizza Neapolitan style. She passed on the wine but had decadent tiramisu for dessert. A satisfied sigh escaped as she swallowed the last piece. Giovanni had swiped a small bite and she'd playfully stabbed at his hand with her fork.

"This is good—,"

"Good?" Eyes wide, her mouth matched. Hands raised in a mock fighting stance, Gabby was ready to do battle.

"*Si,* it is good but Adolfo makes better." He had a smirk on his face as he leaned back in his chair, arms folded across his chest.

"No, this is the best I've ever had."

"You will regret saying that when Adolfo makes his."

"If Adolfo's tiramisu is better than this I'll, I'll, well—"

"We have a bet? What is the prize?" Giovanni's confident grin gave her pause. But then she licked her fork and decided if Adolfo's tiramisu was better than this, it was worth what?

"I don't know what the prize would be." The pause became a small doubt.

"We go to Ireland together if Adolfo's is better. If not, you take the flight already booked."

"But my work?" It was feeble to bring up because she didn't plan on going back to work until November fourth.

"Your work will still be there or you will have better work. You are writing, *no*?"

"Yes, I am writing."

"Maybe you finish the book?"

Was it possible to finish? *If I write every day the first draft may be done by Samhain. But Adolfo's tiramisu can't be better than this. No worries.*

"Deal." Gabby reached across the small table to shake Giovanni's hand. He grasped her fingers, raised them to his lips. A light brush over her knuckles was all but the tremors it set off ran deep.

"How you say in America 'sealed with a kiss'?" He leaned back in his chair, his eyes now in shadow. Uncertain what she'd see in them, Gabby retrieved her hand, put it in her lap and said, "Yes, that is a saying. I don't know if it's only an American saying though."

Giovanni waved his hand in the air and immediately their waiter was there with the check. He paid the bill and by the look on the waiter's face, added a generous tip.

As Giovanni stood, the waiter pulled her chair back. Without really thinking about it, she took Giovanni's offered arm as they left the restaurant. Instead of taking a taxi, they walked the half-mile or so to Giovanni's house. The hour was late but she was not tired.

Tomorrow they would leave for the villa. What time?

As if he read her mind, Giovanni said, "We leave for my villa early. I have an appointment in the afternoon."

"What time should I be ready?"

"Eight."

"I will be ready."

"We have light breakfast. Cook here will fix something for us to eat along the way."

"That will be fine."

Up in her room, Gabby slipped on the cotton nightgown. Before going to bed, she set out the outfit she'd worn when coming to Rome three days ago. She debated on leaving the other two outfits here but in the end decided to take them. There was room in her suitcase so she could take them home.

The pair of stylish jeans and multi-colored green top would get lots of wear. The silk tank-top style turquoise blue dress that didn't come close to reaching her knees was an indulgence. Because she didn't really know any Italian she'd been at a disadvantage as Giovanni and the shop keeper carried on a conversation.

She wasn't even sure it was a used clothing store and she had no idea what the prices were. Giovanni assured her that the marked price had been heavily discounted for her. The marked prices? She barely saw the tag before it was whisked away.

"There's no point in getting or being upset about it. He agreed I would pay him back when we get back to the villa. It isn't like he bought these things for me." She muttered a few more words about being at a disadvantage and she should have insisted or learned Italian or... .

Everything in order, she turned off the lights. Before going to bed, Gabby stood at the window looking out over the courtyard garden. The scented air seemed to stir and then she saw him. Glass of wine in hand, Giovanni sat on a bench underneath a flowering bush. He slouched, crossed his ankles and took a sip. She stepped back afraid to be seen watching him. Did he glance up at her window?

Retreating into her room's interior, Gabby stubbed her right toe on the corner of a chair leg. "Ouch!"

She limped the few steps to the bed, sat down and rubbed her toe as tears welled. Sitting in the dark, her right ankle on her left knee, she held the throbbing area. Tears streamed down her cheeks, fell onto her nightgown. Sobs surged from deep within as repressed pain from the horrors in her past surfaced. When all efforts to subdue them failed, Gabby drew her knees to her chest, wrapped her arms around and rested her forehead on them.

Time passed, the sobs turned to gulps, the tears ebbed, she curled into a ball and rocked.

Returning to The Villa

Sound carries in the quiet of night, in the darkness. Giovanni heard "ouch", heard the sobs and after a time, heard the silence. He was a man who loved women no matter their shape, size or color. As a successful man, he was often surrounded by beautiful women but that wasn't because he sought them out. He'd been attracted to Gabriella from the very beginning. She had rebuffed him at every turn. More recently, she'd mellowed or maybe it was because he'd stopped trying to entice her into a relationship.

Actually they'd always had a relationship of sorts because she was Lily's friend and he was Jackson's. He thought they were actually becoming friends…just the two of them. Their time in Rome helped because she was truly interested in sacred geometry, as if it would fix something if she could just figure it out.

One of the secrets about sacred geometry was not the 'figuring out' although some basic fundamentals helped. It was the appreciation of the sacred, the noumenal that is in all things that please God.

He smiled to himself. *She'd add Goddess.* While he didn't believe as Gabriella did, he respected her beliefs and knew her to be a spiritual person. But what to do about the sadness? His heart ached for her. So strong and yet so fragile. *Something very bad happen to her. And by a man. This I know.*

The silence was not restful but the choices before him were limited. He could go up and knock on her door, ask her if she needed anything. But, he already knew the answer. She'd say

"No, everything is fine."

He could send the maid to check on her but that would not elicit a different answer.

He could wait until morning and ask her if she was okay. Again, he knew what her answer would be.

He could tuck away the knowledge that something was wrong and just be her friend.

Rising from the bench, Giovanni strolled back into the house. He had a plan and believed it a good one.

The next morning, the dark circles under Gabriella's hazel eyes bespoke of a sleepless night. Giovanni noticed but said little other than he hoped she'd slept well. She shrugged but offered nothing more.

Gabriella loved the fresh orange juice and he added a splash of champagne. Not enough to be a true mimosa but enough to add a bit of effervescence to the drink. They headed out with a basket of pastries and a thermos of coffee for Giovanni and another one of orange juice splashed with champagne for Gabriella.

Italian opera on the radio, Gabriella relaxed into the leather seats sipping her mini-mimosa from the thermos's cup. The sights held her interest and after an uneventful four hour trip, they pulled into the villa's drive.

Silvio and Margretta greeted them, taking luggage and basket inside. Giovanni suggested she set up her laptop on the veranda assuring her it would not bother his client who was coming in an hour.

Gabriella rejected the suggestion. She was going to write where she always did—in her room. Since she didn't know if she'd come down for lunch, he was pleased she agreed to have something brought to her.

"I'll see you at dinner," Gabriella said as she started up the stairs.

While he wanted more, he kept a friendly smile on his face as she left the foyer for her room. He watched Gabriella until she passed from his view up the stairs.

Margretta soon followed with a tray with bread, cheese and large blue mug of liquid. He guessed it was the orange mint drink Adolfo had created for her. As Margretta passed by, Giovanni noticed a fresh flower in a small vase.

Calling out to Silvio to bring him coffee and something for his soon-to-arrive client, Giovanni headed to his office. He stood in the bowed windows of his work space and plotted. Plotted how to ease her pain or at least break through her defenses.

Holly's Story

Holly was struggling. Struggling to find her way. Everywhere she turned there was someone she knew who reminded her she was worth nothing, worthless. The energy to stay the course flagged. Staying off the streets was too hard. She'd take her chances. Maybe she could find someone to team up with and together they'd make it.

She made an appointment with the social worker who worked with girls like her who were trying to make different choices. She had to give thirty days' notice and that was what she planned to do.

Waiting for her appointment, she was surprised to see Doc S.

"Hey there Holly," Doc called out in her cheery voice. "How's it going?"

"I'm giving my notice." She looked away unable to meet Doc's gaze.

Of course the seat next to her was vacant, an open invitation for Doc to join her—which she did.

"So tell me what's going on?"

Now Doc was in her concerned mode. Tears threatened and Holly turned away.

"That bad, eh?"

Holly nodded, gulped before trusting herself to speak. "I-I-I can't do it alone."

"You don't have to do it alone."

"I'm not going to the groups here. All they talk about is what happened to them. I can't do that. If I don't look ahead, I just want to die."

Ms. Waterson, the social worker, appeared. "I can see you now." She glanced at Doc, raised her brow, gestured and added. "Why don't we go in here?

"Doc, why don't you join us?" Ms. Waterson asked, both brows raised which widened her eyes. "I think both Holly and I could use your input."

Gabriella took a break and scanned back over the chapter looking for her name instead of Holly's. There was a time a few months into the program that she'd lost hope, was ready to quit. Between the support of Ms. Waterson and Doc S she'd stayed but Holly? Holly was a composite of many of the girls she knew and because of that, she would send Holly back to the streets.

At least for a few days or maybe a week, possibly a month. It would depend, of course, on how the story played out. If that magical person appeared and together they could make a go of it that was one thing but what if…

"'What if' can give life to a story." Her mind raced with a dozen possibilities of 'what if's' on the streets.

But when she turned back to her laptop, the words for Holly to take off and go back to the streets wouldn't come. It was tempting to quit but she didn't make it off the streets to where she was now by quitting.

Gabby started a new chapter, a chapter where Holly made a different choice. *I can always come back and write about what happens to her. I can't face those stories now. For me, I must go forward.*

Doc S, Ms. Waterson and Holly sat at a round table. Holly's back was to the wall. Doc and Ms. W sat on either side. Together they formed a triangle.

Gabby stopped typing. They did make a triangle and Giovanni had told her that was one of the first sacred geometric shapes. Hands poised over the keys, Gabby mentally wandered back to her own meeting with Doc S and Mrs. Mortenson, her social worker. Had they been seated as a triangle? Had that configuration helped her see a way forward? She'd been so alone then, so disconnected to other people. It didn't matter that she worked as a server in a restaurant and lived in an apartment building. In fact it was worse to be surrounded by people and yet feel so desperately alone.

Doc S invited her to spend her day off with her. They went out to the cabin in the woods Doc had just purchased. Hard back-breaking work was needed to clear the land enough for the flower beds. She'd been outside often enough but never in the woods.

Sitting back in her chair, Gabby remembered the hard work, the burning muscles, the sweat dripping off her nose, the calloused hands, the sense of accomplishment as she and Doc S stopped at the end of the day. Sitting on the porch, ice cold lemonade in hand, starving and yet satisfied.

Doc had drawn out the garden. Raised rectangular beds for the vegetables. Round beds for the flowers. She'd investigated what she could do to protect the plants from the deer in particular. She put bird netting over the raised beds, added a drip system and decided to take her chances with the flowers. They were transplanted from the land and, she thought were native.

Gabby stood and stretched. On the balcony she looked out over the gardens to the sea beyond. *Doc would love it here.* A light breeze caught the sweet scent of the plethora of flowers below. Closing her eyes, Gabby reveled in the aroma as it wrapped around her. *Yes, Doc would love it here.*

She jerked her eyes open as the next thought popped into her mind. *No! I will not even contemplate it.* Stalking back to her computer, she plopped down and stared at the screen.

Holly was still in the room with the two women. She'd let her memories and imagination take her out of the story. Sipping her orange mint tea she took the mug and a piece of fresh bread out to the balcony. This mini-break would help her get back into the story, back to Holly's life, back to the interview room.

Nibbling on the delicious bread and Adolfo's wonderful honey butter, her gaze unfocused, she heard voices. Giovanni's musical baritone saying something in Italian. Moments later a higher female voice responded. Who did he have here? And if she'd been working on the veranda, would he have introduced her? And if he did, what would he say?

A knock on her door jolted her out of her thoughts. "Come in."

"Signore Giovanni invites you to come to lunch if you can."

"Tell him I will be there *un minuto, si*?"

"*Si*, I tell him."

Gabby brushed her hair, tucked her shirt in her jeans and slipped on her one pair of sandals. At the bottom of the stairs she paused. Voices came from the veranda. For a second she doubted herself. Doubted this was a good thing to do.

Before she could turn and go back upstairs, Giovanni appeared in the doorway.

"Ah, there you are." He came across the floor to where she stood. "*Grazie* for coming," he said in a lowered voice. "I need your protection."

With that he took her hand and walked back to the veranda. The beauty of the woman almost took her breath away. Around the eyes, she looked like Sophia Loren. Her hair looked like Julia Roberts in *Pretty Woman* except it was black.

Gabby hung back but Giovanni's grip was strong and he towed her forward.

"Magdalena, please meet my friend, Gabriella. Gabriella, Magdalena is a client of mine. We are redesigning a house for her."

Gabby stepped forward and extended her hand. "I'm pleased to meet you." Magdalena responded with a regal and a limp shake. Giovanni gestured for Gabriella to precede him to the table where he pulled the chair to his right out for her. Once she was seated, he rounded the table and offered Magdalena a chair on his left.

As soon as they were settled, staff brought the food. Magdalena, it seemed, did not speak English but Gabby wasn't so sure she didn't understand it. Giovanni divided his time talking to both of them, interpreting some of the conversation.

The meal over, she excused herself intending to return to her room and her writing. Giovanni, his hand on Gabriella's elbow, led Magdalena to her car. He casually draped his arm around Gabby's shoulders and waved as Magdalena backed up and drove off.

"I am in your debt," he said as they returned to the house.

"I don't understand?"

"I am her architect and can offer her nothing more."

"I see." Words that came automatically but meant nothing.

Back in her room, Holly's story beckoned. She pushed aside any thoughts of Magdalena, of Giovanni, of everything except Holly. The laptop beckoned as did a pitcher of lemon water and four of Adolfo's delicious nut bars. *If I keep writing I can eat one every half hour.* That bargain made with herself, she set to work.

Holly's Story

Holly scanned the ten by ten cement room. Her chest contracted on an indrawn breath and exhaling was difficult. Tears blurred her vision. Her legs trembled, her feet stuck to the cement floor.

"I know it isn't much," Ms. Waterson began.

Jolted back to the present, Holly stepped into the room.

"It's everything." On a shaky breath and wobbly feet, Holly entered the room. Right behind her, arms piled with two boxes each, were Ms. Waterson and Doc S. All four boxes were quickly stacked in a corner of the room.

Ms. Waterson took the one box from Holly that she'd carried. Since the door had opened and she'd stepped into the room, she hadn't moved. Her shoulders shook and tears fell but all was quiet.

Doc S stood beside her, a silent, comforting presence. "Do you have your room key?"

Holly nodded, pulling the plastic card from her pants pocket.

"Remember the building code?"

"7-6-0-3," Holly whispered.

A quiet knock on the door frame announced someone else. The security guard stood in the entry way, a brown paper bag in his arm. "Everything okay?" he asked.

"You can set that down on the counter," Ms. Waterson said. "And yes, I believe everything is okay." She'd checked that the lights and water worked while Doc had checked on Holly.

"Do you want us to help you get settled?" Doc asked, laying a hand on Holly's arm.

"No, no I'll be okay. I-I-I just can't believe all this is mine."

Doc S and Ms. Waterson exchanged telling looks, their own eyes glistened with unshed tears.

"I'll stop by and see how you're doing tomorrow," Ms. Waterson said as she turned toward the door.

"Be right with you," Doc S said. When the door closed, Doc turned toward Holly. "I want to see you in a couple of days."

"I'll be okay."

"I know you will but I still want to see you. This is a huge change for you and I want to keep track of how you're doing."

Holly turned to Doc and smiled. "You don't think I'm going to go to the groups here?"

Doc cocked her head and raised an eyebrow.

"And you don't think I'm going to talk to the counselor here either."

"Am I wrong?"

"Probably not. But I'll be okay."

"And you'll do me a favor by letting me see that for myself."

"It's just so hard to come to the clinic."

"I know it is but that's part of your healing process. Coming to the clinic and then coming back here. Finishing school. Getting a job, making friends."

"But who'd be my friend if they knew about—,"

Doc interrupted. "What have we talked about?"

"I know, I don't have to tell anyone about my past unless I want to. I can't imagine ever wanting to tell anyone."

"Then you don't have to."

A faint smile tilted the corners of Holly's mouth. "You sound so ferocious."

"Determined is a better word," Doc replied.

"Ms. Waterson is probably waiting for you."

"She probably is."

"And it's okay if the two of you talk about me." Holly grinned at Doc's fake look of outrage. "I know you do and because it's the two of you, it's okay. I don't have the words to tell you both how important you are to me. This wouldn't be mine without your help." Holly gestured at the small room as if it was a palace. "I can't believe this is really all mine."

"Well, it is." Doc said as she took the few steps to the door. "I'll see you in two days."

"Okay, Doc. I'll come by."

After putting the chain on the door and turning the dead bolt lock, Holly perused the room. To her left was the kitchenette with a counter top, microwave and sink. A small refrigerator was underneath along with two cabinets. There were upper cabinets also.

She unpacked the paper bag and put the milk and cheese in the refrigerator. A loaf of bread, a jar of peanut butter and another one of jelly went in an upper cabinet. The place came furnished with two sets of microwave safe dishes and silverware, four glasses and two serving sized spoons. There were two larger bowls and a platter.

Under the windows was a futon couch that folded down into a bed. A small table at one end held a lamp. Crossing the room, Holly checked her view. She was on the third floor and while the stairs would be challenging when she had her arms full, she was high enough to look into the trees and see the sky above.

The kitchen counter continued along the wall at varying heights. Under the lower height was a wooden chair. That would be her study area. A small alarm clock, a pad of paper and two pens were in her backpack. She set them on the counter along with two textbooks.

Not entirely square, the bump out into the room housed a toilet and a wash basin. Showers were down the hall. The building's security system was predicated on room keys. When she was in the shower, no one else could come in. That was comforting to her because it was a co-ed building.

Unpacking the two boxes took longer than it might have another person because Holly carefully considered where each item was placed. On the shelf in the bathroom she set her shampoo, toothpaste and toothbrush. An extra roll of paper was placed on the back of the toilet.

A small closet easily held her three tops, one jacket, one hoodie and two pair of jeans. She had three changes of underpants, four pairs of socks including what she had on. The drawer at the bottom of the closet was used for her underwear. The shelf on the top? She broke down the two boxes and set them up there. Who knew when she'd have to move? Better to be prepared.

On the window sill, she put two rocks she'd carried in her pocket. One she'd found when she and Doc S were out on the land. It was a plain piece of sand-colored stone shaped like a bird. The other was a small cluster of crystals, a gift from Ms. Waterson. She'd followed Ms. Waterson's directions, holding it in her hand, concentrating on what she wanted in life—her goals and aspirations.

Now when she focused on the sparkling piece, she could see herself finishing school, getting a job. But that was as far as she'd allow herself to dream. Life was harsh and it was important not to want too much or the pain of disappointment sliced deep.

Holly did a slow turn, scrutinizing the room. She crossed to the study area and repositioned the pad of paper a few inches to the right. The crystal was moved to better catch the light. With precision, she arranged the hangers in the closet and the personal hygiene items in the bathroom.

Finally satisfied, she sat on the couch. The room was warm enough she'd be okay at night. *I can fold my jacket for a pillow and wear my hoodie. Maybe in time I can get a real pillow and a blanket.*

Holly jerked at a knock on her door. Startled she stood and went to the door. Looking out the security hole, she saw the security guard. He held up his identification.

She unlocked the deadbolt but left the chain on as she opened the door.

"Yes?"

"I have this package for you." He held up a brown paper wrapped bundle.

Holly stepped back and shut the door. Taking the chain off, she cautiously opened it. The security guard was still there and he still held the package.

"Who is it from?" Holly was nervous and not sure she wanted to accept it.

"Doc and Ms. Waterson came back with it."

Holly took the bundle, thanked the guard and placed it on the kitchen counter while she relocked everything.

Taking the bundle to the couch, she sat and held it. It was soft and sort of squishy. A frown wrinkled her forehead, scrunched her brows together. *I can sit here and wonder or I can open it.*

Careful not to rip the paper, Holly opened the package. A material in a pattern of greens, reds, yellows and blue was on top. Hugging the bundle to her chest, she sobbed.

When the tears abated, she was shaky and still overwhelmed with the day's events. She'd moved from the youth hostel to her own place. She was enrolled in college. She was moving forward with her life.

Above all she was safe. No more curling into a tight ball to stay warm. She shook out the fabric, knowing what she'd find. A set of sheets, two blankets, a pillow and a pillow case.

Tucked in between everything was a small box of laundry detergent and another of dryer cloths. Her tears returned when she saw the chocolate. Two chocolate bars!!!

Not only was she safe, she was rich.

Taking A Break

Gabriella wiped her eyes with the back of her hands. She snuffed her nose but then decided to just deal with it. Getting up, she got a tissue and blew. Another tissue to wipe her eyes. Another tissue. She grabbed a handful and stepped out on the balcony in an effort to distract herself from how writing Holly's story affected her.

Leaning on the railing she stared out past the gardens and pool, out past the gleaming white balustrade to the sea. It sparkled in the brilliant sun. White foam skimmed along the dancing waves. There were no boats within her line of sight and that gave her pause. Usually the water was alive with bright racing sails.

She let the sun and sea, the floral fragrance emanating from the gardens below wrap her in a cloak of peace. *Is this what I should be doing now?* Doubts assailed her battered soul.

While she wanted to stop writing, delete Holly's Story and maybe try her hand at describing the indulgent setting in which she found herself, as soon as that thought surfaced a thread of panic countered.

Compelled for reasons unknown to her, at least consciously known, she believed she must write Holly's Story. It might help another girl off the streets, inspire another young woman to change her life's path, to believe it possible to be safe, to have a good life. Perhaps not as good a life as her circle sisters—*but Sophia isn't married either. But when she was, she was very happy.*

Below her balcony she heard Giovanni talking to Silvio. He stepped out on the path and looked up at her.

His face lit with a genuine smile of pleasure. He lifted a hand in invitation.

"*Si,* you take break and come with me."

As usual it was a combination of request and order, a combination she wasn't sure was a result of English being his second language.

"Where are you going?"

"It will be of surprise to you."

Gabby looked out at the sea again, boats now flitting to and fro, sails flashing under the Mediterranean sun. Too drained to write more, she considered the offer and knew a surprise would lighten her mood. If she didn't do something, nightmares would invade her dreams.

"I'll be right down." With speed she shoved her feet into her sandals and grabbed her purse.

He was waiting for her at the bottom of the stairs. "*Mia Cara,* you look tired. The nightmares?"

She looked away before he saw more. As it was, he saw too much.

"You said I'd get a surprise," she challenged in a too bright voice.

"*Si,* I did promise." He held out his hand.

Later she'd wonder why she didn't hesitate but slipped her hand in his. The warmth of his hand, his clove and sandalwood scent wreathed around her. Distress melted away.

Her hand in his, she matched his stride and let him lead her out to his car.

A Sacred Geometry Lesson

Surprised by how quickly Gabriella agreed and disconcerted by how quickly she took his hand, Giovanni changed his original idea to take a drive along the coast to where he now steered his car.

Twenty minutes later, he pulled into a private drive. Getting out, he rounded the car and offered his hand to an unusually quiet Gabriella.

"We are here," he announced.

"Where are we?" Gabriella took his hand as she stepped out of the car. Looking around her all she saw was a ten foot tall wall with a door to one side.

"Come, I show you something to help." He was going on instinct and hoped he'd guessed right. She had an interest in sacred geometry although she didn't really understand it. If he was right, the likelihood that would change was good.

Leading Gabriella, they passed through the door, traveled past the house to the gardens beyond. Although he said nothing, he was aware of her every movement as her head swiveled left and right taking in the sights.

Climbing a set of stairs at the back of the house, they stood on a veranda with a panoramic view of the gardens. "What do you see?" Giovanni stood to her right, hands clasped behind his back.

"A formal garden with designs in the planting. It's very different from Sophia's garden."

"But you do not see Sophia's garden from this vantage. Every garden has designs, even the ones planted by nature." He leaned forward on the balustrade. "Do you find this pleasing?"

"It's beautiful in its own way. Your garden seems a bit wilder when seen from my balcony."

"Ah, it is less formal but it still has form. The size of plants is important to me. Taller plants in the middle of the bed, I like. Shorter ones circling the taller ones and getting shorter and shorted until the low border plants. Color is also important."

"Is this more of a traditional Italian garden?"

"When you read the history of my country, you see the richness going back to Roman times and even before then. The form of the gardens also have a touch of the English in them in some of the design."

He offered his hand. "Let's look more closely."

As they strolled along the crushed granite paths, Giovanni pointed out flowers that were in his own garden. Because of how they were grouped here, they seemed lusher. "It is because my garden is smaller and I wanted some of various flowers. Some, to me, was better than none so my garden does not have the drama of this one.

"Look at this flower?" He paused and held his hand under the blossom of a medium size sunflower turning the head so it faced her.

"What do you see?"

"Sunflower seeds?" Gabriella peered at the blossom.

"There is a design, look to see it."

She looked up at him, confusion in her hazel gaze.

Giovanni took her hand and using one finger traced the curve of seeds. "This is a double helix. If you look at the other sunflowers you will see the same pattern."

A look of wonder widened her eyes as she traced the pattern. Pulling her hand from his, she checked other flowers seeing the pattern repeated.

"In ancient times people were curious about the world around them. They studied all forms of life and from their studies, devised the shapes we are familiar with today. You know very well the first shape."

"The circle?"

"*Si*, the circle came first. Straight lines, triangles, rectangles, squares are all shapes we find every day in nature.

"The ancients saw harmony as pleasing the gods and disharmony as not pleasing. Sacred geometry is buried in the part of geometry that is not mathematical but is pleasing to the gods."

"I don't think I can understand sacred geometry. I never did well with math."

"*No, Cara*, you already see sacred geometry. It already brings you peace."

"I don't understand?"

"You told your friends about the spruce cone and how magical it was." Seeing her quickly look away, he added, "And maybe still is.

"What draws you to the cone?"

"I don't really have words to describe it."

"*Si*, the sacred is noumenal – we feel it but cannot see or touch it. We know it is there but we cannot describe it."

They meandered through other parts of the garden. Giovanni encouraging Gabriella to see patterns in the flowers, in the design of the leaves.

"Now I show you the Fibonacci spiral." He stopped next to an olive tree. "Here you look down the stem and looking at the placement of the first leaf, count how many leaves until there is one directly below it."

"What does this mean?"

"Every plant has a pattern in its flower and in the arrangement of leaves. The way the leaves are spaced, the angle of protrusion from the stalk, how long the stem before the flower—all these things are part of the Fibonacci spiral."

"This is such a peaceful place." Gabriella sat on a stone bench along the side wall.

"*Si*, because it is a place of harmony. It is a place built upon the sacred geometry. It is a place pleasing to the gods."

Giovanni stayed by her side but said nothing more. It was good to see her so relaxed. At one point she even closed her eyes and rested her head against the back of the bench.

The sun's rays no longer reached the garden blocked by the shadow of the house. It was curious she'd not asked whose place this was. It was a good sign she trusted him enough to be alone with him.

Progress. He was right to stop pursuing her and become her friend. It wasn't that his interest had waned. No, in fact it was even stronger. He knew he could not overtly show his interest, at least not yet, or she would bolt and be lost to him forever.

She is worth my waiting.

The Shift

Boneless was the word that filtered through Gabriella's mind as the soft scented breeze drifted across her face and her hands rested on her thighs. The weight of them comforted. When was the last time she'd been this relaxed?

Nothing came to mind.

How did he know she was wound tight and about ready to come undone?

Did it matter? Maybe—maybe not. Thoughts floated like currents. The warmth of Giovanni's shoulder, arm and thigh close to her own eased her further into the depths of calm.

She never wanted to surface from the place of peace.

She never wanted to leave.

She never wanted this to end.

Of course it must end. His hand closed around her own. His thumb stroked the top of her hand and then stopped. A stray thought to ask him to continue glided past and was gone.

A shadow of something darkened the light shining through her closed eyelids. She didn't jerk or startle but an alertness was now evident and the place of peace less. Not gone but not as it had been.

When it didn't pass, Gabriella knew the time had come to open her eyes, to see where the shadow came from, to join in the world she'd escaped for a few minutes.

"Oh!" She sat upright when her opened eyes revealed it was late and the shadow was because the sun was going down. "I'm sorry—."

"Do not be sorry for coming under the spell of a garden." Giovanni gestured to the sight before her. "We can stay until it is dark if you wish it."

A rumble, her face flushed.

"I think we eat now." He stood and because she'd never removed her hand from his, easily helped her to her feet.

Lightheaded but whether from being so totally relaxed or from standing too quickly or from needing food Gabriella didn't know and didn't care. He caught her swaying and held her until she was steady. "I think food is a good idea."

"There is little restaurant a few minutes from here. We go there."

"What about Adolfo?"

"He would put something together for us if we went back but I tell him we go out and not know when to be back."

Hand-in-hand they strolled back through the garden. Gabriella paused to sniff at different plants one last time. The scent was heady and she was lightheaded again. When she weaved, his hand slipped to her elbow and then around her shoulder. It was so easy to lean into his strength.

He escorted her to the car and handed her into the passenger seat. As he backed around, she saw the clock on the dashboard. They'd spent several hours in someone's garden.

"Where have we been?"

"*Villa Pace*. Villa Peace. It belongs to a good friend. He is in Zagreb for now."

"He doesn't mind people coming into his garden?"

"No, he doesn't mind when I come."

"But—"

"Do not worry. The staff know me. They know my car, they saw us on the veranda."

"So we were watched?" A note of panic coated her voice, inching it higher.

"No, we were not watched. When they see it was me, they went about their duties, which when my friend is gone, is mostly watching television or reading."

He pulled out onto the road. Ten minutes later he parked on a side street. A block away tables and chairs were outside a very small restaurant.

The aroma of sauces and fresh bread carried on a light breeze. Her stomach growled in anticipation of the treat ahead. A smile split her face when she heard Giovanni's stomach's answer.

"You're sure this place has good food?"

His brow quirked he looked down at her. "You doubt Giovanni's choice of where to eat?"

A laugh escaped and she shook her head. "In this I don't doubt you at all."

The stars were out when they finished dinner. In the old part of this little village, the street lamps were dim. Light enough to see the curb and safely cross the streets but dark enough she could see the stars. It would be beautiful to sit by the sea tonight. The stars bright in the sky, the sound of the water on the rocks, the scent of the flowers. Maybe tonight she'd accept the glass of amaretto over ice and sip it while she took in the ambiance.

Gabriella waited for Giovanni to come around the front of the car, open her door, hand her out and lead her into the house. Something had happened today. She wasn't sure what it was but his touch warmed her and his closeness, instead of raising alarm signals, brought her a sense of safety.

She did accept the offer of the amaretto over ice with a splash of Irish Cream and Kahlua. Drink in hand, she wandered out to the veranda, past the pool, through the garden to her favorite spot on the balustrade.

He did fix his own drink.

He did follow her.

He did sit beside her.

In another place and time she'd have been nervous or have left. Tonight she sat next to him and when she shivered in the cooling breeze she did not bristle when he put an arm around her shoulder.

Yes, something had definitely changed.

For the better? Maybe? Perhaps?

For now? Yes. She liked the sense of safety and comfort surrounding her when he was near.

When she leaned back to see the stars above, her head brushed his shoulder. It was tempting to lean back, rest her head there but she didn't. And she didn't question herself. Well, in a way she did because she noticed what she was doing and compared it to how she'd reacted in the past.

Her drink finished, she shifted to face him.

"Thank you for a magical day and evening." His dark chocolate eyes were unreadable in the night light but their intensity communicated he was totally in the present.

"You are welcome. It is my pleasure to show you the garden."

"And teach me more about sacred geometry, and take me to dinner, and spend time with me watching the night sky and listening to the sea."

"*Si*, it is all my pleasure to do for you." He leaned toward her and then back as if he was going to do something and then changed his mind. "Tomorrow I go to Rome for a few days to work. You will write while I am gone?"

"Yes, I will write."

They stood together and started back to the villa.

"Giovanni, do you think sacred geometry can help a person heal from their past?"

"*Si*, it is difficult to stay in the dark when we start looking at the light, the beauty around us."

She thought he might kiss her good night, a brush of his lips on her cheek or forehead. Instead he bowed at the foot of the stairs and turned away towards the hall that led to his work space.

Gabriella made her way up the stairs to her room. The bed was turned down, fresh flowers on the night stand, the door to the balcony open so she could hear the sound of the sea. Diana had mentioned something about being seduced by the place and how the staff, once they got to know her, anticipated her every need. *I guess they've gotten to know me.* She slipped into her nightgown and after brushing her teeth and hair, sat on the balcony.

She saw him come from the side of the house, wander through the garden and out to the wall. He sat where they had sat, looking out at the water. No boats. No birds. Only stars high in the sky and the rhythmical swing of the lighthouse beam.

What was he thinking about? *Probably about the client he'll see tomorrow.* Although she was back in the shadows, she didn't want him to see her watching him so she crept back into her room.

It was painful to be so aware of someone else. Even though he never looked her way, Giovanni knew she was on the balcony, knew when she went inside and knew he'd escaped her lure several times. The impulse, the desire to kiss her, to wrap his arms around her and kiss her until she was breathless had dogged him all day. But he was a man of immense self-control. He knew today something had shifted between them. He knew he needed to maintain control of himself if he was ever to win her.

And win her I will. At last he looked up at her balcony and the door to her room beyond, ran his hand through already rumpled hair and strode inside. Being in Rome for a few days was just what he needed.

27 Connections

Something jerked her from deep numbing sleep to heightened awareness. Gabriella stilled her breathing and her body even though the urge to run was strong. Reminding herself she was in Italy and no one from her past could reach her helped. But why? Why had she awakened with a jolt of awareness? What had happened? In the darkness—she opened her eyes to see that it wasn't totally dark. The room was beginning to brighten as the sun rose.

Morning.

Taking her time, Gabriella shifted to the side of the bed and stood. Nothing had changed in her room and yet something had changed.

Out on the balcony, the shadows of night slid away to be replaced by the dewy light of dawn. Nothing had changed in the gardens below and yet something had changed.

Fully awake, Gabriella showered and dressed all the while searching for what was different. She could feel the difference but couldn't name it.

Sitting outside in a chair on the balcony, she combed her hair, taming the unruly auburn curls as best she could. Her hands moved in a familiar rhythm while her mind sought answers.

I've not checked in with any of the others since Sophia left. Maybe something has happened.

But that didn't feel right.

It wasn't a nightmare that had awakened her. She'd been sleeping better this past week than she could remember. Of course she had good nights here and there but to string this many together was a real gift. This was what being well-rested felt like!

There was an energy to being sleep deprived but it was harsher. Well-rested energy was quieter and more powerful because it didn't take so much effort to access it.

The sun fully up, her hair dried and pulled back from her face with clips, she went downstairs. Maybe she'd see Giovanni before he left for Rome.

One of those surprises that wasn't a surprise—Giovanni had already left. In fact he'd left the same time she woke. He was gone.

Sitting on the patio, a small bowl of fresh fruit and a pot with tea on the table, she sipped her orange juice and nibbled on the croissant from her plate.

She'd write more of Holly's story today but first she'd check in with people back home. Sophia had checked emails every other day she was here. Gabriella wanted the closeness of being connected with the women who were the sisters of her heart.

Finished with her morning meal, she asked about checking emails. In the small room with a computer and a view of a blooming hibiscus, she logged on.

Time warp.

Her inbox was full with hundreds of emails because it had been close to six weeks since she'd checked it.

Methodically she went through and deleted as many as she could. She left work-related ones closed. There were three from Jordan's personal email.

He was going to be in Fremont and wanted to see her.

He was going to be in Fremont and hoped they could have coffee.

He was going to be in Fremont and hoped they could have dinner and catch a movie. Her choice.

What to say? She stood and stretched not because she was stiff but to give herself a chance to think from a different perspective.

When she sat back down she clicked 'reply' on the last one.

"Sorry to have missed you. Out of town."

She deleted that message and tried again.

"Out of town."

She shook her head and deleted that one.

"Hi Jordan, Thanks for thinking of me when you are coming to Fremont. I'm not in town at this time but should be back to work in early November."

After spending an inordinate amount of time reworking it, she made one last change and clicked "send".

"Hi Jordan, I'm not in town at this time but should be back to work in early November. Gabriella Moncrief"

A short email to Doc S followed.

In the end, Gabriella decided to send one group email to everyone. It was tempting to say "having a wonderful time, wish you were here" but that actually would not be true. She valued her time alone, her time to write, her time to sit and contemplate the sea and the rocks and the shadows of the sun by day and the sea and the rocks and the stars and the unwavering signal from the lighthouse by night.

Assuring everyone she was well, Gabriella then talked a bit about her writing and that the story was coming along. She said the villa was a magical place, the food was indescribably fantastic and she was sure she was gaining weight. *But that's not true. If anything I've lost a few pounds.* Rereading what she'd written, she deleted some of the mundane comments and focused on what she was doing. She made sure to mention that Giovanni was spending time in Rome so she had the place to herself.

Ending with she was looking forward to seeing everyone in Ireland she then added a short sentence or two directed at each circle sister.

Satisfied she'd connected with them and knowing she'd see them in a week, she added PS: Because I'll see you so soon, I'll most likely not be emailing again. Back to writing!

Gabriella logged out of her email account, leaned back in the chair and looked at the blank screen. *So this is how Elizabeth feels living in Ireland while the rest of us are in Fremont. She really does still feel connected to us. I miss seeing everyone in person but I know they are with me.*

After a brisk walk three times around the garden, Gabriella headed upstairs to her room and Holly's Story.

28 Holly's Story

Holly ducked into the doorway, shrinking into the darkness, slanting her body to hide her face. If only she hadn't taken this short cut back to her apartment but—

She stiffened her knees and prepared herself to fight her way free if she needed to. There were only two of them and she thought if she could break their hold, she could outrun them the two blocks to the well-lit main street. She'd be safer there but worried they could follow her back to where she lived.

Her mind raced with options, her body still as stone.

When they passed by without even a glance her way, her knees gave out and she crumpled to the ground. The shaking started in her gut and rumbled out to her extremities. At that moment in time she couldn't have stood up much less run away if her life depended upon it.

Arms cradled around her knees, she buried her face and silently wept. Would she never be free of the streets? Would she never feel safe?

Holly waited until she heard a voice talking to someone. Peeking around the corner of the doorway, she saw a couple out walking their dog. Safety in numbers. Standing, she turned and acting as if she was just coming out of the building, stepped onto the sidewalk.

"Great dog," she said to the couple, reaching down to give the pup a chance to smell her. When the pink tongue gave her a lick, she scratched behind soft floppy ears.

The normal chatter about pets in general and dogs in particular soothed her frazzled nerves. Two blocks later they reached the main street. When they turned to the right, she waved good-bye and headed to her place.

Nightmares had her up and studying in the middle of the night. Finishing up a term paper and outlining two chapters for a test the next day, she was bordering on exhaustion as she loaded her backpack with books, papers and pens and headed to class.

Class over. Holly leaned against the hall wall. The desire to slide down, curl into a ball and sleep was strong. *I'm a survivor. I can do this.* She chanted the phrase over and over as she headed back to her room.

Thankful her day was over and she could sleep, she was in a daze as she neared the building.

"Hey Holly, miss you babe."

Her heart pounded in terror as the voice of her abuser registered. Hands fisted she prepared to fight.

Looking into his pock-marked face, sandy greasy hair hanging to his shoulders, brown cold, hard eyes burned.

Head up, chin tucked Holly stood her ground. His arm was slung around a young girl—probably sixteen or so, dressed in a skimpy top and shorts. Her brown hair was pulled back into a high pony tail. Her garishly made-up face had a dazed look. The young girl had been drugged and he was taking her out to sell.

What could she do to stop this from happening?

Mrs. Waterson was striding down the street toward her. Holly waved and stepped in front of the couple to keep them from moving on.

"Holly, so good to see you."

"Mrs. Waterson, I think there's a problem here. This young girl looks ill. I think you should call 911 to get her some help."

Mrs. Waterson already had her phone out. "I've already done that. Both the police and ambulance will be here in seconds."

He grabbed the girl's arm and started to take off. Both Holly and Mrs. Waterson held on to her. As the sirens came closer, he gave up the fight and took off. He disappeared around the corner as the police cruiser came into view.

"Take care of her," Mrs. Waterson said as she jogged over to the police car.

Moments later the car took off and Mrs. Waterson came back.

The ambulance arrived and the EMT's were checking the young girl out.

"Anyone know what she's on?" one asked.

"Not exactly. The guy who was with her gave her something so she wouldn't fight being prostituted out." Holly knew that much.

"So she's a prostitute?"

"I think this is her first time out on the streets with him." Holly hugged herself. *That could be me.*

"If the police catch up with him, you may get more information but right now, that's all we know," Mrs. Waterson added. "I'll contact child protective services to meet you at the ED. I doubt she's of legal age.

"I'll be along shortly," Mrs. Waterson added after learning which ED they were going to.

Holly stood next to Mrs. Waterson as the ambulance drove off. "Will she be okay?"

"I hope so. I hope that whatever drove her onto the streets can be fixed."

"Do you think it would be okay if I saw her?" Holly couldn't explain the need to stay connected to the young girl but it was important to her to do so.

"I'll talk to the CPS worker and let you know." Mrs. Waterson stepped so she faced Holly. "You did a very brave thing. How are you doing now?"

"I'm terrified he'll know I live here and he'll be waiting for me next time I come out."

"I'll be back in a couple of hours and we'll talk. One way or another we'll find a way for you to feel safe."

Mrs. Waterson did come back and she brought Doc S with her. The building had a 'no harassment' policy. They had security and other residents who were willing to act as escorts to and from places. Holly was matched up with two guys who had classes in the same building she did.

She didn't feel threatened by them but she didn't feel safe. The nightmares continued. Doc S prescribed something to help her sleep. Sometimes it worked but other times the nightmares were too strong.

Counseling?

She tried two sessions and not only were nightmares worse than ever before, she also had panic attacks and found herself either crying or vomiting for no apparent reason.

"Stress." Doc S and Mrs. Waterson concurred. "It will get better if you continue counseling."

Holly was losing weight, couldn't sleep, couldn't eat and was in danger of failing her classes.

For her, counseling wasn't working.

She stopped.

Her nemesis had not gotten caught by the police. She knew that because he hung around campus and when he spotted her, would smile and crook his finger, beckoning her to come to him. Thankful for the escorts, she outwardly ignored him.

It was only a matter of time.

He knew she went to school.

He knew in which buildings she had classes.

He knew where she lived.

Her choice was to live with the constant fear, unable to leave her apartment without escort, afraid to look out her window in case he'd spot her. It was one thing for him to know which building she was in, another for him to know which room.

Holly worked hard and made up the work so she passed all her classes. She even got an "A". Doc S and Mrs. Waterson took her out for dinner to celebrate.

Both women noticed she picked at her food. Was there something wrong with it? Did she need to send it back?

Finally she told them she'd seen the creep when they'd left her building. Her voice trembled and a tear slipped down her cheek.

Doc S and Mrs. Waterson discussed filing a stalker report and asking for a restraining order. The main problem with that plan was serving him with it.

Doc S's pat on her arm reengaged her. "Let's get you moved to another place. It is the end of the quarter and you can even change schools."

"But—,"

"As long as you live where you are and attend that school, you are in danger of him catching you unawares and dragging you off. Of course we'd look for you but we'd rather not have to do so."

"But where would I go?"

"I'll check out a couple of options and check in with you tomorrow." Mrs. Waterson's smile was bright and cheerful. "Who knows what you're capable of in school when all this is behind you?"

She invited Doc and Mrs. W up to the apartment after dinner. On the shelf over her study area was a small box wrapped in red tissue paper with a white sparkly bow. Picking up the present she turned to Mrs. W. "Will you be able to give this to Mercy?"

"Her worker will want to know what it is."

"Nothing much. I saw this little crystal at the holiday gift bazaar at the church down the street. When it's in the sun, it sparkles. I thought of her when I saw it." She pointed to the small table at the end of her couch. "It's like that, the one you got me when I first moved in here. When all seems dark, I hold it up to the light and see the rainbows. And I feel better."

Finding Peace

Gabriella stretched. Flexing her fingers she glanced at her word count and sighed. Another section she'd have to pay particular attention to because it was so easy to type her name instead of the made-up Holly's.

The sound of the sea called to her. Out on her balcony she faced the water. Now that she was out of the story, she felt the heat. The pool would be cool—very inviting.

No suit. Improvise. Back in her room she changed into a pair of shorts and a plain white cotton bra. Towel in hand she trotted down to the pool. Sitting on the edge, her feet dangled in the cool blue water.

A limb from a nearby bush seemed to lean towards her. Scrutinizing the branch, she scanned the pattern looking for the Fibonacci spiral. The lush foliage blocked her efforts to track how the leaves circled the stem. *But I know there is a pattern and that pattern is a spiral and it is part of what makes this plant unique.*

Gabriella slipped into the pool and relaxed, letting her weight take her under the water. On an exhale she surfaced and struck out for the opposite side. It felt good to stretch her muscles a different way, give her body a chance to recover from the sitting that came from writing.

Did Holly swim?

Did Holly even like water?

Did Holly feel the healing power, the energy of waves crashing on the rocks?

Back and forth she swam until her muscles burned. She paddled to the shallow end where steps allowed her to walk out of the pool. Picking up the towel, she wrapped it around her hair. With the sun beating down, she'd be dry in no time.

Mindful of her fair skin, she sat at the table with an umbrella. Waiting for her was a glass of lemon water. Startled she realized she'd been so oblivious to what was going on around her, she hadn't even noticed when the lemon water and accompanying pitcher had been brought to her.

Gabriella paused. No she didn't feel panicky or frightened. Confused? Yes, very confused she'd been so unaware of what was happening around her.

From her vantage point she couldn't see the sea although the sound of the waves was audible. If she went back to her room she could shower, dress, sit on her balcony and enjoy the view.

In a minute.

Seagulls twirled overhead, their raucous calls drowning out the sea.

Still at ease, Gabriella watched their antics as they swooped out of sight and then glided up on the breeze. Shivering as a gust of wind blew by, she wrapped the damp towel around her. Was she as relaxed as yesterday in the garden with Giovanni? No. Not even close.

But as the chapters she'd just written played over in her mind she knew she was more at peace than she'd ever been. There was something magical happening to her here in Italy, here with Giovanni, here writing *Holly's Story*.

The fear that had roared back when she wrote about her abuser was gone. She didn't fear having nightmares tonight because for the first time since she was very small she was safe. Even last night with Giovanni in the house she knew in her gut she was safe.

It wasn't that the house was impenetrable although it was well-built.

It wasn't that she was thousands of miles away from those who wished her harm although that maybe was a factor.

It was simply that she trusted Giovanni.

Stunned, she staggered to her feet and headed for the balustrade. Sitting in the place they both loved, she could feel his presence, feel her hand in his.

How?

When?

As Gabriella took stock of the truth that she did trust him, images of her circle sisters and their husbands hovered in her memory. These men were all safe. She'd trust them with her life. With her secrets? *They know some of it and they've not turned away from me. But more important they've never tried hitting on me.*

As she studied her thoughts, she accepted that even Giovanni hadn't "hit on her". He'd flirted. Outrageously at times. But he hadn't felt her up, suggestively brushed against her, or implied he wanted to have sex.

The closest any of them had come to that was Diana's first husband, Dennis. He'd leered at her. She'd glared daggers back—that had been the end of it.

It wasn't that they were so in love with their wives they saw no one else. When Diana, Ashley and Hunter needed help, the men were right there. For a fact she knew if she asked, any one of them would come to her aid.

But asking?

Right now she couldn't imagine asking any man for help.

But then I never thought I'd feel safe, truly safe ever.

Without a backward glance at the dancing waves on sparkling water, Gabriella strolled back to the house.

Not sure what she'd do after she showered and dressed, she decided she didn't have to know. That was one of the benefits to being on sabbatical or extended leave. It was her time to recharge her batteries, to find what fed her soul.

Humming to herself, she trotted up the stairs. An idea was forming. Why she hadn't thought of it before now didn't matter.

Holly's Story

Excited, she read back through the last couple of chapters of *Holly's Story*. Her idea would fit nicely into where the story was now.

Her fingers flew over the keys as she wrote about Holly's journey through school. She'd easily finished her GED and even her two year course at the community college. Moving had become a normal part of her life. Now finishing her senior year at a four year college, she still moved but not every term as she'd done at the community college.

Immersed in her book on women's issues in the 20th Century, Holly marked her place when she heard a knock on the door.

"Come in."

Cathy stuck her head around the door.

"Something you need to deal with."

Holly jumped up and headed out the door almost knocking Cathy over. She jogged down the hall toward the shouting coming from the lobby area. As the on-site manager of the small dorm, it was her job to handle 'issues'.

Entering the lobby, her gut twisted at the scene before her. An angry young man was looming over one of the female residents, shouting obscenities. The terrified young woman cowered, her sobs and pleas to stop yelling going unnoticed.

She wished this was something that never happened and while it wasn't a common occurrence it wasn't that rare.

When she approached, she smelled alcohol.

"Who's called campus police?" she asked in a strong voice.

The man turned toward her. "Stay out of this, bitch," he snarled.

How she wished she could back down, slither away but if there was one thing she'd learned it was to pick your battles. Here in the lobby with the campus police on their way, she was confident she had the upper hand.

"Move away from her," she ordered keeping her gaze fixed on him, looking for any sign he was going to swing.

He didn't move.

She did.

"Edie, you must go to your room right now." The young woman's fear permeated the room. Other residents formed a loose circle around the pair watching to see what happened.

"One of you take Edie to her room. After he leaves," she said, not taking her eyes from him, "I'll be right along."

When no one came forward and Edie had not moved away and the campus police had still not arrived, Holly knew it was up to her.

Standing at her full five foot five height, she imperiously pointed to the door. "Get out!" At the same time, she stepped in front of Edie and pushed her back.

He was drunk. His eyes dilated. The fumes so strong her eyes watered.

She stepped back and used her body to push Edie away. His hand came up and she prepared to duck if he followed through.

"I will press charges if you follow through," she threatened. "And, this will be all over campus by morning."

"That teasing bitch," he roared. "I'll make sure every guy on campus stays away from her." A wild look on his face, he turned and sprinted for the door just as the campus police pulled up.

Holly's knees shook but her indignation at the lack of response from the others was palpable. Whirling around, she reached out for Edie and put her arm around the young woman's waist.

Afraid she'd just sputter, she stared at each person in the room, her displeasure evident. It took some effort to say nothing to the others but her focus now had to be on the young woman next to her.

"Edie, let's go to my room and talk," she soothed. Holly's arm still around Edie's waist, she led her away.

When all said and done, it was obvious Edie had gotten in over her head. It had been heady to be invited to a private party. She'd figured there would be drinking but had misjudged what would be expected of her.

It hadn't taken long for her to realize she was expected to have sex with at least the guy who'd taken her if not one of his friends. That's when she'd run off.

Pom, the guy who'd taken her, noticed she was gone and came after her. Holly figured it was more about not letting some girl make him look bad than that he had any real feelings for about Edie.

Through decreasing sobs, Edie assured her that Pom was really a nice guy. With Holly's questioning, that assessment was amended to 'when he wasn't drinking'. What disturbed Holly the most? Edie's willingness to give Pom another chance if he apologized for what happened tonight.

Secretly Holly hoped he didn't apologize. She saw the beginning of what happens to women like her mother, trapped in a cycle of domestic violence. How many times had she heard "But he apologized" or "He didn't really mean it?"

Too many.

Once Edie had settled enough to go to her own room, Holly got ready for bed. Through the hellish evening, she'd had her own feelings surge. Feeling very vulnerable, she wrapped herself in her oldest and most comfortable robe and curled up in her chair—not the one she sat in at the desk but the other one tucked into the corner.

From this vantage point she easily saw her room. One picture of a blue jay, the bright iridescent color glimmering in the sunlight. The other picture of a sunflower. Neither was very big and both were recent additions courtesy of Doc S and Mrs. Waterson.

On the window sill was the crystal cluster she'd gotten from Mrs. W when she had her very first place. It was dark now but there was also a sense of life within the stone. Fascinated with it, she'd spent hours looking into the depths to see various images depending on how she held it and how the light hit it.

If she had to leave, the pictures would stay but the crystal cluster along with the crystal she'd bought for herself at the Christmas Bazaar when she'd purchased one for Mercy as well as the other pretty reddish stone she'd found on her walks would always come with her.

It was comforting to know she didn't have to leave everything behind.

It was comforting to know she would always be reminded about people who cared about her when those rocks were with her.

It was comforting… .

At a time when things seemed at loose ends having those three pieces helped her make it through.

Signs and Transitions

Gabriella's hands rested in her lap but her eyes caressed a small crystal, a piece of citrine and a small amethyst city that held pride of place to the left of her computer. To the right were three different rocks: a naturally polished agate from an Oregon beach she'd found after a storm; one from The Sacred Grove blessed by The Lady and another she'd found along the pathway in Giovanni's garden.

Of course the semi-precious stones had their own histories but the others were plain stones, ones that had been passed over by hundreds if not thousands of people over the years.

There had been something about each that had drawn her eye. It was true she'd been beach combing after the storm but had only seen chips of agates. This one was about an inch in size and it was amazing to her none of the other beach combers had seen it. Her conclusion? It was waiting for her.

When in Ireland and in Ceremony in The Sacred Grove, things took on a magical quality. They glowed with an aura and some had a spark of light shooting from their core. This stone seemed to brighten when she was near and fade when she passed by. Drawn back to it over and over, she'd bent to touch it. The Lady appeared, "It is yours." Held in her hand, it warmed and transported her back to that peaceful healing place of love.

The pathways in the Villa's gardens were made of a crushed granite. Why this one stone in the middle of the path seemed to call to her was a mystery. At first she'd thought it nonsense—not nonsense that a stone could communicate but nonsense that it would with her—here. But after paying attention during several walks, she knew it was the same stone. Why she needed something from this place and time she didn't know. But she'd learned to trust that inner place of knowing.

While Holly was a composite character of many young girls she'd known, there were autobiographical elements as well. These six rocks formed the core of her sacred items. She'd tucked the three semi-precious gems into pockets more than once as she hurried away from a no-longer-safe-to-her living situation.

The three newer stones had all been found since she'd joined The Circle and to her represented the sacred in her life. Just holding any one of them in her hand brought with it a sense of peace or connection to its source. *If that's really true, why then would I want or need a connection to this place?*

So many thoughts and feelings charged through her these days as she wrote *Holly's Story*. But at night she slept. No nightmares. Only dreams. Ethereal feelings. Vague thoughts upon waking but nothing solid enough to remember.

She'd be surprised if Giovanni wasn't a part of her dreams at some point. He was a constant presence in this place, his home. While his energy was softer—was that the right word or maybe it was just different? The point was, when he was here his energy was palpable. When he was gone it was noticeably less so.

He was gone now and while she'd not told him anything about the story she was writing, he always asked how it was going. She liked being able to report she'd added XXX number of words and finished XX chapters. He would smile and nod and say "*Bene*". She would smile and nod and say "*Sì*".

Gabriella shifted the rocks to form different patterns. Three stones naturally fit into a triangle. If she put them all together they could more easily make a circle. *Maybe I can add a few more? Not so many that I can't easily carry them in a pocket. If I kept them similar sizes I could easily carry four more. That would make ten. What was it Giovanni said about that number in sacred geometry?*

Ten it is the number of completion. She heard him say, his voice in her mind.

Yes, that's what I'll do. I'll be on the lookout for four more. Her brain had already started to plan out where she could find them when she halted. *No, these all came to me as they were meant to be. I'm asking The Universe for four more. There is nothing more I need to do than ask. They will come in right time.*

Two days later Gabriella was halfway across the pool when she passed under a shadow. Treading water she looked up to see Giovanni toeing off his shoes. A glance at the table told her he'd already emptied his pockets. Transfixed she watched him tug his shirt from his pants and pull it off over his head.

His muscles rippled with the motion, the dark arrow of chest hair tempted her gaze lower.

"What are you doing?" Gabriella hoped the note of panic she felt didn't show in her voice.

"Joining you." A mischievous grin tilted his lips as his hands unbuckled his belt and slowly slid it from the loops.

"But you'll—,"

His smooth dive into the pool plugged her words. Frantic, she looked around for him. Panic lodged in her throat and she stifled a scream.

Four feet to her right he popped up. Shaking his head to whip the water from his face and hair, the grin still on his face, he kept pace with her.

"*Si*, it is much better here." He struck out in the direction she'd been headed.

Her heartbeat nearing normal, the panic subsided. He wasn't going to attack her in the pool. He was having fun, teasing her in a challenging way.

Could she keep up with him?

She'd been swimming for thirty minutes and he was fresh in the water. Not today—she wouldn't let him challenge her today because she wouldn't lose to him.

Flipping onto her back, she swam to the opposite end. Hand on the pool side, she looked back. He was nowhere to be seen.

Movement under the water.

Giovanni surged out of the water three feet away.

"Did you swim the length of the pool underwater?"

"*Si*." He managed the short word, but his breathing was labored.

Maybe if she challenged him now, she could beat him. Her innate sense of fairness came to the fore. Winning when your opponent was weakened was not a win.

He recovered quickly because in the few moments she was sorting through challenging or not, he had his breath back.

She knew that because he glided under the water, surfaced eight feet away and stroked to the far end. A fluid turn and he swam back to her. At the pace he was keeping now, she could keep up with him—but not today.

Thankful she was at the end closest to the steps, she went up them and to the table. Picking up the towel she patted herself dry and then wrapped it around her head tightening it to wring some of the water from her curls. She kept her back to the pool not wanting to watch Giovanni's tan body slicing through the blue water.

However, if she was going to sit down and have her glass of lemon water, she either needed to move the chair so it was turned away from the pool or face it.

In the end she sat facing the pool and watched the rhythmic strokes take him back and forth. Was he counting laps, was he waiting for a sign from his body that it was time to stop?

There was so much about him she didn't know and so much about which she was curious.

She'd been here just over three weeks and other than the few days here and there when he'd been in Rome, he'd been a perfect host. Maybe he wasn't the womanizer she'd always thought him to be. Diana had said he wasn't, going on to say there's a difference between a man who enjoys the company of women and a womanizer. But then, he had been in Rome enough that if he had women he was involved with—.

The thought unfinished she watched as Giovanni mounted the steps out of the pool. His slacks clung to his legs and buttocks. If she'd been a sculptor, he'd make an amazing model.

Cheeks flamed with embarrassment and she quickly looked away when she saw his brow quirk in question. He slouched down in the chair on the other side of the table, reached over and took a drink from her glass.

"*Grazie.*" He crossed his ankles and stared out over the pool. She filled the glass and handed it to him. He shook his head.

A sudden thirst dried her throat. Careful to keep the side he'd used away from her, she drank her fill. The glass was half gone when she put it back on the table. Looking at it she wondered if it was half empty or half full.

It was hard for her to think of the world around her as full of opportunities, of possibilities. Easier now than when she'd first come off the streets but still—.

She took the towel from her head and finger-combed her curls into some semblance of order. Keeping to her routine was for the best so she stood and wrapped the towel around her like a shield.

"I'm going in to shower and change," she announced and turned toward the path to the house.

"I see you at dinner then."

Upstairs she stood back from the doorway to the balcony and looked out toward the pool. He was back in the water, swimming laps. Every ten laps he got out and dove in again, swimming the length of the pool underwater. After watching him for longer than she'd planned, Gabriella turned away and headed to the bathroom and shower fully aware at how aroused she was feeling just watching him swim.

Giovanni was old enough to know he would not die from the arousal that had hit him hard when he'd come upon Gabriella swimming. Shorts and a bra…

Did the woman have no clothes?

Obviously she didn't have or didn't bring a swimsuit. His guess was she didn't have one, didn't allow herself—what? The pleasure of being in the water? The pleasure of having certain items of clothing for various events? Thinking back on all the times he'd seen her, it wasn't that she always wore the same garment but there was a sameness to what she did wear that went beyond color and style.

When he'd gotten out of the pool and felt her eyes rake over his body, it was exhilarating. An exhilaration that was short lived because of the look of panic that followed.

She was interested or at least had feelings for him but it was clear she was nowhere close to acting on them. But then again, he was in it for the long haul. He looked forward to coming home to the villa knowing she was here. While away, he imagined her writing, and now could add swimming, to the scenario in his mind.

And, he loved showing her Rome, teaching her bits and pieces about sacred geometry. Yes, his long term plan would have her here with him. He would no longer be jealous of Jackson or even Michael, Matthew, Daniel and, if he knew him better, Grant. An inward smile, *maybe they be jealous of me.*

Gabriella had been relatively gracious about losing the tiramisu bet which meant they'd fly to Ireland together. It took a bit more effort for Giovanni to convince Gabriella to spend three days in Rome with him before they left.

What won her over was his argument that he would expand her knowledge of sacred geometry, going into more depth about how men had taken the concepts of sacred geometry and used them in art and architecture.

Sitting in the garden at his Rome house on the last evening, she studied the nature around her.

"So you are saying that sitting like this and observing the natural world was the entertainment of the ancients?"

"*No e Si.* Not entertainment but study that they enjoyed. Seeing a figure and then looking to see if it is replicated was something these men of science enjoyed. It wasn't everyone's pastime."

"But were they scientist first and went looking for answers or were they ordinary people who were a bit more aware of their environment and because they saw things became scientist?"

"They were seekers of knowledge. Curious as to how their world worked."

"What I find magical is that what they discovered centuries ago is still valid and used today. I remember studying about Pythagoras' theorem in geometry. I might have paid more attention if I'd understood its history. A simple triangle was used to map out property lines."

"Eratosthenes who lived 275 – 194 BC used a stick and string to measure the circumference of the earth. His measurement is 1.7 percent off from the results of sophisticated tools at our disposal today."

"That still amazes me. Even though I'm amazed by all you are showing me, what sings to me is seeing the patterns in the earth around me. I can hardly wait to return to The Sacred Grove and see it through the eyes of a novice learning sacred geometry."

"You've come a long way from being a novice." Giovanni looked down at Gabriella sitting beside him on the garden bench. The flush of excitement on her cheeks and in her eyes called to him. The urge to lean in and brush his lips against her soft lush lips parted on a sigh had him leaning away and fisting his hands instead.

She must have sensed something because her mood changed in an instant. Shifting away, she stood and started walking down the path toward the house. Knowing it was better this way didn't ease Giovanni's disappointment. Tomorrow morning they'd fly to Ireland and meet up with the other women in her circle. His time with her would be limited.

Could he convince her to return with him at the end of the holiday? He was basically an optimist but in this case, he was certain she'd refuse. Of course he'd ask and even try to persuade but with the other women around her, he knew he had no chance.

Happy confusion and turmoil! Their arrival at Shannon was less than two hours from when everyone else had arrived. When they came through security, Gabriella was rushed, surrounded by her circle sisters.

Standing to the side were husbands with satisfied looks on their faces. Also with the men were the male children. Giovanni looked again and saw Logan, Rose and the baby tucked in the center of the welcoming committee.

Although he knew Diana's son Bill and had met Lily's son Charlie on his visits to Fremont, they hadn't been to any of the ceremonies in Ireland so he was a bit surprised to see them.

Daniel had his hand on the shoulder of his step-son, Anthony, who looked ready to bolt. James, on the other hand, hung on to every word the men exchanged.

Somehow the boys in particular all seemed to have grown in some way. Bill and Charlie looked more mature. Of course Bill was 21 but Charlie, at 19 also looked older—with that stronger look to his face and jaw. Ashley's oldest son, James was shaving now and wore his hair in the same short style Daniel did. *Mirroring himself after Daniel is good thing.*

However, Anthony was a different story. He'd heard from Jackson that Anthony still wanted to go live with his father when Art got out of jail. An event that would happen fairly soon. On the one hand he was glad Ashley and Daniel were not fighting Anthony over hair and dress—at best a losing battle. The long shaggy hair and torn shirt and jeans, tennis shoes with untied laces? At least he was clean.

Logan was definitely her mother's daughter with long dancer legs. He thought Rose had grown a foot in the last month! Madison Michelle was clearly wanting down and to move around. The Circle handled that by passing her around, each woman giving her special attention before handing her off to the next person. It was a bit selfish of him or maybe even a lot selfish but he hoped he wasn't in the van with the baby. Perhaps if she had a chance to wear off some of the pent up energy from having her movements restricted on the long flight he'd reconsider.

As it was he needn't have worried. The men traveled in one van with extra luggage and Michael driving. The women in the other with Seamus at the wheel.

They stopped at The Winner's Circle, Michael's pub in Kinsale. The Manor wasn't that far away but it felt good to stretch and have something to eat. In the pub, they congregated around several tables pulled together.

The younger ones decided to walk on to The Manor a couple of miles up the road. Hunter and Grant followed, keeping their distance, holding hands and at one point, Hunter twirled under Grant's upraised arm.

In the van to The Manor, he found himself sitting next to Gabriella as if they were a couple. She seemed totally unaware of their seating arrangement and he decided it wise to say nothing. He caught the raised brow look of Jackson and answered with a quirk of his own. In Michael's study there would be questions.

Giovanni considered Jackson's raised brow a warning of some sort. His friend knew he would not take advantage of Gabriella but maybe the other men weren't so sure.

As the van took the sharp turn into the long drive, Gabriella leaned into him. When it straightened out, he thought she might not shift away.

Wishful thinking.

He wasn't counting but if he had been, she'd moved away in less than a minute. *But she didn't jerk away.*

She also allowed him to help her down from the van. She did have her arms full of Madison Michelle paraphernalia but she smiled and said thank you—not a bristle in sight!

The Manor was a place of miracles. He'd seen the miracle of Michael and Elizabeth finding their way to happiness. As Diana took her daughter from Matthew, he knew she'd started on her journey to her current life while visiting here. Ashley's children had shown everyone how special Daniel was when they were all here for the Sabbat celebrations. And Grant, the newest husband with only six weeks or so experience in that title, had that extra time with Logan just this past summer. Logan was his daughter but without her love and acceptance, he'd never have Hunter as his wife.

Lily had her arm around Sophia who still did not look like her old self. Gabriella joined them and the threesome headed toward the main entrance to the house.

He turned back to the vans. The walkers had already arrived because the riders had taken their time. A workforce was in place to see to the luggage. He pitched in, helping the men unload and assigning luggage delivery duties to the boys and Logan. Even Rose pitched in, taking a backpack to Diana.

Giovanni considered taking Gabriella's one suitcase and backpack to her but decided against that. She'd been at his place for three weeks, going on four. It was her time to reconnect with The Circle. He'd been waiting for her for almost three years, he could wait a little longer.

Grabbing his own suitcase, he followed the other men into the house. "My study at four. The women are meeting, the kids are going riding. It'll be just us men," Michael said over his shoulder as he strode down the hall.

Giovanni calculated he had ample time to unpack. A smile on his face, he whistled a jaunty tune as he strode down the driveway to the road. Plenty of time to plan how he was going to answer the questions he knew would be waiting.

The Men and Giovanni

His head clear from the walk and his suitcase unpacked, Giovanni strolled into Michael's study a few minutes past four. He fixed two fingers of Irish whiskey on the rocks and took the only empty seat at one end of the two couches. Sipping his drink, he waited for the interrogation to begin.

And he waited.

And he waited.

What was wrong with these men that they weren't checking out his interest in Gabriella?

Michael and Matthew were comparing baby stories. Daniel and Grant were comparing kids and school stories. Jackson had stood and ambled over to look out the windows at the view of the paddocks. Confused by the others seeming to ignore him, Giovanni joined Jackson.

Horses grazed on the lush green grass, their shining coats striped by white fencing. Standing next to Jackson, the silence was just there. No hidden messages. Giovanni shifted from one foot to the other, a restlessness shimmied through him as the pent up energy he'd built to deal with questions looked for an outlet.

"Are you okay?" Jackson asked.

"*Si.*"

"Sure nothing's wrong?"

"*Si,* nothing is wrong." Swallowing the last of his drink, he considered pouring another. *No, stupido.* He did fill his glass with ice and water and added a slice of lemon garnish before resuming his seat.

Relaxing against the corner of the couch, he listened as the conversations wound down. It wasn't that he envied the other men, neither he nor Jackson had fathered children. For that matter, neither had Daniel. But, he was the only one who had no children in his life.

He quashed an image of an auburn haired little girl with his chocolate brown eyes before it fully formed. Did Gabriella ever consider having children? While he harbored the idea of himself as a father, it would not be a deal breaker if she did not see herself as a mother.

She'd be a good one. Serious, conscientious, intensely so. More like what he'd seen between Hunter and Logan than Ashley and her three.

Lost in his own thoughts, the question caught him by surprise.

"So, how did things go with Gabby at your place?" Michael asked the seemingly innocuous question.

Giovanni was aware all ears were primed for his answer even if all eyes were not riveted on him.

"She writes her book. I work."

Now heads turned toward him. Michael didn't blink, his gaze steady, he smiled. "You expect me to believe you were gone the entire time?"

"You believe what you want." He heard the defensiveness in his tone and checked the irritation growing in his chest.

"You forget Elizabeth and I dropped by for a few days."

"No, I don't forget your visit." Giovanni managed a smile. "But that was only a few days out of several weeks. Gabriella begins writing when Sophia leaves. Every day she writes for hours. And, I do have a business, clients to see. Some in Rome so I am gone."

"Gabby never went to Rome with you?" Grant asked, a mock amazed look on his face.

"I go several times, she goes thrice if you count taking Sophia to the airport, coming here as two times. She writes. She not share about the story but I think it is good for her to be writing. She should finish it before she goes back to work."

"So you want her to go back to Italy with you?" Jackson asked this bombshell.

Giovanni took a sip of his lemon water, glad he'd not chosen another alcoholic drink. "It is Gabriella's decision. If she wants to come back and write, of course she is always welcome.

"I'd say any of the women are welcome to come and stay at my villa or at my Rome house but I am not sure any of you," he gestured with his free hand, "would want that so I do not extend an open invitation to them.

"But Gabriella and Sophia do not have men to answer to, nor do they have children to consider so my invitation is only to them." He smiled confident he'd said just enough and not too much.

"They may not have men to 'answer to'," Michael quirked his fingers as if they were quotation marks, "but they do have men watching out for them.

"And I am glad to know that."

A gong sounded. Dinner would be ready in thirty minutes. Giovanni stood. "I go wash up. I'll see you at dinner."

Without a backward glance he left, leaving the door open as he passed through.

"Well, that was enlightening," Daniel said as Giovanni's footsteps faded down the hall.

"I'm fairly sure I've no idea what's going on," Grant said, looking at the others.

"Giovanni has been attracted to Gabriella since he first met her when Lily was recovering from an automobile accident at my place in early 2003." Jackson said, bringing Grant up-to-date. "We've all noticed that this past year or so he's backed off. While she wasn't jumping for joy to spend time in Italy with Sophia at first, she wasn't as adamant about not going as we thought she might be."

"She's softened toward him," Michael added. "E and I noticed that when we were in Italy. She engages with him. He's very careful not to watch her when they are spending time together but if you stay aware, you catch him looking at her as if she were a prize."

"She is a prize," Grant added. "I don't know what shape Logan would be in or if she'd even be alive without Gabby. And, I'd never have Hunt in my life without her."

"We all agree that we'll support him in his efforts to win her?"

"Jackson, what makes you think he's trying to win her?" Matthew asked.

"Because I know him. We've been friends for almost twenty years. He hasn't changed his mind, only his tactics. Gabby rebuffed his more overt efforts but she hasn't rebuffed his offer of friendship.

"I'm not talking about throwing them together as in making sure they can only sit next to each other. I'm talking about paying attention to when they are together and not just barging in."

"Maybe she will consider returning with him and finishing that book. She's talked about being an author ever since I met her," Michael added. "That's something we can support if there is ever a discussion."

Empty glasses on the tray, the men left the study to find wives and kids and dinner.

.

The Women and Gabriella

Smudging as they came into Elizabeth's parlor, the women formed a circle. The center contained a black cloth with a round platter of swirling red, orange and yellow colors in the center. Candles marked the four directions. Before they sat, each of them added an object to the altar.

Gabriella put the piece of granite from Giovanni's garden in the north and her piece of citrine in the south. Lily added a piece of amethyst to the west. Sophia placed a ripe apple next to Gabby's citrine. Hunter took two shells from her shirt pocket. One was from the Rhode Island beach of her youth and one from the Oregon coast. Gabby thought she'd put them in the west, the void, with water as its symbol but she didn't. It did make sense when she saw one in the north and one in the east. Ashley's dragonfly pin sat in the east next to Diana's sunstone ring.

Elizabeth studied the altar before she selected items from her shelves. A dolphin carved from lapis lazuli joined Lily's amethyst in the West along with a small ceramic frog. To the north she added a small painting of a snowy owl. To the south she added a small bag of seeds. "Now each direction has three symbols," Elizabeth said rounding the circle and sitting in the east.

To her it had been a very long time since all seven of them had sat in the same circle together. She, Sophia and Elizabeth had set up a little circle when they were together in Italy and no matter who wasn't there in person, they were always represented energetically—but it was different when they sat face-to-face and shared their lives, shared their energy and shared their hopes and dreams.

Elizabeth, her dark hair pulled up in a careless knot on top of her head, started the sharing, using a palm-sized stone from The Sacred Grove. "Maeve is doing so well! In many ways she is an easy baby and Michael is a devoted father. Almost sleeping through the night but at five months, while I'd love it, I'm not actually expecting it.

"Since she's been born, I still spend time with The Lady but not every day because someone must be here with Maeve and during the summer months with racing season—well, I will say having Eleanor here for a couple of months along with Logan was a huge help.

"I've talked to Shannon and she is going to organize and run the workshops after the first of the year. I'll be more active once Maeve is a year old. But, I also plan on traveling to the U.S for some of the races Michael's horses will be in. You can count on seeing more of me next year.

"Not now, but before everyone leaves after Samhain, we need to talk about Winter Solstice. I know I said we'd come to Fremont for the Yule celebration but I'm not sure I'm comfortable traveling with Maeve. She'll just be six months old and it will be winter. Something to talk about and plan for."

Finished, Elizabeth passed the talking stone to Diana on her left.

"We'll work things out," Diana, her violet eyes shining with happiness, patted Elizabeth's arm. "Madison Michelle handled this trip better than either Matthew or I thought she would. Matthew asked me a few weeks ago if I would consider having another child. That's probably my biggest news. I am considering it although the idea of having another baby at my age is daunting. Of course I'll talk to my doctor and have tests, but with an invested husband and father, I'm not totally opposed to the idea.

"I'm still teaching classes and have my consulting business. Those two activities and taking care of M2 as well as spending time with my husband pretty much fills my day." She grinned and winked, "And nights."

With a light laugh Diana handed the stone to Ashley.

"I'm almost back to normal," Ashley said, running a hand through her short blond hair. "Still can't do heavy lifting but that's more because it will upset Daniel and James. And more than that, I'm not strong enough. But I'm getting there. Being released to drive again was a gift. I know better than I ever did what not being able to drive was for you, Lily.

"As y'all can see the kids are doing well. Even Anthony forgets that he's unhappy some of the time. Daniel and I are reconciled to his going to stay with Art next year. If that's what it takes for him to understand that Art won't ever be satisfied with him, I guess that's what it'll take. At least we both hope that Anthony figures that out instead of trying his whole life to please Art.

"I'm grateful to Lily for work and love spending time with her people. They tell me such wonderful stories. I'm writing them down and James has taken on the project of typing them up. Rose wants to make covers for them and I think giving them their stories back—all typed up and all will be a great holiday gift."

Ashley held the stone out. "I'm actually looking forward to being back to work," Sophia said taking the stone in her right hand. She rolled the stone from hand-to-hand before adding, "Having a few extra days here with Elizabeth and Maeve has helped. I'm hoping to find a direction for my life while in our Sacred Grove ceremony. It feels as if there is something I'm supposed to be doing but I can't figure it out logically so I think it may be a spiritual journey I need to take.

"Thank you all for your support and for your gentle persuasion to go to Italy for a few weeks. My time there and then here allows me to return to the classroom full time.

"Fair warning. I plan on a cooking and baking binge when I get home. My freezer will be stocked with apple, peach and berry pies, cinnamon rolls and pecan sticky bun dough and brownies. Well before Thanksgiving I'll have so much I won't have to bake anything until after the first of the year."

"Even if you're sharing with us?" Lily asked taking the rock.

"Even if I'm sharing with you all. For some reason I feel like I need a stockpile of sorts."

Lily shook her head in disbelief, setting her blond shoulder length hair swinging. "It'll be strange walking into your place without the aroma of fresh baked something."

"There will always be freshly baked bread. I'm stocking up on the sweet stuff, not the bread, rolls and biscuits." Sophia waved for Lily to continue.

"Jackson is thrilled Ashley is able to help out so much. He isn't actually cutting back but it feels like he is because we have so much more time together. We saw Eleanor off to her daughters' where she plans to spend time until Jackson's annual New Year's Eve Party. She'll be home for that.

"I do miss her but now that I'm traveling more with Jackson, it is better that she is back east with her daughters and their families. She's lost touch a bit with her grandchildren and this will give her a chance to really reestablish those ties that mean so much to her. They are already planning on spending Thanksgiving at the house on the shore that she and Archie always went to. Lots of memories. Jackson and I've been invited for Thanksgiving but we've decided we'll sort of see how things are going. Most likely we'll fly out for a few days."

Seeing the looks from the others, she added. "I know, plane tickets and all since we're less than a month out, but we've lots of flexibility. Jackson's actually been contacted by some people who've heard about him from some of his California clients so he's looking at how to add business appointments into the mix."

Hunter laughed and leaned over to hug Lily who passed her the stone. "I can see there being an east coast Montgomery Architects office now. Depending on where the appointments are, I'm sure you can use the Rhode Island house.

"Do any of you ever think back to where we were last year at this time—or the year before?" Hunter leaned forward, her chestnut hair pulled into a pony tail accented turquoise blue eyes that searched each faces. "Our first meeting was on Samhain over ten years ago. So much has happened in our lives, so many changes. Not all of them have been good but in the end, we've stayed true to our beliefs 'harm to none, do as you will; see the divine in everything including each other'.

"I know I messed up worse than anyone on these earlier this year when Logan was missing but without The Circle, without the years we've been together, I don't know that I ever would have made my way through that dark time and back into the light.

"I'm ever so grateful to have each and every one of you in my life. I'm ever so grateful to have my daughter in my life. I'm ever so grateful to have Grant in my life." She turned to Diana. "I don't know if Grant and Matthew have been talking but Grant has broached the topic of our having another child. Logan would be ecstatic. She's hinted more than once. But I'm not sure that is what we need or should do. I see how you and Matthew are raising Madison Michelle and Bill's a young man now. If you see me staring with a thoughtful look on my face, that's most likely why."

Gabriella's hand filled with the warm stone. It was nondescript when it came to rocks or stones, a blackish brown, palm-sized, warm from being held in so many hands but there was something else to it if one stopped long enough to feel it. A radiant energy came from its core. She held it up and confirmed it was opaque. Turning it over she saw faint lines circling the middle. If she'd been alive in ancient times, would she have seen this stone amongst all the others? Would she have noticed the almost invisible markings? Would she have felt the warmth, the life in it?

"You all know since I've been in Italy I've been writing. It's one of those strange compelling things. My other forays into authorship failed and I really don't know what's going to happen with this story but it really doesn't matter.

"It a story that keeps me up at night, that energizes and exhausts me. It is compelling in that there are times I must write. I'm probably two-thirds of the way through. No notes, no outlines, no plot, no character studies—all those things I did before I'm not doing now. I'm just writing.

"Some of you may remember my talking about the spruce cone I found under the Douglas fir tree. Giovanni has been teaching me about sacred geometry. The ancients used it to find the harmonies in nature, in sound. Amazing as it seems, they came very close to determining the actual circumference of Earth with a stick and string.

"As I learned more about sacred geometry I can see it appearing in Holly's life. Holly is the heroine of this story. I've been writing bits and pieces of it into the story. Some of it is very mystical to me because I'm staying focused on sacred geometry in nature although Giovanni has shown me how man has taken these ideas and used them to build pyramids, The Parthenon, cathedrals and stone circles.

"What I'm hoping to sort out while I'm here is how I'm going to finish the book if I return to Fremont. Giovanni has said I can stay at his villa until it is done but I'm not sure that is a good plan. I have my job and then there is the house. It's been vacant for almost a month now. I'm very grateful to be here with all of you and to have the time to sort things through. It feels like I'm at a turning point in my life and until I finish this story, I won't be able to see what direction to take."

Gabriella placed the stone back on the altar. By consensus they agreed to leave things as they were so they could easily return later in the evening if that was what they wanted to do.

The gong sounded announcing dinner in thirty minutes as they stood and said closing prayers.

A Walk After Dinner

Dinner was a lively affair. Seamus had outdone himself with steamed vegetables and a tossed green salad with lettuce and tomato all fresh from the garden. The pasta casserole which served as the main course had an Alfredo sauce with chunks of ham. Peas, carrots, broccoli and cauliflower added color and texture. Dessert? A decadent peach cobbler with or without ice cream.

As one they agreed a bit of exercise before dessert was a good plan. Gabriella and Elizabeth wandered off in the direction of the gardens surrounding the gazebo while the others headed down the drive or to the paddocks and barn.

Hanging baskets of flowers showed the signs of fall with faded blooms interspersed with bright ones. Gabriella inspected each blossom and leaf looking for signs of sacred geometry. Delighted to see the patterns of circles and spirals she'd come to know, she showed them to E explaining as best she could what they were looking at.

"This is a Fibonnaci Spiral." Gabriella held up a fuchsia stem that had lost its flower. "See how the leaves are spaced? It will be the same on each stem of this plant.

"There is a beautiful integrated spiral in the seed heads of sunflowers. And when you look at a cone, you can see the precision of the placement of each bract.

"Our rocks and crystals are also comprised of the sacred forms. Why the round stone we used in circle today has faint white marking around the middle."

"Where did you say you were learning about this?"

"Giovanni mentioned sacred geometry when he was last in Fremont and overheard me telling the others about this spruce cone I'd found under a Doug fir miles away from any spruce tree. And while I've been in Italy, he's shown me other things. We went to a couple of museums in Rome and of course there are the cathedrals. I can see the beauty in the harmonies of the man-made structures but what calls to me is seeing it in The Mother.

"We've always seen Mother Earth as a sacred place but to see the infinite and infinitesimal beauty in each living thing takes my breath away. I know that's a clichéd saying but literally I find myself holding my breath as I take in the beauty, the intricacy of what is before me."

Leaving the gazebo, Gabriella and Elizabeth walked arm-in-arm through the garden with Gabby happily chatting on and pointing out different patterns. Coming to an area that was muddy, she exclaimed, "Fractals!"

"What?"

"Don't step here," she gestured to the muddy area. "I think this is a fractal. I'll ask Giovanni to come see it. He'll know."

"What is a fractal?"

"When you first look at this, it looks random but look closer and you'll see a pattern in the way the water moved through the dirt to create this design. I think fractals initially look disorganized but if we look closely we can see the magic."

"You mentioned that you are including sacred geometry in your story."

"Well, I've not included fractals but I have included rocks and crystals, flowers and leaves. My heroine finds solace in a bright red autumn leaf and she has a crystal on her window sill where it catches the sun's light. When she's troubled, being out in nature soothes her.

"Think about here. The Lady? The Sacred Grove? The old stone circles, wells, you know the holy sites? There is an energy there that we can feel if we pay attention.

"In ancient times people were more attuned to that energy. And there were others who were curious as to how their world worked. Someone had to notice circles, triangles, squares."

"So you're telling me that geometry is not just a form of mathematics. There's more to it?"

"Yes, that is what I'm saying." Gabby's enthusiasm shone in her voice. "There's this concept of noumenal that is a foundation for the sacred in geometry. Noumenal is about that which we feel or instinctively know but can't define or see, touch, hear. We feel the energy at the stone circle but we can't see it, touch it, or hear it. I'm calling it the God/Goddess source energy."

The two women turned back toward the house. "It's good to see you so excited about this."

"I feel so alive when I'm exploring sacred geometry."

"Then you must keep on this path." Elizabeth stopped and gently tugged Gabriella to a halt. "Do not make your decision about writing based on the Fremont house. Do not make your decision about writing based on your job. Trust your heart, Gabby. In this it will not mislead you."

"But it might not sell."

"So, even if it doesn't sell, you will be the better for having written *Holly's Story*. I know you well enough to be quite sure you have money in savings should you need something. Giovanni would welcome you back to Italy and he would not charge you rent. You could stay here and write although your learning more about sacred geometry would be severely hampered.

"I can't explain it, Gabby, but there is something transcendent about you when you talk about *Holly's Story*. You were always excited about the other stories but this one is different."

Gabriella hugged Elizabeth, stepped back and held her hands. "Thank you for your words of wisdom. It feels different but it also feels scary."

"Then finish writing *Holly's Story*."

They continued toward the house. "Ask the others what they think. I'm fairly certain they see what I do—there is something about this story that only you can tell."

Samhain

Monday
October 31, 2005
Samhain

Gabriella took her time preparing for their Samhain ceremony. None of them totally fasted but they all ate sparingly. She had tea and a couple of Seamus's scones. After a warm shower, she rubbed rose oil on her hands and feet before dressing in a loose fitting ankle length dress. There was still time before they were to gather so she sat at the window in her room in a meditative state—just being.

Elizabeth was right. Each of her circle sisters confirmed there was something different about her when she talked about writing this story. Michael had approached her and told her she was welcome to stay and write there and not to worry about the house in Fremont. He reminded her there was a property manager who took care of repairs, yard maintenance, etc.

And, he'd added, Grant and Hunter might be persuaded to move in there until she returned. Their time at Sophia's was about over and this would give them another experience to help them decide if they were going to build a house, find a house already built or do a massive renovation of the building above the dance studio.

I hope to find clarity in my time in Ceremony.

Meeting up with the others at the appointed time, she was pleased to see Logan, Bill, Charlie and James join them. Rose was a little young and seemed to sense that on her own because she chose to stay and help Seamus with Madison Michelle and Maeve. Anthony did not want to participate and arrangements were made for him to spend the night in the stables with the grooms. Joining their group was Shannon, an old girlfriend of Michael's, now friends with Elizabeth.

Down the narrow path to the sacred grove they went. Shannon led the way, Elizabeth brought up the rear. Ferns and fuchsias brushed her skirt as Gabriella followed Lily. Moonlight lit their way along the well-worn footpath.

Stopping at the bottom, they reassembled and started the ceremony at the south entrance. Arms raised over their heads, the women chanted "We come in peace, we come in peace, we come in peace to celebrate this time of the thinning of the veil."

Three times they circled the grove chanting at each opening. One quarter around brought them to the west opening. Entering, they followed the winding passageway to the center where the glow of the fire lit the space. Bubbling of the spring and the soughing of the breeze through the trees filtered through the silence.

As they formed a loose circle around the fire, a shimmering light appeared just beyond the flames. Within the radiance The Lady, dressed in the blue robes of her calling, appeared in their midst. "I welcome you on this sacred night. May you find the answers you are seeking." *Is she speaking to me?*

"May you find a connection to one who has gone before.

"May this night bring you peace."

The Lady raised her arms, hands uplifted to the sky.

"We are the light

"We are the source

"Through us flows love to all the world."

They chanted the prayer times three. The Lady faded and they were left alone. Everyone found a quiet place and opened to the energy around them. Gabriella didn't know anyone who'd died—well, no one close to her so she hunkered down on the log by the fire.

Mesmerized by the flames, she drifted off, dimly aware of the low murmurs from people around her. *Don't forget me.* The whispered entreaty was so close, Gabby looked around. She saw a faint shadow-being hovering a foot away. The anguished look on her face—yes, it was a girl, her long hair floated around her body. *"Don't forget me."*

"But who are you?"

"Don't forget me."

"I won't forget you."

"Tell my story. Don't forget me."

"Holly?"

She was gone. The shadowy-being was gone. The name Holly had barely been said when the vapory being disappeared. It wasn't that she faded away like The Lady. She was there and then she wasn't.

Gabriella shook her head to clear the confusion. Still in a trance, she'd returned enough to notice that some of the others were standing and moving around.

Jackson held Lily in his arms. She nodded when he whispered something.

Michael and Elizabeth had bright smiles and cuddled together.

Grant looked poleaxed. Hunter held his face in her hands and was quietly talking to him.

Sophia's look was thoughtful.

Daniel and Ashley exchanged looks. They were on either side of James who had a stunned look on his face.

Bill and Charlie were obviously still in a mild trance. Seeing Lily and Diana go to their sons, talk to them in quiet voices and noting both boys nodded was a good sign.

Remembering their first Samhain Ceremony in The Sacred Grove brought with it the realization of how far they'd all come in the past three years. Each of them were much more confident in their ability to handle this energy.

"It's time to go," Elizabeth announced. As it was the first time, she was the last to leave.

Gabriella waited for her on the path and together they left the grove. Shannon had already started the others up the path.

"She is a godsend." Elizabeth gestured toward Shannon.

"I'm so glad you have someone here to do ceremony with. If I returned to Italy to finish the book, I'd be on my own. How did you manage until you and Shannon formed a friendship?"

"I had Michael and The Lady. I knew whenever you were gathering so I could sit and pretend I was there with you. I missed you all terribly. But, I always knew when I'd see you next."

"I didn't remember that."

"No, it wasn't something I talked about. But in my heart I've always known that being with everyone on Samhain, Winter Solstice, Beltane and Summer Solstice is my goal. Of course with Maeve that has changed some. But, it is still my goal."

"If you were in Italy, you could come here and I could go there. That isn't a hard trip with a baby. And there is staff at the villa to watch Maeve while you and I do ceremony. We might even convince Shannon to join us. That would make three of us."

"I've never done Ceremony alone."

"But you can. There are solitary practitioners of Wicca," Elizabeth said as they reached the top of the path.

"We don't practice Wicca although we've incorporated some elements from that tradition." Gabriella sighed. "I'd never done anything like the Ceremonies we have before The Circle."

"Me neither. And, having said that, I have faith that what we need for our spiritual growth comes to us when we are ready for it. That has certainly been the case for me."

Gathered in the kitchen, food was distributed. The women would come together in Elizabeth's parlor while the men gathered in Michael's study.

Diana carried the soup tureen and ladle. Sophia the basket of bread. Lily picked up the small tray with fresh butter and jam. Ashley grabbed the plate of cookies. Gabriella, her hands full with a tray of bowls, spoons, glasses and napkins, followed Elizabeth who led the way.

The men had obviously changed plans. They were dishing up and sitting around the kitchen table. Michael, who had disappeared was coming back with a decanter of Irish whiskey. At least Gabriella thought that was the amber colored liquid in the crystal container.

Jackson sat on one side of Grant and Michael slipped in beside him on the other.

Lily was talking to Hunter who was reluctant to leave. Hunt strode to the table, leaned down and said something in a voice too low for Gabby to hear. Michael and Jackson nodded. The men moved so their shoulders were touching Grant's.

Physical contact helped bring people out of the trance. Physical contact and voices. The rumble of male voices trailed down the hall as the women left the kitchen.

At the end of the table where the men sat, Giovanni leaned heavily on his elbows. Grant was definitely still under the effects of the trance. He knew the man had been warned about what could happen and had also been given extra energetic protection. Why was he in such shape?

Michael and Jackson were taking turns talking to Grant. When they talked, each initiated physical contact. Michael tapped on Grant's hand and Jackson patted his back.

Matthew, who sat directly across was also involved. He urged Grant to take a sip of soup. The spoon he offered was barely coated with the liquid to minimize the possibility of choking.

The other men ranged around the table or stood at the counter eating by rote. He surmised they were lost in their own thoughts. He'd obviously been worried because he noticed a change in his own physiology when Grant took a deep breath, shook his head and stared at everyone, a confused look on his face.

"What happened? I mean how did I get here?"

Giovanni heard a slight note of panic in the east coast American accent.

"You've been in a trance," Michael said tapping Grant's hand. "You're coming out of it now."

"What do you remember?" Jackson asked patting Grant's back.

"Very strange dream."

"You don't have to tell us if you don't want to." Matthew pointed to the soup bowl. "Take a couple of bites. Share or not. It's okay."

Grant swallowed a couple spoonful's of soup. Leaning back in his chair he looked at the other men now gathered around the table.

"You guys do this every year?"

They all nodded.

Daniel said, "You don't have to. It's always our choice now that we're invited."

"What do you mean? You've let those women do that by themselves?" Grant started to stand, wove to and fro and sat with a thump. His hands massaged his temples. "I just can't get my mind around this."

"Remember, you don't have to. It's their thing. If none of us ever went, they'd be fine with that." Jackson shifted in his chair and looked at Grant. "This is not a requirement to have a relationship with them. They were a circle long before any of us came on the scene. It took them months to even consider including us in something as tame as Beltane when they basically just sing and dance."

"This does seem to be the most intense ceremony." Daniel stood and started toward the stove. "Anyone want more soup?"

After everyone's bowl was filled and another loaf of bread sliced and on the table, Jackson said. "You know they are upstairs sharing their experience. Is that something we want to do?"

Grant rubbed the back of his neck before moving his fingers to his temples and along his forehead. "I just need to know if it's normal to see dead people."

"Didn't Hunter—?"

"Of course she did. But I guess I never believed her. My great grandfather and grandfather were there. They both talked to me as if they were here. I mean I heard their voices and saw them. They were a bit faint but it was clearly them."

"That's not abnormal," Michael assured him. "My grandmother and grandfather have visited me in this way as has my mother."

"What do you make of what they say to you?" Grant stared at his soup bowl. Hands fisted he continued. "These are the men who started the law firm. They are Parker I and II. I've always been told, as Parker IV, that the family name is everything. I was raised to always consider the family name in everything I do. My finding Hunter, Logan and then moving to Fremont are the only decisions I've really ever made in my life that hasn't put the family name and reputation first.

"They both told me I've made a good choice. My grandfather said he had regrets that he didn't spend time with his family and do things with people he loved. I could see a woman behind him, she wasn't my grandmother. She smiled when he said that about people he loved.

"I just don't know what to make of it all." Grant moved his bowl away, bowed his head in his hands and was quiet.

"In the morning you can talk to Hunter and Logan or if that seems too long to wait, Hunt said to come and get her. She was worried about you." Michael waited as did the others for Grant's reply.

"So what are they doing now?"

"They are sitting in a circle with pillows and blankets piled around them taking turns sharing their experiences. Depending, they may take a break and eat or they may finish sharing and eat afterwards. Then they sleep," Daniel supplied the basic information.

"And in the morning, we knock first and wait for invitation. We help straighten up and get their things back to their rooms. Of course with little ones it can be different this time." Giovanni added, remembering the past and the tousled auburn haired beauty with the glaring hazel eyes who'd rejected his offer to help.

Charlie and Bill were also first timers to this powerful ceremony. Giovanni thought it was because they'd lived so many years with their mothers and knew on some level what was going on that they weren't quite as affected.

Both talked about friends who'd been killed in drunk driving accidents. Both heard a similar message. It really wasn't an accident because both knew they were impaired and decided to drive anyway. If it hadn't been that day, it would have been another one because they saw their lives so bleak that drinking was their way out of the pain.

Giovanni kept his counsel. His grandmother and great aunt had visited him. They were pleased he'd finally found someone to give his heart to. Don't dawdle they'd said as they faded away.

36   The Women Share

Upstairs Hunter paced around the room.

"Mom, Dad will be okay. If there are any real problems, Jackson or someone else would come and get us."

Gabriella watched Logan try and calm her mom down with reason.

"I shouldn't have let him—,"

"Mom, he wanted to be with us. It isn't right to keep him away if he wants to join us."

Logic wasn't working. Diversion might.

"Shall we eat first or start sharing?" Gabriella asked the key question.

"I don't think I can eat anything right now," Hunter stated.

"Right. Then, I think we'll start with sharing." Elizabeth followed along the direction Gabby had started.

"Hunt, if you want to keep moving, that's just fine. I'll save a spot for you next to me." Ashley patted the empty place as everyone gathered into a circle.

Sophia talked about the visit from her friend who'd just died. "He looked hale and hearty and assured me he'd lived the life he wanted to live with few exceptions. He asked me to consider volunteering to help other people like him. I'm not sure I can do something that requires several months or years and ends in death but I will look into maybe short-term volunteer programs."

"My aunt wrapped her arms around me and kissed my cheek." Diana's hand brushed a spot on her right cheek. "So real I can still feel it. She is watching out for me and my family. I remember our first Samhain here and she was warning me about living my life in misery. She reminded me I had a choice. My gratitude for my life now is immense. With all of you, Matthew, Bill and Madison Michelle my life is complete." She winked, "Or not. She did say another little soul would come if called."

"As you know I've had several clients die in the past six months. They all stopped by for a brief moment to say they were well. Seeing them so frail at the end of their physical lives, it is such a gift to see them glowing in the afterlife."

"I remember our first Samhain ceremony here too," Ashley said in her soft Alabama accent. "I feel I've come full circle because my Mom and Gran are happy and the pain in their lives here is gone. They are paying attention to my life and my children's lives. If Anthony goes to Alabama, they will be there with him in spirit. I can't ask for more."

"Hunt? Do you want to share now?" Elizabeth asked as Hunter settled next to Ashley.

"I wasn't as involved as I usually am because I was so aware of what was happening to Grant. I could see these men, smiles on their faces as if they were pleased about something replacing their original frowns. It felt like they were approving of something by the time they left. And that's what they did. No fading. They just vanished."

"I was on dad's other side and, even though I didn't see what mom saw, I felt the shift in energy from negative to positive. Dad was stiff and then he relaxed. There was also a young girl with long hair in the distance. I didn't recognize her and don't know why I'd see her." Logan shrugged. "All in all it was a pretty awesome experience. I'd like to do it again next year."

Interesting that Logan saw the same young woman. Gabriella took a sip of her water and looked at Elizabeth before starting. At E's nod she caught Logan's gaze and began. "I think the young woman you saw is the same one who came to me. I'm writing a story about Holly, a composite character made up of many of the young women I knew when I was on the streets and as a volunteer. Too many young girls are beaten to death by the men who are trying to pimp them or are just mean. While I didn't recognize this young woman, when I asked if she was Holly, she instantly disappeared.

"I have dreams about this story. I hear voices in my head as the characters talk to each other. I feel a kind of guilt if I'm not writing or doing something to further the story. And sometimes the compelling urge to write wakes me at night and I must write a chapter or two before I can go back to bed.

"But," Gabriella took a deep breath, "I've a job waiting for me. I don't know that I can get more time off. I don't know that I'm brave enough to turn in my resignation, live off my savings and finish the book. And even if I did that, do I have the courage to stay the course? Will this story catch reader's attention? Will I ever be able to support myself from my writing?

"I'm beyond grateful to have this time to figure things out."

Elizabeth reached across Sophia and patted Diana's knee. "I got a similar message from Michael's Grandmother. Another little soul is waiting for us. We have decided to wait until Maeve is a year old before trying. But it is comforting to know, given the problems in the past, that it is possible to have two children in our home.

"I am struck with how far we've come as a Sacred Circle. Think back on when we first met ten years ago at Sophia's. Consider the ceremonies we've created, the skills we've learned and mastered. No longer are we afraid of our own power." She turned to Gabriella. "You are a strong and powerful woman who has a compelling story to tell. I can see it coming forth. I can see it is a story only you can tell. I can also see that you must believe in yourself for it all to manifest."

Silence.

Elizabeth's voice was soft and had a hint of the Irish in it. "The Lady and I welcome you to join us tomorrow at sunset. We are the light, we are the source, through us love flows throughout the world."

The others joined in and three times three the prayer was said.

As food was consumed and bedding laid out, Gabriella's mind whirled with the reality that the death of someone needed to be inserted into *Holly's Story*. Elizabeth's words and the fact that Logan had seen the young woman compounded the importance of adding that actual authentic real life event.

37 Crossroads

The specter of the young woman haunted Gabriella. She was in her dreams and twice her presence was so strong she turned to her—the space was empty.

At sunset she and the other women along with Logan and Rose went to the Grove. Rose was young but this was a simple time of giving thanks for the day. Gabriella and Ashley were on either side of Rose. Lily and Sophia behind.

Prayers, a time to meditate or reflect, a song and they were done. Before leaving, they stood in a circle and times three repeated

"We are the light,

"We are the source,

"Through us love flows throughout the world."

Out of the Grove, Gabby turned to look back into the woods. The path that clearly glowed as they walked along was dark, so dark she saw no path at all.

"We've never come out so quickly," Gabriella remarked to Elizabeth.

"Everything flowed as it did because The Lady watched Rose. Our time was shorter because Rose did what she came to do."

"That makes sense."

Rose joined them in Elizabeth's parlor along with the babies. Madison Michelle and Maeve were in the center of the circle. Ten month old M2 crawled from woman to woman, sometimes climbing into their laps and other times just babbling. Maeve, at five months turned over and over or rocked on her hands and knees. She studied Madison Michelle but couldn't quite put hands and legs together. Lurching forward, she'd land on her forehead and move several inches.

Gabriella watched the babies, only five months apart in age, but at very, very different stages of development. Amazed at how different and yet how much the same they were, a longing crept into her heart. In her thirty-five years, she'd never seriously considered having children.

Until now it had never bothered her she would go through her life without a child of her own. Dinner threatened to make a reappearance. Tears crowded her eyes. *I'll only be an aunt and an honorary aunt at that.* Tamping down the unfamiliar emotions, Gabby tuned back in to the conversation.

The next morning she booted up her laptop and opened the file for *Holly's Story*. Reading the last two chapters, she picked up the thread of the story. Holly was still the dorm monitor. *Is this where Holly dies?* That didn't make sense because Holly was a composite of the street youth she'd known.

"Should I go back and put it in before now?"

That didn't feel right.

Gabriella wrote two more chapters about Holly's dorm experiences, how she stood up for the young women when young men were the problem and also when they got into altercations among themselves.

What now?

Where does the story go?

I should have written down those ideas.

Tears of frustration wet her eyes. The story that had flowed so easily in Italy was gone.

A knock on the door.

"Come in." Gabriella stood and turned to the door, blocking the laptop behind her.

Elizabeth and Sophia did just that. They came in and came across the room and wrapped her in hugs.

"Oh, you are writing." Elizabeth grinned and looked at the laptop.

"You look frustrated or disappointed," Sophia said. "Or am I off base?"

"I wish you were off base. I just don't know what to do now. The story seems to have petered out and I can't even remember the ideas I'd had, the scenarios I wanted to include."

Elizabeth stepped in front of her circle sister and placed her hands on her shoulders. "Then this is not the place for you to finish your book. I won't lie and say I'm not disappointed because I was looking forward to having you here with us. But—," she looked over at Sophia who had nudged her side.

Sophia put her arm around Gabriella's shoulders when Elizabeth stepped back. "If you can't get back into the story here, without the distractions of work and everything, how do you think you can write when you are in Fremont?"

"But my job—." Gabriella started to protest.

"If they won't give you more time off, there will always be another job," Sophia reasoned.

"This is your time to leap into the void." Elizabeth stood on Gabriella's other side and laid a hand on her back. "I know you have money in savings. And I also know you don't have bills. Michael has already checked with the property manager about seeing to the Fremont house and keeping the yard and utilities up."

"If there is anything you need from there, I can pack it up and send it to you."

Gabriella whirled away, hazel eyes shooting fire, jaw clenched, hands fisted and faced them. "Send it to me where?"

"Wherever you are writing," Sophia said, her voice calm and reasonable, her gaze steady.

"Wherever your story comes to you," Elizabeth added her voice and posture communicating she was not intimidated by her friend.

"But... ." Gabriella looked beyond her friends out the window to the cloudless sky. "I don't think I can stay there." A thread of panic and tears woven in her voice.

"This is your void," Elizabeth said, coming to stand directly in front of Gabriella. "This is where you leap in to the unknown. This is where you find the trust to do the impossible because of the possible reward.

"It's never a guarantee. But there is the promise that if we do the impossible we'll have our heart's desire. Your heart's desire was to write a book. And you have written books. Perhaps because none were published your heart's desire is not yet satisfied.

"Your energy around *Holly's Story* is different. We've all seen it and so have you. This, Gabby, this is the story only you can write. This is the promise of your heart's desire if you only go for it."

"Giovanni… ."

"Has extended an open-ended invitation to you. You can stay at his villa any time. He also mentioned to Michael that if you were available, he had clients who were interested in house totems. You'd be paid in US Dollars. It could work out that you would have a better income there than in Fremont—if you take the leap."

She was at a crossroads in her life. Not the first time and maybe not the last but—. She hesitated not sure what to say because the terror of spending more time at the villa was eating her inside out. How could she when Giovanni had become a friend? She didn't want to anticipate his coming home—she didn't want to think of the villa as home! What was happening here!!!

It had been difficult but she'd not met Elizabeth or Sophia's gaze. She did now. "I'll think about it. I have until tomorrow to decide."

"If you want to call work, you can use Michael's phone in his office or if you want to email, we'll see that you are on The Manor's router."

"How about breakfast?" Sophia looped her arm through Elizabeth's. "I'm starved."

Gabriella joined her friends, looping her arm through Elizabeth's. They turned sideways to make it through the door without letting go. Down the hall they were joined by Lily, Hunter, Diana and Ashley. It was obvious they'd all been waiting to see what had happened, whether she'd capitulated and was returning to Italy.

While in her mind she chanted "It depends" in her heart she was already on her balcony looking out over the garden to the sea beyond, the beam from the lighthouse sweeping past her as the fragrant breeze wrapped her in its embrace.

 More Time To Write?

Gabriella did check emails, reading each one that had to do with work. Jordan was checking in with her each week. His last one certainly told her he was waiting for her to get home. She double checked the time difference and if she just did it, could call personnel right now.

Heart in throat, she dialed the number. A part of her hoped no one answered and she got voice mail. The other part of her just wanted to talk to someone and figure out what her options were.

"Justine, speaking."

"Hi Justine, it's Gabriella Moncrief calling from Ireland. I hope our connection is strong enough you can easily hear me."

"Gabby, you're in Ireland? You sound like you're next door. How are you?"

"I'll send you an email with news, Justine. I'm using someone else's phone and don't want to run up their bill. I'm calling because if possible, I'd like to extend my sabbatical until the end of the year. I want to know if that's possible and if not that long, how long I might be able to extend it."

"I'm pulling up your personnel file now, Gabby. Just so you know, we're in a downturn and there is talk of layoffs. You don't have to worry because of your seniority and because Jordan West has put in a request to have you transferred to our Seattle office.

"Looks like you were to return to work this next week. You want to extend your leave for eight more weeks?"

"Most likely through January 5th or 6th. I don't have a calendar in front of me but the Monday after the holiday weekend is what I have in mind."

"I've written your request up and will send it to your supervisor, your department head and the personnel committee. Do you want me to add a new reason?"

"No, nothing new to add. I just need a bit more time. Things have come up and have delayed my finishing up."

Gabby smiled at Justine's soft chuckle. "Vague enough?"

"Perfectly vague. Your supervisor and department head are still in the building. I'll take this to them right now. The committee is set to meet in the morning so you should hear from me tomorrow."

"An email response is just fine. You won't have to figure out the time difference and tomorrow will still give me enough time to get home and over jetlag if I'm turned down."

"So being turned down isn't a deal breaker?"

"What do you mean?"

"If your request is turned down, you won't quit?"

"I hadn't thought that far ahead, Justine. I'm keeping positive thoughts it's approved and I won't have to think that far ahead."

"Good idea. I'll get back to you tomorrow as soon as I know something."

"Thanks, Justine. Bye."

"Bye, Gabby. Oh and Gabby,"

"Yes?"

"I hope you are having a marvelous time in Ireland."

"I am. I've friends here and the time is just flying by."

"Tomorrow then."

It wasn't as satisfying a conversation as she might have liked. The news about layoffs was particular disconcerting. But the timing was right. She'd know tomorrow by this time what her immediate future held.

Justine had told her Jordan wanted her in Seattle and had planted the idea of quitting. She couldn't see herself moving to Seattle and traveling each weekend to Fremont. She'd done so when Logan had been missing but it was not something she wanted to be doing each week.

And where would she stay? She'd have to impose on Sophia or one of the others because if she didn't return, Hunter and Grant would most likely move into Murphy House until they sorted out their own living situation.

Shaking her head to clear the tumbling thoughts, Gabriella went in search of the others. She found them crammed into the small room Michael's grandmother had used as her study. No room for everyone to sit, they were standing around the room perusing the books.

When she entered the room, six expectant faces turned her way. "Where is everyone?"

"We're all here," Lily said.

Gabriella smiled. "To be more specific, where are Madison Michelle, Maeve, Logan, Rose and the guys?"

"The guys are hanging out with Michael at the stables. The guys includes all males regardless of familial connections. Rose and Logan are with them. M2 and Maeve are taking naps."

"So the moms have a little free time?"

"We do," Diana and Elizabeth answered in unison.

"I could go for a cup of tea and something sweet if Seamus has cookies or something," Gabriella said turning toward the door. "Anyone want to join me?"

Of course they all did and shortly The Circle was seated around the kitchen table, a plate of shortbread cookies in the middle and a pot of tea nearby.

"I know I'm being nosy," Elizabeth started. "But I'm dying of curiosity about your phone call. How did it go?"

"Okay. I'll know more tomorrow."

"That's cryptic," Sophia said.

"Not really. I called, talked to a woman in personnel I know and she is circulating my request to extend my sabbatical. It has to be approved by my supervisor, department head and a personnel committee. She thought she'd be able to get back to me tomorrow afternoon, Fremont time."

"How much more time off did you ask for?" Lily leaned forward, her hands wrapped around her tea cup.

"Until the Monday after the New Year's Eve holidays. The worst that will happen is I won't even be finished by then." She paused. "Actually the worst that will happen is I can't pick up the story again no matter what and I'm not working either."

"You can stay with us," Elizabeth interjected. "We'd love to have you. I miss having you with me in the flesh. Energetically is better than nothing but this is a real gift." She reached out and held the hands of Diana and Lily. "Being able to reach out and touch you, to hold your hand, to give you a hug is a precious gift you've all given me this Samhain."

The back door burst open and Rose, Logan, Anthony, James, Bill and Charlie tumbled inside.

"We're starving!" Rose announced in her most dramatic fashion.

Heads nodded.

"Where is Daniel and the others?" Ashley asked.

"Right behind us." James gestured with his thumb over his shoulder.

"And they'd be inside by now if the doorway wasn't blocked." Even though they couldn't see the speaker, the Irish brogue gave Michael away.

The younger set moved on in and the men followed.

Hands reached across to the plate of cookies. Noses sniffed the air searching for food.

"Seamus is not cooking today. When the babies wake up we'll go to the pub for dinner." Elizabeth stood, crossed the room and gave Michael a hug and a kiss on the cheek.

As if on cue, baby monitors burst to life.

"Guess that means no one will starve to death." Diana headed toward the door.

"Thirty minutes before M2 will be ready," Matthew said.

"Even if you help?" Charlie asked.

"Even if."

"Everyone check your clothes and change if you need to, wash up, get your better jackets and meet up in the front foyer," Sophia suggested. "That way we won't be waiting while you go off and do that."

The younger set headed off, chattering as they went.

Jackson sat down next to Lily, Daniel next to Ashley, Grant next to Hunter and Giovanni next to Sophia. Gabriella was still at the table but in between Matthew and Michael. The conversation was focused on the horses. First foals were due in January. A side conversation between Giovanni and Sophia was quiet and she couldn't hear a word of it. Matthew and Michael started talking about babies and children. Daniel joined in.

Gabrielle was grateful when the thundering feet on the stairs, echoed down the hall.

"I'll go check on everyone." Gabriella stood before either Michael or Matthew could move her chair and headed down the hall. *Being an honorary aunt is not such a bad thing.*

Decisions, Decisions

It was dark when they headed back to The Manor. Gabriella decided to walk, time to think and time to work off the extra food she'd eaten. The Winner's Circle barman, Patrick, fixed the best brisket she'd ever eaten and after two helpings, along with a salad and a decadent bread pudding with brandy sauce, she was full to the brim.

Giovanni kept pace with her but did not break the silence. When the others stopped by to see if they wanted a ride, she'd told him to go on. He just shook his head and waved them off.

Well, they weren't really alone because Hunter and Grant along with Logan, Bill and Charlie were also walking back. Their pace was faster and they were fading into the distance.

The ambling pace was just right. Movement without rushing through the quiet night fit her mood. And whether she wanted to acknowledge it or not, the quiet presence, and Giovanni's signature clove scent was welcomed.

She could do this walk alone, even at night. Kinsale was a safe place and everyone knew they were Michael's guests but—having Giovanni next to her, knowing he was alert and watchful allowed her mind to wander.

Wander down paths she'd walked.

Wander down paths she could have walked.

Wander down paths—no she wasn't ready to wander down possible future paths.

As they turned down the long drive to the house, she heard an owl hoot in the night, the rustle of underbrush as critters moved around in the dark. Night sounds were different here than in Italy or where she lived in Fremont.

There were night birds in Italy but to her, their song was softer. *Where did that come from? An owl's hoot is not harsh.*

Giovanni had remained silent during the entire walk but when the lights of The Manor House came into sight, he spoke. "Your invitation to finish your book at my villa is firm. Even if you return to Fremont, if in future you want to come back, you let me know. I see you met at the airport if I cannot be there."

"I appreciate the offer. Right now I don't know what I'm going to do, whether my request to extend my time off work will be accepted. There is a possibility I could be laid off or fired if I don't return."

"Do not let fear make decision. If you come to write or even if you do not, I will see you have work. A few of my clients ask about house totems. If you were there or even here, you could do the work."

"I thought Elizabeth was helping you with that?"

"She has done so but with baby, her life is full. I ask one of the others to come? *No,* everyone but you and Sophia have children."

He opened the door and held it. She stepped inside.

"Trust all is well. Trust whether you stay here or come to Italy all will be well. Trust your path not to be hard or harsh. Your path can be of peace, of calm." His voice dropped an octave. "And, of love," he whispered.

Her brain whirled as his words registered. He was so close, too close. She shivered. Nameless words stuck in her throat.

Instead of following her in, he closed the door and disappeared into the night. Her first instinct was to go after him, tell him he was wrong.

But his was just one more in a line of messages she was getting. Messages that all told her to believe, trust and leap. All will be well.

As Gabriella headed for the stairs and her room, she mused that with her history, "all will be well" was virtually impossible.

A restless night led to a groggy day. Gabriella shuffled through the motions of getting up, dressed and going to breakfast. The others returned from morning prayers in The Sacred Grove. And after breaking their fasts, went into town.

Gabriella stayed behind. Ostensibly to make sure she was available when she got the call about work. In reality, she just needed time and space to regroup.

The attraction between Giovanni and her was different now. She'd always seen him as physically handsome. The fact he was wealthy, while a lure to some was not so strong of a one to her. Her needs were simple. Traveling light her mantra.

But while in the beginning she saw him more as a predator, a man who used and abused women, after all this time and especially after spending over three weeks at his villa she knew differently. He did like women and while he obviously appreciated them, he really wasn't the flirt she'd thought. When they were out together, he paid attention to her. Even when he flashed that devastating smile at the waitress or sales clerk, he was not hitting on them. Diana had been right about him.

But to believe she could have a relationship with him beyond the friendship that had developed, to trust her heart to him and to leap into the void of being with him and living in Italy full time? That was more than she could envision.

Besides, he would want a physically intimate relationship and it had been a very long time since any man had really touched her. Her doctors were women. And she didn't count handshakes as physically intimate.

Would he want to know more about her past? After all this time, she knew that secrets hurt intimacy, hurt relationships but details could hurt more.

Or could they?

None of The Circle members or their husbands had pulled away from her after she divulged she'd lived on the streets.

Toting her laptop to Michael's study, Gabriella booted it up and waited for the phone call. She opened the file for Holly's Story and read the last chapter. Fingers poised over the keys, she waited for the words to come.

Nothing.

Just write!

She started another file and typed. Rambling, free-flowing words strewn across the page. Not stopping to go back to read anything she typed on. Gibberish now.

Steady typing for twenty minutes produced rambling gibberish.

Page break and beginning again.

Samhain: She came to me as a vision or a specter (need to check the dictionary to see what the difference is). "Don't forget me" is really all she said. When I asked if she was Holly, she vanished. Not faded away but Vanished! And Logan saw her too. Definitely a thread to add to the story but how? When? Where? I know the 'why'.

Gabriella looked away, out the window at the green fields, the white fences, the horses. Overlaying that reality was the blue sea. Boats with multi-colored sails flew across the white caps. A lighthouse in the distance.

Blinking back tears, she saved her work and powered down her laptop.

It made no difference what the response was about her job. She could not forget Holly because she did not forget the young women who died on the streets…even the suicides were an abstract murder.

Obviously not murder in the eyes of the law but murder by society's belief that these young people wanted to be there, wanted that lifestyle.

Society not understanding that as dangerous as the streets were, the streets were safer than where they'd been.

Society not understanding the stigma they cast on these youth…the shame they poured over them by their disdainful looks or worse, not even seeing them.

But there were actual murders. The pimps who beat them, the dealers who, once they were hooked, gave them dirty drugs. The johns who strangled them in order to reach their own orgasm.

Needing activity, Gabriella took her laptop to her room before walking outside. Her steps took her to the stables where she roamed between the aisles of horses. Social animals, they poked their heads out of their stalls to see the stranger.

Dickens, the head groom approached, his head cocked to one side. "Ride?"

"No, I just wanted to see them. They're so beautiful. I saw a barrel of apples as I came in. Is it okay if I gave one of them an apple?"

"Have you done this before?"

"No."

"Then I show you."

Dickens walked with her to the apple barrel. She stuffed a couple in her pockets and held two in each hand.

He pulled out a pocket knife, cut an apple in half and placed it on his palm. Holding his hand out flat, he stepped up to the stall door. His voice smooth and soft, he held his hand out. With his free hand, he smoothed a hand down the horse's face.

Gabriella watched as the big animal nibbled the apple from Dickens' hand.

He gave the horse the other half. Patted his neck and moved to the next stall.

"Now you." He took the two apples from her hand, put one in his pocket and cut the other one in half.

"Hold your hand out flat," he instructed. "Be prepared to be sniffed because they do not know you."

Her breath held in her chest, Gabriella tentatively held out her hand.

Whoof. The horse's warm breath caressed her hand. Warm whiskery lips nibbled the apple. Her smile bloomed at the crunching as the apple was chewed.

"You can pat her neck if you want," Dickens said.

"She won't bite me?"

Dickens laughed. "She will be trying to get to your apples. Not bite you."

Gabriella fed the horse the other half of the apple, patted her neck and moved on.

They continued down the aisle, Dickens cutting her apples and Gabriella doling out the pieces and patting necks and an occasional nose.

"Why are some so much bigger?" She asked the head groom.

"The bigger ones are jumpers, Mick has both," Dickens explained.

It took her a second to remember who Mick was because she'd only known E's husband as Michael but everyone in Ireland had and still did call him Mick.

The curiosity of the stables' inhabitants, the intelligence shining in their eyes intrigued her. She'd never ridden a horse and it was a daunting thought to be on a large animal so high off the ground but as she met the resident of each stall, the idea she might want to learn began forming in her mind.

Dickens returned just as she was finishing and thanking the second groom.

"Thank you, Dickens. I needed a bit of a break and meeting the horses was just the thing."

He walked beside her as she headed for the barn door.

"Is it hard to learn to ride?"

"To ride well, to jump fences, to race—it is."

"Do the children jump fences and race?"

"No to the jumping. Mick would fire us all. But racing? They do, but on trails, not across the fields. And a groom is always with them. None of them know the horses or the area well enough to be out on their own.

"If you want to try, you come tell me and I'll see that you get the chance."

"Thanks, Dickens. Maybe when I come back. I can't now because I'm going back to Italy tomorrow."

Gabriella ambled back to the house. She'd told Dickens she was returning to Italy and the words hadn't stuck in her throat nor had nausea claimed her. Her pace was slow but steady. Instead of going through the side door she rounded the house to the front. Last night replayed in her mind as she went up the steps and opened the door.

The foyer had not changed. The altar with the horses and crystals sat center-stage. The black and white tiles echoed when booted feet crossed them.

But something had changed. She was going back to Italy. *Holly's Story* must be told.

Return to Italy

Gabriella hugged everyone good bye before walking down the concourse with Giovanni. When she'd gotten back from the stables, there was a message for her. She was laid off. Relief that her decision to return to Italy had come before the message buckled her knees. Grabbing the back of the chair kept her from crashing to the floor. Everything in her world pointed her to Italy. And while she still had reservations, she was going.

On shorter flights, especially if like today, he was returning to his villa on Italy's west coast, Giovanni preferred landing in Florence. Silvio met them and efficiently loaded luggage into the trunk while Giovanni ushered her into the limousine's backseat.

Turning into the circular drive of the villa, a sense of peace overlaid the anxiety. Gabriella, her backpack slung over one shoulder, her laptop in her opposite hand, was greeted by

Margretta as she came in the door. Giovanni followed a few steps behind Silvio who had their luggage.

Margretta followed her up to her room. As soon as Silvio dropped Gabriella's bag at her door, the maid pulled it inside and put it on the bench at the foot of the bed and opened it.

"I'll unpack myself," Gabriella said turning toward the young woman a smile on her face.

"*Si, Signorina* Gabby. I get your lemon water now." Margretta was gone in a flash. Rapid Italian drifted in from the open doorway.

"You are settled?"

Gabriella dropped the blouse she'd taken from the suitcase and was hanging in the closet.

"Mea culpa, I am sorry I scare you."

"You didn't scare me, you startled me." She bristled as she picked up the garment, shook it out and proceeded to hang it in the closet.

Giovanni leaned against the doorframe, watching her cross from her suitcase to the closet and back. He wasn't staring, just watching. The last item put away, she zipped the bag closed and tucked it in the back corner of the closet.

"Is there something you want?" There was a snappish edge in her voice. Hands fisted on her hips, she glared.

"*Si*, I am to ask what you want for super."

"You could have asked while I was unpacking. I am capable of talking and unpacking at the same time."

"*Si*, but I like watching you do these simple things."

"Giovanni—,"

"Dinner?"

"Whatever is most convenient for Adolfo to fix is just fine."

Giovanni smiled. "But he wants to please you. He is very glad you are back as are the others."

"I still feel like I'm intruding and a bother for them."

"No, they like having someone here. Keeping busy is better than being bored, *si*?"

Gabriella smiled. "*Si*, being busy is better than being bored." She walked the few steps to the table she used as a desk and set up her laptop.

"I really like the way he fixes the tomatoes, basil and mozzarella cheese."

"He make a very fine pasta dish with the tomatoes, basil and mozzarella. A little olive oil and maybe a bit of fresh parsley."

"That sounds delicious."

"He will have tiramisu for you tomorrow. Tonight maybe the rum cake?"

"Actually I don't need a dessert." Gabriella saw the look of consternation on Giovanni's face. She patted her belly. "I ate too much at E's."

"You gain not one pound."

She started to challenge him but the serious expression on his face struck her silent. In his eyes, she was perfect just as she was.

The effect of his words tightened her chest. *He can't see me like this.* She turned to the doors to her balcony. Opening them, she stepped out and breathed in the sea air.

Composed once again, she turned back.

He was still in the doorway, still watching her but now concern wrinkled his forehead. "I mean not to upset you."

"I'm just tired. I didn't sleep well in Ireland."

"We make an early night of it."

"Yes, we make an early night of it."

Holly's Story

Holly thrashed awake. Strangled by her bedding, she hoped at the least her scream had been muffled. Silence suffocated her but she remained still, listening for the footsteps, the knock on the door that would tell her someone had heard her cry out.

The nightmare was so real. Becca was dead. Holly had found the young girl lying in the gutter, the needle in her arm. When she'd called to her, then bent over her, she'd still had hope. But when she touched her, she knew she was dead. Tears tracked down her face blended into the raindrops falling from the sky. Where else did raindrops fall from?

Holly remembered someone telling her rain was the tears of angels. Would angels cry over Becca? Did God even know she was in trouble? Was there even a God? She didn't think so. Because why would the God of love she heard people talk about have let her be raped; let her be beaten, let her mother choose disgusting boyfriends over her? Why would God have let Becca die in the rain in a gutter?

To the faithful there were answers. But she wasn't one of the faithful. A loving, just God would not allow children to be treated so. Would not allow children to be thrown away.

"May wherever you are be a safe and peaceful place." Holly straightened and walked away. There was nothing more she could do except try to save herself.

As soon as daylight crept through the slit in her curtains, Holly was up. Showered, dressed, teeth brushed, she gathered her books and headed to her classes. It was growing dark when she got back to the dorm because of the hours she'd spent at the library doing research.

Checking on the other residents, seeing all was quiet and in order, she paced the halls. Something was calling to her. Something was compelling her to go out once again into the night.

After making another round, she asked the assistant dorm monitor to take over. "There's something I need to check on."

Holly ran toward her past. Terrified and yet unable to not continue, she turned a corner and ran headlong into a melee.

"Stop!" she shouted, swinging her bag with both hands. "Help! Help! Help! Call the police! Someone call the police!"

One of the assailants turned on her and her living nightmare became a living horror.

"Got you," he snarled, grabbing an arm.

She swung her bag at him with all her might, hitting him on the side of his head.

"Fucking bitch!" He let go to punch her but she ducked and then pushed him from behind. Sirens in the distance seemed to get closer.

I just have to hang on a few more minutes.

Holly continued to swing her bag, duck and kick out if someone tried grabbing for her.

Does time slow down in a crisis? For Holly not only did time slow down but everything seemed in slow motion.

The police car skidding to a halt.

The thugs running away.

The officers in pursuit.

But there was one thing that was not in slow motion. One thing that was still.

The young girl on the street looked to be nineteen but Holly knew she could be younger. Life on the streets took a toll on a body. Did she know her?

No, she didn't think so.

Maybe Doc S or Mrs. Waterson did but Holly was fairly sure she didn't. But then the girl's face was unrecognizable, nose broken, hair matted. The ring in her nose had been ripped out. Clothes muddy and bloody.

"Miss?" The police officer stood on the other side of the body.

Holly raised her gaze and met his questioning one.

"I don't think I know her."

Another siren in the distance announced an ambulance was on the way.

"What happened?"

"I came around the corner and saw that someone was down on the ground and still being hit and kicked. I tried to break it up."

"Are you all right?"

"I'm fine."

The officer crouched down next to the body, placed two fingers against the girl's carotid artery. "She's still alive."

When the limp body was loaded on the gurney and the light from the ambulance illuminated the face, Holly thought she might know her. Not well. She'd been off the streets for over a year now. But, if this was who she thought it might be, she came and went. They'd been on the streets together in the past and she hadn't seen her for over a year. She was about nineteen with a background similar to her own except the abuser was her father, uncle and older brother depending on who her mother let in the house.

"I don't think she's going to make it." Holly heard the EMT tell the police office.

"I need to get a statement from you," the officer was now talking to her. "I can do it here or at the hospital."

"Hospital."

"You'll have to sit in back but I can take you," the officer said.

In the Emergency Department they let her sit with Louise and hold her hand as she answered the officer's questions. Who might know her? Doc S, the Youth Shelter staff.

"What happened?" That was the hardest question. What she knew about Louise was she didn't do drugs but did have sex with guys for money in order to eat or get a place to sleep. She didn't consider her a prostitute because Louise didn't just have sex with anyone who approached her.

"My guess is these guys wanted her to have sex with them or to watch her have sex with some of them or something else kinky. Louise wasn't into kinky. Maybe oral sex and different positions but not bondage and that kind of stuff. If she refused, they'd figure it was four against one.

"One of them is real mean. I know him. I didn't recognize anyone but him." She gave the officer Seth's name and description. "I'm sure he has a record."

"We'll check him out."

Holly sat with Louise throughout the night. The hospital let her call the dorm and let her assistant know where she was.

At one point a nurse came in and told her they'd reached family but no one would be coming. The nurse's voice cracked and her eyes welled with tears.

"If it's okay with you, I'll stay with her."

The nurse nodded and left.

Holly stayed with Louise, talking to her about a place of peace. A place of safety. A place where you never had to worry about someone turning on you, hurting you. She described the picture of the sunflower on the wall in her room and the crystals on her window sill catching the light and casting rainbows on every wall.

In the early hours of morning. Holly was describing a green meadow filled with flowers of every color, their fragrance swirling on the gentle breeze and warmth from the sun caressing them. Words from the Bible that had been made into a folk song came to her. In the quiet of the hospital room, she hummed and then sang the words she knew. "To every season turn, turn, turn…a time to live, a time to die… ."

Louise's hand was still warm but there was a difference. *She's gone.* Tears balanced on Holly's lower eyelids but she did not cry. Bile churned in her stomach but she did not vomit. Rigidity that had held her upright faded but she did not crumble.

Holly heard someone come into the room.

Surprised? No.

Grateful? Yes.

The nurse appeared on the other side of the bed and someone stopped next to her. When she glanced up, it was Mrs. Waterson.

The nurse made a note in the chart. There were unshed tears in her eyes as she pulled the sheet up over Louise's face. "I'll let the police officer know."

"Thank you," Mrs. Waterson said to the nurse. She rested a hand on Holly's shoulder. "When you're ready to leave, I'll take you."

The nurse came back in and Holly lifted her bowed head. "Does it hurt to die?"

The nurse startled but quickly recovered. From across the bed, she caught Holly's gaze. "Your friend's suffering, her pain came before death. She's at peace now."

"But when she died?"

"You mean at that moment in time when her body totally shut down?"

Holly nodded.

"No, she was on pain medication. Because of her injuries it would have taken a miracle for her to survive and I'm not sure she wanted to live."

"No, no, I'm sure she didn't want to live anymore." Head bowed, her chin on her chest, Holly cried. Her body shook with the sobs. Her lungs gulped for air. Her tears fell. And fell. And fell. At one point she raised her legs and with her heels resting on the chair seat, hugged her knees. And still her tears fell.

Exhausted.

Pain-filled.

Heart-broken.

Dried up.

Finally the tears dried and she was aware of her surroundings. Mrs. Waterson was still there but had moved to a chair next to her.

Her voice shaky, Holly asked, "Where do tears come from?"

"In this case, they come from your heart."

"But I barely knew her."

"You barely knew this Louise but you know a lot of other girls like Louise. And there was a time not so long ago when you were Louise."

A moment passed before Mrs. Waterson spoke again.

"If you still need to stay here with her, you can. If you are ready to leave, I'll take you."

Her legs rebelled when she stood but Holly steadied herself with the bed's side rail.

Outside, Mrs. Waterson led Holly to her car, opened the passenger door and waited until Holly was seated before she closed the door and rounded to the driver's seat.

"Are you able to eat?"

"I don't know."

"While you check with your stomach, put your seatbelt on."

A loud growl filled the car.

Holly's laugh was as shaky as her legs. "I think my body has answered."

Another surprise was in store. Mrs. Waterson drove to her home, parked in the driveway and got out. "Come along in."

"I can wait in the car," Holly started.

"I'm fixing us breakfast." Mrs. Waterson started toward a side door and gestured Holly to follow.

It could have been awkward but instead it was dreamlike. Mrs. Waterson's husband was pouring eggs for an omelet into the frying pan. The house smelled of yeast and cinnamon. Holly smelled the cinnamon rolls before she saw them.

"Orange or tomato juice?" Mrs. Waterson asked.

"Tomato if it isn't too much trouble."

Mrs. Waterson made the introductions. Her husband's name was Robert.

"What all do you want in your omelet?" Robert asked.

"Tell her what her options are.

Robert listed off vegetables and meat and shrimp. Overwhelmed was what she was. Overwhelmed and exhausted and unable to make a simple decision.

"Do you like shrimp?"

Holly nodded.

"Fix her a shrimp omelet with mozzarella cheese and some veggies."

"You mean make two of them?" Robert turned from the stove and grinned at his wife.

"Yes," she said and laughed. "That's what I mean."

Finished with breakfast, Holly drifted and her eyes closed.

"Come with me," Mrs. Waterson's hand was on her arm.

Holly stood and in a daze followed Mrs. W to another room with a day bed.

"Sit here."

Holly complied and sat on the edge of the bed.

"I'm taking your shoes off," Mrs. Waterson said as she followed her words with action.

"You rest. I'll be in the next room."

"I can go back to the dorm," Holly lay down already half-asleep.

"You have an appointment to talk to the police at three today. I'll take you there and then take you back to the dorm afterward."

"The police?"

"It'll be okay, Holly. The officer knew it was important for you to be with Louise last night so he stopped asking questions when the nurse asked him to."

"I don't remember anyone asking him to stop."

"Rest. I'll take you and stay with you and then take you back to the dorm."

True to her word, Mrs. Waterson woke her with enough time to stop by the dorm and change clothes after the shortest shower in history.

She stayed with her while the officer asked more questions.

She stopped at a Thai restaurant and Holly had her first taste of Phad Thai noodles and coconut ice cream. And then she took her back to the dorm.

"Will you be okay by yourself?"

"Sure," Holly's response was full of a bravado she didn't feel but that wasn't new. To be safe on the streets, it was important to act tough. Not that acting tough guaranteed anything. She knew that from experience. But acting tough had gotten her out of more scrapes than she cared to count.

"I'll check in with you later," Mrs. W. said as Holly got out of the car.

Slinging her bag over her shoulder, she waved as Mrs. W. drove away.

Back to work. Holly squared her shoulders, lifted her chin and with purpose in her stride walked into the building. Grateful for the routine of work, she notified her assistant dorm monitor she was back. Making her way along the hallways, she spoke to the girls who were either in the hall or whose doors were open.

In her own room, she closed the door and sank into her chair. The framed sunflower did not lift her spirits. The dark pall of death hung over her and filled the small space.

She had dozed at Mrs. W's but the effects of being up all night slammed her. Through the open curtains, a ray of sunlight pierced the crystal on her window sill. A smile crept across her face as rainbows danced over her walls.

Toeing her shoes off, Holly stretched out on her bed to watch the exuberant display. *Maybe they are dancing today because Louise is with them?* That thought comforted. Closing her eyes, she saw the colors skip by. *I'm on the third floor, my door is locked, a chair is propped under the handle. I'm safe.*

Regrouping

Clicking "save", Gabriella leaned back in her chair watching the blinking cursor at the end of the paragraph. Swiping at her gritty eyes, she brushed a lingering tear from her chin. Holly was safe in her room but not safe in her life outside her room. Gabriella knew Holly faced more dangers.

Powering down her laptop, Gabriella rose and crossed to the balcony. The breeze off the water was cool. It was the beginning of November and sitting outside in the evening without a jacket would be too chilly.

I can always wrap up in a blanket.

The garden and sea wall were empty. If she'd seen Giovanni out there pacing along the garden pathways or sitting on the wall looking out across the water, she wouldn't have the hollow feeling of loneliness that left her adrift.

That's silly. He's here in the house somewhere and even if he'd left, there are always staff about. Perhaps it was a silly thought but there is often truth in a silly thought.

Writing Holly's Story wasn't easy. Half catharsis and half semi-biographical and half—can't have three halves.

Why was she writing this painful story?

Why was it important for her to write it? There was no doubt in her mind that this was a story she had to write.

Why?

Her best answer was because it was a story that needed to be told. Society had turned its collective back on too many throw-away children. America saw itself as this great country and in many ways it was but the plight of these throw-away children was real.

She was lucky.

She got out.

She had a life.

Tears fell again as a picture of Elizabeth and Maeve and Diana with Madison Michelle took root in her mind. She'd never seriously thought about having children. Her heart ached with grief because she never would.

For one, she wouldn't trust herself to be a good mom. And then there was the whole work and child care. Having a husband? *I don't have to be married. I could do invitro-fertilization or find a surrogate?*

Tears fell.

Her nose ran.

Her shoulders shook from deep racking sobs.

Gabriella held a pillow to her mouth to keep the sound in. She was falling apart, shattering into small pebbles of herself.

A knock on the door, Margretta's voice announcing dinner in fifteen minutes.

She managed a muffled "okay".

In the bathroom she blew her nose, pressed a cool damp washcloth to her swollen eyes and eventually ran her brush through her hair. It was still obvious she'd been crying.

Her stomach grumbled. She really did feel hungry and since she'd never tell Giovanni she'd been crying, she decided she'd deny tears and fall back on the "I'm just so tired" excuse so she could come right back to her room after her last bite.

Having a plan in place, she headed down to dinner.

Giovanni knew she'd been crying but consciously decided to say nothing. He stood when she came into the room, held her chair out for her and after she sat and the food was served, engaged in idle chitchat.

The weather should be fair with cool nights. Was she warm enough?

He needed to go into Rome on business in two days. Would she like to go with him?

The garden seemed to be doing well. Didn't she agree?

Enough! Giovanni muttered to himself.

"I'm sorry. I missed that," Gabriella said.

"No *problema*. I talk to myself."

Her mouth formed an "o" and the urge to take her in his arms and just hold her obliterated all other thoughts. He sipped his wine and gathered himself together.

"You are writing again?" *That should be safe because I know she is writing. Simple 'yes' or 'no'.*

"I'm sorry. I'm just tired and a bit teary from it—,"

"You miss your friends." *That should be safe to say.*

"I do miss them and—," Gabriella stood before Giovanni could pull back her chair. "I'm tired and should—."

Giovanni had stood when she did. He took the few steps to stand in front of her. With a finger he tilted her head back and looked into glistening hazel eyes. The hand that had rested on her arm, slid around her back. The hand that held her head, let go of her chin and cupped the back of her head. A slight tug and she was in his arms.

Her tears dampened his shirt.

Her jasmine mixed with his clove and sandalwood.

He would never use the word weak to describe his Gabriella but at this moment he would use the word fragile.

Gabriella relaxed into his strength. She was being held by a man and crying her heart out. What was it about *Holly's Story* that affected her so? *It could have been me. I was on the streets, I was beat up. I could have been Louise.*

Her feet left the floor when Giovanni lifted her and cradled her in his arms. The air cooled and the waves sounded closer. They were outside.

When he sat down, he didn't release her but settled her on his lap.

Gabriella felt something warm and soft. He was tucking a blanket around them to keep her warm.

A note of panic tensed her body.

His hands stroked her back. Nothing more than the rhythmic motion of him touching her through a blanket and her clothes. The tears subsided. Drained, empty and quiet were the words drifting into her mind as she tried to sort out what had happened. But then a thought formed and grew... *I feel safe.*

At that realization, she jerked away.

Giovanni let her go, resting his arms on the chair.

"I listen if you talk. Talk will help."

"I don't know that it will help." Gabriella's throat was scratchy and her eyes itched. A hiccup erupted followed a moment later by another one.

Giovanni handed her a glass of wine. "Hold a sip in your mouth and swallow slowly holding your nose."

She cocked a brow.

"Trust me. This works."

Gabriella followed his instructions and the hiccups did go away. "I've tried that before and it didn't work."

"Perhaps because you are in Italy with me is why it works." He flashed that cocky grin. The one that drew countless women to his side. Why here she was, sitting in his lap.

The very idea! She squirmed to get off.

"Here, stay still. I help you get untangled."

When the blanket fell away, even though she was free, she did not immediately jump up and scurry off. Balanced on his thighs she said, "The story is in a very emotional place and I'm not handling it very well. Thank you for holding me."

"But you are handling it, as you say, very well. All the emotions on your surface are now on the pages of your book where they need to be." He'd not moved his hands to recapture her, to pull her against his chest.

It would be her decision.

If she asked, he would hold her.

If she asked, he would make love to her.

If she asked—

"It's been a very long day." Gabriella scooted and shifted until she could easily stand. "I'll see you in the morning."

"*Cara*, you remember. Giovanni has good ear and listens very well."

He spoke to an empty space because Gabriella had vanished. He listened to her faint footsteps on the stairs, the quiet closing of her door. He may have imagined all that because she was quiet and fast. But he did not imagine her in his arms, the feel of her tears soaking through his shirt and wetting his skin. A hand over his heart confirmed she'd cried enough this shirt was still damp.

They had come a long way since he'd first met her at Jackson's house. Was it possible to have her in his life, here in Italy?

Giovanni stood, folded the blanket and laid it on the chair. Strolling through the garden he eventually arrived at the sea wall. From here he could look back at the villa and see her balcony, see if she was still up, see if she was watching him, see if she was sitting in the dark or maybe writing more.

He sat on the sea wall, his back to the house. When he chilled, it was time to go back. Taking a side path that led back to the villa meant he did not see her room unless he purposefully looked up and turned his head. The urge to check on her was strong because something was clearly wrong, clearly bothering her. But she did not yet trust him enough to talk about it.

Time.

Time was his friend. In time she'd come to trust him even more than she begrudgingly did now.

"Can time be my friend but not her enemy?" He hoped the answer was "yes."

Holly's Story

Gabriella curled into a tight ball, covers pulled over her head. She'd created a cocoon for herself. Could she be like the caterpillar that turned into a butterfly? Could she open herself enough to allow someone close?

She did allow people to be close. Doc S, her circle sisters, the children. But with men it was different.

Or was it? She'd known Bill and Charlie since they were kids and now they were young men. Had her feelings toward them changed?

And then there were Ashley's boys, James and Anthony. Well, Anthony was a loose cannon right now because of his need to be—to be what? She wasn't sure what Anthony needed but he certainly thought he'd get it if he was with his dad, Art. *There's no way Art can give that boy what he needs.* How could she be so sure?

When was it she stopped wishing for her mom to protect her? When was it she gave up on that dream and fended for herself?

She wasn't always successful. But at least she'd tried.

Had her mom ever tried to protect her? She couldn't remember a time when she had.

A memory surfaced. *She used to leave me alone. Tie a blanket over my crib so I couldn't get out. Lock me in my bedroom when I was older. Maybe she thought she was protecting me when she did that. Keeping me from getting hurt.*

Vivid memories, almost like flashbacks except she knew where she was—one step away from that time and space.

Why?

Because I'm in Italy. The physical distance helps me separate myself from the memories.

Where does Holly's Story go from here? Gabriella snuggled under the covers after making a breathing hole. The fresh air soothed her lungs and cooled her face. Sleep tugged at the corners of her awareness. *I'll have the answers tomorrow.*

Morning came early. Gabriella woke while it was still dark. She pulsed with energy and leapt from the bed. Pulling on her clothes, she traipsed down to the kitchen and heated water for tea. Taking her mug and teapot, she ascended the stairs and got to work.

Holly's Story was racing from her mind, through her fingers and onto the computer screen. Being with Louise when she died was a turning point in Holly's life. She made the decision to live each day with joy in her heart. She was not Becca, she was not Louise, she was Holly and she could control the outcome of her story.

Holly knocked once on the door and stepped into the room where Mrs. Waterson, Doc S and a person she didn't know were seated around a table.

"Come in, Holly," Mrs. W said, gesturing her to the only vacant chair.

Holly perched on the seat, keenly aware of the young man sitting beside her. He wore his dark brown hair pulled back into a pony tail. His ears sported two rings on one side and three on the other. She'd bet real money there were tattoos under the yellow and green print long sleeved shirt he had on over well-worn jeans.

"This is Simon Perkins," Mrs. W. said as an introduction.

Simon held out his hand. "Pleased to meet you, Holly."

His grasp was warm, firm and matched the smile on his face. An interesting face, rather on the long side but when he smiled his crooked nose looked like it belonged to him.

"Pleased to meet you, too." Holly saw a ripple of humor in Simon's dark brown eyes.

"Thank you for joining us today." Doc S spoke, leaning toward her across the table. "We've something to discuss and I assured Simon here that your input was needed."

Holly's posture was erect, rigid, her hands clasped tight. Mentally she knew where the door was and how many steps she'd have to take before escaping.

"Simon heads up a new program at the youth shelter." Mrs. W gestured to Simon and nodded. "Go ahead and let Holly know what you're doing."

He shifted in his chair to better face her. "I'm heading up a team of people to approach youth on the streets to see if we can offer them an alternative. We're especially focused on the young girls. Louise was the seventh death so far this year. Our goal is to bring that number down to zero. The other demographic we're targeting is young boys, especially gay boys. They aren't being killed at the same number as girls. More of them are showing up in the Emergency Departments, beaten and brutally raped."

"But girls are beaten and brutally raped, too," Holly challenged.

"That's true. By showing them options to being on the street, both their death rate and their beaten/raped rate should go down also."

"How do you expect to do this?" Holly was interested yet skeptical about this idea.

"One idea is to put together street teams. They'd spend time out on the streets, visiting the places we know homeless youth congregate. The goal is to establish a trusting relationship so that a youth would confide in the street team that they wanted out."

"I don't see how I fit into this plan."

Doc S spoke up. "You'd be perfect to head up a street team. It's gotten around you tried to save Louise that you stayed with her. You're a role model because you've successfully left the streets. You're in school and are creating a good life for yourself."

"If the police hadn't come when they did, I could be where Louise is. Seth was one of that gang and he'd kill me in an instant without blinking an eye." A shudder racked her body and her teeth chattered as she remembered the hatred on his face. She rubbed her arm where he'd bruised her when he'd grabbed her and tried to haul her off somewhere. Somewhere he could beat her, rape her, torture her until she wished she were dead.

"I don't think I can do this." Holly's fear oozed through her words and filled the small room.

Simon leaned forward, his movement caught her attention. Turning toward him, she opened her mouth to say more.

She paused at his upraised hand.

"If you'd help me set up the program and interview the people who apply to be on the street team that would be immensely helpful. Under no circumstances should you be a member of a street team unless you are comfortable with the idea. Under no circumstances will we put any of our teams in danger."

Her laugh was hollow. "Then you'll have them sitting in a well-lit building with bullet proof windows and locks on the door as well as security cameras outside."

"There has to be a way to talk to these young people, let them know what their options are and still be safe."

"They'd have to be out in the daytime and they'd have to be in sufficient numbers to give anyone who wanted to harm them pause," Holly shot back.

"We'd thought of special personal defense training so if there was an attack, they'd be better able to defend themselves."

"Hand to hand? They could disarm someone who had a brick, a bat or a knife?"

"Special phones keyed into the police so that they only have to push one button to be automatically connected to 911."

"But how will the police know where they are?"

"We could provide the police with a list of locations the teams were visiting."

"But how would the police know which of the teams needed help?" Holly tapped the table, her tone urgent. "And, you'd have to be very careful arming them. If anyone saw a gun, that would be a prize and that person would be targeted, followed and attacked as soon as they were vulnerable."

The room was quiet. Simon had a grin on his face. Holly looked over at Doc S and Mrs. W both of whom smiled like a satisfied cat having its belly rubbed or its ears scratched.

"What?" Holly glared at the women.

"This is why we suggested Simon meet you." Doc S leaned forward, rested her arms on the table. "You'd know how to set up the street teams so they have the highest possibility of success."

"But I'm in school. And I'm a dorm monitor. I don't have time to add something else."

"You graduate in four months," Mrs. W said. "More planning is needed before anything is implemented. Except for finals week, you would have time to meet up with Simon for a couple of hours each week."

"And, you'd be paid for your time." Simon added. "Doc and Mrs. W were right. You are perfect for the position of assistant director. You don't have to go out as a team member unless you want to. You can point out the risks inherent not only in the job itself but in meeting up with youth in different areas."

Holly sat back in her chair, her mind racing with ideas and questions. She had wondered what she'd do in four months. Being dorm monitor gave her room and board and nominal pay. She had financial aid paying for most of her education but there was still a student loan she'd had to take out to cover some additional costs.

Turning to Simon, she met his gaze. "How much?"

"Ten dollars an hour."

"How many hours a week?"

"How many can you work?"

Holly looked away but as she glanced around the room, she saw Doc S and Mrs. W with neutral looks on their faces. "I'm not sure. I'll figure it out and let you know."

She started to stand but Simon was already on his feet. As she shoved her chair back, he pulled a card from his shirt pocket and handed it to her. "Here's how to reach me."

Sitting back down in her chair, she took the card.

"It was a pleasure meeting you," Simon said, taking the few steps to the door. "I'm looking forward to hearing from you."

Her 'it was a pleasure to meet you too' was said to his back and the closed door.

"You will do well at this job," Mrs. W was saying when Holly tuned back in.

Doc S was watching her, that calculating or was it all-knowing look on her face.

"Does Simon have any idea what he's in for?"

A glance passed between Mrs. W and Doc S. They nodded in unison but said nothing more.

That evening Holly sat in her chair looking out at the night. No rainbows sparkled around the wall of her room but the crystal glowed in the moonlight. She'd been trying to puzzle out what had happened this afternoon. How had she agreed to a job with a man she didn't know? What was it about Simon that wasn't threatening? *Maybe he's gay? Stop it! Don't be such an idiot.*

There was something about him that poked at her and said she was safe with him. *Be on guard. You know how to do that.* Holly opened the textbook on her lap and started to read.

A job. Using her finger as a page marker, she closed the book.

A job. She'd hoped she'd find a job and a place to live but she'd been too busy to seriously look for either. *I've asked my crystal to show me the way forward in my life. I wonder if… .*

The two blocks from the bus stop to the Youth Drop In Center were the longest two blocks Holly walked. She'd graduated, found a room to rent and gotten her first pay check. Distracted with the image of a real check made out in her name, she almost missed the young girl huddled in the doorway.

"Enid? Is that you?" Holly stopped and peered into the shadow.

"Holly?" The little girl voice whispered past her.

"Come on, Enid. Let's get you into a warm place with some hot food." Holly, her hand held out, stepped closer to the opening.

A damp and dirty hand grasped hers. "Come on, Enid."

Holly's tug was gentle.

Enid emerged from the shadows.

"Let's get you taken care of." Holly started toward the shelter in the next block.

A man stepped out of the next doorway and Holly's way was barred by a familiar pock marked face—Seth.

Shoving Enid behind her, Holly attempted to step around Seth. He just moved when she did, a smile—more like a snarl curled his lips.

"Remember what we planned, Enid."

"Enid, don't listen to him. We're going to the shelter and you'll be safe there."

Seth's harsh guttural laugh was a punch in Holly's gut. When he'd beater her so badly, he'd made the same sound. If she didn't escape, he'd kill her for sure.

"Enid?" The warning was clear. Enid better do what he'd told her to do or—. The image of Louise's battered body fresh in her mind, Holly still couldn't let go of the young girl and save herself.

"Come on, Enid. We can do this. We can get away if we try together. We've only to cross the street ahead and we'll be safe." Holly prayed her voice was strong and Enid would hear the promise of a future if she came with her.

Her eyes never left Seth's face. She was a couple of steps back from him so her peripheral vision saw his hand raise.

"Enid, you fucking bitch. Do it now or I'll make you so sorry you'll wish you were dead!" Seth had raised his voice in an effort to get Enid to act.

Holly felt Enid's grasp firm and start to twist her arm up behind her back. The reality of what was happening spurred her to action.

She tried to pull away from Enid but her arm was already half-way up her back. "Enid, let go of my arm."

Letting Seth know he had the upper hand meant her death.

It would not be quick.

It would be painful.

It would be inevitable.

I have a job.

Where did that come from?

I'm going crazy.

Pain shot up her arm and into her shoulder as she twisted in an effort to escape Enid's grasp. Enid held on with both hands and Holly could not break her hold.

When Seth's arm came up, his hand fisted, his ring glinted in the street light, Holly ducked.

His blow landed on the side of her head, above her ear. Her balance off Holly stumbled. Pain lanced through her body.

It was Enid's hold on her arm that kept her from falling to the ground.

"Let her go, bitch," Seth shouted at Enid as he slapped her face.

Enid reeled back, dropping Holly's hand.

Holly's balance still off, she flailed about in an effort to grab hold of something to keep from falling.

A knee came up and hit her in the chest. Air whooshed out of her lungs. She dropped like a dead body.

Seth gripped her hair and pulled her head up. His foot back, he was going to kick her in the face. That had happened to Louise. It was going to happen to her.

She closed her eyes and prayed it all be over soon. Her luck had run out. She'd had a couple of good years, got her education and had a job. She was a success.

Oof!!! A heavy weight landed on her and then was gone. She curled into a ball to protect her face. Would her parents come to her funeral?

"Got 'em," a male voice said.

"Thanks." She knew that voice.

"Holly? Holly? It's Simon. You're safe now, Holly. The police have him and the girl."

"No, not her." Holly managed to speak through gritted teeth. "Not Enid. She was... ."

"Don't try to talk now. Let's get you to Doc S."

Strong arms helped her to her feet. She was lightheaded and wobbly but with Simon's arm around her waist she stood. Leaning against him, she looked for Enid. The young girl was huddled on the sidewalk.

"Come with me, Enid. I need you with me. Remember, just cross the street and we'll be safe." Holly's knees buckled and Simon let her slide to the ground.

The fire truck cruised around the corner. The EMT's jumped off grabbing gear, pulling on gloves.

"I'm okay," Holly said as one crouched next to her. "Nothing's broken. Just a little shaken up. Check Enid out first."

"Miss, we've enough folks here to check both of you out."

"I just need to get to the Shelter Clinic. Doc S will take care of me."

"Can you stand?"

"I'm just a little lightheaded. I'll be okay. How's Enid?"

"I'll go see. You stay here, on the ground. Do not get up." Simon strode the half-dozen steps to where the EMT's were checking Enid out.

Holly couldn't hear the conversation but knew it was intense by the tone and postures of Simon and the EMT's.

Her blood pressure and heart rate were elevated. She wanted to say "Duh" but bit her lip and stayed quiet. Her goal now was to get to the Clinic and see Doc S.

"What's going on here?" Tears welled in Holly's eyes at Doc S's familiar voice.

"Hey, Doc," the EMT next to her said. "This one has been hit at least once in the head. Heart rate and blood pressure are elevated. Respiration rate is slow and shallow."

"Like someone in pain?"

"Most likely."

"And the other one?"

"She's on something. Won't say what. Just rocks and moans."

"Let's get them both to the clinic. I'll take care of them."

Simon was by her side. "Can you stand now?"

With his help Holly did stand. The wooziness was better and she took a couple of steps to make sure everything still worked.

Holly held her hand out, "Come on, Enid. Doc S is here and we've only a little ways to go to the Clinic." She looked around. Seth was in the back of the police cruiser. With the door closed and windows up. Neither she nor Enid could hear the hate spew from his mouth.

Doc S put her arm around Enid. "Come along, Enid. We'll get you fixed up in no time. Seth is in police custody and with you and Holly talking to the police, he won't be around here for a long time."

As the little procession headed toward the shelter, a different police officer approached. "We'll need statements."

"Come to the clinic. We've got coffee and cookies tonight. You can talk to them there."

The officer walked on the other side of Doc S, her head bent as she introduced herself to Enid.

Holly held on to Simon as they followed Doc's party. "How did you know?"

"I can see the bus as it pulls away from that stop. By the time I count to fifty, I see you. Tonight I didn't. Had staff put a call in to the police and headed out to meet up with you."

"You watch for me?"

"You're special and I want you safe."

The warmth of his arm around her waist spread throughout her body. "You only want me safe?"

"I want everyone safe but if something happened to you, a bit of me would die."

"You don't know me."

"But I do. We came from the same place—the streets. We've found our way out. Together we can offer hope of a better life to the others."

Holly looked up at Simon. He was looking ahead but he was serious.

"You lived out here too?"

"Five years."

She wanted to ask him how he'd survived, what had happened to him that the streets were safer than home or foster care or wherever else but she didn't. He'd done what he had to survive as had she.

He was right, they had a chance to work together and help others come off the street.

"Thank you." Holly slipped her arm around Simon's waist.

"You're welcome I guess."

"You saved my life. And, most likely saved Enid's too."

"You saved my life."

"I've done nothing."

"You've shown up in my life. You've brought smiles and laughter back."

"But you've always smiled and laughed."

"You can ask Doc S. I don't think she's seen me smile or laugh in years."

"But you smiled when I first met you?"

They were standing just outside the Clinic's door. The light from within spilled out onto the sidewalk. A soft smile graced Simon's face. "I know. That's when I knew how special you are and how much I want you in my life."

He slipped his arms around her and held her close.

She melted into his embrace and held on tight.

He rested his cheek against her hair.

She sighed.

The door opened. "You two need to come in." Doc S said in a stern tone.

Holly's faced flushed with embarrassment but when she looked at Doc, she saw a smile dancing in her eyes.

With Simon holding her hand, Holly walked into the clinic ready to talk to the police, ready to support Enid, ready to face a new future. The warmth of his hand holding hers sent the message that her future could have Simon by her side.

Village Shopping and Sacred Geometry

Gabriella leaned against the back of the chair, her hands still poised over the key board. Holly was safe. Seth was in police custody and would be charged with Louise's murder.

I never had to testify in court. So much evidence, the defense attorneys' plea bargained. Guilty for a lesser crime.

Her Seth was back on the streets. She shivered when the image of her seeing him a few months ago popped into her mind. He was a reminder that being safe was a myth. All she could do was her best to protect herself.

Grateful she'd seen him before he saw her, she talked to the shelter staff about counseling the young girls on how to protect themselves from him. He had a smooth line and even with his pock-marked and scared face, he was seen by some as ruggedly handsome.

She was certain if he found her, she'd be dead. That fact had fueled her asking for a sabbatical leave. She needed to get her head screwed on right. She needed to make peace with her own death if she continued to volunteer at the youth shelter. At the very least she needed to be clear that she'd accomplished all that was most important to her in this lifetime.

Writing *Holly's Story* was her way of sorting things out for herself. Now that the first draft was done—or was it? She needed to read it through from the beginning, fill in any blanks and make sure that the current ending made sense. After all, Holly and Simon had not known each other all that long.

But she feels safe with him.

Gabriella powered down her laptop and closed the lid. In November the air was cool enough she kept the door to the balcony closed. Crossing to the French doors, she opened them and breathed the sea air deep into her lungs.

Who do you trust?

That question nagged at the back of her mind. Did she even totally trust The Circle? Is there even one man I trust?

The feeling of being held, comforted, cared for swelled as images of her meltdown last night and Giovanni's tenderness replayed. *Awkward.*

It was awkward and a bit embarrassing but also wonderful. Her chest expanded and warmth filled her core pushing out a modicum of the deep cold that had been in her center for so long.

Even though she still had nightmares, they didn't terrify her here. She felt safer here in this villa than she could ever remember. Why?

In part it was because she was in Italy and she knew none of her past would find her here. But it was also because she knew that Giovanni spoke the truth. If she wanted to talk, he would listen. Not lecture. Not disbelieve. Not judge her. Just listen. He would hear the meaning beyond the words. He'd proven that when he'd come to her room at Lily's. He'd sat in the chair and listened at a time when she needed someone in her life that would do only that.

Of course the other women in The Circle would also just listen. That was part of what being a sacred women's circle was all about—listening, with no judgement, offering suggestions only if asked.

She'd never had a man in her life she could talk to. Giovanni was the first. *Will he be the only one? Will he be the last?*

Gabriella stepped back into the room and closed the doors. Her feet were cold and she pulled on a pair of socks. After dressing in her warmest clothing, she stuffed her feet into shoes and headed downstairs for a cup of hot tea.

Giovanni stood when she entered. He remained standing even when she waved him back to his seat. Begrudgingly she allowed him to pull out her chair and seat her at the table.

"You really don't have to do that, you know. I can seat myself."

"*Si*, you can. But I like doing so. I like showing you respect and that you are special."

"Thank you." Gabriella busied herself with a piece of toast spreading on butter and jam. Margretta appeared with a plate of scrambled eggs, a bowl of fresh fruit and her daily glass of fresh squeezed orange juice.

"Something hot to drink, please," Gabriella requested.

Five minutes later a steaming mug of tea was brought in. Gabriella held the pottery in her hands to warm them and sipped the fruity liquid. Heat slipped down her throat and warmed.

She sighed. "I'm being spoiled."

"You are being cared for." Giovanni settled back in his chair. "There is a difference between being spoiled and being cared for, *no*?"

"There is a difference but I've done nothing that warrants being cared for."

He said something in Italian. Margretta did also. She wished she knew at least a few words so she'd know what that was all about. When Giovanni leaned forward, rested his forearms on the table and speared her with his intense gaze, she knew she'd been the topic of that exchange.

"My staff be with me for many years. In that time, many people come to stay. If they voted, you would be their favorite." He negligently waved a hand. "You, Diana, Sophia but you are here the longest which is why you are first."

Her mouth open to reply. He stopped her with a palm out hand.

"Why you a favorite?"

"I can't understand why the three of us stand out. We don't even speak Italian."

"But you are kind and considerate. You go to the kitchen to get more lemon water."

"I need to get up and move—,"

"You say polite words 'please' and 'thank you' for example. You have a smile on your face. You appreciate what they do. You compliment cook—every meal is 'the best'."

"I'm only telling—,"

"It makes no difference why you do these things. They are unusual here. Most servants are not appreciated."

"I know you compliment them." Gabriella's hackles raised, her posture defensive. Why? *He is only telling me positive things.*

"*Si*, I do more now because I saw how Diana's compliments improved their dispositions. Of course the quality of work is the same because they value their positions, but it makes a noticeable difference if staff is happy or not.

"And I do even more with you here." He grinned and Gabriella's defenses weakened. "I have even been known to pick up my clothes from the floor and place them on the chair."

She leaned forward and in a conspiratorial tone asked, "What about putting them in the laundry hamper?"

Giovanni's laugh came from his belly. He leaned back in his chair, a hand on his stomach, his face scrunched as the roar of delight erupted. Tears brightened his dark brown eyes and a lock of dark hair flopped over his brow. He was devastatingly real.

As his mirth subsided, he wiped his eyes with his napkin and leaned forward again. "*Si*, you are a good influence on me."

And he was a good influence on her.

A sense of satisfaction filled her. She was spending time with Giovanni this morning and only now did last night's memories enter her mind.

Her worry she'd feel awkward or embarrassed never materialized. Instead she felt comfortable and secure. Secure in the knowledge that he genuinely liked her and so did his staff. She was more herself here than most anywhere because she was not looking over her shoulder for danger.

Safety. She could go into the little town and feel safe. If she learned at least a bit of the language, she'd feel freer about exploring. What surprised her the most was the realization that if Giovanni was with her, she trusted all would be right.

She trusted him?

Looking back over the years she'd known him it came in bits and pieces. Even in the beginning when he teased Jackson about Lily coming here to do house totems with him, it was apparent he was teasing. There was always an underlying element of respect.

And he participated in their ceremonies. It was a foregone conclusion that when the other men were invited, Giovanni would be included.

Like clicking the refresh button on her computer, a new picture of him came into focus. He was her friend. A shiver shuddered through her.

"You are cold." He stood, shook off his jacket and smoothed it across her shoulders. "When you are through with breakfast, we go shopping."

Her mouth open to protest, she stopped sensing the steel underneath his usual friendly façade.

"But I pay for my own purchases."

His non-committal shrug telegraphed his "we'll see" attitude.

I'll be at a disadvantage because I don't know the language. But, she inwardly smiled, *that can change.*

Using her most innocent voice and look, she kept her gaze on her plate as she asked, "How do you say 'how much?' in Italian?"

He chuckled. "I give you lessons while we shop."

She didn't like feeling in debt to someone but when she wanted to bristle, it didn't come out right. In the end, she said "Thank You, I'd appreciate that.

"And maybe another lesson in sacred geometry?"

The trip into the small village equipped her with a jacket, sweater and lunch. Giovanni helped her pay for the items but purchased their lunch. She learned "how much" or "quanto?"

She was treated differently if she was in the shop and Giovanni was not by her side. He always materialized before she paid for anything. When the clerk saw she was with him, the price on the jacket changed and a matching scarf joined the sweater. He bought her two pair of warm socks before she realized he'd made the purchase.

Lunch was at a little bistro. They sat inside by the fire. She had been there a few times before and the owner remembered what she'd ordered. A glass of red wine, a local blend, was set before her; a matching glass in front of Giovanni.

Pasta primavera with a side of garlic bread was her order. Mouthwatering when it was set before her, Gabriella allowed herself to breathe deeply of the aroma before picking up her fork and spoon.

A soft moan escaped as the pasta and vegetables warmed her mouth and after a couple of chews, slipped down her throat. The taste, temperature and flavor were sensual. Not like Sophia's desserts but different—more basic or earthy. It was hard to differentiate when she was lost in the pleasure.

"You enjoy." Giovanni's statement elicited a smile.

"I enjoy this food very much."

"As good as Adolfo's?"

Gabriella looked at him. His brown eyes held a hint of amusement.

"If you tell Adolfo I like the Pasta Primavera here better than his, I'll deny it."

Giovanni laughed. More of a chuckle than a guffaw but she had to smile at the sound. Even trying not to react, there was something in his laugh that drew her out of herself.

"How is your story now?"

Gabriella, her forearms on the table, leaned closer. "I thought I might have finished it but something feels off. Holly, the heroine, just met Simon a few months ago and a romance is blooming. I didn't think she'd let herself be close to him this soon."

He lounged against the back of his chair, his wine glass twirling in one hand, the other resting casually on the table's edge. "She has had a hard life?"

Gabriella nodded.

"She would not trust so easily then." His gaze held hers, a warm understanding easy for her to read.

"No, you are right. I don't think she'd trust this soon. I have more work to do."

"And, you have time to do it. All the time you need."

"That isn't entirely true. I have some time to finish it but I will have to go home and find a job if I'm not rehired after the first of the year."

"When you have the time. When you take a break, I arrange for house totem appointments."

"But Elizabeth—"

"Elizabeth has a baby, a husband and enough to do without coming to Italy for a few days to do this totem work. You are already here."

"I'll talk to her. I can always split the fee with her."

"If that is what you need to do, so be it. I know she be greatly relieved not to feel obligated to come here. You hear she and Michael are to have another child—well, once Maeve is a year old—." He stopped and she saw a soft blush highlight his cheekbones.

"What you're saying is that Elizabeth has other priorities, like raising a family and serving The Lady and that coming to Italy is low on that list."

"*Si* that is what I say."

"I'll let you know tomorrow how things are going. If I'm still struggling with where the story goes next, maybe sensing a house totem or two will help."

For her sacred geometry lesson, they walked the few blocks to the village center and the old church. Giovanni talked about the size, shape, dimension, proportions, symmetry and harmony.

"But what about the stained glass windows?"

"Most people see the beauty in the colored glass but to see the sacred in the structure—? People acknowledge the sacredness of the triangle of the Great Pyramids but this church is a rectangle. How many people see the sacred in that?"

"People also acknowledge that circles represent the sacred. But you are correct. I've never heard anyone talk about the sacred rectangle or square."

He also pointed out how the village plaza was laid out, showing her how different buildings added to the importance of the church. Nothing was higher than the steeple and only one other building was as high as the church roof—that was the building that housed the local government offices.

A chill was in the air when they started back to the villa. They stopped on the way back to the car and Giovanni took her jacket from the bag and placed it around her shoulders. Instead of taking his arm away, he left it draped there.

They'd taken several steps before Gabriella registered the weight and feel of his arm, the heat from his body, the scent of clove and sandalwood she would always associate with him. She watched for the panic, waited for the need to pull away to swamp her but it never happened. They were at the car, Giovanni opening the door and ushering her in and, although alert, panic never appeared.

Resting her head against the back of the seat, Gabriella allowed thoughts to swim through her mind. She'd known Giovanni for almost three years and only recently saw him as a friend. How could Holly already trust Simon? *If I'm just learning to trust Giovanni, Holly can't trust Simon yet.*

Sorting Things Out

The realization that Holly's relationship with Simon either had to slowly grow or was most likely doomed to fail kept Gabriella occupied for the next couple of days. She wanted Holly to heal, to be whole, to be able to love another, to trust and to have these miracles happen quickly. She didn't want Holly to have to struggle for years as she had. She had been off the streets for over a decade and yet she still did not trust easily. *And maybe I never will. But at least now I can trust more than ever before.*

To know the reality that she was more trusting soothed. Maybe she didn't trust everyone, but she did trust the women in her circle, their husbands and children. It was comforting to know if she decided to tell them everything about her past, they'd still want her in their lives. They'd still love her.

Spending this time in Italy, being able to write *Holly's Story* was a gift. But what stuttered her heart beat and fractured her breathing was when she acknowledged she trusted Giovanni.

He was like the other men connected to The Circle. Not only would he protect her but he also wouldn't knowingly hurt her.

But love her?

Every friendship had an element of love. A happiness at being with that person who, with unconditional acceptance, was safe and someone with whom she wanted to spend time.

Hope stirred in her heart as memories flooded in of Giovanni's arm around her shoulder as they walked to the car, of him holding her while she cried, of him sitting and listening as she talked about her nightmares. There'd been no one in her life outside of Doc S and Ms. Mortenson, her first social worker that she talked to like that. Certainly no male and to be honest, except for The Circle with Logan, not even her own circle sisters.

Her knees buckled and she grabbed the balcony railing to keep from falling when, with stunning clarity, she knew with certainty he wouldn't push her away even if she told him everything.

But romantic love? Her logical brain pointed out: how can you write about something you know nothing about?

That thought took residence in Gabriella's mind. Of course she knew about research but she didn't need research to know about sex. What she didn't know about was sex in the context of romantic love. There was no way to know about that herself unless she was willing to open herself up to the possibility.

Pictures surfaced in her inner mind of each of her circle sisters' in the depths of despair when they realized they loved another and even though he might love her, it still might not be enough.

Shaking her head free of those dark images, she focused instead on the radiance their faces showed when married. *If I want a chance at that, I need to face the reality I'll likely feel despair.*

She hadn't allowed herself to feel anything for a man for a very long time, had actually shut down that part of her until she'd met Giovanni. Until this past year when he learned of her past and remained her friend. Her guard had been up because she'd always been attracted to him.

Here in Italy, in his home she'd seen him in a different light. He was still charming but she saw beyond the surface charm to the man. He was kind, caring. He took the time to really listen beyond her words to what she was trying to say. He treated her and also everyone he met with respect. He was teaching her about sacred geometry in such a way that she did see the wonder in it even if she didn't really understand it. She smiled and even laughed when with him.

While Gabriella struggled with her thoughts and *Holly's Story*, Giovanni disappeared into his studio first thing, then emerged obviously distracted for a quick lunch before going back until dinner. This morning she'd suggested he have lunch in his studio, assuring him she was most likely going to write and would have lunch in her room.

His brow had arched and he'd opened his mouth, she knew to assure her it was good for him to leave the studio. She'd cut him off by repeating herself and turning to Margretta who had brought a fresh pot of tea to her.

"*Signore* will take his lunch in his studio today."

Presumptuous of her but Margretta nodded and left ostensibly to let Adolfo know. Giovanni gave her a considering look but said no more.

Her own lunch now eaten, laptop open and booted up but no new words on the page, Gabriella stood on her balcony and considered her options in finishing *Holly's Story*.

One: she could leave it rather as it was with a few minor additions about how Holly never dreamed someone would love her, etc. She left this one as a possibility while she let her mind roam freely with other possibilities.

Two: she could use her mother's trail of boyfriend upon boyfriend—instantly she discarded that one because Simon was basically a good guy.

Three: she could patch something together based on her observations of other people's healthy relationships. *Another possibility.*

Four: she could let her guard down while in Italy and see what developed between Giovanni and herself. It might not be a lasting romantic love but it would be a romantic affair. And in that moment she was clear that Giovanni would be a caring, giving lover.

Although her list had four options, there were really only three. *I'm going to let it sit for the rest of the day and see if anything else comes to mind. I can always stop for now, go home and see what develops with Jordan. I think he'd be a caring lover also.* But when she imagined Jordan's arm around her shoulders, the warmth and sense of being cherished wasn't there.

She leaned on the railing and looked out over the garden toward the sea. Triangle sails were visible in the distance. The waves marched in rows towards the shore. Symmetry today because the weather was mild. Chaos by nightfall if the forecasted storm arrived. *I've never watched the sea in a storm. Maybe there is a symmetry, a harmony as in sacred geometry I've just never noticed.*

The beam of the lighthouse swung across her view. *Maybe the lighthouse's light brings a balance to the storm.*

The triangle sails disappeared and dark storm clouds gathered on the horizon as if they were an invading army showing their strength to the opposition. A brisk wind whipped across the garden and whirled around her. She retreated to her room, closing the French doors and locking them as another gust buffeted.

Chilled, Gabriella decided to go down and fix herself a fresh pot of tea. As she started down the stairs, a happy whistle came from the corridor to Giovanni's studio.

They met as if the stars or The Universe or whatever it was that managed mortal lives watched over them. Giovanni casually slung his arm over her shoulder and she slipped an arm around his waist.

"You are in a good mood."

"*Si*, my project is done except for a few details I already know." He paused in the central room and looked at the cloud-filled sky, the garden's trees dancing in the wind. "We eat in tonight. Perhaps a fire?"

"I'd love a fire."

Giovanni called out in Italian and moments later Margretta appeared with a bottle of wine and two glasses. Minutes later Silvio came in with a canvas carrier filled with wood.

Gabriella and Giovanni settled on the couch in front of the fireplace, a glass of wine and the beginnings of a warming fire. His arm was along the back of the couch. With little effort he could play with the ends of her hair. She was close enough his heat and scent of cloves and sandalwood warmed her.

Comfortable, relaxed and safe. *Without being on guard, alert, tense, I'm alone with a man. I'm relaxed and I feel safe.*

"Are you okay?" Giovanni asked.

Gabriella tipped her head up, saw concern in his eyes and nodded. "I'm very okay."

"*Molto bene.*"

No need to talk, the two sat in front of the fire watching the flames twist and turn, ebb and flow devouring the logs as if feasting on a delicacy. Something about her was different. What exactly Giovanni didn't know. She wasn't snuggled up to him but she was close enough her curls brushed his hand and her jasmine scent stirred when she turned her head.

"Do you write today?" He asked his question with his gaze centered on the fire.

She shook her head first but then murmured "no".

"It is good you take some time to step back then."

"I want it finished."

His heart skipped a beat and he paused before responding. "Because?"

"I'm not sure. I don't like this limbo, this in between place. I'm not sure how to go forward."

"Ah, I know that place."

"You?"

"*Si*, me. Not so much now but when I was first starting out, I reach a place where I wasn't sure which direction to go. It was important to get everything right so my clients are pleased. I always know what they want in general with a few details but there is much to a building that most people never think about.

"You take the time you need. The story will be finished when it is the right time for it to happen."

"You used to take time to figure something out but now?"

"I still take time when it is needed. Sometimes creativity must rest before it can produce the best ideas or in your case, the best words. The story, it is in the back of your mind?"

"It is all over in my mind. I just can't figure out where the story goes next? Or if it is really finished except for a bit of ending."

"But you will figure that out."

"But how do you know that?"

"Because this is your story. There is no one else in the entire world to tell this story, who knows it is finished except you. I guess there is more to tell or you be done."

Gabriella relaxed against the sofa, her eyes closed, she enjoyed the light of the flickering flames against her lids. When was the last time she was so relaxed almost boneless alone with a man? In the garden? No other scenario came to mind. In neither case was she really alone. However, because there were staff didn't take away from the sense of rightness settling in her.

The bell rang announcing dinner was almost ready.

They bestirred themselves and washed in the guest half-bath before sitting down to dinner. By now they had "their" spots and staff had place settings set so they sat across from each other, the better to observe the other when in conversation.

Dinner was Pasta Primavera with warm bread and garlic butter along with a simple salad of lettuce and tomato with an olive oil and balsamic vinegar dressing. Dessert, Giovanni knew, was tiramisu, Gabriella's favorite.

Conversation interspersed with laughter, it didn't take long to finish the simple meal and await the decadent dessert. After clearing away the dinner dishes, Margretta returned with two plates with generous pieces of tiramisu.

Before she took a bite, he asked, "If you had to choose, would you pick Adolfo's tiramisu or Jackson's make-it-yourself ice cream sundae?"

"What a diabolical question." Gabriella tipped her head to the side as if this was a difficult question. She took her time responding although the scent of her tiramisu beckoned. "I know Italians love their gelato but that in comparison to Jackson's ice cream? Jackson wins—no contest. But tiramisu? Now you are comparing apples and oranges and that isn't a fair comparison."

"So you do not choose?"

"So, when here I choose tiramisu because Adolfo's is the best ever. And," Gabriella chuckled before continuing, "Jackson's ice cream isn't anywhere near." She forked a bite of the dessert into her mouth. Her eyes closed, a transcendent look on her face, she moaned as the bite of amaretto and chocolate and cream slipped down her throat.

Giovanni watched her sublime pleasure of the treat. Adolfo fixed it every now and then. *Not often enough.* Giovanni watched her throat move in sensual enjoyment of the dessert.

"Does Adolfo know you are smitten with his tiramisu?"

Gabriella smiled. "He does. He found me in the kitchen snitching a bite. He told me he would fix it for me but I'd never know when because anticipation is part of the joy." She leaned forward, her arms on the table. "Do you believe that? That anticipation is part of the joy? That waiting for something adds to its desirability?"

He contemplated that question. He'd been waiting for Gabriella for almost three years now. His arousal had tented his pants and his heart had speeded up while watching her pleasure with that single bite. She would be that beautiful in his arms, in his bed. Internally he shook his head and struggled with words to answer but not reveal too much. To be honest? To give a simple answer?

"Anticipation is like a torture if what you desire is never to be yours. It is important to find a way in your life so you always have some things to enjoy, to look forward to."

Gabriella's gaze remained fixed on his. "Like when Sophia's husband was killed and more recently her friend died. Of course she had us but we were not Jonathan.

"When he died, Sophia moved from Diana and Ashley, who were married, to Elizabeth, Sophia, Lily, Hunter and me. We were single. But Lily and Hunter had children. Now Sophia and I have no husband and no children." Her gaze focused past his shoulder to an empty spot on the wall.

"Wishing doesn't make it so. It takes courage to create the life one wants to live. Just because you want it, doesn't mean it will happen." Her voice soft she continued. "You have to be prepared for disappointment. If you try someone's tiramisu and it doesn't measure up, you have to be prepared for pain and possible despair. If you open yourself up, you have to—."

Gabriella's hand flew up and covered her mouth. She jumped up from the table and ran from the room.

Giovanni heard her footsteps on the stairs, the door to her room close. He looked where she'd sat mere seconds ago. Her piece of tiramisu, only one bite missing, still sat at her place. He picked up their plates and forks and carried them into the living room where he deposited them on the table in front of the fire.

Slouching on the couch, he watched the flames leap into the void, stretch higher and higher as if they just tried hard enough they could escape up the chimney. She did want a family, a husband and children. He was sure of that. He was also sure she'd just shared more than she'd planned.

What to do? What to say?

He crossed his feet at the ankles, folded his hands behind his head and let the images form. The clock struck the time. She'd been gone the better part of an hour and the fire was burning low.

Giovanni picked up the tiramisu-laden-plates and headed toward the stairs. Simple words filled with his truth was what he had to offer. He could only hope she could hear them without panicking, without throwing her belongings in her suitcases and running away.

Anticipation, desire, torture, joy?

Not knowing the outcome did not deter his focus. At the top of the stairs he turned toward her room. He paused, made sure he was willing to accept the consequences if his reading of her was wrong, then shifting, he gently knocked on the door with his elbow.

Fumbling Forward

He wasn't surprised when his quiet knock was met with silence but he was determined. He balanced one plate on the forearm so he had a hand free to knock a bit more loudly.

Again no answer.

When he knocked a third time, he called out. "Gabriella I have something so you feel better."

A rustle and then the door cracked open.

No surprise her eyes were puffy and her face streaked with dried tears.

With his free hand he grabbed the plate of tiramisu. "I bring you this. Your favorite. It will help, *si*?"

Gabriella saw the hopeful look in his eyes and the outstretched hand with her plate of tiramisu.

"I suppose you want to come in." Her voice held defeat and exhaustion to her own ears.

"I want to finish our dessert together, *si*. But if you would prefer downstairs in front of the fire, that is good too."

She stepped away from the door but quickly returned, slippers on her feet and a scarf around her shoulders.

He carried their plates down the stairs and set them on the table. After stoking the fire and adding another log, he joined her on the couch. Worry coursed through him when he noticed she hadn't reached for her plate. He handed it to her.

"Cook thinks you no longer like his tiramisu if you don't eat." Giovanni took a bite and although he looked at the fire she was in his peripheral vision.

"You know that his name is Adolfo."

"*Si,* I know that."

"But you often refer to him as Cook."

"Because when I hired him, I ask him what he wants to be called and he say "Cook" so that is what I call him. It is the same with everyone in my employ."

"But no one calls you Giovanni."

"True, because they not invited to do so."

"Why do you keep the distance between you and them?"

"What do they call you?"

"Miss Gabriella or *Signorina* Gabriella."

"That is a sign of respect and I would guess you have given them leave to call you Gabriella or even Gabby."

"I have but they just shake their heads and continue to call me Miss Gabriella."

The iron bar across Giovanni's shoulders slipped away. There was a focus to this conversation, something Gabriella was trying to sort through by talking about how his staff addressed him and now her. He shifted a few inches so he was turned more toward her.

"What bothers you about this?"

"Why do you think something bothers me?"

He shrugged, a quintessential Italian movement of his shoulders. "I feel it." He laid his palm on his heart. "Something bothers you and you talk about my staff."

Her spine ridged, her shoulders squared, her chin raised, Gabriella faced him. "Do you never get upset? I've only ever seen you calm, complacent, happy."

"Then you don't see 'me'." He punctuated that last word by stabbing a finger on his own chest. "You don't pay attention to me, to my moods—I do have them. When I sat in your room at Jackson's and you talked, you remember me as complacent, happy?"

"You were calm," Gabriella shot back resisting the urge to stand and stalk away.

Anger spiked through him. His gut churned and emotions too numerous to catalogue clogged his throat. His fists clenched as he cleared his throat. *It is now or never.* Setting his plate on the table with enough force he feared it would break, he swiveled to fully face her.

"And would it have helped you if I show outrage? Would you understand my rage was for *what* happen to you and not *about* you? Did you think I have no feelings when Logan was missing? Or Ashley's children stolen away?

"What kind of a monster do you think I am? And more, why you spend time with such a man who only feels calm, complacent and happy?" He spat the last three words at her but somewhere during his tirade, he'd also reached out and taken her hands.

His voice softened, his thumbs caressed the backs of her hands. "You have no idea who I am to think so little of me. But, if you allow, I would like you to know me better."

Her chest painfully tight with pent up air. Her cold hands clasped in his warm ones, Gabriella looked up. Her hazel gaze met his dark chocolate and after a brief second, searched for something behind his shuttered lids. There was something there but it was hard for her to decipher what it was.

Even though she couldn't see what was in his eyes, she could feel him. Feel his restrained energy, feel his passion, feel him teetering on the edge of something.

Tears welled and she sniffed to keep them from falling. She shook her head because this time it didn't work. So she sat on the couch, her hands held by Giovanni and let the tears fall. "You've always frightened me," she whispered as the salty drops dripped from her chin. "I know you would never intentionally hurt me but—.

"You are temptation, Giovanni. I've never felt so safe with a man in my entire life and it scares me so—." She gulped in air, the tightness in her chest increased. "I want—."

If she didn't let go of the pain inside, let the tightness in her chest ease, she'd die. Tears freely streaming down her face, her stomach in turmoil, Gabriella leapt into the void. "Hold me?"

Two words that changed his life. How long had he waited for the invitation? Years.

Slowly he drew her into his embrace. With one hand he cradled her head against his shoulder, the other gently stroked her back. He'd offered her comfort before and she'd accepted. What was different was she'd asked. Actually said the words inviting him into her life.

While his body clamored for more, he kept his touch gentle. His shirt damp from her tears, he relished the closeness.

Slow, you must go slow, he reminded himself. Taking a slight risk, he pressed soft kisses in the curls on top of her head.

She lay in his arms for several minutes after the tears stopped. He'd had a bit of time to consider what he'd do when she pulled away.

"*Un minuto*. A minute. It is easier for me to say my words with us like this."

No words but she subsided and seemed to nestle more closely to him.

"I remember I see you first time at Jackson's house. So beautiful, so fiery and yet not. Always I have seen a contradiction in you.

"I flirted with you. Did you notice I didn't flirt with anyone else? You bristled." He chuckled at those memories, his hand still cupping her head against his chest, his other hand caressing her back. "Always you fascinate me. Always you hold me at arm's length.

"I am a slow learner." Another chuckle. "But I can learn. I am what is called 'trainable' or 'teachable'." His laugh was soft and then he sighed.

"So I think, maybe we can become friends? Do you know when I decided that?"

Her head nodded under his hand.

"I have treasured this time of friendship. You here in my home for the last weeks is a dream come true for me."

He paused, his hand rhythmically stroked her back. Another deep sigh. "But my Gabriella, I wish for more. I wish to be more than your friend. In time I wish for us to become lovers. In time I wish for you to be my wife."

He felt the panic well in her and when she struggled to free herself, he let her go but slipped his hand from her back across her shoulder and down her arm to hold her hand.

"You can't want that!" Panic infused her features, her eyes were wild with fear and something more. "You don't know me."

"I know I love you. I love you a very long time. I know you carry a past with you but I also know who you are in the present. You are a loving, caring, loyal friend. You are passionate to protect those who are your friends. You are a hard worker. You persevere even in the face of your own doubts. You are brave."

She pulled on the hand he held attempting to separate them.

"Please do not leave me." A plea in his voice, he looked at their joined hands. "Per favore."

Finding A Path

Gabriella knew in that instant she was going to be sick. Sick as in vomiting all over him. Sick as in falling to her knees from the pain in her heart. Sick as in blocking the image of being with him for all time.

It wasn't possible to accept his love because just being friends was excruciating. She'd die if the feelings were even more intense.

No longer struggling, Gabriella quieted and then in the silence and stillness she opened her eyes, connected with his dark brown gaze and lost all—her heart and her soul.

His truth shone brightly. She saw his love, his passion, his desire, his wanting more. She saw it all including his restraint. The choice really was hers to make.

Her mind raced with possibilities. While she had had sex many times, she'd never made love, never been intimate with someone who truly cared about her. What would it be like?

Her mind raced with possibilities. Would it be more physically satisfying? Would she be able to withdraw, to return to her life in Fremont and be happy? Would she change so fundamentally she wouldn't know herself?

Her mind raced with possibilities. What if she couldn't satisfy him? What if she felt nothing when he touched her? She shook her head crossing that idea off the rambles in her mind. His touch already healed her at some level. She felt safe in his arms and that was a first—a first to even allow herself to be held in someone's arms.

As the panic subsided, fear came rushing in to fill the gap. Vulnerable, inadequate, a fraud—those were the words that described her.

Who was she to think she even deserved to spend time at a villa in Italy to write a story about throw away kids?

Who was she to aspire to having a family that included a husband who loved her?

Who was she to believe—?

Chaos reigned. Her stomach felt as if a million beads were roiling around. Her brain felt as if a zip-line was strung tight and someone else was sending thoughts and feelings careening. Her body shook with the enormity of emotions churning through her.

And still, through it all, Giovanni remained. He held her hand, his thumb slowly stroking its back. His gaze never left her face. Even when she turned away, he still watched her. Every time she turned back, he was there, his gaze gentle with understanding.

His rhythmic caress of her hand was a point of symmetry, of clarity in the chaos of her body, mind and soul. Her gaze locked with his, she held on to his hand and mimicked his touch with her thumb. The slow, steady pace calmed. Her rapid heartbeat slowed, her roiling stomach eased, her careening thoughts coalesced into a quiet chant. *I am a Beloved Child of The Universe. I am watched over this day and forever more.*

Tranquility replaced the churning emotions.

Giovanni witnessed the internal battle Gabriella waged. What he wanted more than anything was to pull her into his arms and make the pain and turmoil disappear. Instead he watched and looked for any sign that his words could be welcomed. It was very obvious they weren't initially welcomed, but perhaps, in time, they could be.

When the shaking stopped, when she held his hand and matched his stroke with her thumb, hope swelled. Maybe?

Chaos was powerful and it always felt as if it was stronger than symmetry, than peace but that was a myth. Symmetry and peace were also powerful. The ancients used symmetry to create peace through their drawings, buildings and observations of the world around them.

When she drew quiet, he knew she'd conquered chaos.

Not sure what to do next, he waited. What was a few more minutes after all these years? Not that it was easy to do. Words flew through his mind but he held them in.

Because he was studying her so closely, he saw the slight sag of her shoulders, the minute nod of her head. But even with some warning, her words stunned.

"Please hold me."

Three simple words that were as magical as if she'd said 'I love you'.

Moving slowly he shifted, drawing her into his arms. Again he cupped her head to his chest, moved so his free arm encircled her back. He shifted again, reclining on the couch with her tucked against him. Pulling the throw from the back of the couch, he covered them both because the fire was dying out and he did not want the cool night air to disturb this time with her.

"I-I-I can't do more." The words were muffled against his shirt.

"You don't have to do more. Allowing me to hold you is the gift you give me tonight."

"I-I-I-".

"Shh, there is nothing more that must be said tonight. I hold you, maybe we fall asleep or maybe we don't. When it is enough, you tell me and I let you go." Inwardly he added 'for now'.

Gabriella's breathing slowed and she melted against him. She was just low enough on his chest that he couldn't easily kiss the top of her head without moving. He settled for finger combing her curls and massaging her scalp.

Giovanni relished her weight and breathed deeply of her jasmine scent. She hadn't dashed out into the night. Instead she had stayed and asked him for comfort. She was safe with him and from what he knew of her background that was another gift she'd bestowed on him.

Somewhere in the wee hours of the night, he fell asleep hopeful that in the light of day, they could move forward and create the relationship that worked for both of them, that allowed them to marry and create a family. A warning bell sounded in the back of his mind as sleep won out.

A New Path

The consistent thrumming was the first sound Gabriella registered. Approaching soft footsteps came next followed by whispered Italian and then receding footsteps. Warmth enveloped her. A soft fabric under her cheek, a warm hand on her back.

As her brain catalogued the sounds and textures, her body remained relaxed, at rest. Scanning her physical self, Gabriella sighed when no sign of distress or fear much less panic surfaced.

There was no time in her life that she could remember feeling safe and relaxed in a man's arms. Sexually sated? Yes. Being sexually sated and feeling safe and relaxed were very different. This new way, to her at least, of being with someone, being with a man was not as difficult as she'd imagined it might be.

Why?

Because we're friends.

That was part of it, but there was so much more. She trusted Giovanni. Trusted that if she said she wanted nothing more from their relationship than what they had, he'd honor that without pushing. Trusted that he would still be her friend and would still hold her if she asked. Trusted that she could remain here and finish *Holly's Story* and even return to write again.

Even if he went on to another relationship, she thought they could still be friends. *But would either of us want that? It would take a special woman to welcome another woman.*

She thought of Michael and Shannon and knew it could be done. Elizabeth and Shannon had become friends themselves and because of Shannon, Elizabeth was able to have the life she wanted with Michael and Maeve and also serve The Lady.

But Elizabeth is special. She's always been compassionate and caring while I—?

The thought was interrupted by a rumbled under her ear. Her lips quirked and she lifted her head. "I think someone is hungry."

"Someone is hungry and I believe you are too." He patted her back and dropped the hand that had rested on her curls to his side.

Disappointment swirled when Gabriella was gently moved to the side and Giovanni shifted to stand. He stood beside the couch and stretched, male muscle disguised in rumpled clothing.

She saw the dark shadow on his face as he turned toward her and, bending, dropped a kiss on her forehead. The scratchy beard gone before it fully registered. Gabriella reached up and ran her fingers over his chin.

"*Si*, I need shave. Shave, shower, clean clothes." He sniffed under his arm. "I return when I'm presentable." He pivoted and strode away. Away to the stairs where he charged up them taking two at a time. He was whistling as he crossed the upstairs corridor to his room in the wing opposite hers.

Snuggling down under the throw, Gabriella stared at the fireplace. Not even embers glowed but she still felt a warmth coursing through her. There were nights she slept well. There were nights with no nightmares. But there were never nights when she woke so slowly, so sure of her safety. Even in her own place with the doors locked and the alarm on, she woke with a start. But not this morning.

What time was it?

She didn't even know but what was more telling, she didn't even care. When was the last time she was so comfortable with just being?

The closest I come is when I'm at a Women of the 14th Moon ceremony or in Ireland with The Lady. Of course The Circle is with me but then, they are with me in Fremont and yet I'm never this content. Always there is an undercurrent of alertness, of awareness or readiness.

The footsteps on the stairs warned her she was not alone. Looking in that direction, she witnessed Giovanni coming down the stairs, his feet bare, his whiskers gone and his dark brown hair still damp from his shower. His shirt tucked into the low hung waist of his jeans. He was magnificent and part of that magnificence was in his casual manner.

He stopped at the bottom of the stairs and let his gaze roam over her. A smile tipped the corners of his mouth and lit up his eyes.

"You are still abed?"

"I'm still acouch," she said and struggled out of the throw and onto her feet. "And now I'm up."

"You are up and beautiful."

"I am up and a mess."

He took a step in her direction. She saw when he changed his mind and, instead, headed for the small room where they ate breakfast.

"I'll be there shortly." She headed for the stairs without looking back. It crossed her mind he liked the mussed look of her although, once she was in her room and looked in the mirror she couldn't understand why.

A quick shower later, she dressed but before heading downstairs she stopped to look in the glass. Her auburn curls ran rampant. As she ran her fingers through her unruly hair, she saw herself as never before.

Something has changed. I'm different. I can see it in the mirror. I wonder... . She let the thought drift away. An eagerness in her step, she headed to the stairs and breakfast with Giovanni.

Halfway down she stopped as *what if's* assailed her. I have choices and whatever I choose, I know Giovanni will support me. But—no, I don't have to decide now if we will ever be lovers. I know in my heart he will never physically, mentally or emotionally force himself on me. I am truly safe.

With that thought uppermost in her mind, Gabriella completed her way down the stairs and crossed to the breakfast room. As she entered, Giovanni rose as he always did. This time she approached him, raised on her tiptoes and kissed his cheek before sitting down on his right.

Giovanni's hesitation was slight but she noticed it. *"Buon giorno, amore."*

"Buon giorno," she replied.

Use Your Words

Giovanni sat when Gabriella did. Not sure what to do next, he picked up his coffee cup and after taking a drink, started back on his breakfast. Usually Gabriella had fresh squeezed orange juice and tea with either a croissant, muffin or toast. Today she asked for two eggs scrambled on the dry side along with a croissant as well as her juice and tea.

"Your plans for the day?" Gabriella asked when the gnawing hunger was somewhat abated.

"I go to Rome."

Startled and instantly on guard, Gabriella wrapped an arm around her waist her free hand clutching her tea.

Giovanni reached for the hand nearest him, the one wrapped around the mug. Instead of taking her hand, he rested his on her arm. "I have two clients to see. I be back tomorrow night." His chocolate brown gaze held her hazel one. "You know what I want between us. I will miss you but it is good for us to be apart for a short time so you have space to see what you want for us." He kept his eyes on her, a soft smile tipped his lips. "I am a mere man and to be here while you decide would try my control."

She started to pull away.

He let her go.

"I know myself and I would want to influence you to my way of thinking. This way, you have time and space to come to your own decision." He pushed back from the table. "I finish packing now but I will see you before I leave."

Gabriella's heart thudded, her hands shook. *He is leaving me!* She argued with herself. *No, he is giving me time and space.* But the cold crept from her toes upwards.

Finished with her breakfast, at least all she could eat, Gabriella padded to the living room. Sitting on the couch in front of the cold fireplace, she waited. A part of her wanted to go upstairs, go to his room and tell him to stay that she desperately wanted him to stay but the saner part of her knew he was right. She did need time. She wasn't sure she could be his lover even though she thought she was in love with him.

A dry sobbing laugh erupted. Gabriella clamped a hand over her mouth to stem the hysteria that threatened.

When Giovanni came down the stairs, suitcase in hand, she rose and met him at the bottom. He didn't reach out to touch her, to hold her hand, to give her a hug.

Defensive, Gabriella's voice was harsh when she said, "So no hugs, no hand holding? You're just going to walk out?"

"If you want hug, I give you one. If you want me to hold your hand, I will. But I need to hear the words, Gabriella. I will not impose what I want on you."

She stood like a silent statue, immobile except for a beating heart and words screaming in her mind. Her feet were itchy as if they needed to move but the only direction she wanted was forward.

It occurred to her that he was hanging on to his control by a thread and if she leaned in, kissed him with passion, palmed his penis, she could change his mind about leaving. The image was hot in her head and her own body responded to it. With concentration, she pulled back because he mattered. She did not want to lose whatever they might create by using the old tricks she'd used to survive on the streets.

She reached out and took his free hand. "I'd like to walk with you, like this to your car." She nodded toward their joined hands. And I'd like a hug before you leave."

Giovanni closed his hand around hers and tugged her closer. "I would like that too."

After stowing his bag in the trunk, Giovanni leaned against his vehicle. Taking her hand, he guided her closer until she was standing between his legs. His arms enveloped her in a warm hug. "Is this what you wanted?" His chin rested against her forehead, his voice husky.

Gabriella nodded.

"I must go or I be late."

Gabriella pulled away. "May the Goddess be with you. May you come back to me safely." She reached for him, wanted desperately to kiss him, saw the desire flare in his eyes and instead of stepping forward, took a step back.

"Your words, Gabriella. Use your words." His gaze burned and her face flushed.

"I can't. I can't ask yet."

His mouth opened to tell her she could demand instead of ask but he let it go. He wanted her forever but she had to decide and be clear enough she could ask or demand. He cared not a whit which way.

In his car, he backed around and headed out. His last view of her was of her standing in the drive, her hand on her lips.

What was she to do with herself until tomorrow night? Ideas for the direction of Holly's story popped up in her brain. The idea of going up to her room to write cancelled all her creativity.

"Does Miss need something?" Margretta asked.

"I'm just thinking. I need to write but I don't want to be in my room right now."

"Miss can write here. Silvio will build up the fire and I can bring tea and scones."

Gabriella looked around but didn't see any place that would work. She shook her head and sighed.

"You can put your computer here." Margretta pointed to the sofa table. "There is a chair that suits so it is a good height. *Signore* builds it so he can enjoy a meal in front of the fire without leaning over low table."

"I'll get my laptop." Gabriella trotted up the stairs, a spring in her step. *Maybe I'll find my own answers as I write Holly's Story today.*

Holly's Story

HOLLY'S GAZE FOCUSED ON SIMON'S FACE. "I KNOW. THAT'S WHEN I KNEW HOW SPECIAL YOU ARE AND HOW MUCH I WANT YOU IN MY LIFE."

HE SLIPPED HIS ARMS AROUND HER AND HELD HER CLOSE.

SHE MELTED INTO HIS EMBRACE AND HELD ON TIGHT.

HE RESTED HIS CHEEK AGAINST HER HAIR.

SHE SIGHED.

THE DOOR OPENED. "YOU TWO NEED TO COME IN." DOC S SAID IN A STERN TONE.

HOLLY'S FACED FLUSHED WITH EMBARRASSMENT BUT WHEN SHE LOOKED AT DOC, SHE SAW A SMILE DANCING IN HER EYES.

WITH SIMON HOLDING HER HAND, HOLLY WALKED INTO THE CLINIC READY TO TALK TO THE POLICE, READY TO SUPPORT ENID, READY TO FACE A NEW FUTURE. THE WARMTH OF HIS HAND HOLDING HERS SENT THE MESSAGE THAT HER FUTURE COULD HAVE SIMON BY HER SIDE.

Gabriella read the last paragraphs she'd written of Holly's Story. No, she couldn't leave it here and type "The End". But where to take the story? That was her dilemma.

Settled in the chair, her laptop situated on the sofa table, she stared into the flames now dancing before her, hoping inspiration would come.

Her fingers settled on the keys and without looking she began to type.

Holly trudged into her apartment building and up the stairs to her apartment on the second floor. Even though she was exhausted, it was easier to walk up a flight of stairs than wait for the ancient elevator to creak and groan from floor to floor. All she wanted was a hot shower and sleep.

Unlocking the door, she entered, shrugged out of her jacket and dropped her bag on the floor. She kicked off her shoes and by stepping on the toes of her socks, pulled her feet free. Hands on the snaps to her jeans, she paused when her phone rang.

"Hello?" She continued to take the pants off while holding the phone to her ear.

"I'm really tired, Simon. It's been a long and stressful day. A hot shower and bed…"

She padded into the bathroom and awkwardly worked her shirt over her head. With it hanging around her neck, she bent to turn the water on.

"Yes, you are hearing water running. I said I was tired and taking a shower and going to bed." Holly heard her own voice. It wasn't a pleasant tone and her words were clipped.

"I do hear that you miss me and want to see me."

"No, I'm not saying I don't want to see you. I just need to take a shower and go to bed. Simon, please listen. I just want—." Frustration edged her voice. "Okay, if you insist, come on over but remember, I only want a shower and sleep. Nothing else."

Simon had heard her, had held her as she fell asleep but somewhere during the night, he'd started to make love with her. She pushed him away but he persuaded her that she wanted what he wanted.

When she woke up, he was still there looking very pleased with himself. "You always sleep better after making love."

Did she? Holly only knew she needed to shower before she dressed and she was running late. Starting the day stressed out and in a rush was not what she wanted.

When Simon started into the bathroom to "help" with her morning shower, Holly's distress erupted. "Get away from me! Don't touch me!"

Simon's confusion was written all over his face from his question marked brow to his open mouth stare. "Hey Babe, what's wrong?"

"I'm late and I still have to shower and you want to have sex. What do you see wrong with that picture?"

"I thought you liked having sex with me?"

"That isn't the question, Simon, and you know it. I'm standing here as the clock is ticking and you can't see that pressuring me to have sex with you is a problem?"

Simon strode to the door. "Fine. If you don't want me, I can deal with it." The door slammed behind him.

Holly stood in the doorway to the bathroom, tears streaming down her cheeks. Slowly she turned into the room, turned on the water and stepped into the shower. *Am I wrong to not always want to have sex with someone, even if I like them?*

As she dried off another thought crowded in. "I know Simon was really angry but if I invite him over for dinner and then offer him sex, maybe he'll forgive me."

When she got to work, Simon was already there and busy at the computer. No welcoming words or smile, not even a wave. He was polite, business like and when she suggested they have dinner that night, at her place so his roommate wouldn't interfere, he declined.

The week was long and strained. At the end of it, she again tried to talk to him but he brushed her off with "What did you think would happen when you kicked me out? Did you expect me to come back begging?"

"No, I didn't expect that. But I thought we could talk about what happened and why."

His response? "I know what happened and I don't care why."

That evening Holly started looking for another job. The program was set up and because of Seth, she wasn't doing the street outreach.

On Saturday she called both Doc S and Mrs. W about being references. Vague about why she was looking, neither woman pushed.

Tuesday, Mrs. W came into the center to talk to her about her job search.

"What are you looking for?" A fundamental question that had a plethora of answers.

"I need to get away from the streets. I don't know what I can do but I know I can learn or even go back to school."

"Come to dinner tonight. My husband has some ideas but it would be best if you talked directly to him."

"And I wouldn't be working down here, I mean downtown where I might be seen?"

"No, Holly, you would be far away from here. I doubt any of the people you know from here would ever be where you might work."

"I'll come. What time?"

"I'll pick you up outside at 4:30."

Holly's life changed that evening. Mr. W. worked for a large construction company that did work around the world. They had entry level positions that she could easily do because she was familiar with Word, Excel and Power Point programs. That night she completed the application on the Waterson's computer.

Two days later she had an interview and was offered a job in the communications department, a fancy name for the mail room. That afternoon she gave her two week notice both on her job and her apartment.

She would be working out by the airport and the commute from her apartment would be long. The Waterson's offered her a place to stay for a month while she got her bearings, got two paychecks and found a new place.

Life was good.

Holly blew out the candles on the birthday cake. She was twenty-five years old, had a career, new friends and a new place to live. Her work ethic and determination to learn all she could had been noticed. Now she was working in the proposal unit where they scoured the internet and trade papers for information about new construction contracts. Once identified, they checked out whether it was a good fit. One of the things she liked about this company was they only went after business where they excelled.

She had friends and money in the bank because she lived a simple life. Holly purchased a new-to-her car when she'd saved enough to pay cash. She regularly shopped sales and thrift stores but most importantly, she lived with one foot out the door. Moving at the drop of a hat was just what she did.

Since taking this new job she'd moved twice. It seems with the light rail system, homeless youth did not just stay downtown. Both times, she'd been packed and out of her apartment within the hour. Staying in motels until she found another apartment, debating whether a smaller complex was safer than a large one, she'd finally decided smaller suited her. It was easier to notice someone new.

More than satisfied with the life she'd constructed for herself, Holly celebrated her twenty-fifth birthday and three plus years off the streets. Doc S and Mrs. W were there along with Mr. W. Studying her old social worker's marriage had become a habit. It wasn't that everything was always roses. She knew they had disagreements but they never seemed to really fight and she was positive they didn't hit each other.

Why hadn't Doc S gotten married? Why hadn't the Waterson's ever had children? She still had her secrets, experiences she'd never shared with anyone, so while she was curious, she never asked.

Lots of cake and ice cream left over because they'd had a wonderful Thai dinner courtesy of Mr. W. Sitting around the Waterson's family room, a fire blazing in the hearth, Holly felt her life was complete. What more could she ask for? She had a home, was safe, had a job she enjoyed and was good at.

Out of the corner of her eye, she saw Mr. W give Mrs. W a kiss on the cheek and put his arms around her. He kissed her temple and she snuggled against him.

The pain was swift and sharp. No, her life was not complete and never would be. While she longed to have someone hold her in his arms and kiss her brow, she'd have to trust him to only go as far as she wanted.

Never did she want to have sex with a man because he wanted it when she didn't.

Never did she want to have sex with a man in payment for dinner or drinks or dancing.

Never did she want to have sex with a man who didn't respect her at the very least and love her at the very best.

Never—."

Gabriella stopped mid-sentence, tears streaming down her face, dropping off her chin, dampening her shirt. There were a few other "never" but this was the crux of the matter. She wanted desperately to be loved but even more, to feel safe and respected. Without that. Without a certainty that he would listen to her—.

She made sure she saved what she'd written and then powered off her laptop. The mug of tea was cold but the fire still burned brightly.

Getting up, intending to go to the kitchen and fix a fresh pot of tea, she was met by Margretta.

"I get your tea. You rest on the couch."

Gabriella did just that. She pulled the throw from the back and wrapped it around her shoulders. Tucking her feet under her, she let the tension from writing about Holly ease. Giovanni's clove and sandalwood scent clung to the blanket and soothed. *If he was here?* If he was here, she could talk to him. He'd listen and maybe comment but most important, he would listen and maybe ask her questions. He'd only comment if she asked.

She trusted what he said to her about this story.

It wasn't the same, being wrapped in a blanket that smelled of him but that was all she had right now. Footsteps announced Margretta's return.

Coming around the end of the couch, a tray in her hands, a smile on her face, she said, "Signore say to take good care of you."

She set down the tray on the low table and poured a mug of tea. Also on the tray was a covered dish. With a flourish, she removed the cover. "Adolfo says this will help. Everything is better with this."

Gabriella laughed as her eyes beheld one of the biggest pieces of tiramisu she'd ever seen. "Tell him he's right. I already feel better and I've yet to take a bite."

Picking up the plate, she took a forkful of the decadent dessert in her mouth. A soft moan escaped as she relished the sweet amaretto-flavored cream and cake. As she ate a second bite, the pain from the insights she'd gained from *Holly's Story* faded. Giovanni would be home tomorrow night. She had about twenty-four hours to find the words to tell him what she wanted.

Finding Their Way

The bedraggled man who came in the door bore no resemblance to the Giovanni Migliori she knew. Never had she seen him look so tired, so disheveled, so—. Something horrible must have happened while he was gone.

His staff appeared and were even now divesting him of coat and suitcase. He remained just inside the door as if he wasn't sure whether to even come the rest of the way in.

Gabriella approached him, slipped her arms around his neck and raised on her tiptoes to kiss his cheek. Her lips registered he hadn't shaved.

"Come." She took him by the hand and led him to the couch.

"Sit." Her hands on his shoulders, she urged him down.

Gabriella curled next to him, wrapped him in her arms and waited, waited for the tension in his body to abate, waited for words to help her understand what had happened, what she could do.

After minutes of silence, his tension had not ebbed. Clearly out of her element, Gabriella considered calling for help from his staff. For an unknown to her reason, that didn't feel right so she improvised.

"I've done a lot of thinking since you left yesterday. Thinking and writing and eating sum up how I've spent my time. It won't surprise you that Adolfo fixed tiramisu but what might surprise you is the size of the piece he sent me after you left. The biggest piece of tiramisu I've ever seen and," she paused for dramatic effect, "I ate every bite. It probably is a good thing you weren't here because I'm not sure I would have shared. But then, if you were here Adolfo wouldn't have given me such a large piece.

"I wrote a couple new chapters and I did started reading *Holly's Story* from the beginning. So many spelling and grammatical errors. When I stopped for the day, I had more notes on where the story might go next. When you are rested, you can tell me which one you think will work best.

"You gave me lots to think about. You told me to use my words and while I've thought of many, many words saying them out loud is really hard. But I've practiced them in my head and whispered them to myself.

"I'm rattling on and on because I'm worried about you and I don't know what to do right now."

Gabriella rested her head on his rock-like shoulder. She'd wager not an iota of tension had subsided from his body. An idea struck and she shifted to move away.

His hand gripped her shoulder.

"I'm not leaving. I have something for you I think you'll like but I need a little space."

When his hand relaxed, she knelt, and taking his arm from around her, placed it on his lap. Standing, she pulled the foot stool over and sat. Bending, she removed his shoes and socks.

Picking up his right foot, she started a rhythmical massage of his foot.

"You may not know this, but Elizabeth and I took a beginning reflexology class together to learn how to give foot massages. That was many years ago and I may be a bit rusty but I think, well, I hope this will help whatever is bothering you.

"Did you know that there's a place on your foot that corresponds to every point on your body?" One by one she flexed his toes before she pressed the knuckles of her fingers into the ball of his foot. "I use my knuckles because my hands aren't as strong and deeper pressure on these points is best."

Her head down, she concentrated on what she was doing, giving him a running commentary so he'd know what to expect. At one point his foot twitched. She smoothed her hand over where she'd been working.

When she'd finished with his right foot and before she started on his left, she looked up.

Giovanni's slitted eyes gleamed. His face was still darkened from his beard, he was still disheveled but the exhaustion or whatever had weighed him down when he'd come in the door had eased.

"Better?"

"*Si.*" His voice was as soothing as a sip of hot dark chocolate.

"Well, then, I'll just take care of this foot." She patted his left foot. "You do know it isn't good to only work on one side of your body and not the other. It throws things out of whack. Be sure and let me know if you want me to do a little more in one place or a little less in another."

Head bent she diligently worked the same pattern she'd used on the right foot.

He watched her.

Even with her head bent she knew for a certainty he watched her. In some ways she'd always known when he watched her, when he entered or left a room, where he was in proximity to her. What had for so long been frightening now comforted.

When she finished ministering to his left foot, she looked up. His eyes were closed, his breathing deep. Whatever had been plaguing him was no longer visible on his face or in his posture.

Gabriella rose and made sure both of his feet were securely on the foot stool. The throw she'd been wrapped in when he arrived was still on the corner of the couch. She shook it out and laid it over him. A lock of hair had fallen across his forehead. She brushed it back, sifting her fingers through his soft locks.

Curling her feet under her, she sat sideways on the couch the better to watch him as he slept. To her, he'd always been sinfully handsome but more than the external looks with which he was abundantly blessed, there was a goodness she'd seen even in the beginning. That goodness had terrified her and while it still intimidated, she trusted that when she said her words, regardless of how he heard them, he would be kind.

He stirred and his hand, which had been under the throw was now resting on her knee. Not grabbing or groping, just there. The heat of his palm penetrated her jeans and the warmth radiated up her leg and settled deep inside.

She allowed her imagination to run free with pictures of lying with him, both naked, their legs entwined, lips feasting on lips, hands questing to learn each other's body. Her gaze locked on his face, focused on his lips. It took all her willpower not to lean in and kiss him awake.

He needs his rest. As those words resounded in her mind, his eyes opened. The first seconds of confusion vanished when he caught sight of her.

"You are here," he said in a sleep-graveled voice.

"Yes, I am here. I've practiced my words and tomorrow I will say them to you."

"Come." Giovanni reached for her. "Come be with me here."

He pushed the throw aside and angled himself on the couch so his back was in the corner. Swinging his legs up, he patted the place between his body and the back of the couch. "This way you don't fall off when I move."

"Does that mean, you'll fall off when you move?" Gabriella grinned.

"If I move too much, *si*, I will fall to the floor but you will be safe." He beckoned to her.

She moved to nestled between him and the couch. "We've done this before."

"*Si*, I slept very well that night."

"If that is so, you left as soon as you could the next day."

"In the morning I listen to your words and you listen to mine, *si*?" Giovanni arranged the throw to cover them.

"*Si*, in the morning." Gabriella closed her eyes and shifted to a more comfortable spot. A smile blossomed on her face and she sighed.

"You laugh?"

"No, I sighed. Sort of a hiccup sigh."

"You explain?"

Gabriella struggled until she sat up, leaning forward she folded her arms on Giovanni's chest. "Do you know the last time I slept in the arms of man? Really slept?"

His gaze darkened, a frown appeared between his brows. "Do I want to know?"

She rose up and kissed his cheek. "Two nights ago, right here with you."

Settling back, she rested her hand on his chest. He covered it with his with own. His breath ruffled her curls and then his lips pressed against the top of her head. Some yet unreleased tension slipped away and he held her loosely in his arms.

As she drifted off to sleep, her wish was for the chaos of her past life to not interfere with now. In her mind's eye she conjured up the image of the spruce cone and relaxed into dreams of being in Italy with Giovanni.

Confessions

The urge to stay snuggled and sleep or at least pretend to sleep was strong but fortified by a peaceful night, Gabriella opened her eyes. She knew he was already awake, could feel the alertness in his body even though his hold of her was gentle. The image she'd held in her mind as she woke, still lingered. Her personal totem, the blue jay sitting on her spruce cone.

It had been some time since she'd seen her totem, felt its energy. Each of them had personal totems. Lily's was the lioness, Elizabeth's the swan and Diana's was a Siamese cat. Ashley's dragonfly totem had been critical to her beating back the cancer and Hunter's stork had helped her through the time when Logan was missing. Sophia's was the blue bird. Even though she and Sophia's totem sounded almost the same, they represented very different traits and protections.

Because her personal totem and what she was beginning to call her work were together, confidence that she was on the right path and could accomplish what she'd planned all day yesterday soared.

Tilting her head, she opened her eyes. Her gaze took in the thicker bristles of his darker beard surrounding sculpted lips. His dark brown hair was sticking out in random directions except for the one lock that seemed to always fall over his forehead.

His eyes opened and reflected the smile now curving his mouth. *"Buon Giorno."*

"Buon Giorno to you." She reached up and caressed his whiskered cheeks, the texture of beard across her finger tips a mixture of prickle and tickle.

"Will you kiss me so I know how it feels to be kissed with your face covered in whiskers?"

He took her hand and kissed her finger tips before shifting his weight and looming over her.

Panic slammed into her and Gabriella kicked and scratched, pushed and shoved, writhed to put her knee in his groin.

Giovanni pulled back, slipped off the couch and knelt beside it. He never let go of her hand.

Her breathing harsh, her stomach in turmoil, blood pumped through her veins like a bilge pump trying to keep afloat a boat filling with water.

His gaze never wavered in the neutral mask he'd put on his face but his eyes. In his eyes she saw what? Pity? Disgust? Shaking her head to clear the words, she looked again and saw compassion and concern.

"I'm—," he cut her words off with the index finger of his free hand.

"You owe me no apologies. I owe you one."

She held onto his hand still by her face. "I practiced the words but I'm not sure how many of them I can say to you."

He rose to stand. "I sit again?"

She scooted around so she sat as she had before, legs tucked to the side and looked at him as he slanted his body onto the couch facing her.

"I listen to whatever you can say."

Gabriella glanced toward the fireplace before bringing her gaze back to him.

"When I was seven, one of my mother's boyfriends wanted me to touch him. He made it seem like a game. What could I do to make him grow? That sort of thing. At seven I didn't really understand what was happening but one day my mother walked in. She was furious—at me.

"I was sent to live with a friend of hers. After a couple of months, I went back to my mother's because the boyfriend had left. You must understand, she didn't send me away to protect me. She saw me as competition.

"When I was ten, another boyfriend tried to rape me. I screamed and screamed. A neighbor called the police. I was taken into protective custody and put in foster care. I wasn't obedient. I didn't like being there. An older boy in the home tried to seduce me.

"The courts sent me home. This was my life for the next five years. Mother's boyfriends coming on to me. I was raped by one when I was thirteen. Terrified I'd become pregnant, I ran away. Of course I was found almost immediately and was in foster care less than a week before returned home. Mother knew how the system worked and had kicked the guy out.

"By the time I was fifteen, I'd run away a dozen times staying away for longer and longer periods. I figured out how to survive for a day, then two days and then a week. When mother brought a new guy home, introduced us and then said she was tired and went to bed, shutting the door, I knew she would never protect me. I excused myself, went into my room and shut the door. I propped a chair under the knob like I'd seen on television but also pushed the dresser partway in front of it. I got out my backpack and stuffed it with clothes and some money I'd taken from my mother's purse over the course of several months. I had about thirty dollars.

"He did try the door handle but when the door didn't easily open, he stopped. I imagined him sitting outside waiting for me to come out. Terrified and angry, I went out the bedroom window. I never looked back. I've never been home and I've never seen my mother since."

Gabriella's heart pounded, nausea threatened. She wiped her sweating hands on the knees of her pants. Her breathing was rapid as if she'd just run, sprinted away from evil. She'd kept her eyes open and pointed toward Giovanni but the images of the past had taken over and she stared in his direction unseeing.

"Living on the streets—I know I didn't really have more control but it felt like it. For a girl to survive, she has sex with guys who have money or a place to stay or extra food. That is really the only thing she has to offer, her only value unless she can panhandle or is lucky and gets a job. At fifteen, I needed a work permit, needed my parents to sign permission. I did have my high school identification card but that really didn't count and I was no longer going to that school—no longer going to any school.

"I hooked up with different guys. By the time I was eighteen, I was very street savvy. I knew my way around the streets and alleys, could spot a cop blocks away. I had also started going to the homeless youth drop in center. I'd met Dr. S because I'd been sick a couple of times.

"This one guy had wanted me for a few months. I didn't really like him. There was something about him I didn't trust. But when the guy I was currently with was beaten up and in the hospital, I was alone and had no protection."

The shaking had started when she began talking about her life when she turned eighteen. The bile rose so swiftly into her throat she knew she was going to hurl the contents of her stomach all over the couch and the man still sitting quietly across from her. Hand on her mouth she bolted. She barely made it to the guest bathroom around the corner from the stairs.

Giovanni found her half-propped against the wall, her head resting on the toilet. His heart ached for her, for what she'd endured as a child. He stood in the doorway leaning to the side so as not to block the entire space.

"I help now?"

No bright, liveliness shone in her hazel eyes, just pure misery.

He decided to take no answer for a possible 'yes' and stepped into the room. Dampening a small towel, he squatted down so he was eye level with her and handed it to her. She looked at it as if she couldn't figure out what it was or what to do with it.

"I help." He took the towel and first wiped the sweaty hair back from her face before continuing to gently erase the tracks of tears and vomit. "Better?" When she didn't answer, he stood and got a glass from the counter, filled it with a couple of inches of water. "Rinse your mouth and you will feel better." He handed it to her, keeping his hand around hers to help her raise the glass.

Giovanni grabbed two large bath towels from the rack by the shower and tossed them over his shoulder. Bending down, he took Gabriella's hands and in a quiet voice said, "Come with me now. It is best if we leave this room."

The pain of seeing her so lost, so alone welled tears in his eyes. He slipped an arm around her back, his hand under her arm and lifted. She looked up at him with unseeing eyes. He whispered in Italian hoping to assure her she was safe. Once she was standing, he took a chance and picked her up. Carrying her back to the couch, he sat down with her on his lap. He placed the towels so that if she were sick again, she didn't have to dash to the bathroom. Cupping her head with one hand, he guided it down to his shoulder. He stroked her back with his free hand.

"*Mio Gabriella. Mia amore. Sei al sicuro.* You are safe. *Insieme si proteggiamo da ogni male.* We protect you from all harm."

But There Is More

The steady beat in her ear soothed, the rhythmic caress on her back comforted. Heat from his embrace and wonderment warmed banishing the cold from her body. Giovanni had not dismissed or left her. He had not turned away from her.

"You are better?" The breath from his voice feathered across her face.

She nodded not yet trusting her voice.

"You humble me with the gift of your words."

He didn't move but she knew something had changed. Of course something had changed. He knew her past. She was grateful he hadn't pushed her away but gratitude wasn't what she wanted to feel. *We will still be friends.* She told herself that was enough. She'd be able to visit him and write if she wanted. They could spend time together without her spitting at him. Now that he knew almost everything... .

She sighed blinking back tears. It was easier and harder than she'd imagine. In some ways she was more prepared to see disgust on his face, to see him stand up and walk away from her than to see caring and compassion in his eyes—or was it pity?

Gabriella shifted in order to look deep into his dark brown eyes. No, it wasn't pity she saw. His intense gaze was warm and inviting. She didn't even see compassion. As she searched his gaze for answers, he dipped his head and kissed her forehead.

Her stomach growled or maybe it was his. He grinned. "We are hungry. It is time to break our fast, *si*?"

Was that going to be it? They'd just move on to breakfast?

Something must have shown on her face because he leaned closer and whispered, "We eat and then we talk. Maybe I shower and shave and then we eat and talk?"

Recognizing that when she lost the contents of her stomach, some had splashed on her shirt, Gabriella concurred with that idea.

"*Si*, we shower and then eat."

Giovanni's smile transformed his beard darkened face. "Your Italian is *molto bene*."

"*Grazie*."

She scrambled off the couch, the cool air emphasizing the loss of his heat. Together they walked up the stairs. At the top, he turned toward his room in the other wing and she continued the short trip to her room.

The door closed behind her, she stripped off her clothes and without looking in the mirror, turned on the shower and stepped in. She stood underneath the water, her skin pinkish red from the heat and pulsing water. Her warm body clean and revived, she turned off the water and stepped onto the mat. Wrapping a towel around her body and another one around her hair, she slathered lotion on her arms, legs and face. Towel drying her hair, she finger combed the curls pulling them back from her face with bobby pins.

A clean pair of jeans and a long sleeved silvery green shirt were pulled on over clean underwear. Slipping her feet into slippers, she pulled the pins from her hair pleased the curls remained in place. A deep breath followed by a deep knee bend, Gabriella opened the door to her balcony. Another deep breath of the fresh sea-soaked air helped calm her now racing heart. Always she'd known if she found the courage to tell him, she'd have to see him afterwards.

Closing the door she let her gaze travel the room. If she left here in a hurry, what would she take and what would she leave behind? She'd accumulated more here than in most places but what was more important, everything she'd added to her life here had a memory attached. The new clothes she had were ones she'd bought while shopping with Giovanni. There were also a couple of things he'd bought and given to her as gifts.

A framed picture of the view from her balcony. She'd have to take it out of the frame or leave it behind. Pain sliced through her heart because she knew Giovanni had made the frame from driftwood off the beach…made it just for her.

The soft knock on her door drew her out of the misery of having to decide what to take and what to leave behind. A wave of despair and exhaustion swept over her.

"Gabriella? I am opening the door on the count of three."

"*Uno.*

"*Due.*

"*Tre.*"

"I'm coming in."

The first thing Giovanni noticed when he opened the door was Gabriella, standing in the middle of the room, a forlorn look on her face. It tore at his heart to see her looking so lost and alone. Did she even know he was there? In that moment he questioned his drive to know about her past if this was what the memories did to her.

"I don't know what to take and what to leave behind." Her look of dismay, of confusion hastened his steps to her side.

"You can take it all, even the furniture if you want it." His heart squeezed and his lungs seized.

"No, you don't understand." She turned to face him. "I only take what I can carry."

"You explain please because I do not understand this."

"If they find me, I have to be able to leave quickly. I can only take what I can carry or take to my car in one or two trips or they'll catch me."

He risked caressing her cheek with the tips of his fingers. "But you are here, in Italy, with me. They will never find you here. And, it they did, you'd still be able to stay because my staff and I would always protect you. They would never be able to take you away. Ever."

"I want to believe that." She leaned into him. "I want to believe that very much."

"But... ." Calm outwardly, inwardly he seethed with anger. If he ever met her mother, he'd—. He'd be tempted to do something he'd never done before—strike a woman.

Gabriella chewed her lower lip.

He'd never seen her do that before. He'd never seen her so distressed. He'd never felt so unsure of himself.

"Why do you think you'd ever have to leave here?" His breath caught in his lungs as he waited for her answer.

When she lifted her face to him, the dazed look on her face tore at his composure.

"You know about me. Not everything, but almost all."

"And I am honored you trust me enough to give me your words, to tell me your story." He'd rested his hand on her shoulder after skimming her cheek. He lifted it and held her chin in his fingertips, careful to keep his touch gentle. "Do you think I would send you away?"

She nodded.

"I want to hold you in my arms." He moved closer and hugged her to him. "I would never send you away. I love you. I want you for my wife. I want to fall asleep and wake up with you in my arms. There is nothing you've said that would change my mind."

His shirt dampened with her tears as she held on to him.

"Did you not hear me tell you I had sex with men for food? For a place to stay. That I prostituted myself on the streets?"

"I heard you say the words but I never thought of you as a prostitute. I still don't. You were and are a survivor. You did what you did to live. You did what you did to stay safe."

She pulled away. Anger radiated from her stiff body, her fisted hands. "I was never safe. I was beaten and almost died," she screamed. "You don't know. You don't understand."

"And you risk yourself every time you volunteered at the shelter and even more so when you searched for Logan. I only have admiration for what you endured, what you survived. I only thank the good Lord for your determination to live, to leave the streets, to find a new life so I could find you.

"Is it so hard to believe I love you and still want you, still want to marry you?"

Her head bobbed. "So hard, I don't really believe."

What to do? Giovanni had no more words to assure her of his love or, more importantly of her worth. But he did still have words. Words that needed to be spoken. A story that needed to be told.

"We are not through but we take a break. We need food and a little space to find our balance before we talk like this again." He knew she was going to argue. Her chin came up, her eyes blazed and her mouth opened.

"It is my turn." He held out his hand. "I have words to say to you after breakfast." He waited, his hand outstretched.

Her internal debate showed on her face but in the end, she took his hand. No words. Maybe too many had already been said or maybe not enough. They'd know more once they'd eaten and maybe sat on the seawall and watched the waves, or walked through the garden looking at sacred geometry.

His prayer as they descended the stairs hand-in-hand, a foot of space between them, was that at the end of the day, they ascended the steps with their arms around each other's waist.

His Turn To Share

Giovanni forced himself to eat something. He sipped at his coffee and drank his fresh orange juice. It did not escape his notice that Gabriella picked at her food while surreptitiously watching him. Foregoing the sausage, he ate scrambled eggs and toast, thinking that would sit better than something spicy. It was important to him to have a calm stomach. Since that was not happening, he modified that thought to not getting sick.

Too soon and yet not, they finished. He pulled her chair back and offered his hand, pleased when she tentatively took it.

"Where do you want to be now?"

Gabriella saw the wintry sky, the trees bending with the force of the wind but still she said, "I want to walk to the wall and watch the sea."

"We will need coats to stay warm."

She shook her head. "We won't stay long. I just want to see."

Grateful she didn't object, Giovanni grabbed the throw from the back of the couch and wrapped it around her shoulders as they headed toward the French doors leading out to the gardens.

The air was brisk but not as cold as it would be in another month. He hunched his shoulders and strode down the path to the white balustrade agleam in the bright sun. A large urn on the wall acted as a partial windbreak so that is where they stood.

White caps graced the curling edges of the waves. In the distance a spear of sunlight sparkled on the water competing with the rhythmical swing of the beam from the lighthouse. But where they were, the water was dark and foreboding as it dashed against the rocks. Gabriella turned her face up to the sky and lifted her arms above her head.

Giovanni stepped back understanding this was the stance The Circle took when saying prayers. He said one of his own, one that asked for her understanding and them being able to work out their differences.

When she lowered her arms, she turned to him.

"Let's go back in before you get sick." She started back toward the villa a quickness in her steps.

She wants to get this over with. Move forward with her life. The stress of wanting something and not knowing how to achieve it was tearing up his insides. He almost doubled over from the pain in his stomach.

Once inside, he opened his mouth to call for his servant to build a fire when he saw Gabriella wad paper and place it just so. On top of that she added kindling.

"I'll be right back," he said as he started up the stairs. Once in his room, he headed right to the bathroom, thankful he'd made it before he'd lost what breakfast he'd eaten. After making sure his innards were empty, he brushed his teeth. The man in the mirror was him but an earlier version. The version that was unsure of himself, uncertain of his own worth, unsure he'd ever be able to build a life for himself and his family.

Scrubbing a hand over his face, a forced smile on his face, he left the bathroom. He paused by the large king sized bed dominating the room. Walls in neutral colors with splashes of blues and red in fabric pillows. Would she like it here?

"I'm making myself crazy," he muttered to himself as he strode to the door.

At the bottom of the stairs, he turned toward the living area and couch. Gabriella sat cross-legged on the floor in front of the fire staring into the flames. She hadn't even heard him come down the steps.

Clearing his throat he called out to his staff. Silvio's head poked through the door. "*Portare una bottiglia di sidro caldo e qualcosa di leggero da mangiare,*" he said.

When he looked back toward Gabriella, she was watching him.

"I just asked for something hot to drink and something light to eat." He took the few steps to where she sat and, head cocked to the side asked, "Do we sit here or on the couch?"

When she straightened her legs and started to stand, he offered his hand and helped her to her feet very aware that she was totally capable of getting up on her own.

They moved the table to the side so they had an unobstructed view of the fire if they slouched on the couch—which they did. When the mugs of cider along with a bowl of nuts were delivered, they held the warm pottery in both hands blowing gently on the steaming brew. On the marble sofa table, the carafe and bowl of nuts along with napkins and small bowls waited for their attention.

"*Grazie, Silvio,*" Gabriella said.

A smile tilted Giovanni's lips as he heard her unconsciously speak in Italian.

They sat side-by-side, shoulders and thighs inches apart. How he wanted to lean into her and touch but he restrained himself. Now was the time for his words. He only hoped the touching would come later.

"This is not easy for me but I want to tell you these things about me. Of course my family knows most of it but no one else. Not even Jackson knows all.

"My father, he was an alcoholic...not kind or gentle. I'm the oldest and only boy so, I protect my mother and sisters, and put myself in his way. I went to work early in my life so I not always home to do so. Being big for my age helped me get work when I should be in school. But if I hadn't worked, we would have no place to live. We went hungry, but I made sure the rent was paid.

"When I was sixteen, my father died. But I work in construction and now make good money. I put some away after paying the family bills. My mother, she gets a job in a laundry so now I put more away.

"The architect of the building I worked on saw me making some drawings. I was seventeen. He asked me what I was doing. I explain to him the changes I make if it was my building. He took an interest in me and after a few months, apprenticed me to him.

"He was in his sixties, well-respected in the field. He showed me this place. It was falling down with holes in the roof, cracking tiles in the floor and a jungle of vines climbing everywhere. But I fall in love with it. With his help, I bought it and in my spare time, I start fixing it up. The bones are the same but I've touched every surface in every room." He chuckled. "'Touched' maybe a bit misleading because all this," he waved an arm encompassing the room, "has been replastered, retiled, repainted. The fireplace rebuilt. I create new doors and windows. Outside walls must be removed which means the structure altered to support the upper floor."

"You did it all yourself?" Gabriella continued to look at the flames.

"Initially, all the clean-up and demolition was done by me and a couple of friends. You have to understand, I was an apprentice to an architect not an architect myself. I hadn't even finished school.

"But that changed. Venicimo, he insists I finish school so I take night classes and do as he wished. Then he enrolls me in design and drafting classes. Once I pass those, he sponsors me to attend college. He thinks I have talent and I become one of his projects. You see, Venicimo has no children and his wife has died. He is alone.

"By now my mother and oldest sister are working and able to better support themselves so I had more of my income for me. I lived a marginal life because saving money was so important to me.

"When I finish my formal schooling, I'm twenty-three. Vinicimo, he sponsors me and I become licensed as an architect. He turned seventy and one day he says to me. 'I am tired and have done all I can. It is your time.' He kiss my cheeks and walks away. He dies two days later.

"Devastated, terrified, grief-stricken? All those and lost. I have no clients of my own. How am I to go on? He had a will. I was left his tools. Here is hours from Roma and not a safe place for what he leaves me. I pack them up and put them in storage. No space in my one room apartment.

"I tell myself I'm okay. I have money in savings. But it will not last long. I need my own clients. I sit down one night and write out a list of all the clients I remembered from working with

Vinicimo. There were about a dozen names. I think of ways I could build upon that list, how I could approach them for referrals, etc. But then, the wind is knocked from me.

"My mother is diagnosed with cancer. She can no longer work. My oldest sister is married but she and her husband have no extra funds. My two youngest sisters and my mother are at risk of being homeless.

"I move back home and pay the bills. When my savings shrink, I panic.

"All this time I'm not pursuing my list of possible referrals because every day has some new crisis. But our prayers are answered and my mother, she responds to the treatment. We have hope she will recover. And, my sisters take heart and do more.

"Time, it was time to start being an architect. I choose a couple for my first contact. They are polite but not friendly. They will not refer anyone to an untried architect. And, I will not insult my benefactor by pointing out my ideas in their home.

"Next I chose a single woman in her fifties. She seems more interested and suggests we meet again. She say she needs time to think who might be a referral. We met at a ristorante for dinner and, it turned out, drinks. She was sophisticated and very beautiful. I feel very lucky to be seen with her. When she tells me she forgets her list. I follow her home. What happens next shocks me."

He stared into his mug, turned it this way and that, tipped it to one side and the other. When he looked up and gazed into her hazel eyes, shame colored his cheeks.

"I say 'no' to her advances and I walk away. But two days later I learn my mother no longer responds well to the treatment. My life shifted in the minute it took for me to hear that news. How was I going to take care of my family if I had no income?

"I am twenty-five. My family's sole support. The tools of my trade are in a storage locker. My list of possible referral sources has only two possibilities. Both are single women in their forties. While they are married, it was obvious their husbands had moved on with their lives.

"What to do? My oldest sister and her husband are struggling even with her working. My middle sister is in school. Did I want her to drop out? My youngest sister is finishing high school. If they are to have any life at all, they need their education and I need them to help care for our mother."

Giovanni smiled, a soft one of remembering. "I leave out one of my favorite past times. Watching old American movies. Cary Grant, Rock Hudson, Fred Astaire always charmed the girl. Maybe I can charm referrals from lonely women? Not my proudest idea but it was one that I thought would be successful.

"So you see, Gabriella, you are not the only one who used what was available to survive. I am not on the streets like you but…I have a mother and two sisters who depend on me.

"I find what these women most wanted was someone who paid attention to them, held their hand, gave them a hug and a kiss on the cheek. Most do not want nameless sex but they do want exclusivity. This is not something I can promise because I am building my business.

"Explaining to each I cannot make that promise is very difficult. One sobbed and threatened despair. One became angry and threw things at me. But one nodded and accepted that was how it would be. Although we are lovers, it is only a few months, then we become friends.

"To be honest, I have used my looks and charm to my advantage. But never have I taken a woman to bed on a lie. Three years of struggle before my client base is strong and I can breathe, put money away, rent office space. Such pride my chest must have puffed up a few inches when I first ask a client if they want to meet at my office or their place."

He paused, shifted and brought her hand to his lips. His dark gaze met her hazel one. "I know I love you because I never before feel this way about any woman. I know I love you because the idea I never see you again is beyond my ability to grasp. I know I love you because you are the first woman I say these words to.

"Our way forward is to have bumpy spots but together we smooth them out. Make the life we want. You do not have to be in Roma, you can be here and write. I can come here to you. We spend time in Ireland and Fremont or invite everyone here. I have idea for wing of bedrooms to accommodate everyone."

His heart was beating a rapid tattoo and he clutched her hands. Worried he held them too tight, he dropped them.

"Our paths have been different." Gabriella reached out and clasped his hands in hers. "But you have made a success of your life. I would imagine you still provide for your mother and sisters. You still take care of others and it wouldn't surprise me if you've found and mentored others as you were once mentored.

"However, my life is still fraught with terror, with nightmares, with struggles. I don't have the money to support myself forever tucked away in savings and investments. I don't have a home of my own. I don't have—."

He stayed her words with the touch of his fingers on her lips. "You sleep better here than anywhere else other than maybe Ireland. I see the terror fading from you. And, it is better you do not have a home of your own in Fremont because it will be better if we have that home. If we pick it out. Your book will sell and you will have the money you need. In the meantime, you can stay here."

"I've always paid my own way."

"Then we work it out so you pay something for being here other than bringing joy to my life."

Gabriella took a deep breath and plunged on. "But I've not been with anyone since I left the streets. I don't know if I can be-be-be intimate. Just look what happened when you tried to kiss me."

"If that is your worry, your only worry, are you saying you love me, will stay with me, will marry me if we find our way to that intimacy?"

"Why do I always feel sick when I think of—?"

"That is not my question. If we can work past whatever blocks us from being lovers, will you marry me?"

She noticed the unruly lock of dark hair had flopped across his forehead and then looked into his chocolate brown eyes. His gaze intense, she thought he even held his breath. Could she? Could she say 'yes'? She wanted to. All she had to do was nod her head or maybe whisper the word. But she was frozen in time and place.

He started to pull away, to rise, to leave her.

Her grip tightened, holding him in place. No words were able to push through the clog in her throat. Eyes brimming with unshed tears she leapt into the void and launched herself into his arms.

Caught between them was his mug of cider. It sloshed and dampened them both. Tugging the mug out of the way, Giovanni pulled her close.

"Ti amo," he whispered. "I love you. We will make this work because our love is strong enough to do so."

I Love You

Gabriella's stomach lurched as her heart soared. The dichotomy of feelings, of sensations running through her body—elation and nausea, relief and terror created an internal conflict she couldn't control. Her hand flew to her mouth. Giovanni calmly handed her a towel and kept up the rhythmic stroking of her back.

"I don-don-don't know why you're still here?" Her whole body tremored with terror. To keep herself from leaping up and running away, she clung to him. Arms locked around his neck, face buried in his chest, even her legs entwined with his. As much as this closeness frightened her, it also soothed.

In Giovanni's arms, one keeping her snug against him, the other stroking her hair, her back she was safe. He would do everything he could to protect her. He would always be here for her. She had come to rely on him, to trust him and because they'd shared their histories, she knew him in a different, more fundamental way.

"Does Jackson know your story?" Why it was important for her to know, wasn't clear. But it was.

"No, not even my family knows what I did in the beginning."

"You are the only one who knows my story, my whole story, too."

And that was why he was safe. He knew and he didn't turn away. He knew and he didn't leap on her expecting sex. It was an effort to battle back the terror and fear, to quell the nausea but Gabriella concentrated on the various methods The Circle had learned to relax and let go, to be in the moment, to savor the now.

At one point, Giovanni pulled the throw over them and it was only then she felt the cool air, so focused was she on what was going on inside her body.

She lifted her head. Her hazel gaze searched his face, ending with his chocolate brown eyes. "You've known so many women, beautiful accomplished wealthy women, why me?"

Before now she would have expected to be nervous in asking but right now, snuggled on the couch in his villa in Italy, his hand still stroking her back while the other arm held her close, it seemed the right time and place to inquire.

"I'm not particularly beautiful or talented or accomplished and I'm certainly not wealthy. I've enough emotional baggage—."

"Shh, you disparage the woman I love. I cannot allow that."

He was serious?

"I'm only stating truths so that's not disparaging."

"False truths then. For I see a beautiful woman, full of life. She is loyal to her friends, she cares about others, about strangers even, she is eager to learn new things, to experience new things. She has an inner light that glows when she talks about her passions. She is careful with her love but when she gives it, she does so whole heartedly."

Tears quivered on the brink of falling. "You see all that in me?"

"*Si*, I see even more. You are a survivor. You have not let your past keep you from living your life today."

"But... ."

"Shh, you asked and now you listen to my answer, *si*?"

She nodded. Tears slipped down her cheeks as the wonder of seeing herself through his eyes calmed the last of the nausea and began to wear away her vision of herself.

"When I listen to you tell me about your past and I remember what you did to find Logan, I am amazed at your strength, your determination, your commitment."

He fell silent, his gaze intense and focused on her.

"I am always afraid. Always ready to run, to leave everything behind to be safe."

"Maybe in the past but no longer. You ran toward your past to save Logan. You are here now, in my arms. You have shared your past with me perhaps to push me away but when that didn't work, you embraced me, *si*?"

Her arms were still around his neck although the original death grip had eased. She was flat out sprawled on top of his body, her legs still tangled with his.

The smug grin on his face, the knowing arched brow—she tensed, preparing to flee. This was Giovanni. Was the grin smug? Was his brow arched in challenge?

Gabriella studied his face again. 'Quizzical' is the word she'd use to describe the way he arched his brow and the grin? That was his charming one, the one he used to woo or invite.

"I kiss your forehead now." He shifted and bent and brushed his lips across her brow. "And now, I would move."

"I'm too heavy. I'm sorry. I should have—."

"Shh." The sound was forceful not soft. "You will not disparage the woman I love." His stern voice was not harsh. "You will treat her with the respect she deserves."

"Does she deserve a kiss from the man who pronounces he loves her?"

"She deserves much more than a kiss, but a kiss will do for a start. But we sit up to kiss." He lifted her in his arms and swung his legs around, settling her on his lap. "Now we are ready to kiss."

Gabriella's breath caught in her lungs, anticipation altered her heart beat. She leaned in to him. Her arms reached for him.

"Would it be better if you kissed me first?"

Gabriella looked at his serious face, a worried look in his eyes, a crease on his brow. "I think I love you, Giovanni." She pressed her lips to his, relaxed into his body and let the world slip away. Aware he was mimicking her, she took the lead and nibbled on his bottom lip, scattered kisses along his jaw from ear to ear. Her breathing rapid, her breasts tingled. His arms were around her, holding her. She felt his arousal nudge her bottom, waited for her panicked response. And waited. And waited.

He broke the kiss. "*Cara*, are you okay?" He asked in a worried tone.

"I am more than okay." A blush pinked her cheeks. "You are aroused."

Giovanni laughed. "But of course. I kiss the woman I love." He sobered and added, "We go no further than you are comfortable. I may be aroused, I may want you with every cell in my body but I control myself. I will not push you—ever. You tell me when you are ready to do more than kiss. You use your words."

"If you are up to it, I'd like to kiss more."

"Oh I am most certainly up to it."

When the double entendre registered, Gabriella's face burned with embarrassment. But it wasn't bad, she sort of liked that she could be embarrassed about kissing and loving. *Maybe I'm not as jaded as I thought I was.*

"You tell me if we need to stop," she whispered just before she slipped her hands in his hair and held him still while her lips feasted. Feeling bold, she licked his bottom lip and then nipped it. When his mouth opened, she slipped inside. He tasted of coffee and eggs with a hint of mint. Probably his toothpaste. And that was the last coherent thought she had as their tongues danced and mimicked what would come in time.

Lovers At Last

They didn't become lovers that night or even the next day. He held her hand, kissed her when she asked and waited. His wanting her was evident in the tented pants, the bulge pressing her bottom, the strained breathing when they tangled tongues. But still he waited, waited for her words.

It was two nights after that morning. Gabriella was in bed unable to sleep. She'd paced, she'd sat on her balcony in the cool night air, she'd had a stern talking with herself. The truth was she missed him, wanted to be in his arms but the other truth was, she was afraid she'd freeze and lash out as she had before.

"He says he loves me. He is respectful and compassionate. I've talked to him about things I've not shared with anyone outside of Doc S." Gabriella closed her eyes and willed the vision of the spruce cone to appear. It did and sitting on top was her blue jay, the iridescent blues and strident call a reminder of strengths she possessed.

Gathering her courage and resolve around her, she marched barefoot along the corridor to his room in the other wing of the house. There was no light and the idea that she'd wake him halted her hand hovering over the door.

"Now what," she muttered, frustration welling. She wanted to stomp her feet and scream but she held on to her control. "How bad do I want this?"

The answer to that question was action. She knocked on the door three times. Not timid taps but actual knocks. It was an eternity before the door opened, maybe even a whole minute.

No shirt, no shoes, barely zipped pants slung low in his hips. He was breathtaking. Virile, handsome, alert—.

"I didn't wake you." It was a statement.

"*Si*, you didn't wake me. Sleep, it comes and goes." He ran one hand through already rumbled hair. "Do you want to come in? or is there something wrong?"

"Both. I want to come in because there is something wrong." She still stood in the corridor willing her courage to stay until she was at least inside.

He stepped back and gestured her in.

She'd never been in his room before and besides the scent of him being stronger here, in the shadows created by the ambient light from the moon and stars and outside security lights, she saw a large bed in the center of the room facing a wall of windows. It must be breathtaking to wake up and look out over the garden trees to the sea beyond.

As she stood, mouth agape, the light from the distant lighthouse swiveled through the room. The walls running parallel to the windows were lined with paintings above and low chests below. She saw the reflection of what was behind her, a door that she assumed led to the bathroom and maybe a closet.

"Gabriella."

She loved the way her name sounded when he said it. A slight roll of the 'r', a different cadence because he was Italian.

The lighthouse's beam slipped around the room again but this time her gaze was on him. "I came because—."

He was stiff. Maybe she'd made a mistake. Maybe it was all a lie.

The warmth of his hand on her shoulder anchored her enough to ask, "Did I make a mistake?"

"Come, my feet get cold on the tile." He took her hand and led her across the room, past the bed to a sitting area at its foot. A lush sheepskin rug lay on the floor before a small sofa. "Sit here and talk to me."

"I practiced my words before I came but they seem to have flown away. I thought maybe—but then you—." She twisted her hands and started to stand.

"What did you think before you came to me?"

"I can't sleep. I ache and I miss your arms around me."

He rested his arm along the back of the sofa, his hand resting on her shoulder. "Is this better?"

"Not really."

"I am not interested in a guessing game, Gabriella."

"I'll go now." She started to stand but his hand on her shoulder tightened.

"Tell me about this ache." His voice lowered and he leaned toward her. His breath brushed her ear and she shivered.

"I want to kiss you and have you hold me."

"And you think the ache will go away if that is all we do?"

She shook her head. "But that is where I need to start. I want to do more but I'm afraid I'll panic and freeze up and you'll hate me."

Giovanni held himself under rigid self-control so he wouldn't frighten her. He'd been excruciatingly aware of her so close and yet—, and then the knock on the door. It is true he hesitated a moment before opening it, afraid he'd grab her and haul her into his room. She'd thought he'd changed his mind because he was so stiff and formal. An internal chuckle resounded through him. He certainly was stiff although certainly not formal.

How to proceed without scaring her? What had worked before was to ask her to tell him what she wanted. He'd started down that path but her insecurity, her inability to trust herself and to trust him in this moment was palpable.

"We have kissed before when you have not panicked or frozen."

"But I want more."

"Then we will start with the kisses and when you want more, you tell me."

"Will you hold me, too?"

"*Si*, I will hold you and kiss you and should you desire, make slow sweet love with you. Come." He patted his lap. "You sit here and I hold you, then we kiss."

Gabriella's brow wrinkled before a sigh escaped. She stood and scooted onto his lap.

He shifted and wrapped his arms around her, settling her against his chest. "Are you comfortable this way?"

She giggled and then wiggled her bottom against his groin.

His erection bulged as his body sought her heat.

"I think I'm more comfortable than you."

"But not for long," he murmured into the space behind her ear. "Not for long." He nibbled her ear lobe and then trailed mini-kisses along her jaw. With his finger on her chin, he tilted her head to better access her throat.

"Kiss me," she demanded.

"But I am kissing you." He made his way to her other ear where his kisses and nibbles stopped for a long moment before he started the return trip.

Before he'd made much progress, she seized his hair and dragged his head up so she could kiss his mouth. Arms locked around his head, her elbows on his shoulders, she tapped his lower lip with her tongue seeking entrance into his mouth. He opened and met her questing tongue with his own.

She rocked against him, rubbing her breasts against his chest, her bottom against his penis. "Touch me," she urged when she broke the kiss.

"Where?"

"Everywhere. I want you to touch me everywhere."

He began a slow exploration of her body, asking if that was what she wanted as he progressed. Her breasts fit in his hands. The already puckered nipples tightened under his caress and she gasped when he rolled the points between his fingers.

"More of this?" he asked moving between breasts, "or do you want me to touch you other places?"

Her 'yes' came on a moan and her body jerked, rising into his hands.

"You need to take your clothes off so I can do better," he suggested.

"Don't stop."

"I won't." He pulled her top up and over her head while still managing to keep one hand playing with her breasts. His mouth fixed on one breast as a hand played over her belly and then dipped lower, under the waist band of her pants.

Lifting his head, he blew on the engorged nipple before moving to the neglected one. "Are you okay?" he managed to ask although his voice was strained.

"Don't stop."

"I want to touch you here." His fingers brushed over the curls at the apex of her thighs.

She nodded her assent.

"Words, Gabriella. I need to hear your words."

"Yes," she choked out. "Yes."

Wet and hot—as his fingers searched for her sensitive spots and welcoming core, she arched against him, pulled his head up and consumed his mouth with her own.

As he inserted two fingers into her heat, her hands seized his head, her tongue thrust into his mouth. Her inner muscles clenched, seizing his fingers as she shattered.

Giovanni held her tight and rocked her until her tremors ebbed and her body relaxed. Withdrawing his fingers from her hot core, he caressed her back.

Quiet and still, she could have slept but the wetness on his chest told the truth. She cried.

Why she cried, he didn't know. She didn't seem panicky or frightened.

What to say? Nothing at first. He hoped she'd raise her head and say something. But, she didn't.

"You are crying."

She nodded and sniffed. "I'm sorry," she whispered, her hand drifting down toward his penis. "What do you want me to do?"

"What are you sorry for?"

"I know I can provide you with your own release."

"Gabriella, look at me."

He waited until she lifted her face and her gaze met his. Her hazel eyes were bright with unshed tears. "What are you sorry for?"

Tears spilled onto her cheeks and she dipped her head.

With his fingers, he tipped her head back until their gazes met. "What do you think just happened?"

"You—I don't have the right words," she whispered.

"I gave you pleasure."

She nodded.

"And now you feel you owe me something?"

She nodded again.

"That is not how love works."

Panic rioted across her face and she pulled away.

"How it works is we do this again and add more. When you are ready, we will join our bodies and bring each other to the heights of passion and pleasure."

"But I can—."

"I've not doubt that you can, but that is not what I want. I want to start at the beginning with kisses and touches and when you are ready, you will tell me and we will come together."

"What if I—."

"We start at the beginning and see where it goes." He kissed her nose and then her eyes. "I know you like my kisses and I like yours. I know you like my touches and I already know I'll like yours. For now you can touch me anywhere above the waist because I am only touching you above the waist."

The need to get this right, to make sure she was comfortable with what he was doing fueled Giovanni through another round of kisses and above-the-waist touches. She did minister to his flat male nipples when she got the chance. But when his hand sought her heat, she stayed him.

"Together you said."

"So I did."

"If you touch me there, then I can touch you below the waist also."

He nodded.

She smiled and kissed one corner of his mouth and then the other. "Use your words, Giovanni. Use your words."

This time instead of his fingers, he gave her a condom. After she'd sheathed him, he lifted her so she could straddle him. Lowering herself onto his shaft, she took her time, inch by inch she drew out the exquisite pain of their joining. He was an experienced man and even to him it sounded trite, but being with this woman, with his Gabriella was different. As she rocked them to completion, the upwelling of emotion overwhelmed him. When his release hit, he clutched her hips, held her tight to him and declared his love for her in Italian and then—eventually, in English.

When he got his wind and strength back, he stood. Her legs were still wrapped around his waist, his arms around her back. The few steps to the bed was as far as he could go but it was far enough. Lowering both of them to the soft surface, he pulled the covers over them. She snuggled against him, her head on his shoulder.

"I love you, Gabriella." He'd whispered the words because he needed to say them. Not expecting an answer, when she sighed and said "I love you, too," hope blossomed.

When Morning Comes

Gabriella slept the deep sleep of a well-pleasured woman. She woke before the sun, waited for panic to strike or if not panic at least remorse. Those feelings had abandoned her. In their place was a surreal contentment buoyed by hope. He'd said he loved her while they made love but he'd also said those words in the sober light of day. The reality that he really did love her wrapped around her like heated gloves on a cold winter day.

The view from his bed wasn't as open as the one from her room although he did have one. Her bed faced the corridor's wall but once she was up, the vista of the garden and the sea beyond still took her breath away.

No curtains darkened the room. As daylight made its way across the garden tree tops, he stirred. Without a word being said, she knew when he woke. The energy in the room changed. Would it always be so? Would she always know where he was, when he was near, when he left a room?

Always. The word evoked a shiver of fear. There was no 'always'. 'Always' was a myth. There was only 'for now'.

His penis nudged her thigh but his hands remained still.

"You're awake." She turned on her side to face him. Air caught in her lungs, words lodged in her throat, hunger burned in her core. Giovanni in the morning was a sight to behold: rumpled, disheveled, sinful. Through his whiskered cheek, she spied a crease from his pillow. A lazy grin graced his sculpted lips. But what caused her arms to slide around his neck, her lips to brush kisses on his nose were his eyes. Half-closed, heavy lidded, with vestiges of slumber in their depths, they held promises she'd never dreamed could be hers.

"I want you again," his voice glided over her like molten chocolate—hot, decadent, delicious.

"Is this how you like to start your day?" She pressed against him chest to toes.

"Only if you are with me."

"Good answer." She licked his chin.

"A true answer." He fit a leg between hers.

"For now."

Giovanni pulled away. No half-closed eye lids now. The dark intense look she recognized that signaled his displeasure speared her.

"You think I take this night lightly? That it means very little to me?" He pulled back from her as he spoke.

Gabriella reached out to touch his cheek.

He batted her hand away and sat up. "We will talk now." Not a suggestion or question but a statement.

Feeling exposed, she also sat, pulled the sheet up and tucked it under her arms. It was a bit unnerving because after making the declarative statement about talking, he said nothing. Just sat and looked at her. She fought the urge to say something to break the silence or leave.

"Is this how you deal with loving someone?"

His voice was soft but the words hit her like a sucker punch. Of their own volition, her arms wrapped around her middle and tears welled. Her first thought was to dismiss his words with a wave of her hand and a laugh.

But she didn't. She sat very still and willed the panic away, willed the fear away, willed the urge to run off away.

Why?

Because she did love him. And, because she loved him, she owed him the truth.

Chin up, defiance lacing her voice she said, "I don't know because I've never loved anyone before."

"*Grazie.*"

"Why are you thanking me?" She spat these words.

"Because you tell me the truth. As long as we are honest with each other, we find our way." He leaned forward and kissed her cheek. "I'm going to shower now. You can come with me or not. I do warn you, if you join me I will touch you—everywhere."

"Is that a promise or a threat?"

His smile grew from a slight tilt of the corners of his mouth to a wide grin that crinkled his cheeks and shone from his eyes. He tapped her wrist, still clutching the sheet. "A promise. Making love in a hot shower is a unique experience—and, I have jets that can massage everywhere else my hands aren't touching."

Left on her own to make a decision, Gabriella waited until she heard the water running. She'd been up once during the night to pee so knew the bathroom was enormous and elegant. Her impression of the shower was dim but it would easily hold the two of them. *What would it be like?*

A more important question to ask herself was whether or not she had the courage to move forward with him. To grasp this opportunity to love and be loved; to feel safe and cherished.

The question of The Circle's survival if she no longer lived in Fremont surfaced as she untangled herself from the sheets. *We found a way when Elizabeth moved to Ireland. If I remain here, we'll figure it out.* With the certainty that The Circle was not in danger regardless of her final decision, Gabriella rounded the bed and headed to the bathroom and what would be her first but not her last shower with the man she loved.

Ireland and Ceremony

Gabriella tucked the last item she was taking with her into the suitcase. She'd finished *Holly's Story* and in addition to making sure she'd saved it on her laptop, she'd sent the manuscript to herself as an email attachment and saved it to a thumb drive. Holly had not needed the years to heal and move on with her life that she had. In a new job that had a career path, in a company that valued its employees, Holly made new friends. The brother of a co-worker turned out to be safe, dependable, caring, loving and—. *That's an interesting list.*

Of course safety and dependability were high on the list, but loving was the fourth? As she zipped closed the suitcase, she thought about her relationship with Giovanni. First had come safety because that allowed her to trust him. Next had come friendship because without that she'd not have seen the other sides of him.

He loved her.

She twirled across the space to the desk and picked up her laptop. Grabbing the suitcase handle, she headed out the door. Before she reached the stairs, Silvio was there to take her luggage and cart it down and out to the waiting car. They were taking the limousine to the Florence airport and flying from there to Shannon where they'd meet up with the others. The Circle was celebrating Winter Solstice with Elizabeth and The Lady.

To save herself the onslaught of well-intentioned questions, she'd emailed everyone a week ago and included in the general news that she and Giovanni were talking about "something permanent."

He always talked in terms of them marrying but he hadn't actually asked her. Perhaps she had a strain of 'old-fashion' in her but her childhood fantasies always had the man proposing. *Funny, I never fantasized about my answer.*

Off the plane and through the airport, Gabriella made a bee-line toward Sophia. She was sure something had happened to her circle sister but no one was saying anything.

Thankful Giovanni knew everyone and was comfortable with The Circle and the families attached to them, she focused her attention on Sophia. Gabriella was not surprised Sophia denied there was a problem. It was a denial she didn't totally believe.

It occurred to her as she was talking to Sophia and the others that had it been Jordan with her instead of Giovanni, this entire scene would have been very difficult. *I need to let Jordan know I'm not available to date or to work in Seattle.*

Room arrangements at The Manor were the same except Giovanni was in the room next to hers. "We didn't want to assume," Elizabeth had said when she and Maeve came to check on her. "But, you'll find a connecting door behind there." She pointed to a wall hanging.

Worry that it would be awkward or more likely she'd be teased evaporated. Everyone was happy for her. Delighted to see them together. Happy smiles were welcomed. Gawking and pointed remarks were not.

Since Gabriella wasn't convinced nothing had happened to Sophia, she asked her circle sister to join her on a walk. It was winter in Fremont, garden chores at a minimum. With her friend now gone, what was she doing with her time? There was only so much baking she could do.

She didn't even blink an eye when Sophia told her she was volunteering with a new pilot program. One evening a week and some weekend time she checked on vulnerable adults. Offices were closed and in these cases concern wasn't high enough to involve the police. The program was a resource for those workers who had a nagging feeling that one of their clients needed to be checked on.

A spring in her step, strong energy in her voice, Sophia talked about how important it was for her to feel as if she was contributing to her world. Gabriella's mention of the garden and baking giveaways was waved off as not really that important.

There was something else going on. Gabriella was positive about that. But since Sophia wasn't elaborating, she strolled along with her friend and commented on the horses in the paddocks and expanse of green everywhere they looked.

When they returned, she got questioning looks from the others but she shook her head. She wasn't the only one who'd felt something but as was their tradition, it was up to each of them to share what they would and it was up to the rest of them to make peace with that.

Wednesday
December 21, 2005

Winter Solstice

The afternoon of the Solstice, The Circle met in Elizabeth's parlor. There were couches and chairs enough for everyone, including Hunter's daughter, Logan, Ashley's daughter, Rose and Lily's mother-in-law, Eleanor, to be comfortable without sitting on the floor. A fire burned and warm rum punch was in a pot on the hearth.

Maeve and Madison Michelle were with their dads who were gathered in Michael's study along with Lily's Charlie and Diana's Bill and Ashley's James and Anthony.

Eleanor was adamant that she was not going to do ceremony and would be just fine watching Maeve and Madison Michelle. "After all, I'll have Anthony to help and if I need it, Seamus will be here," she announced, her British accent still discernable after going to the United States as a World War II bride.

At the appointed time, all the others met on the terrace at the entrance to the path to the sacred grove. Single file they followed Elizabeth down the winding trail and three times around the grove before entering.

The grassy center, the bubbling spring, the eternal fire within the ring of trees—all was as it had always been but this time Gabriella was different. *I've always had my guard up, always protecting myself from something. For the first time in my memory I feel utterly and completely safe.* She sought Giovanni and he opened his arms. She walked into her haven. When he enveloped her in his scent, his heat and his arms, she wrapped her arms around his waist and held on.

A tug on her inner vision brought her back to this place. It was time to say prayers, to celebrate another turn of the wheel. The Lady had appeared and as one the women raised their arms over their heads, saying the words to send love throughout the world.

"We are the light

"We are the source

"Through us love flows

"Throughout the World."

Three times three they said the words before dropping their arms. The Lady welcomed them and bid them to spend whatever time they needed to refresh and replenish the energy they would need when they left.

Gabriella saw The Lady smile and in her mind heard her say, "Your way will have challenges but if you believe he loves you, all will be as it should."

At this point in the ceremony, they each spent some time in silent contemplation before leaving. What did The Lady mean? Did She question whether Gabriella believed Giovanni loved her? *It isn't that I don't believe him. My doubts are about me.*

It was almost time to leave and she was still considering her own worthiness to be loved when said man stood in front of her. He knelt before her, took her hands in his. Leaning forward, his chocolate brown eyes saw into her soul. His voice, when he spoke, quiet so only she could hear.

"My Gabriella, I believe this is the right place to ask you to be mine. Be my wife. Be my lover. Be the mother of my children, God willing."

She waited, waited for the question.

He waited, waited for her answer.

His brow arched and then a worried look crossed his face.

"Was there a question you wanted to ask?" she whispered.

"Come, I try again." He tugged her onto her knees and slipped his arms around her.

"My Gabriella, my love. Will you marry me?"

Her arms wrapped around his neck, her head rested on his shoulder. "Yes, I will marry you if you will marry me."

Their embrace was short-lived, when the others started to leave making enough noise to let them know they were going. Elizabeth stopped next to them. "If you want to stay longer, you may. Just remember to go out the east path and to circle the grove one time before going up the path."

Giovanni rose to his feet bringing Gabriella up with him. He looked at her, a question in his eyes.

"We can go now." She kept her hand in his as they followed the others out the east path, around the grove and up the path. They had not yet used the connecting door but maybe tonight?

Elizabeth and Diana checked on the babies. While the men made sure the dining room had chairs for all of them, the women gathered bowls and plates along with Seamus's split pea soup and freshly baked bread. Dessert was a deep dish apple pie with sharp cheddar and ice cream.

When everyone was settled and enjoying their food, Michael looked over at Giovanni. "Do you have an announcement?"

"It is not for me to say." While he kept his gaze on Michael, he reached for Gabriella's hand under the protection of the table. She squeezed his hand and then gave it a pat.

He looked at Gabriella but said nothing. Lost in each other, no words were spoken.

"Do we have a wedding to plan?" Sophia asked.

Giovanni lifted Gabriella's hand to his lips. Pressing a soft kiss to her finger tips, he cocked his head.

Her faced heated and she figured her cheeks were the same shade of auburn red as her hair. Tears filled her eyes and hovered on the edge. Without taking her gaze from his, she nodded.

Giovanni leaned forward and whispered, "Use your words."

She shook her head as the tears spilled down her cheeks.

"Excuse us," he said and picked her up and carried her from the room. He didn't go far, just to a settee in the foyer.

"I'm sorry," she whispered.

He put a finger to her mouth to stay many more words. "No words right now, *si*?"

She nodded.

"Did I misunderstand and you not want to say anything yet?"

She shook her head.

His hand cupped her head, holding it against his shoulder while the other hand stroked her back.

She hiccupped and sighed. "I just couldn't say anything. I didn't have any words only feelings."

"And now?"

"And now there is a question about a wedding to plan. We really haven't talked about that."

He grinned. "I have it on authority that all I have to do is show up. The Circle will take care of everything else."

"However, I am part of The Circle so it isn't quite that easy for me."

"What would make it easy?"

"I'm not sure. You are right when you say the others will take care of any and all details if we want them to."

"And do you?"

"Perhaps some of them. I really don't want to think about colors and flowers and food."

"So the others can do that for you. What do you want to think about?"

"I've so many odds and ends to tie up in Fremont. I have things at the Murphy house to move or get rid of. I need to let them know at work that I won't be returning. I want to spend some time with Doc S and the Watersons."

"May I?"

She nodded and smiled.

"Leave the Fremont things until after. We can spend time there after the ceremony, find our own house if you want and then you can move or discard or bring back to Italy. There are legal things to take care of so you will be a resident.

"Write email or letter to your work. We invite whomever you want for the wedding. When we travel to Fremont, we spend whatever time you need."

"You have a very practical mind."

"When it comes to having you for my wife, my mind is practical and quick. Michael's man of business can research what needs to be done for your residency application in Italy just like he did for Elizabeth to be here. Do you have a date in mind?"

"Everyone has gotten married on a Sabbat. That means either Imbolc, which is February 1st or Beltane or Samhain?"

"We will not marry on Samhain."

"I agree."

"That leaves Imbolc or Beltane?"

"Yes, February 1 or May 1st."

"But what do these words, these Sabbats mean?" Giovanni's brow quirked a question.

"Imbolc is about light, the strength of the light to overcome the dark. Beltane is about spring, rebirth, growing."

"Imbolc."

She breathed deeply when the decision was made. She'd been barely breathing while they discussed getting married. It was one thing to talk about getting married, it was another to say 'yes' to a proposal. What she was quickly realizing was the enormity of having an actual date. She pressed her hands to her abdomen afraid she was going to be sick.

He kissed her forehead. "It will be okay. We can do Beltane if that is easier for you."

"No, Imbolc is the right one for us. I feel it here." She patted her heart "Let's go back and tell them."

"*Si*, they will be worried, I think."

"Not when they hear our news."

Hand in hand they reentered the dining room. Expectant faces turned their way. Some with worried looks, others more neutral.

"Yes, there is a wedding to plan." Gabriella looked up at the man who loved her. Who wanted her no matter her past.

"Can it be done by Imbolc or do we have to elope?" Giovanni's voice boomed over the excited voices that had erupted with Gabriella's announcement.

Sophia stood. Lily, Elizabeth, Diana, Ashley and Hunter followed. "Six weeks is more than enough time for The Circle to put a wedding together."

Giovanni was pushed aside as Gabriella was surrounded by her sisters of her heart. Hugs, tears, well-wishes rained upon her. Every few minutes, her attention strayed to Giovanni whose news was welcomed by the other men. Underneath it all, a distressing sense of doom penetrated the joy. Did she really deserve this much happiness? To have a man who loved her above all others?

Betrayal

Wednesday
January 4, 2006
Rome, Italy

Gabriella almost ran once off the plane to where Giovanni was waiting. He'd left two days after Winter Solstice because he had clients to see, projects to check on and wanted to tell his family about the wedding. The Fremont contingent of The Circle left on the twenty-ninth. Except for the venue and her dress, all decisions had been made.

Shopping in Dublin for her wedding dress kept her in Ireland until after the New Year. Nothing appealed to her. But, she reminded herself, except for the venue and her dress, all was decided.

The troubling question of why he hadn't said anything to his family about her was sorted out over the phone. It took three calls because she didn't understand his family dynamics. In the end she meditated in the Grove with The Lady. The picture of a boisterous family surrounding her helped.

He'd said they'd descend on her and worried she'd back away. By talking to them ahead of time, he hoped to give his mother and sisters time to settle so as not to overwhelm her.

Striding down the concourse, her backpack slung over her shoulder, her laptop in hand Gabriella skipped once. *Skipped! OMG I have it bad if I'm skipping in airports!*

As she came through a checkpoint, she spotted him. Or at least the top of his head. Her mouth opened, the words "I'm here!" ready to shout. The bustling crowd shifted opening a clear path to him.

What she saw nearly brought her to her knees. It did bring her to an abrupt halt. The business man right behind her plowed into her and she started to fall. He grabbed her before she landed and somehow she managed to right herself.

That was when Giovanni, his arm still around the woman he'd been embracing, saw her. He looked down at the woman beside him who was chattering away and looked back at Gabriella who'd not moved.

The woman, dressed like a Milan model in a red and black patterned suit, her hair in a perfect mussed do with open-toed black high heels, kissed his cheek and patted her hand over the spot as if to hold it in place. With an airy wave, she headed down the concourse Gabriella had just come from, turning back and blowing a kiss his way.

Gabriella's pain and furry held her rigid. Chin high, back straight, she stared daggers at him.

"I can explain," Giovanni said, his hand out to take hers.

She pulled away. "I don't want to hear your lies. I know what I saw. That woman is more than a casual friend."

He reached out again.

"Do Not Touch Me! Do Not Speak To Me!" She tried in vain to work his ring off her finger. Maybe if she threw it at him, she'd feel better. But no, the ring stuck tight.

"Come, we go to my house and talk." He stepped toward her.

She stepped back and then pivoting, she ran, dashed away, her backpack bouncing along, her laptop banging her thigh. In the distance he called her name but she kept going. The sign for the women's restroom was on her left. Gabriella veered in that direction. Once inside, she collapsed against the wall. Hand shaking she got out her cell phone and turned it on.

Thankful the signal was strong, she scrolled contacts and called Elizabeth.

"He, he, he—," she sobbed.

"Gabby? Is that you?" Elizabeth's voice, laden with concern, helped her gather herself a bit.

She nodded and when Elizabeth asked a second time, she said "E, I need your help. I can't—, he—. I don't know what to do."

Tears flowed freely, her stomached cramped and words were hard to speak.

"Where are you?"

"In Rome."

"Where in Rome?"

"I'm still at the airport. He—he—he was kissing another woman, E. He doesn't love me. It's all a lie." Her knees gave away and she slid down the wall, sobbing into the phone.

"Do you need help?" The words were said in a heavily accented voice. Gabriella looked up. A young woman squatted next to her, a concerned look on her face.

"My friend... ." she managed pointing to the phone. "She is helping me."

"That is good. You need someone to help you now." The young woman stood. "I wait here for a little to make sure, okay?"

Gabriella nodded, returned her focus to the phone and heard Elizabeth say "okay?"

"I'm sorry E, I missed that."

"Where exactly are you in the airport?"

Gabriella told her the gate where she'd arrived and that she was huddled inside a women's restroom on the left side of the building once she left the concourse.

"Wait there. It may take some time but Michael and I will find someone to come and get you and take you to a hotel until things get sorted out. You know you are welcome to come back here, but you may decide to return to Fremont. Oh, and how is your cell's battery level?"

"It's still pretty full. I haven't used it since I left you except for now."

"Good. Your job is to just take care of yourself as best you can while we get things in place for you. I'll call you back when that's done. In the meantime, I'll hold you in The Light."

After a woman stopped and told her a gentleman was outside wanting to speak to her, Gabriella moved into a stall.

An hour went by before her phone rang.

"A woman will come to the restroom with a sign that says "GMC". She will know your name. Go with her and she'll make sure you get out of the airport and to the hotel. We've made a reservation for you but it is under the name, Mr. Dickens, with you also being listed.

"By now your luggage will have been taken off the carousel and the woman who is coming to get you will help you get it released. You do have your passport handy, don't you?"

"Yes."

"Any questions?" E's voice was brisk and business-like which helped Gabriella keep calm. "When you get to the hotel and check in, call me."

"I promise."

"And use room service. Don't leave your room for anything unless you've checked with Michael or me."

"Michael?"

"Gabriella, as powerful as you think I am, I couldn't do all of this on my own. Michael has connections who have connections, etc. so he made two phone calls and it's done. If you are worried he'll call Giovanni, I can assure you he will not make that call."

"Thank you, E. I didn't know what to do. I'm not even sure he's still in the airport. If you'd seen him... . I can't talk to him. He betrayed me."

"Call me when you are settled in the hotel," Elizabeth repeated. "We'll talk more then. Always remember you are loved by many."

"Maybe not by many but at least by some."

"Not arguing about that now. You might want to start a mental list while you wait. It would pass the time."

Gabriella paced through the women's restroom, pausing by the opening to peek out to see if a certain dark haired, chocolate brown-eyed man lurked. She saw nothing. An hour passed and as the next one started, a middle-aged woman in a chauffer's uniform holding a sign "GMC" came into the rest room.

"You are looking for me." Gabriella stepped up to her.

"Ms. Gabby?"

She nodded.

"Come this way."

Gabriella followed the woman a few steps out the restroom door. Two other women fell into step on either side. She had an escort. It would be more difficult to see her this way. By the time they'd traveled ten feet, she knew another two women were behind her.

At baggage claim, her suitcase had been taken off the carousel and was in storage. She showed her passport and her ticket stub, completed the form and waited. It didn't take long before her luggage was handed to her.

Outside at the curb, a limousine pulled up when the woman with the sign signaled. She climbed inside, thankful when she was joined by two of her escorts.

Ten minutes later they pulled into the circular drive of Hotel Leonardo. The hotel staff was waiting for her and she was quickly checked in.

"I leave you here," her escort said. "He," she nodded to the bellman holding her bag, "will take you to your room. I wish you well."

Gabriella extended her hand, thankful when the other woman took it. "I don't even know your name."

"Maria will do."

It was like being in a movie, secretively, furtively moving from one place to another, not really knowing the identities of those who helped you—only knowing you were extremely grateful for everything they did.

"Thank you, Maria. I've no other words to express my gratitude."

Maria smiled, tilted her head to one side before saying "I am very glad to be of service to you, miss."

In her hotel room which was more like a suite because the bedroom was separate and the bathroom luxurious, she unpacked and set up an altar.

She had a ceramic blue jay, a Solstice gift from Elizabeth and her spruce cone, pieces of calcite in green and gold, lapis and rose quartz were laid out on the multi-colored silk square. It was a new altar to her because she was using the Solstice gifts from her circle sisters. Lighting a candle, she waved it over and around each object before she set it down.

Altar set up, she held the candle in one hand and with the other, brushed the light and heat from the tiny flame over and around her body. Then she raised her arms over her head and spread her feet to shoulder width.

"I call upon Blue Jay and Spruce to guide me through this time.

"I call upon Blue Jay and Spruce to be with me here and now.

"I am open and willing to let go of chaos and welcome symmetry in this time and place.

"Blessed be."

When the bellman had brought her to this room, she'd asked him to retrieve a bucket of ice for her. Filling a glass with the cold cubes, she added water from the stash in the small refrigerator. The living room boasted a full length couch and two overstuffed chairs situated around a gas fireplace.

The bellman had instructed that all she had to do was flip a switch and it would light. He'd had her do it while he was still there so, even though she held her breath, she popped the switch upright. A second later, the pent up air in her lungs whooshed out as the flames came to life.

Water in one hand, she curled up in a corner of the couch. In her other hand she held her cell phone. Now was the time to call Elizabeth. What she really wanted to do was lick her wounds but E would be waiting.

The push of one button was all it took. The phone rang and was answered on the second ring.

"It's me." She took a sip of the cold water and wished it had a slice of lemon floating in it.

"I've just fixed myself a cup of tea, Maeve is taking a nap and Michael will take care of her if she wakes while we're still talking."

"He has someone else in his life." Gabriella was amazed at how calm she sounded. Defeated, destroyed yet calm.

"Tell me what you saw?"

"He was embracing another woman. She wasn't just another woman, E," Gabriella said, tears in her voice. "She is stunning like a model. Her outfit must cost at least a couple of thousand dollars. Her figure is magnificent. Hundreds of dollars spent to make her hair look so perfectly mussed up.

"He held her in his arms and kissed her."

"Lily saw a woman in Jackson's arms and I even saw Shannon wrap herself around Michael."

"Michael did not kiss Shannon and Jackson did not kiss Susannah. They were horrified those women were even there. He saw me, his arm still around her and smiled." Her voice broke and she put the glass of water down before it spilled.

"He smiled, E. He didn't look embarrassed or disconcerted or dismayed. He looked happy—."

"Happy? Are you sure he didn't look upset or anything?"

"Only when I refused to talk to him."

"What did you say?"

"I told him not to touch me and not to talk to me. I know what I saw, E. This woman means something to him. She isn't like Susannah or Shannon at all."

"You are comfortable in your room for now?" Elizabeth was changing the subject and Gabriella was just fine with that. She didn't want to talk about or think about that traitorous—. And to think she'd let her guard down, let herself love him, let—.

She took a deep breath. "I'm find for now, E. I'm going to order something from room service and have them bring another bucket of ice and maybe something else to drink. Something other than water or juice."

"If it will help, Gabby, then do it. Now is the time to take care of yourself." There was a moment of silence on the line before Elizabeth continued. "Do you want me to call you later, like tonight?"

"No, I'll check in with you in the morning."

"Remember, take care of yourself. Talk to you in the morning."

The line went dead when Elizabeth hung up.

Gabriella sat staring into the fake flames. No, not fake. They'd burn her if she stuck her fingers in there. But they weren't real. They weren't flames from wood, from logs from dead trees she'd helped fell. In that moment, she wanted to be at the cabin in the woods more than anywhere else.

I'll let Elizabeth know I want to go back to Fremont—to the cabin.

Seclusion and Maria Sophia

Gabriella's eyes closed. The spruce cone vision morphed into her inner vision, clear, crisp and perfect with varied colors of yellow and gold shooting from the base. Sitting on top was her blue jay. Although the jay covered the flower-like center of the cone, she could still see it, still focus on it and feel the calm infiltrate the marrow of her bones.

Envisioning this scene and the cabin in the woods had kept her sane and in these rooms. She talked to Elizabeth three times a day but stayed off the hotel's internet so had no direct contact with her circle sisters in Fremont.

And since she was off the internet, she'd not contacted her employer. Being in Fremont with the others and at the cabin was one thing, returning to work another. The idea of transferring to Seattle and seeing what happened with Jason churned her insides. It had taken three years to drop her guard around Giovanni. She couldn't imagine even talking to Jason about her past. And, while she thought he'd read her book, she doubted he'd ever connect anything from *Holly's Story* with her own personal experiences.

It wasn't that he was uncaring. No, she knew he was just the opposite because when she'd asked for time off to help a niece, he hadn't hesitated but worked with her to figure out how she could do that and still keep her part of the project on task.

A part of her missed Giovanni. Wanted to see him, to talk to him to find out what she'd done wrong, what had happened in three days for him to turn away from her. When those thoughts were prevalent, she was in the bathroom, on her knees in front of the toilet. Whatever she'd eaten since the last time she'd been in the same position, flushed down the drain.

Thankful she had her laptop, she pushed herself to concentrate and read *Holly's Story*. Finished, she went back and deleted the last two chapters. The end of Holly's story was still too cookie cutter. *She has to work for her happily-ever-after.*

It was the fourth day in the hotel room and she was going slightly crazy. She'd done some exercises, ran in place, paced from one end to the other all in an attempt to work off the tension gripping her from the inside out.

Something was going on? Or maybe something was wrong? Her last conversation with Elizabeth had gaps in it. She couldn't put her finger on it but something was missing. Every conversation had a similar message. "At least talk to him. Keep an open mind and talk to him."

All of her circle sisters had had a time of darkness and doubts they'd survived. Everyone except Sophia unless you counted the death of Jonathan—which she did.

Her circuitous thoughts were interrupted by a knock on the door. "Who's there?"

"Housekeeping."

Even as she opened the hotel room door, her warning voice screamed. But before she could slam the door shut, she was face-to-face with her.

With the woman hugging and kissing Giovanni at the airport.

"How?" She grabbed the door for support as her knees gave. "Get out!" She stabbed her finger toward the hallway as the woman walked in.

"I am Maria Sophia," the woman said, holding her hand out in a friendly gesture. Seeing Gabriella still stood at the open door, her mouth open in shock, she went on. "Please close the door unless you want others to hear what I have to say."

"You are assuming I want to hear what you have to say." Gabriella was livid with rage, her voice steely. "I said get out."

Maria Sophia took off her gloves, put them on top of her handbag that she placed on the table next to the couch. She strolled over to the mini-fridge, surveyed the contents before lifting the phone. "Please send a bottle of champagne and hors d'oeuvres at once."

"What are you doing?" Gabriella let go of the door which shut on its own and crossed the room. "I don't want you here."

Maria Sophia crossed to the couch but sat in the chair on the left, facing the door. "But I have something to say to you."

"You are assuming I want to hear it."

The sad smile on the woman's face caught Gabriella off guard.

"You think Giovanni and I are lovers but you are wrong."

Maria Sophia's hazel eyes were much the same color as Gabriella's own. Today her multi-hued green dress flirted with her knees, dark green pumps on her feet, malachite jewelry graced her neck, fingers and dangled from her ears. It hurt to see someone so perfect for him, someone he could be seen with who complimented his own good looks.

A knock on the door, Gabriella was closest but she did not move to open it. Maria Sophia rose and with elegance gracing every movement, crossed the room. A cart with a bucket of ice, a bottle of champagne, glasses and a tray of appetizers was wheeled in.

"You will need to sign for this," Maria Sophia said to Gabriella handing her the bill. Turning back, she spoke in Italian. The room service staff opened the champagne and poured two glasses. He took the cover off the hors d'oeuvres before leaving.

Maria Sophia handed a glass of champagne to Gabriella, put some shrimp and crab canapes on a plate and resumed her seat in the chair.

"It is much easier to talk about anything with champagne." She took a sip, nibbled her shrimp and after another sip of the bubbling drink went on. "It is true in the past Giovanni and I were lovers a long time ago. But we remain friends."

"I saw you kiss him. He kissed you."

"I had not seen him in many months. I know now why that was. It was an accident seeing him at the airport. I'm on my way to Paris for a meeting and he is waiting—. He would not tell me anything and since I had a little time, I waited hoping to see what or more precisely who he was waiting for.

"I determined he was waiting for a woman but I knew when he looked away and smiled it was you."

She took another sip. Sighed. Took another one and continued.

"I knew I was not welcome to stay because—well, let's just say I knew he wanted to be with you and you alone. So I kissed him goodbye and left for my plane.

"What you don't know is that I also turn my phone off. I leave it off until I reach Paris and my hotel room. When I turn it on, I had at least a dozen calls from him begging me to call and to come home immediately.

"Of course I call him right then and explained that I was in Paris for an important meeting. I run a modeling agency and my top models are in great demand. There was a problem with one of my best customers and it was not something I could put aside to fly back."

She looked Gabriella over from head to foot. "You would make a very good model for—."

"As I was saying. I had a problem in Paris and as the owner of the company, there is no one else who has the authority to make the changes needed. And, since I want my customers to be happy, there are bonuses to add that, again, only I could provide."

"So, if I understand your story, you and Giovanni used to be lovers but now are only friends?"

Maria Sophia nodded.

"What I saw was more than 'only friends'." She crooked her fingers simulating quotations marks around the last two words.

"More champagne?" Maria Sophia asked as she stood and strolled to the still iced bottle. Filling her glass, she turned to Gabriella, her brow arched.

Gabriella shoved her glass out.

"*Si*, everything is better with champagne."

"Why are you here?" Gabriella rounded the couch and perched on the cushion at the end farthest from Maria Sophia.

"I tell you. Giovanni called and asked me to talk to you. To tell you about how things are between us."

"How did you know where I was?" Cold fury infused each word.

"Why he tells me, of course. How else would I know?" Her shoulders shrugged in the elegant Italian manner that shared more than words.

Maria Sophia waved the question away with one polished hand. "He said I was to come. To talk to you. To answer every question you ask. To persuade you, if I could, to talk to him or at least listen to him.

"And so I am here. I tell you how I come to be here and why the delay. He is very upset that I not leave everything and come back immediately. I offer to call and talk to you but he say I need to talk to you in person. The phone not be good enough. You would need to see me to know I speak the truth.

"So I come as quickly as I can. I had planned on staying in Paris for a few more days enjoying the sights but, Giovanni is an old friend and—." Another shrug.

"Tell me about how you met him?" Gabriella couldn't believe she'd asked. Why was she looking for more pain? Why was she prolonging the agony?

"Ahh," Maria Sophia smiled a faraway look in her eyes. "So many years ago. I was a model then and he was starting his business. He loved the old moldering buildings, loved bringing them back to their old magnificence. I was on a photo shoot at one of those buildings and that's where we met. He asked me to share a bottle of wine when we were done.

"Of course you know how handsome he is, so I say '*si*'. We sit on the stone steps that look out over a central plaza. It wasn't expensive wine, he was too poor for that. But we both had dreams for our future. He is very easy to talk to.

"The next two days, until the shoot was over, he was there when we stopped for the day. Bread, cheese and wine—after the first day I bring the wine and he bring the bread and cheese." She laughed at the memory. "I was making more money than he was. But maybe not. I only had myself to support. He had his mother and sisters.

"Meeting them was an adventure. Immediately they want to know when we get married, how many children we having? They love him very much and only want what's best for him but they did think being married to me was what he needed.

"Thankfully we both knew it wasn't what either of us need. We are lovers for a few months when we discover we really just want to spend time together. We didn't want to break up and never see each other again. But the physical side of the relationship other than hugs wasn't important.

"Initially it was hard for me to hear him say that I was beautiful but he not interested in me as a lover. I certainly thought I'd done something wrong, wasn't experienced enough." She waved her hand as if shoving painful memories from her mind. A wistful look on her face, her gaze held Gabriella's.

"I will tell you true that I have always loved him and still do but he is not for me. We have a good and strong friendship. I would like to continue it but I am sure that if you told him he was never to see or speak to me again, he would choose you."

Words clung together in a black and white stream that flowed through her mind. Pictures came next. This Winter Solstice Shannon had not been there. Gabriella had noticed it but not paid that much attention. Now she wondered if it was because of Maeve. Michael's love for Elizabeth was visible. But if she still loved him, seeing Elizabeth with Maeve and knowing she would never—.

"Have you never imagined being married to Giovanni?"

"*Si.*" Maria Sophia didn't look away. Her gaze was steady, her tone firm. "There was a time in the beginning when I did. But when we decide to remain friends, no. It would be foolish of me to wish for something that would never be. And, while I may be many things, I am not a fool." She stood then and without breaking eye contact, looked over at Gabriella.

"You have the opportunity to more than imagine it. You can make it real for yourself."

"But he—."

"But he is saying good bye to an old friend who is going out of town on a business trip. An old friend he not see since September because his heart and his time is taken up by someone who is more to him than a friend.

"The decision to talk to him or not is yours. And, if you have other questions, I will sit down and answer them but if not I'll take my leave."

"Where is he?"

"He is downstairs—waiting—hoping it is you he sees instead of me."

"Do you know how he knew I was here?"

Maria Sophia smiled. "If that is your only question, you will have to ask him because I don't know."

"Downstairs?"

"*Si,* downstairs."

She looked down at the rumpled shirt and pants, knew her hair was in disarray to say the least. "I need to change. Will you wait for me?"

"*Si,* I will wait but I can assure you, he will think you beautiful just as you are."

"Not compared to you." Gabriella had started across to the bedroom.

"Most certainly compared to me. I promise."

Gabriella turned and looked once more at the elegant woman in front of her. He could have married her years ago and maybe even now but he hadn't. What was there about this beautiful, composed—?

She stopped herself short. "For me, then. I at least want to change my shirt. This one has a stain."

"I wait."

Gabriella was pulling off her top as she went in the bedroom. Pulling a clean bright blue one from the dresser drawer she tugged it on as she went in the bathroom. After splashing water on her face, she patted it dry, cursed as water droplets spattered over her shirt. *It'll dry before I get down there.* Finger combing her hair, she pulled it back from her face with clips. Even though the splotches on her were already drying, she grabbed a light jacket.

Maria Sophia was waiting by the door, her handbag in her gloved hands. "He will be delighted to see you."

Gabriella stuffed the panic down along with the nausea, picked up her room key and followed Maria Sophia out.

To Listen with Her Eyes

Walking beside the elegant and sophisticated Maria Sophia, Gabriella noticed the long-limb graceful way she moved in comparison to her own less than graceful gait. Maria Sophia had been a model and still could grace the pages of any fashion magazine cover Gabriella had ever seen.

Compared to her—?

Of course Giovanni would pick Maria Sophia.

What man wouldn't?

The elevator arrived and they stepped in. Of course the walls were mirrors so she had more time to continue the comparison. *I shouldn't be doing this.*

But she did.

Maria Sophia's makeup was so perfect it looked natural. *Or maybe she doesn't wear makeup.* A horrifying thought when comparing her auburn-haired skin tone to Maria Sophia's creamy complexion.

"You will see him and you will listen to him, *no*?" Maria Sophia had turned to her with three floors left on their ride.

"*Si*, I will see him and listen." Just saying the words out loud left her feeling empty yet heavy inside. She had no idea why he'd want her if he could have Maria Sophia but she'd listen to his lies and then call Elizabeth. Returning to Ireland was too painful. E had everything she wanted including a darling baby.

Fremont held more of the same but she'd have her own place and a little distance. Maybe The Circle would go back to their ceremonies only including themselves. No men.

Gabriella stiffened her spine that was already ramrod straight as the elevator door opened.

Maria Sophia strode out into the hotel lobby.

A reluctant Gabriella followed.

The hotel was luxurious with marble tiled floors, tapestry hung walls, leather furniture in various seating arrangements, a huge bouquet of flowers gracing a tile topped table in the middle of the room.

A quick glance around the lobby.

Giovanni wasn't sprawled in any of the chairs.

"Come this way." Maria Sophia took her arm and steered her to their left. A large opening into the lounge loomed before her. They stopped in the entrance and before her eyes adjusted to the dimmer light, she felt his presence.

Pivoting to her right she found him. Tucked into a corner of the bar, a glass of something on the small table in front of him. He didn't move, didn't make any effort to stand, didn't even greet her with words.

I don't need to be here. She started to turn away when it struck her that he hadn't taken his eyes off her. Here she was, Gabriella Moncrief, an ordinary looking female standing next to

Maria Sophia and he hadn't even glanced the other woman's way.

Running away itched at her feet. Tears tipped her eyes.

"Ah, we find you," Maria Sophia said moving in Giovanni's direction, still holding Gabriella by the arm.

And still he didn't move, didn't take his eyes off her.

Maria Sophia pulled a chair out and encouraged Gabriella to sit by pushing down on her arm.

Gabriella's peripheral vision caught Maria Sophia taking a sip from Giovanni's glass.

"How many of these have you drunk?" Her perfectly manicured nails tapped on the table.

"Only this one."

His voice was gravelly and not the smooth baritone she was used to. He wore a dark jacket (probably his brown one) over a white shirt, open at the throat. She imagined he had khaki pants on as that was a look he favored. He needed a haircut more than usual and, although he'd shaved, he still looked unkempt? No that wasn't it.

It was his eyes. They looked haunted? Lost? Why? Because she'd walked away?

It was dark enough in the bar it was difficult to see the emotions in his eyes but she felt them. Wave after wave of confusion and despair flowed over her.

Maria Sophia patted his arm. "She is here to listen to what you have to say." She added something in Italian, leaned over and kissed his cheek. Patting his hand, she rose. But before leaving she stopped next to Gabriella. "You must give him time to find the words. And for your own happiness you must listen with more than your ears."

She was gone, leaving behind a lingering scent of flowers and sunshine.

She was gone and they were alone.

She was gone and they sat in silence.

Gabriella was here to listen to what he had to say and he said nothing.

A waitress appeared and asked if she wanted anything. She ordered a glass of club soda figuring that would go better with the champagne.

After her drink had been delivered and still no words had passed between them, Gabriella was torn between getting up and walking out or saying something.

Maria Sophia's words to listen with more than her ears echoed.

Maybe she also needed to see with more than her eyes? She closed her eyes to better see. Immediately her mind's eye filled with the vision of the spruce cone, perfect symmetry in stark contrast to the chaos rioting in her body. Her blue jay flew by leaving behind a trail of iridescent feathers.

She saw him then, in his room that first night they were lovers. So careful of her, so caring, so considerate, so loving—how did it all go wrong?

Giovanni drank in the sight of her. From the moment she stepped into the bar, he couldn't take his eyes off her. Had he even blinked?

One hand gripped the glass of whiskey and one gripped his thigh. How to go forward? What to say? He'd spent the last four days thinking about what to say. He'd practiced a speech for hours. But here with her sitting across from him? Nothing.

Where were the words? His words. The words that would fix what was wrong. The words that would bring her back to him or at least keep her from going away.

Maria Sophia had left and still he sat, unable to remember all that he wanted to tell her. His throat so dry even the whiskey didn't wet it. His heart pounding so loud she must be able to hear it. His gut so upset he hadn't eaten anything substantial since she ran from him at the airport, her face etched with hurt and betrayal that even now, even the thought of it, brought curses to his lips.

What to say?

She'd ordered something to drink. And even when it had been delivered and she'd taken a drink, he'd said nothing. Just stared as her throat worked when she swallowed. He knew she had a sensitive spot in the hollow of her throat. Did anyone else know that about her?

"Giovanni?"

She'd said his name. Her voice was soft. He listened for worry but heard none.

He'd been focused on her throat but now looked up, his gaze catching her hazel one. Hazel eyes that appeared to darken when they made love, her pupils flaring as arousal claimed her. Did anyone else know that about her?

"You wanted to speak to me. I agreed to listen."

Her lips moved to form those words. Luscious lips, talented lips, lips that blossomed when kissed. Lips that formed a perfect circle just before she climaxed. Did anyone else know that about her?

"I love you."

He heard his own voice say the words but had no conscious awareness of saying them. Where was the speech he'd rehearsed for hours?

"I need to see you when you talk. It's too dark in here. We can sit in the lobby or, if you promise not to touch me, we can go up to my room."

She was offering him the opportunity to talk to her, to try to make it right. The lobby or her room?

The lobby: they could be interrupted and he wasn't sure they'd be comfortable sharing intimate thoughts in a public setting.

Her room: they would have privacy and he would have to keep his hands to himself. Even now he struggled not to reach across the table and hold her hand.

"We can be interrupted if we talk in the lobby. If we go to your room, we have privacy. But it is your choice."

She rose and he followed. In the lobby she paused and looked around before turning toward the bank of elevators. No words spoken on the ride to her floor, down the hall to her room, or even when they stepped inside.

Michael's man of business had done a good job selecting this suite. It was open and airy and comfortable with a gas fireplace. It also had a view of Rome. He wasn't sure she knew that because the sheer curtains were drawn.

Standing just inside the door, he waited until she turned and gestured to the sitting area in front of the fireplace. He chose one of the chairs. The one that faced the wall so he'd be less distracted by looking outside.

Gabriella chose the chair opposite him. "Do you know that is the chair Maria Sophia chose?"

He shook his head.

She gestured to the room service cart behind the couch. "And that is what she ordered. It seems she likes food and drink available when meeting with someone."

That did sound like Maria Sophia but he did not say that out loud, instead his mind raced trying to remember all the words he'd practiced.

Gabriella perched on the chair, her hands clasped in her lap, her back rigid, her feet square on the floor. She had agreed to meet with him, to listen to what he had to say. She'd also said she needed to see him when he talked which was why he was here, exposed and vulnerable.

You could just get up and leave. The thought slammed into him and he leapt up. He paced to the window and looked out at the narrow and crooked streets alongside the wider boulevards. He loved this city but also loved his villa. He loved Florence and Milan and Venice. He loved his country from the Italian Alps to the islands of Sicily and Crete.

"What are you thinking?" Gabriella asked, her gaze unyielding in its quest for honesty.

"I was thinking how much I love my country. The Italian Alps, Tuscany, Milan, Venice, Florence, Rome even Sicily and Crete. I love my work. It has sustained me for many years. My family is here. A lifetime of friends are in this country."

He crossed the room and knelt in front of her. "I know I promise not to touch you but it is a promise I can't keep." He carefully placed his hand over her still folded ones. "I love you. I give it all up to be with you. I have no other words. I love you. I want to be with you, wherever you are is where I want to be. I pray we find our way because losing you will be the most profound loss of my life."

His touch was not heated. He did not stroke or caress her hand. He was kneeling in front of her and offering her his heart. Offering her everything he had. Willing to give up family, friends, career—all he'd known—for her.

"I have questions." She said not withdrawing her hands from under his.

"I will give you answers. I will give you honest answers."

She did pull her hands away and scooted back in the chair. "You need to sit down."

He rose and returned to the chair he'd occupied, hope that they could work this out started to rise.

"Tell me about Maria Sophia."

"I meet her at a photo shoot. She is a model and I am working on restoring the ruins." He kept his gaze on her as he recounted their dating and becoming lovers. He paused in case she asked for details but she didn't and he went on.

"Do you want to know what happened between us so we are friends instead of lovers?

She nodded.

"It's hard to say exactly. I looked forward to spending time with her, talking over a meal or a glass of wine, walking through the streets and commenting on the buildings. As a model, she saw things differently than I did. One night we slept together but did not make love. Then it was two nights and then… .

"Maria Sophia asked why we were drifting apart. I hadn't seen anything wrong because I still looked forward to being with her. It was difficult conversation because she is used to men wanting to bed her and initially couldn't understand why I didn't. I loved her but more like a sister, as a friend."

Gabriella listened to his words. The story was very similar to what Maria Sophia had said except Gabriella now heard how he saw the relationship. He did not want to continue as her lover if he was never going to offer marriage.

"Are there other Maria Sophia's in your past?"

He almost squirmed but managed to stay still. "Do you mean are there other women I've shared a bed with? Or other women I love like a sister?"

"The latter."

He was grateful that was her question because, while he could have talked about the women he'd bedded, he preferred not to. He'd always liked the women, found them interesting, but beyond like and interesting and sex, there wasn't much if anything more. He sounded like a man with an empty soul when he thought about his past. But that wasn't how he saw himself. He enjoyed women, enjoyed flirting, obviously enjoyed the physical side but he also wanted to marry, to have a wife and children, to create a family.

"No, Maria Sophia is the only one I've been with that I'm friends with. Of course, there are some I still see in social situations but she is the only one I ever spend time with."

"She is very beautiful."

"*Si,* she is very beautiful. And so are you. To me, you are even more beautiful." He saw the denial in the way her face grimaced but plowed on. "Your beauty is different than hers but, to me, you are—." He sighed with frustration. "The lemon tree in my garden, you say is beautiful. But you also say the sea is. Which is it? That is how I see you and Maria Sophia. She is the lemon tree. You the sea. Always changing, bringing fresh air into my life. Maria Sophia is much the same as when we met."

He held his hand out in supplication. "I don't know what to say so you know what's in my heart. I love you. I have for a very long time but I stay silent until we become friends. I hope you can hear what I feel through my words."

Gabriella heard his words and also felt them in her heart. When she considered his juxtaposing Maria Sophia and herself, she was much more like the sea and she would take his word that Maria Sophia was more like the lemon tree.

The first words he'd said while they were sitting in the bar were 'I love you'. He'd admitted he'd made up a speech but couldn't remember the words. She did believe he'd answered her questions honestly. One she had for herself was whether she could be around Maria Sophia without jealousy or rancor. *E has done so with Shannon.*

I am the light

I am the Source

Through me love flows throughout the world

And that is how she did it. Gabriella said the prayer to herself times three all the while keeping her gaze locked with his chocolate brown one.

She was his light.

She was his source.

His love for her transformed her and flowed from her throughout the world.

What to do now?

"Do you still want to get married on Imbolc?" She'd taken a deep breath and the words rushed out on her exhale.

He didn't move for a second or two. And when he did, she thought he might leap across the table. Lifting her out of the chair, he held her in his arms.

No kisses.

No caresses.

He held her tight to him. His arms banded around her. She slipped her arms around his neck and held on. She could feel her hair move as he breathed her in. She nestled her head on his chest under his chin.

Clichés flew through her mind. She wanted to mark this moment with something original but all she could think of was *He loves me.*

He set her down on her feet and stepped back. Cradling her face in both hands he kissed her forehead. "I have something more to say that you did not ask about."

His touch gentle, his expression serious, his thumbs stroked her cheeks once. "I know you were here all along. I called Michael. I think you will call Elizabeth. I tell him to do everything you ask but not tell you I know. I give him the name of this place and the limo company.

"I know it wrong to go behind you like that but I am crazy with worry. You don't come out when I send message to you. I afraid if I try to come into the women's restroom, you would try to run away farther. I want you safe. I worry you be hurt or lost or worse if you were not someplace I trust."

His chocolate brown eyes flooded with emotions, hope and fear. Of course he'd want her safe. He always had and he always would. He'd wanted her safe and yet he'd stayed away.

"But you never called."

"I spend my time between the lobby and my home. It is not so far from here. I wait until Maria Sophia can come back to Rome and talk to you. I'm afraid you will not listen to me."

He was right. If he had come knocking on the hotel room door, she never would have opened if had she known who was on the other side.

"Did E know?" Her stomach clenched at the thought that E would have betrayed her.

"She would know now but not when I first call Michael. I call him when Maria Sophia comes up to see you to let him know it was time to tell her."

"E will be angry with him for his deception."

"*Si*, I know that is true."

"But he did it to help you." Her voice was neutral but the edge of pain clawed her throat.

"To help us. He say we belong together and so he will help because he would not want to be reason we do not get back together."

Well, that sounded like Michael. She remembered Michael calling Jackson for help when he wanted Elizabeth to stay. The men, it seemed stood up for each other in a similar way to the women.

"They'll work it out."

Sometime during their conversation, they had moved, his hands now rested on her shoulders and they were an arm's length apart.

"Thank you for telling me you knew I was here, that you were honest with me. I'm not happy about it but I think I understand why you did it." A rueful smile twisted her lips. "While I was sobbing on the phone with Elizabeth who could barely understand me, you were talking to Michael making sure I would be safe and taken care of."

"I do not like to think about the pain I cause you." His hands had moved up to cup her face, his thumbs gliding across her chin.

"If I believe you now, then you didn't cause me pain. I caused it myself because I didn't stop and listen to you at the time. Although to be honest, I don't know that I would have believed you and Maria Sophia had already left to catch her flight."

His chest rose with an intake of air. He held it for several seconds before he exhaled. His hands dropped back to her shoulders. His gaze bore into her soul. "You asked me a question before I confessed the rest."

She nodded.

"Do you still ask this question of me?"

Did she? Did she trust that he loved her above everyone else? Did she trust that she could be a part of his life here in Italy? Did she believe he'd really give everything up and come live with her in Fremont?

"I do still want to know if you want to get married to me knowing I can be unreasonable, jealous and—

He stepped close, lowered his head and before she finished what she was saying, kissed her. It started as a gentle brush of lips against lips but within seconds had changed. He kissed her as if she was his life's breath, tender and passionate at the same time.

She melted against him, her hands in his dark hair holding his head, keeping his mouth fused with hers.

And then he stopped. Stopped and held her close. Stopped and whispered in her ear. "I love you Gabriella Maria Moncrief."

"And you will not be upset if I continue to use that name?" She asked wanting to be sure they were going in the same direction.

"My ring on your finger and you in my bed, is more than I ever thought I'd have." Passion graveled his voice.

"The wedding?"

"*Si*, what was decided?"

"We need to sit down so I can see you when we talk."

One hand slid to her shoulder and then down her arm to her hand. A light grasp and he turned them to the couch. His brow quirked his question.

"Everything is decided, colors, flowers, food. Everything except my dress and where it will be. If we decide Ireland, Elizabeth and Michael would host it. There is a case to be made for us to marry in Fremont. But there is also a case to be made for us to marry here."

"My family will travel to wherever you decide for us to marry."

"And The Circle will travel to wherever we decide for us to marry."

"But...?" The word was drawn out. He knew something bothered her but kept silent until she spoke.

"The only reason I want to be married in Fremont is because Doc S and my social worker could attend. I don't know if they can come to either Ireland or Italy."

"And if they could, where do you want to marry me?"

"At the villa, by the wall overlooking the sea." The words spilled out, no hesitation at all.

"Then that is what we'll do. We contact your Doc S and social worker so they can arrange for time off. We send them tickets and they can stay at the villa. There is room for a few people. The village inn and nearby bed and breakfasts for everyone else."

"Are you sure? It seems like it would be easier to marry here in Rome or… ." Her words trailed off as he leaned over and kissed her cheek.

"I am sure."

"But your family and friends?"

"Our ceremony is to be more private with just our immediate family which for you is The Circle, Doc S and your social worker. The next day we have a big reception here in Roma. My mother and sisters take care of it. Unless?"

"No, that will be perfect. If Sophia comes a day early she and Adolfo will easily have the food ready for our wedding day." Her belly danced with beautiful butterfly nerves.

"Sophia makes her decadent chocolate cake?"

"And Adolfo makes his decadent tiramisu."

"Jackson's ice cream?"

"You forget Grant now competes with Jackson for 'best ice cream maker'." She laughed aloud, joy bubbling up from the butterfly nerves.

"I never forget that competition." He still held her hand but wanted her closer. He shifted so one arm was around her shoulders, he held one of her hands and rested his head against hers. "And the dress?"

"I know I can't wear jeans and a shirt." She felt his smile.

"It is our wedding, we can wear whatever we want."

"Yes, the groom handsome in a tuxedo and the bride barefoot in jeans and tank top."

"Maybe something a little warmer. It will be February and still winter."

"I've time to find something." She sighed. "I must have missed out on the shopping gene. I'm not someone who likes to buy clothes, especially something I'll only wear once."

"Or maybe twice. You never know when you might want to wear a dress."

Without further words they sat. Her head on his shoulder, an arm around his waist, still holding hands.

"I would offer to help you shop but they say it is bad luck for the groom to see the bride in her wedding dress." He thought of offering his mother. She would love to shop with her soon-to-be daughter-in-law but her English was poor and she was already anxious about making a good impression now that he'd finally announced he planned to marry.

"We did look in Limerick, Glasgow and Dublin when I was in Ireland."

"There are many shops here in Rome."

She pulled away and sat up straight. "I know this may sound crazy, but do you think Maria Sophia would help me find a dress?"

"Let's see." He pulled his cell phone out and scrolled to her number. She answered on the second ring. He'd told her he'd call her and let her know what had happened. Should he have told Gabriella that? *Not now.*

"My dear, Gabriella and I have little problem we think you can help with." He purposefully spoke in English so Gabriella would know exactly what he was saying.

"My bride-to-be needs a wedding dress." Silence. Perhaps he had misjudged?

Gabriella took the phone from him. "Maria Sophia, it's Gabriella. I know it's asking a lot of you so please know that if you can't do this, I truly do understand. And I do hope you can clear your schedule to come to the wedding on February 1. It will be at Giovanni's villa."

He took the phone back and spoke in Italian after directing a quizzical look toward Gabriella.

He hung up after listening to his friend speak for several minutes.

"She is honored you have asked. I tell her when I speak in Italian that the ceremony is only for family. She tells me that you are the right one for me and she is happy I have finally found you."

She snuggled in his arms, kissed his neck, nibbled on his ear lobe. His arousal nudged her thigh. "I'm glad you finally found me too."

 Wedding Dress Shopping

Maria Sophia was gracious as she took Gabriella from one little boutique shop to the next. After the fifth stop, she suggested they have a glass of wine and discuss what they liked and didn't like about what they saw.

Gabriella wanted a dress that was simple but not plain. Something she could see herself wearing at another time. Maria Sophia saw her in an elegant gown.

"I know a designer who is just starting out. Let's see what she can do."

Gabriella heard it for what it was. A statement not a question.

Andrea's shop was small with only room for two people along the main aisle. The shop was empty except for Andrea. This was a very different shopping experience from their first five stops on many levels.

The designer was young. In her late twenties or maybe early thirties would be Gabriella's guess. She obviously knew who Maria Sophia was but tried to look calm and composed.

It was also obvious she knew who Giovanni was because as Maria Sophia rattled off in Italian, when his name was mentioned the young woman's eyes darted in her direction.

"You want simple but not plain, *si*?" Her English was heavily accented and Andrea asked her question as she walked around Gabriella.

"Do you want a white dress?"

Gabriella shook her head.

"Then we look at a simple design with elegant fabric." She marched toward the back of her shop and stopped before a large book of some kind. Maria Sophia followed with Gabriella last.

The two women flipped through the book that actually held swatches of fabric. Andrea turned to Gabriella and asked her to step to the left. She did as asked and found herself in a spot light.

Maria Sophia and Andrea both sighed at the same time. They were looking at a white silk embroidered with multi-colored flowers. A blue thread meandered through the fabric like a stream through a meadow.

"It is white," Maria Sophia said looking at Gabriella. "But I can see you in a simple maxi-gown with blue sandals on your feet and blue flowers or ribbons in your hair."

"In a tank top style with a shawl in the blue?" Andrea suggested.

"Maxi means to my ankles?"

They nodded.

"My feet will show."

They nodded again.

"How tight?"

"I can make it full enough you can easily walk in it. Perhaps not run but definitely take long steps."

"How much will the dress cost?"

Maria Sophia and Andrea glanced at each other.

A smile wreathed Maria Sophia's face and twinkled in her eyes. "Nothing to you. It is our wedding present to you. Giovanni's wedding will make the society pages, Andrea will be mentioned as the designer of your wedding dress, I will be listed as one of the guests."

"That isn't enough," Gabriella started to argue but her words were waved away.

"You do not understand fashion, Gabriella. Your choosing Andrea as your dressmaker will give her much exposure. You will look elegant in the dress and Giovanni will look the besotted groom. She will have new business the next day and thereafter. And, if you have her make you something else, then she will be known as La Signora Migliori's dressmaker."

Gabriella didn't correct them about the name. She did listen to Andrea talk about how she could use the same basic pattern and make her other dresses. They looked at fabrics and Gabriella fell in love with a soft cotton in shades of green and blue.

By the time they left, she'd ordered three more dresses and was in a panic as to how to pay for them. She actually didn't even know how much they cost. Her lessons in Italian on how to ask 'how much' had escaped her. As she and Maria Sophia strolled down the street, a small bag of swatches of the fabrics in hand so she could purchase the shoes or maybe several pair, she thought of her savings. She'd just email the bank and have them take money from her savings and put it in her checking account. Having solved that problem, she relaxed.

They turned a corner onto a busier street and there in front of them was Giovanni. His eyes held hers. His arm went around her shoulder. "How did the shopping go?"

"You will love what she picked out," Maria Sophia said. "We still have shoes and maybe some jewelry." She reached for the small bag, opened it and pulled out the strip of white figured silk. "This is the color for the shoes." She pointed to the blue.

"And that is all I see?"

"That is all you see until the wedding." Maria Sophia chuckled and tucked the fabric back in the bag.

"In this moment, February first seems very far away." Giovanni leaned down and kissed Gabriella's cheek.

"The dress will be very elegant. We looked at Andrea's shop among others. She was the only one to see what Gabriella envisions for her dress."

"Do I know who Andrea is?"

"You will after your wedding." Maria Sophia laughed. "I will leave you two for now." She turned to Gabriella. "I will pick you up in two days and we will find shoes."

"Thank you." Gabriella's words were heartfelt. She stepped away from Giovanni and gave Maria Sophia a hug. "I would be attending my wedding in jeans and a tank top without you."

Gabriella thought Maria Sophia's eyes were bright with unshed tears but she didn't say anything. It would be hard to see the man you still loved marrying someone else. And she had no doubt at all that Maria Sophia still loved Giovanni and what she was doing now was a final gift to him.

She'd enjoyed the time she'd spent with her today and hoped she'd remain a part of their lives. *Perhaps with Giovanni marrying me, Maria Sophia will find someone.*

 The Wedding

Wednesday
February 1, 2006
Imbolc

It was her wedding day. Surrounded by her circle sisters, Gabriella stood in the white silk gown with the blue thread like a stream running through the swirls of multi-colored flowers. The flowers were perfect examples of sacred geometry. A knock on the door was answered by Ashley. Maria Sophia stood on the other side.

"Oh do come in," Gabriella invited. "I think you met everyone last night but just in case—." She pointed to each of The Circle reminding Maria Sophia of their names.

"I bring this to you from your bridegroom." Maria Sophia held a thin oblong box out.

Gabriella took and opened it. Her hand flew to her throat as her mouth flew open. "Oh my!"

Reverently she reached down and picked up a chain of lapis beads interspersed with gold ones. At the end of the necklace was a sapphire blue jay that caught the light and sparkled.

"How did he know?"

"He saw the material and I mention jewelry," Maria Sophia said and smiled.

"He called each of our husbands trying to find out what your personal totem was. Of course none of them knew." Lily laughed. "Of all of us, he ended up calling Elizabeth and asking her to please tell him because he wanted to give you something special on your wedding day."

"I hope you don't mind." Elizabeth did have a worried look.

"I don't mind."

"The best part is that our husbands," Hunter pointed to Diana, "have asked us what our personal totems are. I think we can expect something representing them as gifts sometime this year."

It was time. Her circle sisters preceded her down the stairs, through the villa and out to the patio. At the end of the garden path, chairs had been set up along with heaters because it was February and the air was brisk.

When she saw him standing, Michael and Jackson by his side, she knew she had found someone who loved her above all others. He'd even been willing to move away from his home, from his family, from his career for her.

After shopping in Rome, she'd returned here and rewrote the ending of Holly's story. It was important that she show readers that it takes courage to love again, to open oneself up to the possibility of losing the one you love. She'd learned that from Sophia and the others in The Circle. Each of them had had to face a safe life alone or reach for what at the time, seemed unattainable.

The long walk was over. She stood next to the man she loved above all others. Behind her were Doc S and her social worker and her husband, the Mortensons. She'd given them a copy of *Holly's Story* and asked them for feedback. She knew she had to change Doc S's name before she submitted it but it had been important to name her in this draft.

Meeting Giovanni's family had been an experience. One and all pulled her into long hugs, kissing her cheeks. His mother held her hand and beamed. Even though she had no idea what anyone was saying, it didn't matter. She was wholeheartedly welcomed into the family.

"Dearly Beloved."

They were being married by one of Giovanni's relatives who was a priest. When they'd first met, she told him she loved Giovanni with all her heart and would be the best wife and companion she could.

Whatever Giovanni had added, in Italian of course, brought a grin to the priest's face and a twinkle to his eyes. He asked her how she thought she'd do living in Italy, leaving her life in America behind. She had an answer because she'd thought about it and talked to Elizabeth also.

The Wheel turned. The Circle was changing. However the seven of them were at the center and that would never change.

"I now pronounce you husband and wife."

Giovanni did not wait for the priest to say "you may kiss your bride." He picked her up and twirled her around. The joy on his face brought tears to her eyes. The lighthouse beam swung around and she'd swear it paused, holding them in its light.

When Giovanni set her down, she kept her arms around his neck, pulled him towards her. "I do love you above all others for now and for evermore." She kissed him and then buried her face in his chest.

Beyond them bottles of champagne were popping and people were chattering as chairs scraped and people made their way back to the patio and house where food and drink was in abundance.

They sat once again in their spot on the wall, looking out to the sea. Her back warm against his chest, she clasped his hands that were wrapped around her waist.

"I will never know why you love me, why you wanted to marry me, why you stayed with me so long."

"I see you for first time at Jackson's and I think, she is special. I cannot always find words to describe what makes you special to me but I plan to show you every day for the rest of our lives. I do love you above all others now and forever more."

The lighthouse beam flashed past them. "They will come looking for us if we don't go in."

"I know."

They stood and hand in hand walked toward the festivities. Together they would love each other above any others for now and   forever.

Get the Latest News about New Releases, Special Events, Special pricing/sales

You have just finished *Gabriella* the sixth book in The Sacred Women's Circle series. Be the first to learn about future releases, any pre-release pricing or sales and special events by signing up for my Newsletter here.

For More Information on The Sacred Women's Circle series check out:

My website: www.JudithAshleyRomance.com
My blog: www.JudithAshley.blogspot.com

Other Books in The Sacred Women's Circle Series:
Lily: The Dragon and The Great Horned Owl
Elizabeth: The Lady and The Sacred Grove
Diana: The Queen of Swords and The Knight of Pentacles
Ashley: Dragonflies and Dreams
Hunter: The Drum and The Dance

A request:

If you enjoyed *Gabriella*, please consider telling your friends and family and writing a review on Amazon, Apple, Barnes and Noble, Kobo and Goodreads. Reviews are a wonderful way to support me.

ABOUT Judith

Judith, in her real life, has been a part of sacred women's circles for over twenty years and knows first-hand how important spirituality is when dealing with life's challenges.

Her imagination has always been active and through books she's been a princess res-cued from the tower by the handsome knight, a missionary in India, explorer in the Amazon jungle, a priestess of the Goddess, and a nun to name a few. She's lived with people from all walks of life including different tribes of indigenous people on five continents in tents, wood cabins, igloos, castles, mansions, high-rise apartments, penthouses, dungeons, basements, and cottages.

Then one day in Judith's real life, the stories that make up The Sacred Women's Circle series flooded through her in daydreams, lucid dreams, and conversations so real at times she wondered about her sanity. It was a compelling experience! An experience that was a catalyst to starting her journey to tell these stories and see them published.

Judith's prayer for you:

Each and every day of your life may you find joy, may you see beauty, may you experience wonder, and may you know you are unconditionally loved.

For more books from the heart in fiction and non-fiction please visit Windtree Press

http://windtreepress.com

presenting life with imagination